T

ORPHAN

Silver Linings Mysteries Book 5

A Regency Romance

by Mary Kingswood

The Orphan: Silver Linings Mysteries Book 5

Published by Sutors Publishing

ISBN: 978-1-912167-31-9 (paperback)

Cover design by: Shayne Rutherford of Darkmoon Graphics

V3

Author's note:

this book is written using historic British terminology, so *saloon* instead of *salon*, *chaperon* instead of *chaperone* and so on. I follow Jane Austen's example and refer to a group of sisters as the Miss Wintertons.

The Orphan: Silver Linings Mysteries Book 5

About this book: *The sinking of the* Brig Minerva *results in many deaths, while for others, the future is suddenly brighter. But it's not always easy to leave the past behind...*

Evie Parfitt is almost thirty, penniless and with no prospect of ever marrying. She has her hands full helping turn a jewel merchant's wilful heiress into a lady able to move in good society. When the sinking of the Minerva *leaves her charge an orphan and she selects a notorious rake as her guardian, Evie is determined to protect both of them from his attentions. But faced with the most charming man she's ever known, can she protect her own heart?*

Eliot Armitage is rich, idle and spoilt, whiling away his life with a succession of mistresses. He's not tempted by his eighteen-year-old ward, but it would be an amusing game to seduce her cool and oh-so-ladylike companion. When Evie disdains his approach and challenges him to find the jewel merchant's missing diamonds, he sets out to prove that he's not the worthless rogue she thinks him. But will he ever be able to convince Evie that a rake can change his ways?

This is a complete story with a HEA. Book 5 of a 6 book series. A traditional Regency romance, drawing room rather than bedroom.

Isn't that what's-his-name? Regular readers will know that characters from previous books occasionally pop up. Mr Hawes of Kellingborough was last seen dangling after Fanny in *The Seamstress*, until Ferdy lured him away to London with introductions to all his noble relations. Lawyer Mr Willerton-Forbes, his flamboyant sidekick Captain Edgerton and the discreet Mr Neate have been helping my characters solve murders and other puzzles ever since *Lord Augustus*. Mr Jonathan Ellsworthy, mysterious survivor of the Brig Minerva, and his good friend Miss Ginny Chandry were last seen in *The Clerk*.

About the Silver Linings Mysteries series: John Milton coined the phrase 'silver lining' in Comus: A Mask Presented at Ludlow Castle, 1634

Was I deceived, or did a sable cloud
Turn forth her silver lining on the night?
I did not err; there does a sable cloud
Turn forth her silver lining on the night,
And casts a gleam over this tufted grove.

Ever since then, the term 'silver lining' has become synonymous with the unexpected benefits arising from disaster. The sinking of the Brig Minerva results in many deaths, but for others, the future is suddenly brighter. But it's not always easy to leave the past behind...

Book 0: The Clerk: the sinking of the Minerva offers a young man a new life (*a novella, free to mailing list subscribers*).

Book 1: The Widow: the wife of the Minerva's captain is free from his cruelty, but can she learn to trust again?

Book 2: The Lacemaker: three sisters inherit a country cottage, but the locals are surprisingly interested in them.

Book 3: The Apothecary: a long-forgotten suitor returns, now a rich man, but is he all he seems?

Book 4: The Painter: two children are left to the care of a reclusive man.

Book 5: The Orphan: a wilful heiress is determined to choose a notorious rake as her guardian.

Book 6: The Duke: the heir to the dukedom is reluctant to step into his dead brother's shoes and accept his arranged marriage.

Want to be the first to hear about new releases? Sign up for my mailing list at http://marykingswood.co.uk

Table of Contents

The Armitage Family

Hi-res version available at http://marykingswood.co.uk

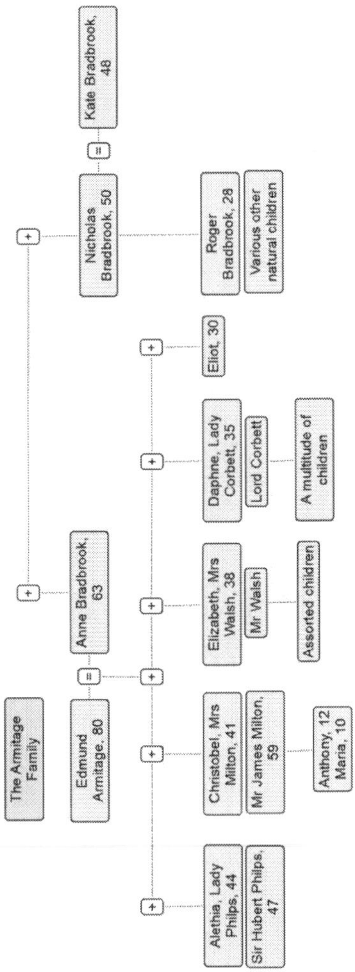

The Folkard Family

Hi-res version available at http://marykingswood.co.uk

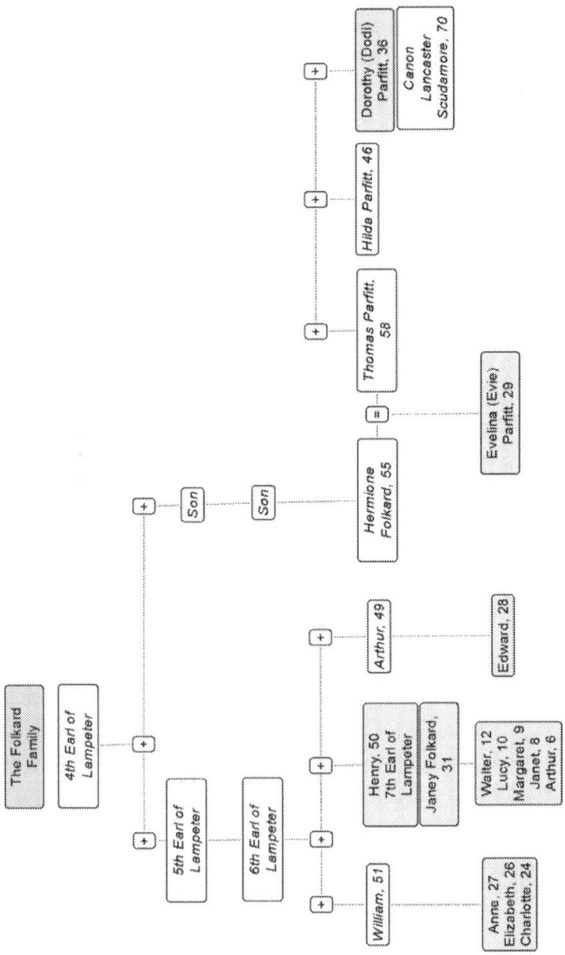

1: In Want Of A Guardian

MARCH

Miss Evelina Parfitt smoothed the soft kid of her gloves, and settled herself on the carved wooden bench in the hall to wait. The carriage was ordered for half an hour before noon, but it would not arrive until ten minutes after that time. Violet would arrive no earlier than ten minutes later. There would be a further delay as she changed her bonnet twice. When the horses had been walked twice down to Berkeley Square and back, and the clock had struck the hour, Violet would be ready to depart. Perhaps.

Green, the butler, and Mrs Bowdler, the housekeeper, hovered anxiously. They knew better than most the price to be paid if the young mistress should find some fault with their management of the household. Heaven forfend that she should deign to be ready and the carriage not waiting for her outside the door.

Evie was of more robust constitution, even though her employment prospects were just as subject to the whims of Miss Violet Barantine. She had been engaged to impart the polished manners of the *beau monde* to the daughter of a jewel merchant, and escort her into those fringes of society which would accept her.

Despite the chance to enjoy London, and the large salary, complete with a generous dress allowance, she would be rather relieved if her young charge should take a pet and dispense with her services, for there was little pleasure to be had as companion and chaperon to a flighty girl like Violet. At eighteen years of age, with a mother long dead and an over-indulgent father, Violet had been for so long the sun around whom the household revolved that she knew no other way.

The carriage arrived, waited, departed. Violet appeared at the top of the stairs waving two bonnets.

"Evie? The chip straw or the velvet? What do you think?"

"When you asked me at breakfast, I suggested the silk as being the most appropriate, and I see no reason to change my opinion."

"But black silk is so lowering, Evie. It makes me look so sallow and ill."

"Black is a depressing colour, it is true, but you would not wish to appear disrespectful of your papa, not so soon after his death. The chip straw is a little too frivolous for town wear, dear, and the velvet makes you look far older than your years, whereas the silk bonnet is perfectly styled to enhance the shape of your face."

"So it is! I look very well in it, do I not? Mrs Carrington said so too, and she knows about such matters, for her bonnets are worn by all the most fashionable ladies of the *ton*. The silk, then."

She whisked away to her room, and the hall lapsed into silence. The carriage returned, waited again, departed, for it was too cold for the horses to stand for long. Green checked his pocket watch for the fourteenth time. Mrs Bowdler paced. Evie sat motionless, hands resting in her lap. The carriage returned, waited. Violet appeared at the top of the stairs.

"Evie? I am not sure about this pelisse. What do you think?"

Evie rose to her feet. "We have an appointment, Violet, we are already late and it would be abominably bad form to keep the gentlemen waiting any longer. A lady must always show consideration for others. You may go and change if you wish, and I will see Mr Camberwell and Mr Baxter on your behalf."

She walked steadily towards the door, but Violet flew down the stairs and reached it before her. "Just button my gloves, will you?"

"You have two lady's maids for the purpose, who would be most offended if I should usurp such a task from them."

Miss Lidderdale and Miss Coleman had followed their mistress down the stairs, albeit at a more decorous pace. After a politely worded dispute as to which of them should have the honour of buttoning the gloves, they settled on one apiece, so that Violet was soon perfectly attired to venture forth. With a final adjustment of the curls artfully framing her face, a last tug at the sleeves of the expertly constructed pelisse, and the lace veil set in place, the two maids stepped back, satisfied. Green sprang forward to open the door and Violet passed through without a glance.

As she followed her charge, Evie murmured, "Thank you, Green."

"Oh yes, thank you, Green," Violet said, turning to him with her most entrancing smile.

"My privilege to serve so charming a mistress," Green murmured.

She dimpled even more. Henry, her personal footman, held open the carriage door. She entered it, Evie followed, Henry jumped up behind and they rolled off, almost exactly on the hour. Evie breathed a sigh of relief. Another effort to cajole Violet into rational behaviour successfully accomplished, and without undue delay. A good morning's work.

"Will young Mr Baxter be there today?" Violet said plaintively. Tedious business meetings were lightened considerably for her by the presence of a personable young man to admire her. They all *did* admire her, naturally. Even in mourning, with her father barely a month dead, Miss Violet Barantine was a sight to cheer any man, and Violet was young enough to enjoy her fledgling power over gentlemen.

"I cannot say," Evie said. "I know only of Mr Camberwell and Mr Baxter, your trustees."

"Will there be ratafia cakes? Last time there were ratafia cakes."

"Too many cakes are ruinous to a lady's complexion," Evie said.

"But I might have just one? That would not be ruinous, would it?"

Evie conceded that a single cake might not be sufficient to destroy Violet's looks entirely.

But when they were shown into the sumptuously appointed office of Mr Camberwell, attorney at law, they found themselves facing a larger group than expected. Mr Baxter, Violet's financial adviser and a joint trustee of her fortune with Mr Camberwell, was well known to them, and the eager face of the young Mr Baxter was there too. But who were the other two gentlemen?

"Miss Parfitt, Miss Barantine, allow me to present to you another colleague from the legal profession, Mr Willerton-Forbes, and this is Captain Edgerton, formerly of the East India Company."

Mr Willerton-Forbes was a dapper man, too fashionable for a lawyer. Captain Edgerton was a more flamboyant dresser, who took one look at Violet and immediately executed a flourishing bow, before stepping forward to hold a seat for her. She responded in her usual manner, with a tinkling laugh, a slight blush and a smile in acknowledgement of his admiration. It was very cleverly done, Evie could not deny, and must be convincingly artless in those who did not know Violet well.

"There is good news, Miss Barantine," Mr Camberwell said, beaming at her with as much paternal fervour as if she were his own daughter. "I shall leave Mr Willerton-Forbes to tell you of it."

The lawyer cleared his throat. "Indeed, indeed! Good news of a most unexpected nature, Miss Barantine. The tragedy of the sinking of the *Brig Minerva* off the Cornish coast, which has so painfully deprived you of your sole remaining parent, has attracted sympathy from many people. One of them has been greatly affected by the great loss of life, and has set aside a sum of money — a rather large sum of money — to compensate all those who survived the disaster, and the next of kin of those who were so unfortunately lost to the world."

Violet blinked at him.

"The sum allotted," Mr Willerton-Forbes said, "is one thousand pounds to each person so affected, to be dispensed in whatever manner is most convenient."

"Is that not good news, Miss Barantine?" Mr Camberwell said. "Is it not splendid news? Not such as to recompense you for the sad loss of your dear father, but is it not a splendid gesture by this unknown person?"

"A thousand pounds? That is not very much. I am worth a hundred thousand pounds," Violet said robustly. "At least!"

"Oh, true, it is but a drop in the ocean," Mr Camberwell said hastily. "But still, an extra thousand pounds will be—"

"What about my guardian?" Violet said. "When you read Papa's will to me, it said that Mr Newbold was to be my guardian, but he is drowned too. So what is to happen now? Am I not to have a guardian?"

"You must have a guardian, Miss Barantine. There must be someone set over you to determine where you live and — should you wish to marry — to give approval, for otherwise you would have to wait until you are of age, you know."

"Oh no, I intend to be married long before then. What a shocking thing to be still unmarried at one and twenty."

Evie smiled, well aware that she herself was regarded as an old maid by her young charge, and therefore much to be pitied, being still unmarried at the advanced age of nine and twenty.

Captain Edgerton put in smoothly, "I am sure that will not be your fate, Miss Barantine."

Violet dimpled at him, with the delicate blush and lowered eyes with which she received every compliment. "Mr Camberwell, you could be my guardian, could you not? Or Mr Baxter?"

"That would not be wise, Miss Barantine. We are the trustees of your fortune, and it is frowned upon rather for the guardianship of your fortune and your person to reside in the same gentleman."

"Then what is to be done? What happens when the lease of the house ends? Must I move? Evie tells me that my guardian would determine such matters, but if I have no guardian—"

Mr Camberwell and Mr Baxter exchanged glances. "You need not worry about that, Miss Barantine," Mr Camberwell said soothingly. "Everything will be arranged, in time, and you may leave everything to us."

"But who will it be? I should not like to be in the hands of someone I dislike, or some dreadfully stuffy person. How will he be chosen? May I have no say in it?" Violet pouted prettily. "That does not seem fair!"

"Such matters are not for young ladies to determine. Since you have no living relations, a guardian will be appointed for you by the Court of Chancery. Naturally, Mr Baxter and I, as your trustees, will make a recommendation, but the court will decide what is best for you."

Mr Willerton-Forbes coughed. "If I may elaborate a little, for the benefit of Miss Barantine, gentlemen?" Mr Camberwell nodded, unable to refuse such an eminent lawyer, although he was clearly not happy about it. "In law, as you are above the age of fourteen, you may choose a guardian for yourself. The court may not agree with you, but generally if a respectable and suitable person should apply to the court to be appointed as your guardian, there will not be any dissent."

Violet's face lit up. "I may choose for myself?"

"In law, you may."

"Then I choose Mr Eliot Armitage."

There was a stunned silence. Evie could not think of a less suitable guardian for a flighty girl of eighteen, but she trusted the gentlemen to scotch the idea. However, her faith in them was misplaced.

"I do not know the gentleman," Mr Baxter said plaintively. "Is he a previously unknown relation, Miss Barantine?"

"No, but is that important? Respectable and suitable, *that* gentleman said, and Mr Armitage is certainly that, is he not, Evie? Why, we met him at Lady Frampton's, who is of the first stare of fashion, so he must be so."

"And that is the only occasion upon which we have met him," Evie said crisply. "He is a single man of some fortune, I was told, who is invited everywhere, but as to whether he is a suitable person to be your guardian, it is difficult to say."

Certainly difficult to say with Violet in the room, but Evie was almost thirty and need not be protected from the realities of masculine life. When she had enquired of the other chaperons about Mr Armitage, they had whispered words that needed no explanation. Lady Frampton herself had added bracingly, "He is rich enough not to prey on heiresses, so you need not be concerned for your charge's fortune. Only for her heart. Eliot is..." She sighed nostalgically. "...quite devastating to female sensibilities. You should permit him one set of dances, no more."

And so Evie had, and Violet had made no demur, but ever since that evening she had talked of nothing but Mr Armitage, and at every evening engagement she had wondered hopefully if he would be there, before her father's death had brought such outings to a halt temporarily. He was not the first charming young man for whom she had developed a *tendre*, and Evie had hoped that this infatuation would go the way of the rest and be rapidly replaced by a new interest, but if he were to become her guardian, who knew how it would end?

"Shall I make some enquiries around the clubs?" Captain Edgerton said. "See what is known about him... his... erm, family circumstances, that sort of thing?"

"That would be most helpful," Mr Camberwell said with obvious relief. "Mr Baxter and I... it is more difficult..."

"Of course, of course! Two gentlemen of your standing in society asking about a man wholly unknown to you would attract some most unwelcome comment, whereas I have some acquaintances of whom the most discreet enquiries may be made. This is just the sort of delicate little undertaking I enjoy."

"That is settled, then," Evie said briskly, rather hoping that Violet's fancy would have shifted before the idea could come to fruition. "Have you made any progress in locating the title to the late Mr Barantine's business, Mr Camberwell, so that Violet's inheritance may be settled?"

"Not as yet, Miss Parfitt, but we are optimistic. Our splendid Royal Navy is currently engaged in retrieving everything that may be retrieved from the wreck of the *Brig Minerva*, and once Mr Barantine's... ah, *effects* are returned to us, we hope to find the title amongst them."

"He carried the title to his business on his person?" Mr Willerton-Forbes said. "That is rather singular."

"Indeed, but Mr Barantine had little faith in the conventional means of security for documents, such as safes," Mr Camberwell said. "He liked to carry all his most important documents with him at all times, in a specially constructed waterproof container."

"What about my diamonds?" Violet said. "Papa was bringing home a fortune in diamonds, and I was to have the largest of them. He promised me."

"They will be found amongst his effects, I make no doubt," Mr Camberwell said. "As soon as everything arrives from Cornwall, you may choose your diamond, Miss Barantine."

Violet smiled, satisfied.

~~~~~

Several days after this meeting, Evie was in the study at Bruton Street writing to her aunt, when Green informed her that Mr Willerton-Forbes and Captain Edgerton wished to speak with her. She laid aside her pen, and stood to receive the two gentlemen.

"How very kind in you to see us at such short notice," Mr Willerton-Forbes said. "Miss Barantine is not at home today?"

"She is busy upstairs with fittings for some additions to her wardrobe," Evie said with a smile. "If, as I suspect, you wish to talk to me about Mr Armitage, then that is a matter best accomplished without Violet's presence, I feel."

"Indeed it is," Mr Willerton-Forbes said. "Captain Edgerton has been pursuing his enquiries with some success. Captain?"

"Miss Parfitt, you said that Mr Armitage is a single man of fortune who is invited everywhere, and I have heard nothing to contradict that. He is thirty years old, he lives in Grosvenor Square and there is an estate in Essex, where his parents still live. His father is very elderly now and never leaves the house. He has four sisters,
~~~~~

all older than he is and all very well married. Everything about him is perfectly respectable and sober."

"But?" Evie said with a smile. "I feel sure that you are about to reveal a flaw."

Captain Edgerton rubbed his chin thoughtfully. "Mr Armitage is a gentleman who holds the female sex in great admiration, Miss Parfitt."

"You mean that he is a libertine?" she said. Mr Willerton-Forbes started, and the captain began to protest, but Evie laughed. "Gentlemen, I am not some green girl fresh from the schoolroom. I am nine and twenty years old, and know something of the world. Mr Armitage is a known rake, and I was warned to keep Violet protected against his wiles, as best I could. He is hardly a suitable person to have guardianship of a girl of eighteen."

"As to that, the court would perhaps see only a man of fortune from a respectable family," Mr Willerton-Forbes said cautiously. "He is of an age to be a responsible guardian. No, the question is whether he would accept such a charge. He is a man who... hmm, likes to enjoy himself, let us say. It is by no means certain that he would wish to undertake such a responsibility."

"It might hinder his pursuit of pleasure, you mean?" Evie said, amused. "Indeed. He sounds like a frivolous sort of man, although when I met him, he appeared to be the model of propriety."

"In public, I believe it is so," Captain Edgerton said. "However, my informants tell me that his house at Grosvenor Square is the scene of parties of a certain type. Of interest to young gentlemen, if you understand me, Miss Parfitt."

"Will you speak plainly, Captain? I should not like to put Violet into the hands of a man who regularly drinks to excess, or who might introduce her into unsavoury society. That would be very dangerous."

"I have heard nothing of that nature. His bachelor parties are very discreet, the gentlemen drawn from the cream of society — the sons of the best families in England. He keeps that side of his life entirely separate from his other activities. He is, as you have already been advised, invited everywhere. Almack's, Carlton House, all the most notable occasions of the season. Miss Barantine could hardly have chosen better, for as her guardian, Mr Armitage will be able to introduce her into a most superior level of society."

Evie chewed her lip thoughtfully. "Even so..."

"Miss Parfitt," Mr Willerton-Forbes said, "May I enquire as to the reason Miss Barantine wishes Mr Armitage to become her guardian?"

"Oh, she wishes to marry him, of course. She is besotted with him at this moment. Next month, there will be someone else, and the month after that... but at present, he is the object of her marital ambitions, and I should not wish the poor man to be forced into marriage against his will. Violet is... quite ruthless in her pursuits, I regret to say."

"Then guardianship would offer him the greatest protection," Mr Willerton-Forbes said, eyes twinkling. "For a guardian to marry his underage ward would be most improper, and the courts would take a dim view of the matter, too. However, this may all be moot, for the very idea may horrify him. Shall I suggest that Mr Camberwell make an approach to the gentleman?"

"Yes, please do," Evie said. "The sooner the matter is settled one way or the other, the better."

But a few days later, Mr Camberwell visited with surprising news. Mr Armitage would be delighted and honoured to become Miss Barantine's guardian.

The other news was less welcome. Violet's father's remains had been returned to London for burial, together with his personal effects recovered from the *Brig Minerva*. Neither the title documents for his business, nor the hoard of diamonds, were amongst them.

2: An Appointment At Grosvenor Square

"Violet, you are not invited," Evie said, for the third or fourth time.

"It must be a mistake," Violet said calmly. "Mr Armitage cannot possibly wish to discuss my guardianship without me. I shall accompany you, naturally."

"The letter is very clear," Evie said. "In its entirety it reads, *'Miss Parfitt, Pray be so good as to call upon me at Grosvenor Square at four o'clock on this coming Wednesday. Yours, Eliot Armitage.'* No mention of Miss Barantine, you see?"

"But why would he wish to see *you* rather than me?" Violet said. "It is clearly a mistake. He is confused, meaning to invite me and addressing the letter to you instead. But you may come with me, naturally, as my chaperon," she added kindly.

Evie gave it up. Once Violet had made up her mind, there was no dissuading her. Besides, she would be accompanied by Henry, her sturdy Negro footman, and his presence would be reassuring. Evie had no intention of visiting a single man in his own home unaccompanied, and without Henry she would have been obliged to take one of the maids with her.

Violet was in an even more than usually indecisive mood, so they were more than an hour late in departing the house, but since Evie had had the forethought to send a footman round to Grosvenor Square to alert Mr Armitage to this possibility, she was not concerned. The distance being so short, Evie insisted that they walk and since Violet had a new walking dress and bonnet to wear, she agreed without protest.

When they arrived at Grosvenor Square, the front door stood open and a distracted footman admitted them at once.

"You are late," he said severely. "Straight upstairs. First room on the left."

"You should announce us," Violet said at once, taking umbrage at this informality. "Miss Barantine to see Mr Armitage."

The footman rolled his eyes, and heaved a long-suffering sigh. "Oh, very well. Follow me, *Miss* Ballantyne."

He set off before anyone could correct him. They trooped up the stairs, Violet directly behind the footman, then Evie, and the heavy tread of Henry at the back of the group. On the landing, a twittering could be heard, like a multitude of birds in an aviary. Evie was struck with sudden misgivings about the visit.

There was no drawing back, however, for the footman threw open a door, announced, "Miss Ballantree!" in stentorian tones, then skipped away down the stairs.

The room was full of colour and movement and noise, that was Evie's first impression. A score or more of women in vivid clothing milled about the room, chattering and laughing and drinking what looked like champagne.

"Oh, a *party!*" Violet cried, plunging into the mêlée gleefully.

Evie knew at once that it was all wrong. She had attended enough routs and card parties and soirées to know what those looked like, and this was nothing like that. The women were fashionably dressed, it was true, but their gowns were cut lower at the front than was usual, their skirts were diaphanous and was that rouge that several of them were wearing?

"Violet, no!" she cried, but the girl was swallowed up by the throng.

There were men, too, although they at least looked to be respectably dressed. One she recognised as the son of a duke, but he was not displaying the manners she had previously observed in him. In fact, he had a female on his knee and his hand was—

"Henry, retrieve Miss Barantine *at once!*"

The footman needed no second bidding. He strode across the room after Violet, her black bonnet and pelisse a stark contrast to the colourful gowns of the other women. She had become entangled with another young man, one Evie thought was the brother of a baronet, who had an arm around her waist and was trying to kiss her. She leaned away from him, arms flailing, but he held her fast. Henry, who was a large and imposing man, picked her up bodily and simultaneously punched her assailant in the nose.

Immediately there was chaos. Women screamed, men protested loudly, one of the house footmen waded into the fight to be soundly thumped by Henry, falling back into the path of another, who dropped the tray of champagne glasses he was carrying. Henry retreated, carrying Violet. And out of the disorder emerged a figure Evie recognised.

Eliot Armitage. His well-fitted coat, pale breeches and gleaming top boots were the standard morning dress of any gentleman, but there was no mistaking the golden head of hair that curled casually about a high forehead. The expression below was not at all welcoming.

"What on earth is going on?" he said to Henry, as he set Violet down again near the door. "Who are you and what do you think you are doing to my guests?"

"Henry is Miss Barantine's personal footman," Evie said, as Violet indignantly straightened her gown. "He was rescuing her from the unwanted attentions of Mr Deptford."

"Miss—? Oh! Oh dear! And you are Miss Parfitt. I gave instructions that you were to be shown into my study. You should not be here."

"I can see why," Evie said feelingly. "It seems to me that you are not at all a proper person to take charge of Miss Barantine. We will leave at once."

"No, no!" he cried. "I cannot apologise enough for the mistake. I do not understand how it could have happened. Pray allow me to make amends. Miss Barantine, I was not expecting you but you are most welcome. Permit me to escort you back downstairs. Ah, William, there you are. What are you about to be showing Miss Parfitt and Miss Barantine up here? Did I not make myself clear?"

"No one said anyhing about Miss Perfect," the footman said indignantly. "Miss Ballantree, she told me. I thought she was like the others, being so pretty and all. I know you like 'em pretty, master."

"Is it a party for pretty ladies?" Violet said. "What a charming idea."

"Do take my arm, Miss Barantine. Miss Parfitt, pray let us all go downstairs at once. Have a care as the stair curves, Miss Barantine. Is your footman following? Ah, good man. You are not injured?"

"No one ever injures Henry," Violet said. "He preserved me from a highwayman once, and took the scoundrel's guns from him and tossed him into a ditch, and not a mark on him. On Henry, I mean. There were *several* marks on the highwayman, and he was hanged after, was he not, Henry? Oh, is this your study? What charming figurines."

"My mother collects them, so every house the family owns overflows with them," Mr Armitage said, and even in this most masculine of rooms, all heavy cabinets and solid leather chairs, there was a display case full of delicate porcelain figurines.

In two of the chairs, rising gracefully to their feet, were a pair of stylish ladies of around forty years whose features proclaimed them to be relations of Mr Armitage.

"Miss Parfitt, Miss Barantine, pray allow me to present to you my sisters. This is Lady Corbett, and here is Mrs Walsh. Daph, Beth, this is Miss Parfitt and my new ward, the Lord Chancellor permitting, Miss Barantine."

There was a flurry of curtsies, and chairs were brought forward, and the ladies settled down as if this were any morning call, and there were not some kind of male party going on in the drawing room upstairs. A flustered housekeeper rushed in with many apologies. She, it seemed, had been set the task of watching out for Evie's arrival and steering her to the study, but a crisis below stairs had caused her to abandon her post for a moment, allowing the mistake to be made.

"Never mind, Mrs Lake," Mr Armitage said. "What is done is done. Bring us some tea, if you will."

"I do not want tea," Violet said, pouting. "The ladies upstairs are drinking champagne."

"Then they are not ladies," Evie said firmly. "No lady of quality drinks champagne at four in the afternoon."

"But they must be ladies, Evie, or else why would Mr Armitage know them?"

This was a tricky question to answer, but Mr Armitage put in smoothly, "Naturally they are ladies, but they are rehearsing for... for a tableau that they hope to present at Carlton House shortly, to entertain His Royal Highness. And that is not champagne, it is soda water."

"Oh," Violet said, deflated. "A tableau... what sort of tableau? I saw a tableau of the Romans at Vauxhall Gardens once, and everyone wore costumes."

"It is a tableau of the French Revolution," he said promptly. "Naturally the ladies are wearing French fashions. Miss Barantine, I can see that you admire my mother's figurines. There is a cabinet of shepherdesses in the card room. Should you like to see them?"

"Ooh, I should like that very much," Violet said, clapping her hands excitedly. "I adore shepherdess figurines."

"Beth, would you be so good...?"

Mrs Walsh rose to her feet uncomplainingly, and led Violet out of the room. Henry, who had stayed in a corner of the room, determined not to leave his mistress, silently followed them.

Lady Corbett burst out laughing. "Really, Eliot! A tableau? Soda water?"

"Heaven forfend that I should begin my guardianship of the chit by explaining to her the *demi monde*," he said ruefully.

"Oh, were they ladies of the *demi monde?*" Evie said interestedly. "I have always wondered what they looked like."

"Miss Parfitt, can you ever forgive me? Such a dreadful mistake! And you and Miss Barantine in deep mourning, too. It is not proper for her to be in this house at all, and to be frank, Miss Parfitt, I was not sure that it would be proper for you, either, but I am going out of town tomorrow, this afternoon is the only time available and I wished for no delay. Beth and Daph persuaded me that it would be acceptable so long as they were here too. I cannot sufficiently express my regret—"

"Enough apologising," Evie said firmly. "I can see very clearly that it was unintentional, and you did not invite Violet, after all. No harm is done, on this occasion."

Mrs Lake returned just then with the tea and an array of little delicacies, which Lady Corbett fell upon with glee. She was not quite stout, but there was a pleasing roundness to her form which, Evie, painfully thin from childhood, could only envy.

When the housekeeper had withdrawn, Evie said, "When you know Violet a little better, Mr Armitage, you will learn that she can never be excluded from any interesting excursion. But since you have contrived to remove her from the room, may I ask you if you are truly willing to undertake the charge of guardian to her?"

"Willing? Very much so. How thrilling to be *asked* to be a guardian, instead of having such a rôle thrust upon one, whether one wills it or no. It is most flattering. I read about her in the newspaper, after the ship sank. There was a great deal about the Duke of Falconbury, naturally, but some of the other bereaved were mentioned also, and everyone knows of Barantine's the jeweller's shop. I have made purchases there myself. I felt a great pity for Barantine's orphaned daughter and wished I might help her, and now I can. I may even be able to put her in the way of a suitable match, in time. But I must ask you one question also — why did Miss Barantine choose me, of all people? After all, we have met but once, and enjoyed one pair of dances together. It seems a tenuous foundation for such an important relationship."

She was both surprised and disturbed by the accuracy of his memory. Was it possible that he had designs upon Violet? Best to tackle the subject directly.

"Violet has developed a *tendre* for you, Mr Armitage, and thinks that by appointing you as her guardian, she will induce you to fall in love with her."

"That is awkward," Lady Corbett said in alarm. "Eliot, you cannot encourage such an attachment."

"No, indeed, and I must assure you, Miss Parfitt, that nothing could be further from my thoughts. Miss Barantine is a charming young lady, but I have not the least intention of marrying soon, and certainly not to a girl of eighteen, and my own ward, at that. Every proper feeling must reject the idea."

"That is excellent news," Evie said. "I should warn you, however, that Violet can be very determined. She will set herself to win you over, and is not above subterfuge. If she is living under your roof, she may try to entrap you."

"I have no intention of settling her in this house, if that is what you mean. She will be based at Marsham Grove, where my parents live. If she comes to London, it will be under the care of one of my sisters or my aunts, and do you think this will be acceptable to her?"

His earnest expression made Evie smile. "Mr Armitage, if you become Violet's guardian, such decisions will be yours to make, regardless of whether they are acceptable to her. She cannot stay on alone in the Bruton Street house, that much is certain, and she will be in mourning for some time. She has always said she would like to live in the country, so perhaps she will enjoy the quieter life there," she added doubtfully. Violet enjoying a quiet life anywhere seemed improbable.

"And what about you, Miss Parfitt? Will you enjoy it, too?" His deep blue eyes were fixed on her with a penetrating gaze.

"I? What have I to do with it? You will not need me if Violet is under the care of your mother, sir."

"My mother is elderly, and fully occupied in caring for my father, who is very frail. It would be best for you to stay with Violet, at least while she is in mourning. She knows and trusts you, and she has sustained a great loss with the death of her father. The fewer changes to her life, the better."

"So will you also retain the services of her two lady's maids, her former governess and her footman?"

"Ah. So you are not her governess?"

"I am companion and chaperon to Violet, since her governess did not feel equal to the task of accompanying her into society. It is my rôle to teach her the demeanour required of a lady."

"And do you find her an apt pupil?" Again his eyes were fixed on hers with an intensity which made her rather breathless. She was unaccustomed to the undivided attentions of personable and wealthy young men. Generally the eyes of such men slid past Evie to rest upon the more attractive sight of Violet.

She could not tear her eyes from his, so she answered hastily, "Results are uneven. She is most amenable when my suggestions accord with her own wishes."

"Girls of eighteen are always thus," Lady Corbett said, breaking the spell. "I was wilful myself at that age. So shall you take on Miss Barantine's entire entourage, Eliot?"

"Certainly," he said eagerly. "Everything must be done for her comfort. Except champagne," he added, which made Evie laugh.

"And introductions to the *demi monde*," she said lightly. "I know I should not enquire, but I should dearly love to know what sort of party involves champagne at four in the afternoon."

"You are quite correct — you should not enquire," he said, but his eyes twinkled with amusement, and she was relieved when Violet returned, a welcome distraction from a dangerously charming man.

~~~~~

The procession leaving London was rather an impressive one. Mr Armitage's travelling carriage led the way, containing Mr Armitage and his valet. Then Violet and Evie in Violet's own carriage, together with the governess, Miss Robart, and Henry standing behind. Then
~~~~~

Mr Armitage's curricle and beautiful pair of bays, driven by his own groom. Finally, the baggage carriage, containing the two lady's maids, as well as Violet's many boxes, bags and band boxes. Two outriders, one leading another sweet-stepping horse, completed the train of travellers. Evie was not a connoisseur of horseflesh, but she could recognise quality when she saw it.

They made the journey slowly, since Mr Armitage disliked hiring horses, but Evie found it restful. Violet was in sunny mood, pleased to have accomplished her aim of obtaining Mr Armitage as her guardian, and not yet aware that this precluded him from any romantic entanglement with her. Every vista was exclaimed over, therefore, every village they passed through was charmingly picturesque and every coaching inn the most obliging she had ever had occasion to patronise. This last was not quite the compliment it seemed, since her travels before this date had consisted of one excursion to Hampton Court Palace and one to Tilbury to meet a ship in which her father had an interest.

Evie had scarcely travelled more than this, and never before in such comfort. At every inn there was a private parlour for their use while the horses rested, and an array of foodstuffs and wines. Violet tried a little of everything, but was too excited to eat much, plying Mr Armitage with breathless questions about his home and his family. Miss Lidderdale and Miss Coleman ate steadily from whatever dish was offered, quite unabashed. Miss Robart, who had suffered abject poverty in her life but would rather die than admit it, ate abstemiously and then eyed the remainder with yearning.

"Come, Miss Robart, do eat a little more," Mr Armitage said genially. "I must pay for all of this whether we eat it or not, and I cannot abide waste, can you?"

"Oh, no, indeed not, sir! How selfish it would be of me to hold back when you have provided such a magnificent spread for us. Such an insult, to leave good food uneaten, when so many poor families are starving."

"That is the spirit," he said cheerfully. "Miss Parfitt, may I convince you also to consider the starving poor?"

"I consider them every time I go to church," she said, although she could not help responding to his smile. "However, I do not think that my eating another slice of ham will do more for them than a penny or two in the poor box."

He laughed, not at all discomposed. "Then, if you will eat no more of this excellent ham, you must pay a forfeit, Miss Parfitt. You must answer a question."

"I have no objection to answering your question, sir, if I can."

"Then tell me, if you will, how you came to be with Miss Barantine. Are you related?"

"Not at all. It was mere chance," she said. "Mr Barantine had business in Winchester, and came to visit the cathedral. I lived in the close there with my aunt and happened upon him. We fell into conversation, and he invited me to help smooth Violet's path into society."

"So on the acquaintance of... oh, five minutes or so, he offered you the position?"

"It was a little more than five minutes," she said, laughing, but a little breathlessly. She was not sure she quite liked the intensity of his gaze, which made her feel as if she were the only person in the room. "It must have been half an hour, at least. I refused at first, naturally, for, like you, sir, I could not believe he was serious. But he enquired about me of the bishop himself, and must have received a favourable report, for he renewed his offer the following day. Again I refused, for I knew nothing at all about him. He was obliged to return to London, but he made another visit to Winchester the following month, accompanied by his business partner and his wife, and armed with letters of recommendation from several respectable persons, and so I was convinced. That was two years ago, and I have never regretted my decision."

"Evie is teaching me how to be a *proper* lady, for everyone else I know is in trade, like Papa," Violet said. "She is very correct on all matters of behaviour, and Papa *so* wished me to behave as real ladies do, although I find it very difficult sometimes, especially when Evie disapproves of all my admirers. Indeed, I think she does not wish me to marry at all, for she herself despises marriage! She wants to belong to no man."

"Indeed I do not despise it in the least," Evie cried. "I wish you only not to rush into matrimony, Violet. Marriage is an honourable career for a woman, if she can find a man who treats her as she should be, and not as a mere possession. There is no worse state for a woman of sensibility and quickness of mind than to be trapped in marriage to a man of little sympathy or bad habits. It is better — far better — to be free than to be caged and treated with contempt. Marriage is not the only option a woman has. So long as she has an income of her own, she may make her own life as she pleases."

"Indeed she may," Mr Armitage said enthusiastically, but there was a gleam in his eye that unsettled Evie, although she could not quite say why.

3: Marsham Grove

Eliot watched her, fascinated. She was not at all the sort of woman who normally drew his notice, for he looked always for the flirtatious gleam in the eye, and perhaps a certain manner of walking that made him think of the bedchamber, not the drawing room. Evie Parfitt was nothing like that. She was coolly ladylike, never rattled, always composed, and she had the most breathtakingly flawless complexion, as pale and smooth as his mother's figurines. Her hair was an indeterminate shade of brown, typically swept into a tidy knot, with a few soft curls around the face. At least she affected no spinster's cap — not yet, anyway, although she must be of an age to do so. And then her eyes, such a gentle shade of brown, much like her hair, the expression in them constantly changing, yet he could not read her moods. Was she flirting with him, when she talked of other careers for women, careers with greater freedom? Did her words mean what he thought they meant? Perhaps she was not at all as cool as she appeared, and was only waiting for the right offer...

His casual questions over their several meetings had elicited the information, mostly from Violet, that Miss Parfitt was the daughter of a country parson, and after his death had lived in genteel poverty with an elderly aunt, the relict of a canon at Winchester Cathedral. She had never had a season in London, or moved in the sort of society that would have put her in the way of a respectable husband. She was nine and twenty years of age, and must feel that life was passing her by. In a few more years, she would be beyond the reach of any prospect of marriage. Yes, she was just the sort of woman who might be responsive to a different sort of offer. It was so difficult to find a mistress who could also provide him with sensible conversation.

It was strange to be returning to Marsham Grove in March. After the frenetic London season, he always spent a few weeks there, enjoying the gentler country society as summer drifted into autumn. He was not fond of hunting, and had lost his appetite for shooting after his father had retired from the sport, but he never minded hosting autumn parties, where the men were out in the fields all day and their wives were left behind, bored and restless. Yes, there were possibilities there. But in March, there would be only the confinement of the local families and the obligation to show himself at church now and again.

Still, the spring colours were pretty, Violet would be an amusement for Mother and Father, and with any luck Miss Parfitt would be an amusement for Eliot himself.

They passed through Epping and within the hour were turning in past the western lodge of Marsham Grove where Matlock's many children all poured out to wave excitedly. Eliot waved cheerily back to them. Then the house was in sight, and there was Powell on the top step, smiling in welcome, and the footmen, James and Richie, bouncing down the steps to open the carriage doors. From the side of the house, a stream of grooms appeared to hold the horses and help with the luggage. And was that the eldest Matlock boy amongst them? Eliot remembered him being born, which made him feel ancient.

"Welcome home, sir," Powell said, beaming, as Eliot dismounted. "The master is taking his nap, but the mistress is in her sitting room."

Violet was all wide-eyed excitement, gazing up at the ivy-clad walls and mullioned windows. Miss Parfitt coolly shook out her skirts, as serene as ever. Eliot was struck with a wild urge to ruffle that calm demeanour. A kiss... surely even the ice-cool Miss Parfitt would melt a little in his arms, with his lips on hers.

Reluctantly brushing such thoughts aside, he left Powell to deal with the baggage and shepherded Violet, Miss Parfitt and Miss Robart into the house, where Mrs Ratcliffe whisked them away to their rooms. He knew he should go to his own room to remove the dust of the journey, but instead he made his way through the house to where a door stood open. He peered round it, and there was Mother, sitting quite alone with her embroidery. Her head was down, a look of intense concentration on her face as she plied her needle, and for a moment he was able to observe her undetected. Was she thinner than at Christmas? He thought she was. Her hair had been entirely white for some years now, and she had ceased to use powder on it well before the fashions changed. She still wore it in the fuller style of her youth, as well as the wider skirts and elegant striped silks that she so loved, which fell in soft folds around her.

By that instinct she had always unerringly had, she was aware of him watching her and looked up at him. "Eliot! Here you are at last! Was your journey tolerable? Come and give me a kiss, my son."

"I am in all my dirt, Mother. I would not put mud on your fine rugs, but I knew you would wish to hear of our arrival at the earliest moment."

She jumped up, still sprightly for her more than sixty years, and made her way to the door to have both cheeks kissed, and to take his hands in hers. "Ah, so cold! Travel is dismal at this time of year. Have you brought your young ward?" He could not miss the brightness in her eye as she spoke.

"Yes, Violet is here, together with her companion, her governess, two lady's maids, her personal footman and a coachman and groom."

His mother laughed merrily. "The house will be full again, as it has not been for too long, and I daresay there will be young men buzzing about her. She has a great fortune, you said?"

"Indeed, but she is very much in mourning and will not be going into company for some time yet." His mother's face fell, so he went on quickly, "And what of Father? Does he go on any better?"

"A little. He has seen a new physician from the north — Scotch, very forward-thinking — who has given him a new regime to follow, which is doing him a little good, I am certain of it. He will be very glad to see you, my son."

"I only hope we will not be too much for him," Eliot said.

"Nonsense! A little company will be just the thing to cheer him up, especially a pretty young thing. She is pretty, I take it, your ward? There you are, then! Every man livens up when there is a young woman to be admired."

By the time Eliot had changed into clean clothes and returned to the sitting room, he found his mother surrounded by Violet's entourage. It was so typical of her to want to meet *everyone*, even the lady's maids and Henry, and make them welcome. The females were all sipping tea, while his mother laboured to make conversation with Henry, who obviously intrigued her. He wondered if she had ever seen a Negro before.

"Where were you born, Henry?" she said brightly.

As always, Violet answered for him. "He is from Africa, Mrs Armitage, but he was taken for a slave at the age of six and shipped to Antigua, but Papa bought him and set him free, so here he is."

"How fascinating!" his mother cried. "What an interesting life you have led, Henry. How long have you been in England?"

"Twelve years," Violet said. "He was just eighteen when he arrived here, and always cold, were you not, Henry? He still feels the cold dreadfully, poor thing! He worked in the shop for a year or two, but then Papa trained him up as a footman and set him to look after me so that I could walk about the streets safely. Poor Papa! He was always so concerned for me."

Her eyes filled with sudden tears, and Mrs Armitage wrapped a motherly arm around her shoulders. "There now, child. You have suffered a tragic loss, and so unexpectedly, too, but you will be able to grieve quietly here for a while until you feel able to venture into company again."

"Oh, I do not mind company. I shall go back to London soon, shall I not, Mr Armitage? The season will begin after Easter, and I cannot miss that!" She must have seen something in Eliot's expression, for her face fell. "Can I?"

"The usual mourning period for a parent is six months, at least," he said. "Perhaps a year."

"Oh, but—" She looked across at Miss Parfitt for support. "That would mean missing the *whole* season! Papa would not let me have a proper season last year, and to miss another year — why, I shall be *nineteen* and positively an old maid!"

"You would not wish the world to think you uncaring of your Papa," Miss Parfitt said quietly. "Accepting the restraints of mourning with grace is the mark of a true lady."

"Oh yes, I wish to be a true lady, but nineteen, Evie! I shall be so old!"

"You will be just as pretty and just as rich as you are at eighteen, dear, and you will have the benefit of another year to add to your poise in society. London ladies are the most elegant and graceful in the world, and you will want to move amongst them with assurance."

"In my experience," Eliot said, "a lady's looks improve with every year."

"Do they?" Violet said hopefully.

"Goodness, Eliot," his mother said with a low laugh. "Then I must be a ravishing beauty indeed."

"As indeed you are," he said, smiling.

"Flatterer! Do you want some tea, my son?"

"I shall leave that for you ladies," he said, moving across to the sideboard where the decanters and glasses stood. Henry was there before him, gesturing with a questioning look at the various wines.

"Madeira, if you please."

Henry poured a glass, placed it on a silver salver and held it out to him with a bow.

"Thank you, Henry," Eliot said gravely.

His mother now delicately suggested that the lady's maids might withdraw. They rose, curtsied in synchrony, turned and marched out side by side, for Heaven forbid that one should place herself before the other. Henry took up position near the door.

The governess rose to leave also, but Mrs Armitage said, "Please stay, Miss Robart. In this house, a governess is part of the family, and I should very much like to know more of Miss Barantine's education, so that we may identify any gaps in her accomplishments and prepare her for her season."

Miss Robart twittered distractedly, half in protest that she was unworthy and far too inferior a person for such condescension, and half in excited gratitude. There was some rearrangement of the seats as Miss Robart and Violet settled themselves nearer to Mrs Armitage. Violet, never reluctant to take the lead in any conversation, began a recitation of all the many subjects Miss Robart had taught her, to all of which the governess nodded and smiled.

"So clever, Violet is," she murmured repeatedly. "None of my doing, I assure you. Such natural ability."

Eliot took the opportunity to sit next to Miss Parfitt.

"She must be the most accomplished girl in England," he whispered.

"Indeed," she said. "Like every other young lady, she plays a little, sings a little, paints a little, embroiders a little, and if she has ever read all three volumes of a book, I should be astonished to hear it. However, if you ask her about the newest styles of bonnet, you will find she can discourse at great length."

He laughed, and said, "She will grow more sensible in time, I fancy." His eye was caught by Henry, standing motionless beside the door, his eyes fixed on his mistress. "Does the footman ever speak?" he whispered.

Her face clouded and she shook her head. He took his cue from her reluctance, and turned the subject.

~~~~~

Dinner was a pleasant affair. There was no doubt that the additional company was good for Eliot's parents. His mother sparkled with energy, and his father... well, he was no worse than before. Even though he looked frail enough to be blown away by a puff of wind like a withered leaf, he still dressed for dinner, stood for the entrance of the ladies and escorted Violet into the dining room himself. Violet was rather overdressed for a simple family dinner, and she was late, arriving in the saloon only minutes before Powell announced dinner, but her youth excused her.

And then there was Miss Parfitt. Her day gowns were plain and unassuming, but in full evening dress, even in black, she was a sight to gladden the heart of any man. She certainly gladdened Eliot's heart, and brought a twinkle to his father's eyes, too. She was no great beauty, and beside Violet's fresh prettiness she looked pale and washed-out, but her quiet dignity and ladylike demeanour were striking, making him wonder just why she remained unwed.

It was his father, with the privilege of age, who asked her the question directly.

"I never met a man I wished to marry," she said at once, smiling. "Not that I met very many men at all, for I have always lived in very confined society. My father was a country parson in a very small village, and we were too poor and insignificant to mix with the
~~~~~

few families of rank in the parish, and yet not at ease amongst the yeoman farmers. A clergyman is a gentleman to those who work with their hands, and yet not the equal of those who do not. It is an awkward position to be in. I had aunts in Winchester and Bath whom I visited from time to time, but no man ever caught my eye."

"But you must have had a great many suitors, I am sure."

"None who could afford to take a dowryless wife."

"How sad!" Mr Armitage said, his aged face distressed. "Every beautiful woman should be cherished by a man."

Miss Parfitt laughed. "You are a romantic, sir. I make no claim to beauty, but I have enjoyed the experience of being cherished by a man — namely, by my father. I shall never meet his equal, and so I cannot lament my lack of a husband."

"Nevertheless, a husband is a woman's best provision against want," he said. "Perhaps you have brothers… cousins…?"

"None, sir. My only relative yet living is my aunt in Winchester, who spends her days making clothes for the workhouse children, and that will be my fate also when my service to Violet is at an end, if I can find no other employment. But you must not pity me, Mr Armitage, for I shall be perfectly content. All I ask is to be useful, to have enough money for my modest wants, and the freedom to select my own path through life. I had sooner be independent than be shackled for ever to a husband."

Eliot listened, smiling inwardly. A woman who wanted no husband, who valued her independence? A woman who asked only money and freedom? She could not have been describing more clearly the life of a mistress.

He spent a quiet half an hour alone with his father talking about estate business, although it seemed to him that his father was depending more and more on his steward, John Curtis. Then there was tea with the ladies before the card tables were set out. Eliot was amused to be the focus of Violet's attentions. Most girls of her age were too young and innocent to flirt, but Violet had an inborn talent for it. She asked him breathlessly for his help with her cards, leaned close as often as she dared, and twice rested her hand on his arm. He was relieved when the supper tray made its appearance, after which they all drifted away to bed.

Eliot changed into his nightgown and robe, retrieved the bottle of wine and two glasses he had placed in the bottom of his wardrobe, then left his room, padding barefoot down the dimly lit passageways until he found the door he wanted. There was still light emanating from the gap around the door and voices within, so he hid in a corner and waited.

After a while, the maid emerged from the room and disappeared. He waited a little longer. The light from within reduced to the level of a single candle. Still he waited.

In some instinctive way, he knew when the moment was right. Creeping down the corridor to the door, he silently turned the handle and pushed on the door. It yielded a bare two inches, and then stopped. He tried again, with the same result. He pushed a little harder, but the door would not open.

"Who is there?" The voice was puzzled, but not afraid.

"It is only I," he said in a low voice. "May I come in?"

The candle appeared in the gap between the door and its frame, momentarily blinding him. "Oh. No, Mr Armitage, you may not."

"I have brought wine."

"Go away," she said quietly. "Go to bed — your *own* bed — and leave me alone."

"I only wish to talk to you," he said. "We can—"

"No." She shut the door in his face, but so softly that he felt, rather than heard, it close.

He turned the knob and pushed the door open its two inches again. "Why does this door not open properly?"

"Because I have jammed a cupboard against it in case of nocturnal wanderings," she said calmly. "A wise precaution, as it turned out. Please go away, Mr Armitage."

She shut the door again.

Laughing, Eliot made his way back to his own room. She wanted to play games, did she? Well, so be it. He never minded the thrill of the chase and a certain reluctance from the female. That would only make his eventual success all the sweeter.

And he would succeed, on that he was determined. Once he had set his mind on a woman, he would not rest until she was his, whether she intended it or not. One day, sooner or later, Evie Parfitt would be his.

4: A Conversation In The Conservatory

Evie paced about her room, seething. She should leave instantly — before breakfast tomorrow. But a few minutes of quiet reflection brought her to a more rational frame of mind. Mr Armitage might, perhaps, be one of those men who tried to get up a flirtation with any available woman, but would abandon the pursuit at the first refusal. There was no purpose in wasting his attentions on so hopeless a case. Besides, she could hardly leave the house so precipitously — a grievous insult to her gentle host and hostess! And then there was Violet. It would be callous to leave her to the ministrations of two gently squabbling maids, a diffident governess and a silent footman. In time, perhaps, Mrs Armitage would take over Evie's rôle as confidante and guide, or perhaps one of her daughters, but until then, she must stay and avoid Mr Armitage as much as possible.

Violet! What if Mr Armitage thought to try elsewhere after Evie had rebuffed him? And Violet — sweet, innocent Violet — might well invite him into her room. Hastily throwing on a wrap, Evie carefully moved aside the low cupboard barring the way and opened the door a fraction. The corridor was dark but for the night light burning on a high shelf. Cautiously she crept along the corridor and down the stairs, where the rough druggets gave way to soft rugs. All was quiet. She hesitated outside Violet's room, not wishing to wake her unnecessarily.

A dark shape clad in an intricately embroidered banyan loomed out of the darkness. For an instant, Evie heart lurched in fear, but almost at once she realised that this man was much larger in both height and girth than Mr Armitage.

"Henry!" she said in relief. "Keeping good watch over your mistress, I see. Has anyone been past her door recently, apart from myself?"

He shook his head.

"Does she keep her door locked?" A nod. "And one of her maids is with her?" Another nod. "Excellent. You are a good and faithful servant, Henry, but Miss Barantine is quite safe. You may go to bed now."

He bowed as punctiliously as if they were in the drawing room, rather than in a dark corridor in their nightclothes, and departed on light feet. Satisfied, Evie returned to her own bedroom, but she carefully checked inside the wardrobe and under the bed for interlopers before she felt it safe to push the cupboard across the door again and retire to bed.

~~~~~

When Evie reached the breakfast parlour the next day, she found only Violet, Mr Eliot Armitage and his mother there, with Henry, as always, hovering behind his mistress. Violet was in full flow.
~~~~~

"But do you not see? Someone must have stolen them, or else they would have been found, do you not agree? Papa would have had them on his person, for he always did, and if they were not amongst his possessions, then some thief must have stolen them."

Mr Armitage, to whom these words were addressed, steadily worked his way through a large plate of ham and eggs, unperturbed, but Mrs Armitage looked distressed.

"Oh dear! It is very worrying. You poor girl, as if you had not enough to worry you without half your father's fortune going missing. Can anything be done, Eliot? Surely something can be done to find these diamonds."

He laid down his knife and fork, and said calmly, "It is hard to see what, however. We do not even know whether Mr Barantine had them in his possession when he boarded the ship, and if he did, they may well have been washed away and lie at the bottom of the English Channel."

"No, that could not happen," Violet cried. "Papa always kept his jewels stitched into the seams of his clothing, and all of it was recovered, was it not?"

"I believe it was," Mr Armitage said, picking up his knife and fork again.

"But perhaps no one thought to look for the jewels!" Violet cried distressfully.

"It would be shocking indeed if his clothes had been given away to the poor," Mrs Armitage said, one hand playing restlessly with her pearl necklace.

"Or given to his valet," Evie said.

"No, that was not possible, for poor Mr Crick drowned, too," Violet said, her soft eyes filling with tears again.

"Oh dear me!" Mrs Armitage said, the pearls clicking under her restless fingers. "So many tragic deaths. So sad!"

"Perhaps Mr Barantine was buried in his clothes," Evie said brightly.

Mr Armitage set down his knife and fork again with a sigh. "This is all very well, but I do not see what may be done about it. The diamonds are gone, and the deed for the business too, and that is an end to the matter."

Violet subsided, although she produced a delicate lace handkerchief and sniffed quietly until she realised that Mr Armitage was unmoved by her tears. Mrs Armitage, more troubled, played with her necklace, her breakfast abandoned.

Into the silence, Evie said cheerfully, "What a delicious array of pastries, Mrs Armitage. Your cook is a treasure."

"Oh indeed, Mrs Flynn is a marvel. Just wait until you have tried her orange puffs, and she has such a way with woodcock and partridge." A pause and then she remembered her rôle as hostess. "I trust you slept well, Miss Parfitt?"

"Indeed I did, thank you. It would hardly be possible to sleep badly in such a comfortable and well-appointed room, and Margie has been most helpful to me."

"And you have everything you need?"

"There is just one small matter... quite trivial, in fact, but the key to my room seems to have vanished. I was certain it was there yesterday afternoon, yet when I retired to bed last night it was nowhere to be found. Perhaps one of the servants took it by mistake. It is of little consequence, but in these large houses it is so easy for a guest to become disoriented and find himself entering the wrong room. I should prefer to be able to lock my door to prevent any misunderstandings."

"Oh dear! Of course, of course, I shall speak to Mrs Ratcliffe about it... or perhaps it is a matter for Powell."

"Let me take care of it, Mother," Mr Armitage said silkily. "Locks and keys are a male province, I feel."

"I do believe you are correct, sir," Evie said evenly, sipping her coffee.

"Thank you, my son," Mrs Armitage said, beaming at him. "What would I do without you?"

Powell came in just then. "Mr Armitage is awake, madam."

"Oh dear! I must go to him at once. Pray excuse me, Miss Parfitt, Violet."

She rushed away distractedly, and the room fell into silence, Violet still morose over her lost diamonds, while Evie and Mr Armitage ate steadily and exchanged neither word nor glance.

The door opened again, and Miss Robart was shown in by Powell. "Thank you so much. So kind! Much obliged. Here you all are! So easy to become confused in these old houses, do you not think? Not you, of course, Mr Armitage, naturally, for this is your home, but for strangers — so many twists and turns, and I found myself descending by the service stairs and not the least idea in the world until I met the housemaid. Although there are those who would say that is my proper place." She tittered. "So kind as everyone is to me! So grateful. Why, thank you, Mr Armitage, so gracious, but there is no need to hold the chair for me... well, if you insist. How affable you are. Oh my, so many varieties of bread and bun laid out for us. Goodness, where to begin? Oh, thank you, Henry. How splendid it all is."

Mr Armitage, having risen for Miss Robart's entry and waited patiently through her apologetic twitterings, now turned to Evie.

"I wonder, Miss Parfitt, if you would favour me with a few minutes of your time to talk in private? If we ask Violet for the loan of Henry, we may talk in the conservatory without the least impropriety."

"Why do you want to talk to Evie in private?" Violet said at once. "Whatever can you have to say to her that we may not all hear?"

"I want to talk to her about you, of course," he said at once. "How else may I plan surprises for you if I do not talk to Miss Parfitt in private?"

"Oh! Surprises? What kind of surprises?"

"If I were to tell you that, they would hardly be surprises, would they?" he said easily, and she laughed and said no more.

"Shall we?" Mr Armitage said, offering his arm to Evie. She could not well refuse, but since she guessed — or perhaps *hoped* — that he wished to apologise, and since she wished to set the matter to rest once and for all, she allowed herself to be escorted out of the room, with the watchful Henry in attendance.

The conservatory was a long, narrow room squeezed between two corner protrusions of the house. Mr Armitage stationed Henry at one end of it and led Evie to a cluster of chairs at the other end. The wind, and a light rain rattling against the window panes, rendered it impossible for Henry to overhear them. Evie chose a seat, and Mr Armitage took the one next to hers, close enough for conversation but not close enough for any intimacy.

"Thank you," he said simply, and she could not mistake the sincerity in his eyes. "Let us first talk about Violet, so that we may truthfully say that we have done so. Does she ride?"

"She does, although not well. Her father arranged lessons, but he was too fearful for her safety to provide a horse for her."

"And you? Do you ride?"

Her eyebrows rose. "A little."

"You must both practise, then. I will make arrangements with Winfield. You both have habits?" She nodded. "Good. And now we may come to what I wished to say to you, Miss Parfitt, for we seem to have got off on the wrong foot. I am sorry if I startled you last night, but I would never have harmed you. All I looked for was a little conversation, nothing more."

His effrontery took her breath away. It was the most paltry apology, considering the offence, and to say that all he wanted was conversation was disingenuous indeed.

"Mr Armitage, when a gentleman tries to enter a lady's bedroom at midnight, a little conversation is not usually all he expects."

"Well, as to that, it would have been delightful, but I should never have forced you. I have never in my life taken a woman against her will, and never shall."

"But you planned to enter my bedroom against my will," she said quietly. "You deliberately removed the key to my door so that you could have your little conversation, whether I wished it or not. That is not the action of a gentleman, sir, and I want your absolute assurance — your word of honour — that you will not try such a trick on Violet."

"Good God, no! I have no taste for ingenues, believe me."

"How reassuring," she said acidly.

"She is my *ward*. Naturally I shall always treat her with respect."

"As you do not treat me."

"You mistake me!" he cried, then, with a glance at Henry, whose eyes were unwaveringly fixed on them, he went on in a low voice, "I have the greatest respect for you, believe me. I am accorded a connoisseur of women, so to attract my attention is a compliment, I do assure you. You should be flattered."

Evie was too shocked to utter a word, and after a moment, he went on, "Let us speak openly, shall we? You have given me reason to believe you would be open to an informal approach of this nature, so—"

"I have done nothing of the kind!"

"No? That is how I read your remarks, but perhaps I was mistaken in this instance. No matter. You may consider the question now. You are of an age when marriage is becoming less likely, and although you live in some comfort at present, you will not always be needed by Violet and your prospects then will not be enticing. I can give you everything you want — money, a pleasant life in good society and some independence. I have a fully staffed suite of rooms in London for the use of my mistress, and I am not a demanding man. In time, you may wish to move on to another patron, but if not, you have my word that you will always be taken care of."

She jumped to her feet, although her legs trembled so violently that she was not sure they would carry her. “Say no more,” she said, her voice hoarse with shock. “What you propose is utterly vile.”

“Vile? No, no, no!” he said, politely standing too. “A mistress has all the fun of marriage with none of the responsibilities. You need not have children unless you wish it. Did you not say that you wanted to be independent? What I offer is exactly that. It is a business arrangement, that is all. Employment, if you like, just as you are employed to help Violet, except that you would be employed by me instead. What is so strange about that?”

“You think because I am poor and unmarriageable, I have no alternative but to accept this... this *wicked* proposal. I had rather be dead, Mr Armitage!”

His eyebrows rose. “Hmm. That is clear enough, if disappointing, but perhaps I may yet persuade you if—”

“Never!” Her legs gave way, and she plumped down onto the chair again, unable to look at him, quite unable to think how to escape from this nightmare. If she tried to walk out, she might swoon altogether, and how feeble that would be! Yet she had no words to set against his absolute assurance in his own charms. He was entirely at his ease, still smiling, not in the least put out.

“Miss Parfitt... Evie...” he said, and his voice was as smooth and soft as butter. “You hide behind this cool, ladylike exterior, but inside there is a passionate woman. How do I know this? Because there is passion inside *every* woman, if only the right man should come along to release it. Have you never been kissed? You make no answer, but I believe you have not, Evie. If you had, you would not tremble so when I speak of it. One kiss... that is all it would take, I swear it. One wonderful kiss... and then you would understand.”

She raised her eyes to his, and that was a mistake, for they gazed into hers with an intensity which made her shake even more violently.

"Will you let me kiss you, Evie?"

"No!"

He gave a low chuckle. "You cannot blame me for wanting to try."

That threat gave her the impetus to rise to her feet again. He rose to face her, and the amusement in his eyes drove everything from her mind but rage, pure, burning rage.

"I am going to pack. Please order the carriage to take me to the nearest stage coach station."

"Ah, no, Evie, do not leave." Now the eyes were anxious. "Violet needs you here. You cannot desert her so soon after her father's death."

It was blackmail, and she knew it, but there was truth in it, too. She had argued exactly so herself, not a few hours earlier. It would look so very particular to rush away on the common stage only the day after her arrival. The world would wonder what exactly had happened to make her run away, and it would not be Mr Armitage who took the blame. No man ever took the blame in such cases. The world would assume that something bad had happened, and that Evie herself had been at fault. That was what the world always decided. However difficult it was, she must stay until she could make an orderly retreat.

"Very well, for Violet's sake, but I warn you, if you lay one finger on me, Mr Armitage, then I shall leave within the hour."

The amusement was back instantly, and he made her an ironic little bow. "It shall be as you wish, madam."

"I have your word as a gentleman?"

"Upon my honour, I swear it. But I am determined to have that kiss sooner or later."

"And I am determined that you shall not."

He chuckled. "That is a challenge that I intend to win handsomely, Miss Parfitt. You see, I have promised not to lay a finger upon your person, but I shall not need to do so, for *you* are going to kiss *me."*

"Never!"

"Indeed you will, because I am going to make you fall in love with me."

5: A Ride In The Country

Evie raged back and forth across her bedroom floor for fully an hour before she felt calm enough even to sit and consider her position sensibly. Then she took the chair at the small table in the window and pondered her options. She must be prepared for flight, she decided. No matter the promises Mr Armitage had made, she did not trust him to keep them, and at the first transgression, she must leave, for her own protection. She would not stay here to become a victim of Mr Armitage's lascivious ways. If he wanted a mistress, he must look elsewhere. Such an insult! How could he so mistake her as to imagine she *wanted* his attentions? The more she considered his behaviour, the more outraged she was.

Again, she made herself be calm. She retrieved her purse, which she kept locked away in her travel box. Twenty three pounds six shillings and fourpence. Was that enough to get her to Winchester on the stage? If need be she could sell something to raise funds — her necklace with the garnet pendant, perhaps. The two bone combs. The ivory fan her father had given her when she first went into society. It would be a wrench to part with any of them, but she would do it if she had to.

She considered her clothes. Little would be needed for a hasty flight, so she carefully packed her small portmanteau and placed it in the bottom of the wardrobe. Thus prepared for any emergency, she felt composed enough to go in search of Violet and pretend that nothing had happened. She found her in an airy room positioned in a corner of the building, so that light entered from two sides.

Violet looked up with an over-bright smile, and Evie realised with a spasm of guilt that she had abandoned her without a thought. That would never do! Miss Robart sat in a corner with a book, and Violet sat at the round table, now covered with the debris of her millinery efforts.

"Oh, Evie, there you are! Do you like this bonnet better so, or should I put the feathers back on? But black feathers are so dreary, do you not agree? What did Mr Armitage say? Is it to be a lovely surprise? Shall I like it very much?"

For a moment, Evie was non-plussed. What surprise? Her mind was so fixed on her own conversation with Mr Armitage that she could not recollect the matter at all, and only with a great effort did she force herself to remember.

"Oh... oh, certainly! But you will see before too long. I think the bonnet was very well as it was. Should you like me to put the feathers back?"

"If you please! Your fingers are much better at such delicate work than mine. Everything I try to rework comes out looking worse than it was when I began."

"Then I wonder that you will so often insist upon making the attempt," Evie said, but she softened the reproof with a smile, as she sat and picked up the bonnet. She was little minded for such work, but it would occupy her hands and the necessity to listen to

Violet's chattering and answer periodically would keep her thoughts from wandering.

She had not been working for long when the door opened and Mr Armitage entered. Evie tried to look composed, and hoped that he would soon go away, or at least would say nothing to her. On both counts she was to be disappointed.

"Miss Parfitt, I have located the key to your room," he said, as casually as if he were talking about the weather.

"Oh, whatever happened to it?" Violet cried at once.

"It was removed in error," he said smoothly, looking not the least bit conscious, with no sign at all that he had himself removed it. "My apologies for the deficiencies of the house." He made Evie a little bow, and laid the key on the table beside her.

"Thank you, sir." It was an effort to prevent her hands from shaking as she tucked the heavy key into her reticule.

"Violet, would you like to see your surprise now?"

She clapped her hands excitedly, so that the delicate curls framing her face bounced in fervent sympathy. "Very much, if you please, sir. Is it a *splendid* surprise? Shall I like it?"

"I hope you will," he said. "Miss Parfitt, Miss Robart, you may come too."

They followed him out of the front door, where the rain had now stopped, and round to the side of the house. Set a little distance away were the stables, and here they were introduced to Winfield, the elderly head groom of Marsham Grove, and shown the many horses there. Amongst the carriage horses and gentlemen's mounts were several smaller animals, which looked to Evie's eyes more manageable for an inexpert rider.

"This will be your first mount, Violet," Mr Armitage said, stopping beside a pretty grey mare. "Her name is Bright Lady, and she is gentle enough for you to learn your way about the estate. Miss Parfitt will ride Dawn Light here. Both of them are used to carrying ladies, so you will not find them too boisterous. Once you are accustomed to their manners and begin to find them too tame, I shall look about for something more suitable for London. If you are to ride in Hyde Park you must be seen on something a little more showy than these gentle beasts. Miss Robart, do you ride, too?"

"Oh, indeed not, Mr Armitage, sir. How shocking for a mere governess to ride about like a lady."

"My sisters' governesses all rode with them, so I do not find the idea in the least shocking," he said, his eyes full of amusement. "Should you like to?"

He turned his gaze fully on her, and she blushed scarlet. "Oh... oh, indeed, how generous, how gracious! Such a kindness to consider me... how very... but I cannot see... it does not seem to me... I should not be comfortable... it would not be... I do not think..."

He stepped in smoothly to cut short her confusion. "Well, if you change your mind, you need only say the word. Violet, there are some rules."

"There are always rules," she said sulkily. "I am not a child, Mr Armitage."

"Indeed you are not," he said equably, "but you are at present unfamiliar with both your horse and also the estate and surrounding terrain, therefore you will not under any circumstances ride without a groom, and Miss Parfitt, if it suits her to accompany you. The groom will direct you, and you will follow his instructions or those of Miss Parfitt at all times. Is that clearly understood?"

She pouted, but nodded briefly once.

"If I hear of even the smallest transgression, your right to ride will be forfeit."

She gazed at him, as if wondering how far she might push him. Her father had been an indulgent parent, easily coaxed into compliance, but on the matter of her safety, he had been unshakable. Perhaps Violet recognised the same implacable tone, for she bowed her head demurely. "I shall be very good. How often may I ride?"

"Every day, if you wish."

"Not on Sundays, I trust," Evie put in.

Mr Armitage bowed his head courteously. "Every day *except* Sundays."

"Today?" Violet said, her face suddenly alight with anticipation.

He laughed, and agreed to it. Nothing would do then but for Violet to rush away to don her habit at once, with Evie following in a more decorous manner. When they returned, their horses were saddled ready for them, together with two other horses, a nondescript hack for the groom, and the elegant long-legged animal Mr Armitage rode. Evie's heart sank. So he meant to accompany them... was this part of his plan to win her over? But he made no attempt to lift her into the saddle, focusing his attention entirely on Violet and leaving Evie to be assisted by Winfield. It was perfectly proper, yet oddly, she was a little disappointed.

Her spirits rose as they rode sedately out of the stable yard, for Mr Armitage positioned himself beside Violet, pointing out the various landmarks along the way, and occasionally correcting the position of her hands on the reins. She for her part flirted outrageously with him, but he took no notice, his manner towards her never less than avuncular. Evie's horse plodded gamely along in their wake, with Winfield slightly behind her. Perhaps after all Mr Armitage had given up his intended assault on her heart?

They crossed the open part of the grounds surrounding the house, which were not large, and entered into a track bordered on one side by fields and on the other by woodland. The track passed a large, prosperous-looking farm and then Winfield opened a gate for them to enter a large, grassy field, empty of stock.

"Violet, would you like to try a canter?" Mr Armitage said. When she nodded, he turned to Winfield. "Take her round, will you? Miss Parfitt and I will observe from here."

They set off at a gentle pace, Winfield riding alongside Violet and keeping a close eye on her, ready to intervene if necessary.

Mr Armitage drew up his horse beside Evie's, and for some minutes nothing was said as they both watched Violet's progress. She completed a circuit of the field and began another.

"She has not been well-taught, I think," he said, frowning. "Her seat is not good, she is lax with the reins and she has too much confidence. Look at the way she waves to me from the far side of the field, when I have told her repeatedly to keep hold of the reins. You would not do so, I fancy, Miss Parfitt. You have had the benefit of excellent tutelage, yet you lack confidence in the saddle."

"It is a long way to the ground," she said.

He laughed. "Very true! Was it your father who taught you?"

"No, Papa could never afford to keep a horse. We had kindly neighbours who took me under their wing when I was a child. I had lessons with their daughters for a while, which included riding lessons." Her tone was flat, and she hoped he would ask no more.

"Kindly and *rich* neighbours, I deduce," he said lightly. "Do you still see the daughters?"

"Not at all. They move in a very different sphere from me."

"Ah, that is sad, when childhood friends are pushed apart by the circumstances of adult life. But you need not regret their loss, Miss Parfitt. True friends would continue to seek you out, no matter where you go or how different your life may be from theirs."

There was unexpected sympathy in his eyes, and for an instant her own eyes filled with tears. She quickly blinked them away, and said, "Very true," in a colourless tone. To her relief, he took the hint and turned the subject.

"I believe Violet has had enough excitement for one day. We will return to the house by the eastern woods."

He resumed his place beside Violet, and Evie quickly recovered her composure. It was a long time ago, after all, and ridiculous to still feel the slight after so many years.

Their route passed a small cottage, and just as they approached, a man emerged, hat in hand, and strode down the short garden path, waiting at the gate for their little group to pass by. He was rather young, no more than five and twenty, but soberly dressed from head to foot in black, and as handsome a man as Evie had ever seen. He bowed politely as they rode past, but his expression was dark, as if he disapproved of them.

"Who was that?" Violet asked, almost before they were out of earshot.

"I have not the least idea," Mr Armitage said. "I never saw him before in my life."

"That's the new parson, sir," Winfield said. "Mr Nettles, from Colchester way."

"The new parson, eh? He looked like a nettlish sort of a man... very prickly."

Mr Armitage laughed at his own wit, but Evie thought it rather an ill-humoured remark. Perhaps Mr Armitage expected Mr Nettles to display a deal more obsequiousness towards the residents of the local great house. Winfield perhaps thought so too, for he muttered, "Nay, he's a good man and a good parson, too," in an undertone that only Evie could hear.

She found herself looking forward to the Sabbath with greater than usual interest.

~~~~~

'Marsham Grove, Essex. March 20th. My very dear aunt, Thank you for your long letter, the very best kind, for I love to hear that you have so much news to impart. I am so glad your little evening party went well, and the new Deacon sounds quite charming, although I do not think you will make a match for him with Miss Brighton. She so despises all men, and particularly men of the cloth, that it seems a hopeless business. I am not greatly enamoured of the male sex myself just now, especially young Mr Armitage. He is just the sort of man I despise — rich, idle and utterly selfish. He lounges about the place all day, hardly going anywhere, except to accompany us on our gentle rides, and even joins us in the morning room most days, which is a great annoyance, for how can we indulge ourselves in discussing his many faults when he is in the room? I do not even know why he is here, for I fully expected him to disappear back to the pleasures of
~~~~~

London at the earliest opportunity, yet here he still is, and looking very settled. He is a good-for-nothing, and I cannot understand why he undertook to become Violet's guardian, for it seems not at all consistent with his character. He seemed quite gentlemanly in London, but now that I can compare him with his father, who is a perfect gentleman in every way, the difference is clear to see. My page is full already! How did I write so much when nothing at all has happened here? I will put a guinea under the seal — try to get a bit of fish for a change, if it is not too dear. It will do you good. Your loving niece, Evie.'

~~~~~

Eliot was quietly pleased with his progress with Evie Parfitt. He had deliberately paid her little attention, but when he had done so, he had succeeded in drawing a moment of emotion from her, and that was promising, very promising! She was such a serene person that it was rather a triumph to have dented her poise even so slightly. He knew better than to press home his advantage, however. She would need delicate handling, not a bullish approach, but he was a patient man.

That evening, when the ladies had withdrawn, his father said to him, "What are your plans, young man? Are you away to London again soon?"

"I thought I might stay for a few weeks," Eliot said, twirling his port glass with one hand. "At least until after Easter."

"Ah." His father took a sip of port. "Then you have some game afoot. Miss Parfitt?"

"Mm. I thought it might be amusing to crack that oh-so-proper veneer of ladylike coolness."
~~~~~

His father chuckled. "Quite a challenge, I should think. She is the daughter of a clergyman, after all, and she was telling me earlier that she lives with the relict of a canon, no less, when she is not playing nursemaid to a chit of a girl."

"All the more entertaining to watch her crumble, then."

"True enough. The chase is never so enjoyable as when it is real, but I hope you will be discreet, Eliot. She is a guest in this house, and I should not like your mother to be distressed by a scandal."

"No scandal. Miss Parfitt is not minded for anything serious, so I am only proposing a little flirtation."

His father nodded. "Very well, but have a care with her. These vicarage girls take things to heart. They are apt to squeal, and start ranting about a wedding ring."

"I will make sure there is no danger of that. No one has caught me yet, Father." He took a thoughtful sip from his glass. "I suppose I should be thinking about it, though. Marriage, I mean."

"Pooh, plenty of time yet. Why, you are not yet thirty!"

"I was thirty last birthday, Father," Eliot said with a smile.

"Were you? Well, bless me, where does the time go to? Seems like no time since you were running around in leading strings. Still, no need to rush it. I was five and thirty before I started to look about me, and that was plenty soon enough. You want to have time to enjoy yourself, you know. Marriage... it changes everything. A man can never just please himself after that, he must always take his wife's wishes into account or else there is the Devil to pay."

Eliot laughed, and said, "Come now, Father, Mother never cramped your style in the slightest, and she certainly never kicked up a fuss about anything."

"Well, no, I suppose not, but a wife is always *there*, if you understand me. Almost everywhere one goes, there she goes too, and there is hardly anywhere a man can take his mistress after that."

His tone was wistful, and Eliot caught an unexpected glimpse of the tensions of a life where a man had both wife and mistress, and none of the three entirely happy with the arrangement. It was unsettling.

His father went on, "If you are to be here for a while, perhaps you will ride over and see Nancy one day? Make sure she is all right, that sort of thing."

"I will do that. Should you like to write a letter for me to take?"

"Oh no... so awkward, because Mrs Armitage is always about, you know, and she would want to know to whom I was writing. But see if there is anything Nancy needs, anything at all."

To lighten the serious tone a little, Eliot told his father about the riding expedition that day.

"We passed the new clergyman as we returned, and a sour-faced fellow he is."

"Is he so?" his father said, chuckling. "The ladies like him, so I have heard, and he is popular amongst the common people for his fiery sermons."

"He is one of those Evangelicals, is he?" Eliot said. "I might have to hear one of those fiery sermons for myself. Whatever made you choose such a man for sleepy Lower Marsham?"

"He came highly recommended, and paid handsomely for the living. I feel rather guilty that I have not paid him the courtesy of calling upon him as I should have done. If you attend on Sunday, you may make my apologies for me and explain that I never leave the house now. But why not invite him for dinner on Sunday? That would be a very proper attention, do you not think?"

Eliot thought it would also be a very proper way to remove any vestige of pleasure from the evening, but he smiled his agreement.

"That is settled, then," his father said happily. "Shall we join the ladies now?"

After tea, his mother said brightly, "Shall we play Speculation again, as we did last night? That was such fun, was it not?"

His father's face fell a little, but he said politely, "As you wish, my dear."

Eliot remembered that his father had grown very tired during the game, but had not wished to spoil the others' pleasure by withdrawing. "Perhaps you would care to play cribbage with me, Father?" he said. "That way, we can leave the ladies to play whatever noisy game they choose."

"Are you a cribbage player, Mr Armitage?" Miss Parfitt said, hearing this exchange. "I should be delighted to challenge you, for it is a favourite game with me."

It was amusing how his father perked up at the prospect. Eliot settled himself at the other table with Violet, Miss Robart and his mother, but he positioned himself so that he could watch Miss Parfitt, and was astonished at how she unbent as the game progressed. She smiled, she even laughed when she made a good play, and he could not deny that there was a certain pale prettiness about her when she was so animated. His father was mesmerised by her, to the point that he was almost flirting, and was so engrossed in the game that he did not leave off until the supper tray arrived.

Eliot himself had a less enjoyable evening. None of the ladies displayed much aptitude for whist and Violet was far more interested in chattering nonsensically about her clothes, interspersed with laments about her missing diamonds, ending every tedious pronouncement with, "Do you not agree, Mr Armitage?" He enjoyed being fashionable as much as the next man, but such an obsession with sleeves or trimmings or jewellery was beyond him. In the end, he was forced to reprove her for her lack of attention to the game, after which she sulked, and played, if such a thing were possible, even worse than before. It was a long, dull evening.

Even so, he was not displeased. He had carefully not shown Miss Parfitt any special attention, and went to bed satisfied that his campaign to woo her had made a good start.

6: The New Clergyman

Sunday in the country was not a day Eliot much enjoyed. In town, no one took too much notice of the restrictions of the Sabbath, and although there were no social occasions of any importance, there would always be two or three invitations to informal dinners, and good company to be had. At home, however, there was absolutely nothing to relieve the boredom.

He dutifully rose early and dressed for church, however, joining the group gathered in the hall. It was no more than a mile to the church, and since it was a fine day, cold but dry and clear, even Violet felt that she could manage the walk and the carriage need not be summoned. The time for departure had been set the evening before, but Violet, naturally, was late. Eliot had never known her to be on time for anything as she fussed over her appearance, but he had presumed that she would make an exception for church. He presumed wrongly.

Miss Parfitt sat composedly, Prayer Book in hand. Miss Robart eyed the long-case clock and twittered nervously. Henry stood immobile at the foot of the stairs. Violet appeared once to ask Miss Parfitt's advice on the matter of a pelisse, then disappeared again.

"Can she not even be on time for church?" Eliot cried.

"Not even for God," Miss Parfitt said equably. "Her father used to say that she will be late for her own funeral."

"And you are obliged to be late also. It is thoughtless of her, very thoughtless. We shall wait no longer. Henry, do you know the way? It is straight through the shrubbery to the gate in the wall, and then down the lane, impossible to go astray." Henry nodded once. "Very well. Miss Parfitt, Miss Robart, we will leave now."

Miss Parfitt sat still. "I cannot do so, sir. I am engaged to attend upon Violet, just as Henry is, and must not abandon my post."

"Such sentiments do you credit, but you are employed by me, now, and therefore you will obey my orders. Violet has Henry and both her lady's maids to accompany her. She does not need you as well."

"Henry and the lady's maids will sit with the other servants. Your scheme leaves Violet to enter church and find her way to the family pew quite alone."

"That is the choice she has made by being late. Come, Miss Parfitt."

Still she hesitated, a little colour in her cheeks, but after a moment she rose obediently. Ritchie, the footman left behind to mind the house, held the door open for them.

"Explain to Miss Barantine that we have gone ahead," Eliot said to him, as they left the house.

They walked briskly through the shrubbery, passing through the gate and thence down the lane to the church, a rather pretty Norman affair with flint walls. A small group of parishioners still loitered outside, turning to bow or curtsy respectfully as their little group passed by, their eyes mostly lingering on Miss Parfitt. Eliot's acquisition of a ward would be well known in the district by now, and the exact numbers of her household, so there would naturally be curiosity to see the newcomers. The drab Miss Robart, scuttling along with her head down, drew no notice, but the graceful Miss Parfitt could not fail to attract attention.

Inside the church, they settled in their pew, Nettles took up his position and began the service. He had reached the end of the first prayer when there was a sudden hush over the back of the church, where those too poor to afford a pew stood.

Eliot peered over the top of the pew wall. There by the door, the crowds had parted and Violet's small, black-clad figure stood uncertainly. Behind her, the imposing shape of Henry and the two lady's maids.

Mr Nettles lowered his Prayer Book. "Do come in," he said, but the tone was coldly disapproving.

Eliot stood so that Violet could see him. With relief on her face, she scurried down the aisle and rushed into the pew. One of the Marsham Grove footmen waved Henry and the lady's maids to the servants' pew.

Nettles raised his Prayer Book and repeated the last lines of the prayer, with some emphasis — *'And grant, O most merciful Father, for his sake; That we may hereafter live a* godly, righteous, and sober life, *To the glory of thy holy Name. Amen.'* Violet sat, head defiantly raised, and there she stayed, unmoving, throughout the long service. The sermon was indeed fiery, extolling the virtues of poverty, which Eliot privately thought a bit much from a man who lived on the tithes of a fine, wealthy parish.

Eventually it was over, and Eliot shepherded the ladies outside. He did not forget his father's request that he apologise to Nettles for neglecting to call upon him, and also invite him to dinner. The clergyman received this without obvious signs of pleasure, looking rather as if he had accidentally eaten something disagreeable, but Eliot was beginning to suspect that this was his habitual expression. He was glad to begin the walk home and leave the church behind.

Violet walked in sullen silence, and it amused Eliot to prod at her ill-humour by maintaining a cheerful monologue as he kept pace with her. She ignored him, and as they approached the house he said light-heartedly, "You wound me deeply, Violet. I am sure Miss Parfitt would tell you that a lady should respond politely to all conversational overtures from a gentleman."

"And so I should, but you are no gentleman, Mr Armitage, to leave me to walk into church all alone. It was a most unpleasant experience."

"If you wish to avoid such unpleasantness you should learn to be on time, but it is my opinion that you enjoy being late so that you will be the centre of attention."

"Oh!" she cried, turning furiously towards him, and even in anger her beauty was undimmed. "You are perfectly horrid, and I have changed my mind about having you as my guardian! I shall choose someone else, someone who treats me with respect and consideration."

"Unfortunately you cannot change your mind now, for the Lord Chancellor has approved the arrangement and so you are stuck with me until you come of age," he said, with out the least sign of dismay. "But do not despair, for I shall only beat you for very serious misdemeanours. Minor transgressions will only incur a week of confinement to your room with nothing but bread and water to sustain you."

Violet was so incensed that she was reduced to stamping her foot in silent rage before stomping away in a huff.

Miss Parfitt muffled a laugh. "You are wicked, sir, to tease her so."

"Perhaps, but at least it may deter her from any matrimonial ambitions in my direction," he said, permitting himself a smile at Violet's disappearing back. "If it stops her from flirting with me, I shall consider this a good day's work."

~~~~~

Mr Nettles arrived for dinner before anyone else was ready, and Eliot had to hustle through his dressing in order to rescue him from his solitude.

"You find us all unprepared, Nettles," he said cheerfully. "Will you take a glass of something? Sherry, perhaps?"

"Thank you, but no."

"As you wish. I did not hear a carriage. Did you walk over?"

"I did. I keep neither horse nor carriage."

"Then you must allow us to order ours to convey you home this evening."

"There is no need, I assure you. I have brought my lantern, and it is no distance." He said no more, turning to examine one of the glass cases containing Mrs Armitage's figurines.

"My mother collects porcelain," Eliot said.

"So I observe," Nettles said repressively.
~~~~~

Eliot gave up any attempt at conversation, and wandered off to the sideboard where the decanters stood, pouring himself a large measure of sherry. The evening promised to be a long one. He was relieved when Miss Parfitt entered the room, and engaged Nettles in polite discourse about his home and parish. Her efforts were little more successful than his own, but she laboured gamely on, and when his mother appeared shortly after, the two ladies carried the conversation between them. Violet was late, naturally, but not so late as to inconvenience the kitchen, for once.

Dinner was unexpectedly amusing, however, and that, too, was because of Violet. Despite the permanent expression of disapproval on Nettles' face, he was the youngest man in the room, and the nearest in age to Violet, and thus became the target of her flirtation. She could not have expended her efforts on a less grateful recipient. Eliot could hardly imagine that any man would be immune to the attentions of a girl as beautiful and artlessly flattering as Violet, for he even felt the pull of her charms himself, but somehow Nettles, a country parson of no great importance, was able to resist her. He answered her monosyllabically, and as often as he could he turned rather pointedly towards Mrs Armitage on his other side.

Nettles was no more fluent a conversationalist without the ladies, and Eliot's father proposed a return to the saloon as soon as was decent. There was no music, being a Sunday, and no cards either.

"Mr Nettles, perhaps you would care to read us a sermon?" Mrs Armitage said brightly. "I have some books of sermons here for you to choose from."

"Oh, I do hope you will favour us with a more cheerful subject than this morning's," Violet said, simpering at him. "Such a *lowering* topic, poverty, do you not think?"

He gazed at her with the slightest lift of his eyebrows. "A young lady such as yourself, Miss Barantine, whose life has been devoted to frivolity and excessive display, cannot properly contemplate philosophical discourse with the required degree of seriousness. That is to be expected. Nevertheless, such sermons are for your benefit, and you should learn from them, no matter how *lowering* you find the subject matter."

Violet lifted her chin. "I am quite prepared to learn, Mr Nettles, but you made it sound as if being poor is better than being rich, and I do not quite see why you should say so. I am very grateful for my fortune, and I do not like being made to feel guilty about something which I cannot help."

Nettles curled his lip in a manner that was almost a sneer. "You are ignorant of the world, so your words must be excused on the grounds of youth, but believe me when I say that there is virtue in poverty and none at all in wealth."

Violet's eyes flashed dangerously, and she would have answered him robustly, but aid came from a surprising quarter.

"Have you ever been poor, Mr Nettles?" Miss Parfitt said in her gentle voice.

"I am far from rich," he said at once, his brows snapping together.

"But you are not poor. Your coat alone must have cost far more than a farm labourer makes in a year, and I daresay you have more than one such. Your parish tithes not only put food on your table and clothes on your back, but they enable you to employ servants and give alms to those poorer than yourself. Mr Armitage's greater wealth provides employment for scores of men on the farms, and servants on his own estates. Is it not better for a few men to use their wealth to the benefit of many more?"

"If that is indeed what they do with their riches, Miss Parfitt, but all too frequently they dissipate their lives in idleness and spend their money on wasteful show, rather than bread for the poor." His eyes strayed to the cabinet of porcelain figurines.

"Wasteful show?" Miss Parfitt said quietly. "Mrs Armitage's collection provides employment for many people."

"One person making ornaments with no useful purpose?" he spat, his tone harsh beside her well-modulated voice.

"Far more than that," she said. "There are those who find the raw materials for such creations, the fuel for the firing of them, and the pigments for the paints. There is also the carpenter who made the cabinet and the glazier who made the glass."

"And Mr King of Piccadilly, who sold me most of those pieces," Mrs Armitage said brightly. "And is it not better to surround ourselves with beauty? Art is a worthy enterprise, surely? May we not admire a beautiful object?"

Nettles' eyes flew briefly to Violet's lovely face, but he said testily, "The beauties of nature, and beauty created to the glory of God, perhaps, but art for its own sake is a dangerous distraction. Wealth creates so much temptation, a veritable forest in which a man may lose himself. Or a woman," he added, again looking at Violet. "Poverty is an inherently virtuous state, and is the ideal for mankind, weak as we all are."

"There is no virtue in poverty," Miss Parfitt said, and for the first time there was a hint of anger to her tone. "I have been poor, Mr Nettles, indeed, I have been entirely penniless, and believe me, there is nothing to recommend the state, nothing at all. Where is the virtue in having too little income and no hope of getting more? Where is the virtue in being dependent on others for charity merely to survive? Where is the *dignity* in that? Few of us aspire to great wealth, but what is wrong with having enough money to live upon without the spectre of starvation constantly at one's shoulder?"

"No one should be in fear of starvation!" Violet cried, distressed. "Mr Nettles, will you not tell me how best I might employ my fortune for the benefit of the poor? I do not wish anyone to starve if I may prevent it."

This was a happy thought, and the remainder of the evening was spent in Nettles elaborating on the theme of charity to Violet, and tying himself in philosophical knots as he tried very hard to despise the wealth which made such charity possible.

Eliot watched them, seeing a new side to Violet. Her wish to do good was entirely genuine, he thought, and yet it seemed to be a novel idea to her, as if the thought had never previously entered her head that her money could be put to any other use than buying bonnets and fans and other furbelows. Seeing Miss Parfitt watching Violet with some interest, too, Eliot crossed the room to sit beside her.

"This is an interesting facet to Violet's character," he said in a low voice. "Has she not previously used her fortune to do some good in the world?"

"Never, for her father always told her that it was to be her dowry, to help her make a good match. She thought no more of it than that."

"And now Nettles has got her thinking of the most elaborate schemes for alms houses and orphanages."

"Which her trustees will never permit," Miss Parfitt said with a smile. "They will not jeopardise her inheritance for such wild ideas. She will have to wait until she marries and hope that her husband is more amenable to giving much of her fortune away. Still, it does no harm for her to begin thinking of others less blessed than she is. She has lived until this moment much sheltered from the worst of the modern world, never knowing what it is to be in want."

"Whereas you have," he said quietly. "When were you penniless, Miss Parfitt?"

"After my father died," she said, and her hands, normally so still in her lap, twisted involuntarily. "He was a country parson, just like Mr Nettles. The living was not a rich one, but we did well enough. There was always sufficient to meet our few needs, and a little more besides, which my father mostly spent on books. How he loved his books! The excitement when a parcel came from London, with two or three new volumes within, and the joy of new words to read, new ideas to discuss. But then he slipped on an icy path and hit his head, and that was the end of it. It was such a shock, for he was not old and had never been prone to illness. But there we are. When God calls us, we must go and those of us left behind must manage as best we can."

"And he had made no provision for you?"

"He left me nothing but the little money he kept by him — not much more than a hundred pounds. And his books, of course. I was fortunate, for I had my widowed aunt in Winchester to go to, and so there I went, with my hundred pounds and Papa's books. Whenever I needed a new gown or something more interesting on the table than mutton, I sold a book or two. That and my aunt's small annuity kept us afloat, until Mr Barantine came along. You cannot imagine, Mr Armitage, you who have always had money in your purse, the thrill of an income of my own. It is delightful, and I shall miss it when Violet no longer needs me."

"And shall you then return to your aunt in Winchester, exchanging books for beef and fowl?"

She laughed. "I shall, unless I can find another position."

"Have you no other relations to whom you might turn? For I must tell you, Miss Parfitt, that it sounds like a precarious life, a widow and a single lady living on a small annuity and the sale of a book now and then, and what will become of you when you have sold your last book?"

"Who can say? It is indeed precarious, and Aunt Dodi lives in the Cathedral Close in a grace-and-favour house, so whenever she dies I shall be homeless. But there is no one else. All Papa's kin are dead apart from my aunt."

"Is there no one from your mother's family who might help you?"

For an instant her face closed up, but then she smiled and said, "No one. But I shall survive, Mr Armitage. Something will turn up, I am certain. I shall never starve."

She spoke lightly, with her usual calm demeanour, but her words were painful to hear. She had no money of her own, beyond her small salary, and no relations beyond one elderly aunt. For all her brave words, her prospects were appallingly limited. Once Violet was off her hands, how might she live? A badly paid position as companion and drudge to a tiresome old woman, no doubt. Governess to a troop of disobedient children. Or she might abandon the life of a gentlewoman and take a position as a housekeeper. A hideous prospect. He sincerely pitied her.

7: A Change Of Heart

'Marsham Grove, Essex. March 30th My very dear aunt, Thank you for your last, and I am delighted to hear that you enjoyed your evening at the Palace. How I wish I had been there! We are so quiet here, with no guests in the house but ourselves, and not even any evening visitors apart from the local vicar, a fine upstanding young man who berates us all for having so much money. Violet is quite chastened and wishes to set up a benevolent home for orphans or injured soldiers or children rescued from the mines — she is not quite sure which yet — and hangs upon Mr Nettles' every word. Did I sound snappish when I wrote about young Mr Armitage before? That is because he makes me snappish. My fears regarding Violet have not been realised, however. He responds to her flirting with avuncular lack of interest, and her infatuation with him has waned with closer acquaintance. Perhaps she now sees him for the lazy scoundrel he is, for he cares nothing about her father's haul of diamonds, which have gone missing, or the legal papers for his business, likewise. Who else but her guardian should make the effort to recover such things? Yet he merely shrugs and says there is nothing to be done about it. It is frustrating, for I do think something might be done, if only he would exert himself. I hope to have more

to tell you soon, for we are to have visitors for Easter, and that will liven us all up a little. Your loving niece, Evie.'

~~~~~

APRIL

Eliot chose a fine spring morning to visit Nancy. It was the first time he had permitted the ladies to ride with only Winfield's tutelage, but Violet was coming on apace and even the timid Miss Parfitt was gaining in confidence with each day that passed. It would do her no harm to miss his presence for once.

He was rather pleased with his progress in that regard, for although he had spent a great deal of time in her company, he had been very careful not to distinguish her by any special attention. He had got her measure, he felt. Overt flirting would not be effective, but, just as with riding, he needed to bolster her confidence slowly and delicately. The first stage was to allow her to grow accustomed to his company, and to observe the pains he was under to ensure Violet's comfort. Before too long, he would begin to devote more time to Miss Parfitt herself, convincing her that he was a thoughtful and serious man, worthy of her regard. Once he had begun to attach her, he would move in to secure her affections fully and she would be his. Then he would have his kiss.

With such pleasant thoughts, the ride passed speedily by, and he hummed quietly as he made his way through the forest, vibrant with new greenery above and colourful violets and primroses below.

Nancy lived in a pleasant house on the outskirts of Epping Street, its neat lawns and shrubbery hidden behind high hedges. As always, she greeted him with a wide smile.
~~~~~

"Eliot! Such a long time since I have seen you, but... there is nothing amiss? Your father?"

"No, no, he is well, Nancy. Not as spry as he used to be, that is all. And you? You are well?"

"I'm not so spry, either." She laughed, the same rich, fruity laugh that had so mesmerised Eliot in his youth. Nancy was everything a mistress should be, in his eyes — richly curvaceous, with a ready laugh and a generous nature. When he had taken his own mistresses, he had sought women who reminded him of his father's, although none of his had stayed as long as she had. Nancy had been ensconced in this house before his father had married, and here she still was, as charming and lively as ever, and with the signs of her former beauty clearly visible, although she was past seventy now.

She found a bottle of claret for him, and had a glass herself, together with three slices of plum cake. For a while, they talked of London, and she delighted in hearing about the goings on in the *ton*.

Eventually, he remembered his father's instructions to him. "How are you situated, Nancy? Is there anything you need? Does your annuity still cover your expenses? Father wished me to tell you that you may have whatever you need."

"Ah, he's a generous man, but money... I have no need of money. He set me up in style all those years ago, and my wants are few now. The only thing I'd like is his company, but that's not possible," she said wistfully.

"Does he never come to see you?" Eliot said. "Yet he was always so fond of you."

Her eyes filled with sudden tears. "And I of him. Your father is the great love of my life, Eliot. I never looked at another man after I met him, and he told me it was the same for him. But he had to marry sensibly, and he never wished to distress Anne. She was not to know about us, so he never used the carriage to come here in case word got back to her through the servants. His man knew, of course, when he stayed overnight, but no one else, and I suppose he no longer rides."

"Is it a long time since you have seen him?"

"Six years and seven months," she said promptly. "After you were born, he said then that there would be no more children, and that if ever anything should happen to Anne, he would marry me, but there, she's a fine lady, your mother, and we neither of us ever wished her harm. But I do miss him, Eliot, and that's the truth."

"But you have your friends, I daresay," he said. "You have your sons for company."

She gave a wry smile. "They're ashamed of their mother, bless them. Such a wicked woman I am, to bring them into the world without the benefit of marriage. In the greatest love, but that isn't enough, seemingly. As for friends, there's a kindly widow who plays backgammon with me once or twice a week, and the vicar and his wife call, but that's all the company I have, and even at church people bow to me, but they don't speak. It's a heavy price to pay for what I've done."

"Do you regret the choice you made?" he said, suddenly curious, for he had never heard her talk so openly before. "After all, you have been well provided for."

"What's the point of regret? Waste of time. You're right, I've been provided every material comfort, I've had your father's love all these years, and I had the joy of my two babes, until they went away to school and learnt to despise me. The only part I'd change is to see your father still, just sometimes. But Eliot, don't make the mistake of thinking that I chose this life freely. No one becomes a mistress from choice, not truly. Every woman would take a husband and respectability over life as an outcast if she could. But I was the youngest daughter of a man clinging to gentility by his fingernails. I had no dowry, no well-married older sister or brother established in a career to help out, no prospect of any life except that of drudge at home, and perhaps, if I were very lucky, a chance as second or third wife to a man with a quiverful of children already. Along came your father — so charming, so handsome, so *rich* — how could I possibly refuse? I don't regret it, but what woman would be a mistress, even a cherished one, if there were any alternative?"

This conversation affected Eliot powerfully. He had had a succession of mistresses in his keeping for so long that he no longer thought anything of it. He took good care of them, made sure they left him better off than they arrived, and waved them farewell without regret. But until that moment, he had always considered the arrangement was beneficial on both sides. Two of his former mistresses had married rather well, two more had moved on to other protectors and one had gone home to her family with a much wanted child. None had ever seemed to regret the time with him. His friends had similar tales to tell, and his discreet afternoon parties at Grosvenor Square had become famous as a place where a man might meet up with a potential mistress. He had never seen anything wrong with his behaviour.

Yet now he wondered. Was he doing a very bad thing by encouraging these women into a life as a courtesan? At least one of them he had seduced away from virtue himself, convinced that if he had not, it would have been some other man. He could always tell when a woman was ripe for plucking. And were they not better off as the pampered pets of wealthy men? So he had always told himself. Now he began to doubt.

When he put the point to his father that evening over the port, his father shook his head. "What would become of them otherwise? Every woman must have a man to take care of her, one way or another, for that is how the world is created. There is nothing wrong with it, Eliot, and no need to be sentimental. A mistress left alone is no worse off than a widow, after all, so long as she has money enough to live upon, and Nancy is very well taken care of. She has wanted for nothing, these many years she has been in my keeping."

"Except your company," Eliot said. "She misses you."

His father's face softened. "Ah, I miss her too, my sweet Nancy! I am very fond of your mother and she is a wonderful woman, but she does fuss me so. I do not truly need so many naps and early nights as I claim, you know." His eyes twinkled affectionately. "Oftentimes I just need to be left in peace to read or to think, and if I am in the library or the saloon, then there is Mrs Armitage too, worrying about whether I am too warm or too cold, and have I enough cushions to my back? Nancy never chafed me that way. She just let me be. Such a restful woman!"

"Would you not like to see her now and then?"

"And how would I get there without the stables knowing all about it? And then sooner or later Mrs Armitage would know, too. I would not injure her so."

Eliot could not help wondering if it would be such an injury to his mother, but he could not press the point any further.

~~~~~

Evie had begun to look forward to her rides each morning. Now that she and Violet were becoming more adept in the saddle, their little party was permitted to wander further afield, discovering an abundance of flower-edged meadows, quiet riverbanks and darkly mysterious forests. The first half of each ride was dedicated to improving their skills, but once they turned for home, the more adventurous Violet often disappeared ahead with the groom, while Evie followed more slowly in company with Mr Armitage.

She had grown to enjoy their conversations, finding him to be a far more thoughtful and interesting man than she could ever have supposed from their earliest meetings. It was hard to imagine that he was the same person who had hosted the disorderly party at Grosvenor Square.

One day, however, she found him uncharacteristically silent. For a while she left him to his thoughts, but eventually she said, "You are very quiet today, Mr Armitage. Is there anything amiss?"

He sighed. "Only myself, Miss Parfitt. My conscience is troubling me, that is the sum of it, and I can blame nothing but my own thoughtlessness."

She could not think how to respond to such a confession, but while she was pondering the question, he began to speak in a low voice.

"You think me an idle, selfish fellow, I dare say, and so I am, but it never seemed to me that there was any harm in my actions. Certainly all was meant for the best. Yet lately it has been borne in on me that there may be injury caused, entirely without intent, to those whom I meant to help. Yet I do not quite see what may be
~~~~~

done about it. It all seems beyond repair now. What is done may not be undone."

He fell silent again, his usually open countenance so clouded that she could see that he was truly troubled by some difficulty. What was done may not be undone? Did he mean Violet? Was he now regretting his guardianship? It was not a matter on which she could advise him, but she felt that she ought to say something to reassure him.

"I do not know the particular case of which you speak," she said slowly, "but are you quite sure the matter is beyond repair? There is usually some amelioration or restitution that may be offered."

"That is true," he said. "I cannot restore that which was lost, but perhaps I may assure myself that there is no lasting damage that may be rectified."

That which was lost? Violet's diamonds, perhaps? "Is it impossible to restore the lost items?" she said.

He burst out laughing. "This is what comes of speaking in riddles, is it not? Naturally you cannot understand me, and how should you indeed?" He pulled his horse to a halt. "I beg your pardon, but it is not a subject that I should have raised at all, not with a lady. Pray forget I ever mentioned it."

"But you have *not* mentioned it!" she said, laughing too. "That is the problem, is it not? I imagined you to be talking about Violet's missing diamonds, but I collect it was another matter altogether."

"Oh... the diamonds." He sighed. "The lost items, indeed. Do you believe they might still be found?"

She frowned. "I cannot say. I know only that Mr Barantine took several made-up pieces of jewellery to Dublin with him to be traded with an American buyer for a supply of diamonds. Whether the trade took place I do not know. Perhaps no one knows, but it would be worth enquiring of Mr Drysdale if he had any communication from Mr Barantine from Dublin."

"Who is Drysdale?"

"The manager of Mr Barantine's jewellery shop in London. There is one in Winchester, also. Mr Clarkson is in charge there. Or Violet's trustees may know."

"Ah," he said thoughtfully. "And you think I should make some effort to find out what became of these mysterious diamonds, do you?"

"Do you not want to know?" she said, laughing again. "Are you not curious, Mr Armitage? Two things which Mr Barantine supposedly had with him on his last fatal journey, the papers for his business and the diamonds, yet neither is to be found. Violet would certainly like to know what has become of them, but it is not within her power to make enquiries."

"Very well. I shall see what may be discovered," he said. "And perhaps, if I meet your exacting standards in this matter, you may reward me with that kiss of which I still harbour hopes." Before she could express her outrage, he went on smoothly, "As to the other matter, let me say only that it has made me reconsider the choices that women make, and why they make them."

"Women have no choices to make," she said in sudden annoyance, so that her horse was startled into motion again. "Their lives are not their own to order as they please. Why should you think otherwise?"

"Ah, now I have angered you, Miss Parfitt," he said sorrowfully, keeping his horse close to hers as they progressed with a skill which she could only admire. "Pray forgive my impertinence, but I speak only what is commonly said, that women may have more limited choices than men, for they may take up no occupation beyond the domestic sphere, but do they not hold the happiness of men in their gentle hands? Is it not women who decide where to marry?"

"Not at all," she said sharply. "It is *men* who choose, men who propose, men who make the offer. A woman may only say yes or no, and if no man offers, then she has no choice at all. The only offer I have ever received was yours, sir, and it had nothing to do with marriage, if you remember."

"You astonish me!" he cried, halting his horse again so that she was obliged to stop also. "No offers of marriage? Is every male of your acquaintance blind and stupid?"

That made her laugh, and restored her good humour in an instant. "Or married already or in his dotage or too poor to marry or too devoted to God or a thousand other reasons, I daresay. Or simply not looking for a wife, perhaps. A man must be both willing and able to consider matrimony."

"That is true enough," he said. "And a woman to consider his offer. But you accepted Mr Barantine's offer of employment and I am curious about *that*. I know precisely what he paid you and it is not enough to put up with that tiresome chit. How do you stand it so patiently?"

That made her smile. "Two hundred a year, and as much again as a dress allowance? Riches indeed to me, which enables me to be very patient indeed as I wait for Violet to choose from amongst her many bonnets. But that is not entirely why I undertook to chaperon her, Mr Armitage. Her company allows me to move in society in a way I have never been able to do before. It is not your level of society, certainly, and it was mere chance that our paths crossed at Lady Frampton's, but amongst Mr Barantine's acquaintances there were evening parties and outings and all manner of entertainments to entice a sequestered daughter of the parsonage. I have never enjoyed myself so much in my life."

"And now you are sequestered again, in the wilds of Essex," he said lightly. "Six months or more of mourning before you can emerge from your seclusion."

"I expect I shall be long gone before Violet is back in society," she said. "You have four sisters, after all, who can help chaperon and advise her far better than I." He frowned and looked about to speak, but before he had the opportunity, she went on, "But what of you, Mr Armitage? I am curious about *your* choices, in particular, why you chose to take on the guardianship of this tiresome chit, as you call her. There must be more to it than pity for an orphan."

"Ah, I have a cunning plan for Violet, which I hope will benefit her and another in equal measure. I have a friend who is an orphan, just as Violet is, and although he is of good family, he is virtually penniless. Violet might like to connect herself with the family of an earl, and my friend might like a pretty young wife with a hundred thousand pounds."

"You would not force her into marriage?"

"Not in the least. My plan is merely to introduce them and see if anything comes of it. You think me a rogue, I daresay, Miss Parfitt, and so I am, but I like to balance the scales of my wickedness by doing a little good in the world where I can."

"The scales would tilt more favourably if you were to leave the wickedness behind you, sir," she said tartly. "After all, Robin Hood justified his thievery by giving the proceeds to the poor, but he was still *stealing*. Think how much good you could do in the world if you had no wickedness to offset."

"But it would not be near so much fun, would it?" he said, in such reasonable tones that she could not be at all cross with him, despite his outrageousness.

8: An Old Friend

Easter brought with it two of the daughters of the house, together with their husbands, children, nurses, maids and valets, carriages, horses and grooms. Suddenly the house was full, and the nursery floor echoed to running feet and shrieks of glee, while the more formal parts of the house were taken over by chattering knots of people who knew each other intimately, and talked incessantly about acquaintances unknown to Evie. Other guests arrived, too — more distant relations or friends determined to enjoy themselves at someone else's expense for a few weeks, and every day brought other acquaintances to the house, as morning callers or dinner guests.

Violet was the focus of everyone's interest, and she bloomed under such scrutiny, especially in the company of the several young men who made no secret of their admiration for her. She had made no complaint about her retired life in the country, and had practised her flirtation skills on the unresponsive Mr Nettles, but now she had a wider field to enthral and she thrived under their attention.

Evie was happy to melt into the background, sitting quietly in a corner with Miss Robart after dinner, unnoticed and unregarded, as the ladies played the pianoforte and harp, recited poetry to each other or related the exploits of their children. But when the gentlemen joined them, she was unsettled to find herself often sought out by Mr Eliot Armitage himself. There was nothing of the lover about his attentions, however. He paid her no compliments and never made her the object of the sort of gallantry that Violet inspired from her swains. Instead, he seemed simply to prefer her company, talking to her quite as an equal about his plans to catch a local poacher, the dispute between the miller and a neighbouring farmer, and how the warm spring had allowed the ploughing to advance a full two weeks early. Any hint of flirtation would have set her against him instantly, but he had such an easy charm, and spoke of nothing but the most impersonal matters, that she could not object in the slightest. It seemed that his original intentions towards her had been quite forgotten, and she could enjoy his company and the little flutter of a *tendre* that he evoked in her, without any fear that it would be put to the test.

~~~~~

'Marsham Grove, gracious, is it April already? My dearest aunt, We are inundated, for the Family is come to stay. It is only two of the Armitage daughters, and thank goodness the other two are engaged elsewhere for the house is overflowing already. Lady Philps is the oldest of them, very like her mother in both appearance and ways, for they both fret over their husbands with endearing persistence. Mr A tolerates it with gentlemanly forbearance, but Sir Hubert is more robust, telling his wife bluntly that she is a thorn in his side and a fuss-budget, after which he does whatever he likes. She laughs and never minds his words, for he is clearly very fond of her. Lady Corbett is the youngest daughter, and a sweet-natured lady, who never frets over anything. She is increasing, although she already has eight or is it nine children? I am not perfectly sure, for although there are
~~~~~

always two or three of them at her feet or running about the room shrieking, for they seem not to have learnt to modulate their voices, I have never seen all of them together. I shall remember them long after I have returned to your little house in Winchester, my dear aunt. We may occasionally lack for company, and find our long days of sewing irksome and dull, but perhaps that is better than the perpetual riot that is family life for the Corbetts. They do not mind it, however, and both father and mother are doting parents who love to play with their infants and complain that the evenings are dull when the little ones are all abed. Lord Corbett has one other great advantage, however, of which you would have been aware even before opening this missive. He is a baron, and therefore a peer of the realm, with the right to send and receive mail free of all charges. This right he liberally bestows on everyone, and spent the first hour after his arrival franking sheet after sheet of paper. I am now the proud possessor of no fewer than twelve of these magical sheets, which means you will not have to pay to read my news for months, with care. I shall celebrate this largesse by filling two sheets today, for I must tell you of—'

~~~~~

Eliot had waved the Armitage ladies off with Violet to pay calls on the neighbours, and sent his brothers-in-law out with the gamekeeper for some sport. With the children confined to the nursery quarters the house returned to blessed peacefulness. For an hour, he and his father pretended to play cribbage, while indulging in reminiscences of a particularly male kind.

Shortly after noon, however, the rattle of wheels on the drive heralded the arrival of the last guest, the well-connected but impoverished young man of whom Eliot had hopes of making a match with Violet. No one seeing the fashionably-dressed Edward
~~~~~

Folkard arrive in a stylish curricle drawn by a matched pair of prime horse-flesh would have suspected that he survived on tiny allowances from his uncle and godfather, and whatever he could win at the gaming tables.

"Armitage!" he cried cheerfully, as he jumped down from his equipage. "Well met, my friend. What a great kindness to invite me here! I hope you will find some way for me to repay the debt to your family. Some gentle flirtation with the ladies, perhaps, or shall I allow the gentlemen the best stretches of river for their fishing?"

"A little cribbage with my father, and some music for my mother would be all that is necessary."

"You let me off too lightly," he said easily.

But when he had shown Folkard to his assigned room, Eliot said quietly, "I believe it may be in my power to do something for *you* on this visit. You will remember me mentioning this orphan whose guardianship I have undertaken? Pretty as paint, and a fortune of one hundred thousand, it is said. She will be in mourning for this year, but you will have a chance to get to know her."

Folkard's eyes widened. "A hundred thousand! You would surrender her to a worthless fellow such as I?"

"You are the best of my friends, and deserving of a little good fortune," Eliot said, smiling. "I give you fair warning, however — she is flighty, and not exactly a demure maiden, so it will take all your skills to attach her. Nor will I push her in your direction in the slightest, but I would wager she has never met your kind before. Her late father was a jewel merchant."

"Ah, a cit," Folkard said knowingly.

"Precisely so, but you will not set yourself against her on that account, I am sure. You will have two weeks to decide if the lady is likely to suit you. If so, you may return for a longer stay in the summer. She is out visiting just now — in fact I believe most of the ladies are from home, but there is one left behind. I would have you meet Violet's companion, Miss Parfitt."

She was in the morning room and busy writing a letter, he could see, but she willingly laid down her pen and rose gracefully to meet them.

"There you are, Miss Parfitt. As I promised, here is my friend to make your acquaintance."

"Oh but... I already know Mr Folkard."

Folkard beamed at her, laughing in delight. "Why, Evie! How wonderful to see you again. When Armitage spoke of Miss Parfitt, it seemed impossible that it should be you, for I thought surely you must be long married by now. How are you?"

"I am well, Mr Folkard, as you see."

"What is all this formality? You must call me Edward, as you always did."

Eliot looked from one to the other, eyebrows raised. "You know each other well, then?"

Folkard laughed. "Know each other well? I should say we do! Practically grew up together, in fact. Evie is my cousin."

"Your *cousin!*"

"Third cousin, at least," she said at once. "Nothing close, but my mother was a Folkard. She lived at Folkard Hall before she married my father, and the countess was so kind as to allow me to make use of the girls' governesses. That was where I learnt to ride."

"Such good times we had then, do you remember?" Folkard said.

They sat side by side on a wide sofa, and there was no stopping the flood of reminiscences. Eliot watched them, bemused. He had never suspected such an acquaintance between them, and now he was not at all sure what to make of it. To his eyes, the very composed Miss Parfitt surely seemed warmer with Folkard than he had ever seen her before. She smiled, she laughed, her eyes shone... it was not just his imagination, was it? And was Folkard's manner more eager than usual? It was disconcerting, and he was pleased when the ladies returned from their morning calls and the little tête-à-tête on the sofa was broken up.

~~~~~

'Dear aunt, I scarcely know what I was about to say to you, for the most extraordinary coincidence has occurred which has driven every other thought out of my head. Edward Folkard is here! His godfather is Mrs Armitage's brother, Mr Bradbrook, with whom he presently lives in town. He is to be a lawyer, he tells me, and is presently engaged in eating his dinners, as he terms it, and hopes to be called to the bar two years from now. He is the same personable man he ever was, so he will do well in his chosen career, I am certain, and I wish him every success, but I could have hoped never to be obliged to meet any of that family again. However, I must put up with his presence for two weeks, for he is a guest in the house and will be quite unavoidable. Mr Eliot Armitage has hopes of a match between Violet and Edward. I should have said that he was too serious a man to attract her, for she has previously been drawn to frivolous, not to say, roguish charmers like Mr Eliot himself, but lately Mr Nettles the
~~~~~

clergyman has induced an unexpected degree of sobriety in her behaviour. She is presently deeply involved in a number of charitable works in the neighbourhood, including the making of beef broth and pigeon pie for anyone sick, the provision of swaddling garments for new infants, and the knitting of stockings for wounded soldiers. There is even talk of a school for the children of farmers and millers and smiths, which will no doubt irritate their harassed parents when they are wanted to help out and are nowhere to be found. However, it keeps her out of mischief, and she will assuredly have moved on to some other fancy in a month or two. In the meantime, Edward may serve to amuse her in the evenings, and with Violet as a distraction I may hope to avoid him altogether. It is time to change for dinner, so I will close now, dearest aunt. Do try to keep out of this nasty easterly wind. I have had my salary for Lady Day, and having no expenses here, will contrive to convey most of it to you as soon as I can. Your affectionate niece, Evie.'

~~~~~

Evie's days were busy. Even though she was seldom needed to chaperon Violet, she found many other ways to make herself useful. She and Miss Robart helped with the nursery children, taking small groups of them on long, bracing walks to collect an array of leaves, buds, catkins and strange caterpillars, all of which were recorded in sketchpads. The older girls practised the pianoforte or harp, or painstakingly worked samplers, while the boys read in Latin or, if left unsupervised for five minutes, fell to fighting on the upper landings. They were, Evie supposed, not quite so bad as they had appeared when they had first descended on Marsham Grove, but she still looked forward to the day when they went home and the house fell back into its habitual repose.
~~~~~

The evenings were more to her taste. Almost every night saw extra covers laid at dinner, or else there would be an invitation to some neighbour's house, in which Evie was included more often than not. How she loved such evenings! Each one was a memory to be stored up against the day when she returned to Winchester and the prospect of no social engagements whatsoever, apart from a quarterly dinner at the Bishop's Palace. Very often the carpets were rolled up after dinner and there would be dancing. Evie was seldom called upon to play for the dancers, so she sat happily and watched.

Violet was still in deep mourning, so she did not dance either, which restriction she took in good part, especially as it meant that her admirers must necessarily sit out the dance if they wished to be beside her, which they often did.

Evie had company, too, although describing them as admirers might be stretching a point. Mr Eliot Armitage always sat out at least one dance with her, relaying whatever scurrilous rumour or anecdotes of the company he thought might amuse her. He seemed very curious about her relationship with Edward.

"Was it true, that you grew up together?" he asked her once.

"Indeed it was. He is only a year younger than I am, and his cousins only a little younger than him, and all of them lived at Folkard Hall, so the five of us were often together. When the girls acquired a governess, I was invited to join them for lessons, and Edward shared the schoolroom with us until he went to Eton at the age of twelve."

"He is a cousin to you — a third cousin, or some such?"

"Something of the sort. We worked it out once. Edward and the three girls are first cousins, since their fathers were brothers, and my great-grandfather was brother to the Fifth Earl, which I think makes me their third cousin."

"But how was it that you lost touch so comprehensively?" he said, leaning forward with a slight frown, his deep blue eyes fixed on her, so that she caught her breath.

"I... I am not very sure," she said, moving away from him a little, so that their conversation looked less intimate. It would not do for anyone to think their acquaintance was becoming too particular. She had the greatest abhorrence of being thought too forward. "As we all grew up, we... drifted apart, I suppose. Our destinies were very different... mine looking after Papa at the parsonage, and the girls to London and the season and dazzling marriages."

"And Edward?"

"He went to London, to his godfather — your uncle. By the time he was sixteen, he was no longer in any danger of inheriting, so it was thought best he consider a career, I suppose."

Mr Armitage frowned. "I never knew he was ever in line for the earldom. He never mentioned it. His father was the youngest of several brothers, as I understand it."

"Three brothers, William, Henry and Arthur, but William only had daughters and Henry married late, so for a long time Edward was the only male in the next generation."

"Even so, it was abrupt, was it not? He was simply told to pack one day. Or so my uncle said, for Edward never spoke of it."

"It was after the old earl died, and William had died less than two months before," Evie said colourlessly. "Everything changed."

"Hmm, I can see that," he said thoughtfully.

To her relief he asked no more. Not that she could have answered his questions, but she was uncomfortable talking about Edward at all. Yet, there he was in the house and as her connection with him became known, she was the focus of considerable curiosity and speculation. Edward himself did nothing to damp down such talk, for even though he was there to pay court to Violet, it sometimes seemed that his attention was far more towards Evie. In the evenings, he frequently escorted Violet in to dinner but afterwards, as if he felt he had done his duty and might now please himself, he then sought out Evie, joining whatever card game she was involved in, standing near the instrument if she played or sang, or else engaging her in quiet conversation if she were sitting with her needlework.

"Mr Folkard is very attentive to *you*, Miss Parfitt," Lady Corbett said to Evie one day when the gentlemen had gone out for some sport and the wind was too brisk for the ladies to venture outdoors. "Such a personable young man! I was quite struck last night when he was turning the pages for you as you played — such a handsome couple you make. Do you not think, Alethia?"

Her sister laughed. "Now, you must not be matchmaking, Daph. Take no notice of her, Miss Parfitt. She has only to see a smile exchanged between two people to be hearing wedding bells ringing."

"And is not that how every match begins?" Lady Corbett said, dimpling cheerfully. "A smile and then another and another... what could be more natural? Two young people who get along well... it is the most natural thing in the world."

"Natural but imprudent," Evie said, laughing. "Neither of us has two pennies to rub together. One cannot live on smiles, Lady Corbett."

"Oh, pooh! Uncle Bradbrook is a wealthy man and will leave him comfortably situated, I am sure."

"I do not think he has any expectations in that direction," Evie said, puzzled, for she had not known that Edward's godfather was wealthy. "He must needs earn his bread."

"Yes, Daph, surely you remember," Lady Philps said in a low voice, so that Violet would not overhear. "Uncle Bradbrook has an heir already — his... *you know."*

"Oh yes!" Lady Corbett's eyes widened, and she mouthed, *"Natural son,"* at Evie. "So that would not do," she went on in her normal voice. "He will have to make his own fortune, then." Her eye fell on Violet, placidly knitting a stocking. "Or marry one." With only the slightest pause, she said, "What do you think of Mr Folkard, Violet? Is he not a charming man, and *so* handsome?"

"Do you think so?" Violet said, wrinkling her nose slightly as she pondered the question. "He is not so handsome as Mr Nettles."

9: To London And Back

Easter came and went, and the guests began to leave. The children were the first to be bundled into carriages and waved away down the drive, for Eliot's mother said firmly that his father had had enough of their noise for the moment, and they might return in the summer if they were very well behaved. Then, gradually, the adult guests drifted away. Not Edward Folkard, for as the last to arrive so he was also to be the last to leave. Not Daphne either.

"I hate this part of it," she told Eliot, patting her stomach with a rueful laugh, as they sat on a bench in the garden one day. "I do not mind increasing, not at all, for every child is a welcome gift, but I feel so horrid just now and no one cossets me like Mama does. If she would only come to me, as she used to... but there, she will not leave Papa now, and so I must come to her. You do not mind? I shall keep an eye on Violet for you while you are in town."

He had not thought much about London. "I am not sure I shall stay there long," he said. "Folkard and I will travel up together, but I may only stay a week or so."

"Oh?" She eyed him with sudden interest. "Miss Parfitt? She will not become your mistress, you know, if that is your little scheme."

He laughed. "Now, why should you think so? I enjoy her company, that is all, but I have no designs upon her beyond that." And it was true, for he had long since forgotten his earlier intentions towards her. A kiss, perhaps... but that hardly counted.

"None at all? When a man forgoes the amusements of London to rusticate in Essex, there is usually a strong motive. You are not thinking of marriage, are you? For I should have said—"

"No, no! Lord, how you do take a fellow up, Daph. I have new responsibilities with Violet, and I wish to keep a close eye on her, that is all. Miss Parfitt has nothing either to fear or to hope from me."

"Well, do not break her heart, that is all. She is not used to flirtatious rogues like you."

"Her heart is made of solid stone," he said easily. "She is entirely resistant to my manifold charms, I assure you. If anyone can melt her, it is Folkard."

"Do you think so?" She frowned, pondering that idea. "I would have said she pushes him away, if anything. Not you, although she does not encourage you either, but she is definitely not putting out lures towards *him*. But he likes her, that much is certain."

Eliot thought so too. He had noted the dutiful way Folkard had attended on Violet even as his eyes often strayed to wherever Miss Parfitt was, and when he felt liberated from Violet's side, he would instantly make his way to the companion. And there he would stay, if he possibly could. Yes, that much was clear.

Yet he had never seen Miss Parfitt repulse him, until one day when they gathered in the hall for a walk to the village. It was one of Violet's charitable ventures, taking baskets of pork jelly and chicken wings and knitted children's clothes to those in need, inspired by Violet's newfound admiration for the pious Mr Nettles. Miss Parfitt sat calmly on a seat, bonneted and gloved, awaiting Violet's arrival. Folkard bounced down the stairs, and at once sat down beside her, leaning forward to say something in a low tone. Her expression did not change, but she shook her head slightly and then stood, crossing the hall to where Eliot lounged, one arm against the marble mantelpiece.

"I wonder if we shall be able to carry all this?" she said, eyeing the several baskets the footmen had deposited on the floor.

"Should you like me to order the carriage?" he said. "Or my curricle, perhaps?"

Folkard followed her across the hall. "Is anything amiss?" he said, with his usual smile.

"Miss Parfitt is concerned that there may be too many baskets for us to carry," Eliot said.

"Perhaps your curricle may be of service, Mr Folkard?" she said smoothly.

He responded without the slightest hesitation. "Of course." A delicate bow. "I shall attend to it at once." He disappeared to send word to the stables, gentlemanly and polite, giving no sign of reproach for the way she had manoeuvred him into it, but Eliot found it interesting. Yes, she had definitely repulsed Folkard.

Violet and Miss Robart appeared at that moment, closely followed by Daphne, and for a while the ladies were engaged in checking the contents of the baskets and discussing the best means of distribution. Eliot felt it politic to keep out of such discussions, his rôle being to fetch and carry as instructed by the ladies. Once Folkard had brought his curricle to the door and the baskets had been secured to it, the walkers set off on the path through the woods to the village.

At first they all travelled in a loose group, but it was not long before Violet took the lead, with Daphne's long stride matching hers, while Miss Robart raced to keep up. Miss Parfitt was too ladylike to race, so gradually she and Eliot fell behind, and Violet's high, clear voice diminished in the distance.

Eliot could not resist the opportunity to say, "Have you fallen out with Folkard?"

"With Edward? No!" she said, with her ready smile. "How could anyone fall out with him? It would be impossible. But..." A shadow crossed her face.

"But?" he said encouragingly.

"He is too well-mannered, or perhaps it is that I am unaccustomed to move in such levels of society, but I cannot read him in the slightest. It is most disconcerting. He is all polite attentiveness, and perhaps that is only because he feels safe with an old friend such as I am, and yet... it would distress me to think that there were more to his attentions than friendship."

"Should you like me to warn him away from you?" Eliot said lightly.

To his surprise, she took the question seriously. "Would you? If the subject should arise... he may speak frankly to you, and you could say that I do not view him in that light."

"Do you not? Not at all? He is a very personable man."

"Indeed he is, but we grew up together," she cried. "I see him quite as a brother, nothing more."

"As a brother... I shall tell him so."

"Only if the subject should arise," she said quickly. "I should not wish him to think—"

"No, no. Only if the subject should arise."

"Thank you!"

They fell into what he hoped was a companionable silence. He watched her covertly as dappled sunlight through the trees lit up her delicate features now and then, before plunging into shade again. She was so serene, and it was restful to walk beside her in tranquil silence, but the opportunity to procure more confidences was irresistible. "Do you not wish to marry one day, Miss Parfitt?"

"Well, of course!" She turned to him with such a teasing smile that his breath caught in his throat for a moment. She had a dimple — just one — but he had never noticed it before and was enchanted. "Every girl dreams of marriage from the age of twelve onwards," she went on. "Or perhaps not so much the abstract idea of marriage as the more realistic goal of a man. Handsome, naturally... tall and broad-shouldered, with shapely calves to show to advantage in the dance. He would ride well and drive a curricle and matched pair and dress stylishly but without ostentation."

"He is rich, then, this man?" Eliot said, smiling.

"But of course! A comfortable independence, with a pleasant estate and a snug little house. He would be well-read, of a serious, not to say bookish, character, but able to make me laugh. And he would have a poetical turn of phrase. He would tell me that my eyes were the colour of storm clouds on a winter's day, and my skin is as soft as a dove's wing. He would adore me, obviously, yet still listen respectfully to my opinions and treat me as a friend, and if ever you should encounter such a paragon, you must send him my way at once, Mr Armitage."

He laughed and agreed to it, although he suspected that Folkard came closer to her ideal than perhaps she realised. They walked on very comfortably for some distance before he said, "Porcelain."

"I beg your pardon?"

"Not dove's wings. Your skin is as smooth and white as porcelain, and your eyes… definitely *not* storm clouds. They are as clear and brown as a mountain stream." Her mouth was an 'O' of surprise. "Your hair is more difficult to describe," he went on blandly, "but I had a pointer exactly that colour once."

She burst out laughing. "For a moment there I thought you were flirting with me, sir, but I acquit you!"

"I should not dare," he said. "Now you may tell me that my hair is the colour of corn or some such, and my eyes like a summer sky."

"Your hair is more golden than corn-coloured," she said in serious tones, although her eyes shimmered with mischief. "It is more the colour of the tassels on your mama's bell ropes. And your eyes — we had curtains that colour once at the parsonage."

He shook with laughter. "Touché, Miss Parfitt. Curtains!"

"We had a sofa to match," she added kindly.

And so it was that they arrived at the village in fits of giggles, and quite unable to explain the joke to the others. And his head was filled with porcelain skin and pool-dark eyes and lips that invited a whole host of delightful comparisons. Cherries, he thought... yes, they were as red and soft and full as ripe cherries.

~~~~~

MAY

Evie gazed at her reflection in the hand mirror. "What colour are my eyes, would you say, Margie?"

"Hazel, madam," the maid said firmly, pinning the last strands of hair in place.

"Do you think so? I would have said brown, myself. Like mud." No matter how hard she stared, she could not see the colour of a mountain stream in her rather ordinary eyes.

Margie giggled. "Nonsense, madam! Are you done, now? May I go and help with poor Lady Corbett's bath, if she's awake now?"

"Oh yes, do go."

It was always *'poor Lady Corbett'* to the servants since the onset of queasiness each morning which left her pale and listless. The lady herself laughed at her infirmity, but she liked to lie abed each morning until she felt better, and often she retired soon after dinner each evening, while her mother and the servants fussed around her, and the kitchen sent up possets and broths and little delicacies to tempt her ladyship's appetite.

Evie was confirmed in her belief that she was better off a spinster than perpetually increasing, but when the invalid had withdrawn at night, taking her mother away with her, Mr Armitage said mildly, "She loves to be fussed over, but there is nothing much amiss with her. Shall we have another rubber before the supper tray?" Evie smiled, seeing how much more he enjoyed the evenings when he himself was not the object of his wife's fussing. He would
~~~~~

play whist with Evie, Violet and Miss Robart until close to midnight sometimes, and only the suppressed yawns of the footmen reminded him of the hour.

The house had returned to some semblance of normality. The guests had left, and even Mr Eliot Armitage had gone off to town, taking Edward Folkard with him, their two curricles and a carriage behind making a fine procession. They would be enjoying the season, Evie supposed, and tried to imagine them moving gracefully through the saloons and ballrooms of London. At least, her imagination was fixed more on the graceful movements of Mr Armitage, for she seldom thought of Edward except to be glad that he had gone. But Mr Eliot Armitage… he was a very different matter.

It was not until he had left that she began to realise just how much she had come to depend on his company. After his earliest shameful approaches, he seemed to have accepted her wishes and had made no effort to flirt with her, or make her fall in love with him, as he had threatened to do. He had never tried to separate her from the company, or steal a kiss. His eyes had not lingered on hers as he passed her the buttered lobster. He had never held her hand a few seconds longer than necessary as he handed her into a carriage. He had paid her no extravagant compliments, or sought her company before that of other ladies with a better right to his attentions, or deliberately drawn her from her quiet corner after dinner. He had simply treated her as a sensible person whose conversation he enjoyed.

And yet… she had never met anyone like him. He had what her father had described as *'town bronze'*, that sophistication that denoted the gentleman of the *ton*, elegant, mannered, poised… She had never been much exposed to his kind before, and the few such of that type who had crossed her path had never turned their gaze on unworldly, retiring Evie. But Eliot had done so, had dazzled her with his gentlemanly charm and she had no defences against it. So it was that after barely two months' acquaintanceship, she found herself helplessly deep in love with him.

Her hopes of a respite for the duration of the season were soon blighted, however, for not ten days after his tearful mother had waved him away, he returned.

"Town is very dull this year," was the only explanation he offered. "You are not missing anything, puss," he added to Violet, giving her an avuncular pinch of one cheek. "Have you been good while I was away?"

"Of course," she said, sounding astonished that anyone might suspect otherwise.

He laughed, said he was glad to hear it and sat down to relate all the society gossip to the ladies over cups of tea before disappearing with his father into the library. About an hour later, a footman came up to Evie where she was knitting yet another stocking for Violet's schemes.

"Begging your pardon, madam, but Mr Armitage and Mr Eliot would like to talk to you in the library."

That was ominous. They were sat either side of a low-burning fire, with a candelabrum lit, for the spring sunshine penetrated only to the conservatory outside the windows. Mr Eliot gave her his leather wing chair, pulling over a small chair for himself.

"Miss Parfitt, I hope to obtain the benefit of your advice in a matter that is rather troubling," he began. "It concerns Violet, but she need not know of it yet... not until I have better news, at least. Will you tell me what you know of the Newbolds?"

"Mr Newbold was Mr Barantine's business partner," Evie said. "He travelled to Ireland with Mr Barantine on his last fatal journey, and so was lost at sea also. He left a widow and… two children, I believe."

"Yes, a son and a daughter. Newbold also had a brother, much younger than he was. This brother is now laying claim to the whole of Barantine's business—"

"What!"

"—on the grounds that Newbold funded the entire enterprise. He professes to be protecting the interests of the boy — his nephew. Since the papers detailing the business are lost, it is impossible to prove one way or the other. Did you ever hear Barantine speak about Newbold's share of the business?"

"I did not. Mr Barantine's original business was in Winchester, but Mr Newbold's investment permitted him to set up the much larger shop in London, with the vault in the basement. Mr Barantine disliked banks, so everything was kept on the premises."

"So it would seem," Mr Eliot said, with a rueful smile. "My solicitors have been looking into his affairs for me, and there are no bank accounts, no investments elsewhere. Everything is in that vault, the finished items of jewellery and uncut gems, naturally, but also the money. All the profits of the business for the last fifteen years reside in those vaults, Miss Parfitt."

"Even Violet's dowry?"

"Even so, seemingly. Apart from the contents of the Bruton Street house, every penny piece Barantine owned is in that vault, and Newbold is claiming all of it."

"But… that is outrageous!" Evie cried.

"It is indeed," said the elder Mr Armitage. "It is my belief that the fellow hopes that Eliot will make him an offer — half the value, or something of the sort. Even a quarter of it would be a considerable sum to such a man."

"Surely such a claim may be contested?" Evie said.

"True," Mr Eliot said, "but without proper documentation, the case could drag on for years, with the lawyers growing fat and the business dwindling. I will take a legal opinion, of course, but there is no knowing how the law will decide."

"Then Violet may not be an heiress after all," Evie said sadly.

"Let us not be so pessimistic," Mr Eliot said, with his warm smile. "It is unlikely that Newbold will be able to take everything, so there will still be a considerable sum for Violet's dowry, just not quite as much as she had supposed."

"Oh dear," Evie said.

10: Only A Kiss

Violet surprised Eliot by taking the news of her possible impoverishment with surprising equanimity. "Wealth is not important," she said airily. "It is the use to which it is put that matters, and now I shall not be able to accomplish my more ambitious schemes, but there is still much that may be achieved. Fifty thousand pounds will do almost as well as a hundred."

"That will depend upon your husband," Eliot said repressively.

"My husband? What has that to do with anything?"

"The fortune your father left you is for your dowry, to enable you to marry well. It will be in your husband's control, to dispose of as he sees fit, or to add to his own estate."

"Oh yes, but I intend to marry a man who wishes me to do charitable works. That is what a great lady does, is it not, Evie? And I intend to be a great lady, and very charitable."

"That is commendable, Violet," Evie said, but she sounded doubtful.

Eliot wondered how long this urge for benevolence towards the poor would last. He set it all at the feet of the dour Mr Nettles, who might be handsome but had not a jot of charm about him. Still, if he could induce generosity in Violet, a girl who had grown up with nothing but her own pleasure to consider, then Eliot would regard him with gratitude. He had even brought Violet to a degree of respect for punctuality, which was a thing never before seen in her. Not only did she contrive to be on time, but she had willingly refused a shopping expedition to Epping with Daphne, who planned to visit a linen draper there. It was a miracle, he considered, and hoped Violet's penchant for Mr Nettles lasted for some considerable time.

Even so, Miss Parfitt had suggested that he make further enquiries regarding Mr Barantine's wealth.

"Those diamonds are still missing," she said, "not to mention the paperwork regarding the business. You might write to the attorney who handled the transfer of the diamonds in Dublin. Also, Henry might know something of the way matters lay with Mr Newbold."

"Henry? What would he know of it?"

"He often attended the gentlemen when they discussed business affairs."

"But even if he knows anything, how will he tell me of it?"

Miss Parfitt laughed merrily. "He may not talk, but he can read and write perfectly well, Mr Armitage."

And so he could, but even Henry, writing in a surprisingly neat hand, could not shed any light on how much of Barantine's business was owned by Newbold.

Part of Violet's charity consisted of the setting up of a school for poor children in the village, and she had received permission from Eliot's parents to send some books from the schoolroom that might be of use.

"We can always get more," his mother said airily. "Besides, we have no great need for them at the moment, do we?"

Eliot took this comment on his lack of a growing family with aplomb. With no entail on the estate, and a horde of cousins and nephews as potential heirs, should the need arise, he had never felt pressured into marrying. He knew he would do so eventually, but that pleasant duty could wait until the perfect woman should come his way. Occasionally, he wondered what she would be like, this perfect woman, and lately his imagination had veered towards alabaster skin and hair of a rich auburn, but he was in no hurry. He liked Evie Parfitt, that was undeniable. He had thought her rather plain at first, but when animated she was rather pretty... no, more than that, she was beautiful, he conceded, and her cool, ladylike composure was enticing to a man who was used to women falling into his arms. He would very much have liked her to fall into his arms! But she had not, and he had long since given up his attempts to woo her. He might enjoy her company, and he certainly enjoyed looking at her, but he had no thoughts in his head beyond that.

One day, however, the other ladies being out, he found himself alone in the schoolroom with her, selecting books for Violet's little school. Such a comfortable pastime, and they were in complete harmony with each other. She was not treating him with chilly disdain, had not for some time now, and he had no thought of her beyond the shared occupation. They had simply been sorting through books, selecting this one or that one, and returning the others to the shelves.

Somehow, as they had moved this way and that around each other, they had ended up quite in the corner of the room, she with her back to the wall and he not a foot away from her. He could not quite tell how it had happened, for he had not been trying to make a move against her, that much was certain. But there they were and for some reason he could not take his eyes off her lips. Such lush lips — why did they distract him so? When she disapproved of him, they thinned almost to nothing, but now... now they were soft and warm and unbearably, distractingly kissable. Would she...? Should he...?

If he never put it to the test, he would never know. But he must not cheat! He had sworn not to lay a finger on her, and she had sworn to leave if he did, but there were other ways...

Quickly, before she had a chance to move away, he planted his hands on the wall behind her, one on either side of her head.

"Now I have you caught," he said softly. "Shall I have that kiss from you now? Shall I?"

She could have pushed him away. She could have expressed her outrage. She could even have ducked under his arms and escaped him altogether. But she did not. Instead, she waited, it seemed to him, gazing up with those limpid brown eyes, such gentle, clear eyes. He could surely see straight to her soul. She *wanted* it, he realised triumphantly.

Very slowly, he leaned towards her, and still she made no move to evade him. She sighed, and closed her eyes and waited. With infinite gentleness, he touched his lips to hers and to his delight and astonishment, she kissed him back. Not with passion or even expertise, for he had surely been right that she had never been kissed before, but with a touching innocence as she gave herself to the moment.

Eliot had kissed many women, but he had never before experienced so sweet and tender a kiss as Evie's. She stole the breath from his body, and it took all his willpower not to take her in his arms and crush her against him so tightly that she could not breathe either. But he dared not. This was no prelude to something more intimate, this was only a kiss.

Only a kiss! As if there could be such a thing as *only a kiss*. It was a magical moment, when all the regular constraints of propriety were swept aside, a moment when their two hearts, their very souls, were united and nothing existed except Evie's warm lips and the delicate affection that bore the two of them on its sweet tide. Such joy in a kiss that asked nothing in return, that had no deeper meaning beyond that long, exquisite entanglement. For those few seconds or minutes — he could not tell how long it lasted — she surrendered utterly to him, and he was thrilled by her.

Eventually, reluctantly, he drew away, with a triumphant laugh. “There now! Was that not delicious?”

She hung her head, and to his amazement, a tear trickled down one pale cheek.

“Evie? Why the tears? You cannot tell me you did not enjoy that!”

Her face was turned away from him, but she shook her head.

“Evie, look at me.” She turned a little towards him without meeting his eyes. Her face was so filled with misery that his heart lurched in dismay. “What is it?”

“You are cruel, Mr Armitage.” Her voice was hollow.

“Cruel? I gave you a pleasurable experience, a little fun in your dull life.”

“That is all it is to you, a little fun, a game, an amusing diversion.”

"It is only a kiss, Evie. You want nothing more from me, and I respect that, but now you have tasted a little of the future you have rejected. Now you have something to remember."

"Yes!" she cried fiercely. "And I *shall* remember it, always! You told me how wonderful it would be, and I set it down to idle boasting. Just another arrogant man who thinks he has only to kiss a woman to have her at his feet. But it *was* wonderful! Do you not understand what you have done? Whatever I do in my life, wherever I go, whether I see the world or live quietly in obscurity, nothing will ever be the same. Even if I marry, I shall never be able to kiss my husband without remembering you. And if I die a maid, then my old age will be haunted by you, because I shall know *exactly* what I have missed. You have destroyed all my peace of mind, because just once in my life I experienced a glorious, perfect kiss from the man I love. Oh! Go away! I wish I might never see you again!"

Pushing past him, she fled the room, leaving him feeling sick despair, for surely he was the lowest worm in the world. He prowled back and forth, veering from guilt to anger — she had *wanted* him to, after all, so how dare she berate him! — and back to guilt just as fast. He had almost forgotten his plan to make her fall in love with him, had long since abandoned any stratagems against her and yet he had succeeded without even trying. Poor, innocent Evie! He had never meant to hurt her, and yet it was unconsciously done and he could hardly be blamed for it... could he? Would he be expected to offer for her, now that she had fallen in love with him? Surely not! He had not been trying to attach her in the slightest, so it was hardly his fault! Was it? God, what should he do? How could he make things right again?

His wildly veering emotions were interrupted by a discreet tap at the door, followed by Powell's apologetic face. "Beg pardon, sir, but I thought you would wish to know that Miss Parfitt has ordered the carriage to take her to Epping, to catch the stage."

"Damnation! Where is Miss Parfitt now?"

"In her room, sir, packing."

Eliot flew along the corridor and burst open the door. Evie and the maid were kneeling on the floor, folding gowns into a box.

"What nonsense is this?" he cried. "You cannot leave." She stood, her face white but composed, making no answer. The maid looked up at him, astonished. "Margie, leave us."

Calmly, Evie said, "Margie, you will do no such thing."

The maid jumped up and stood beside Evie, her mouth set into a mulish line. "Certainly not, madam."

Eliot clicked his tongue in annoyance. She was right, of course. They could not talk here, not in her bedchamber, not alone. "I must speak with you," he said in more placating tones. "I shall wait for you downstairs."

In the hall, he paced about, while Powell hovered anxiously with the two footmen, awaiting orders. In a very few minutes, she appeared, dressed in her brown travelling gown and pelisse.

He had had time to compose his thoughts somewhat, so he began, "Miss Parfitt, would you step into the breakfast parlour for a moment so that we may talk?"

It was not the most private of rooms, having three entrances, but perhaps she would be more comfortable there. In any event, she inclined her head and passed through the door he held open for her. He closed it behind him as he followed her, and she made no protest. Whatever needed to be said between them, she understood that it must be private. But now he had no idea what to say. An apology? For a kiss? Again he was aware of a spurt of anger — she had not tried to avoid it, after all!

Instead he said, "There is no need for you to leave."

"There is every need, Mr Armitage."

So formal! "You said you would leave if I laid a finger on you, and I did not do so. I was very careful not to do so."

"Sophistry!" she said scornfully.

"You have my word I will not touch you again, if you will stay."

"How can I trust you?" she said simply.

"Are we not friends?" he said gently. "Can we not move beyond this? I know we started badly, but I long since abandoned any attempt to seduce you, or affect your heart. All that was forgotten, it seemed to me. Today was... a mistake, I can see that. A misunderstanding, but surely we can put it behind us, for Violet's sake."

"I must go, and today. If you wish to explain my sudden departure to the others, I received a letter from my aunt this morning, so you may say that she is ill and I have been called away to her."

"If I wish? Is that what you want me to tell everyone?"

"I do not care. Tell them the truth, if you prefer, for I shall not be here. Tell your mama and Violet that I shall write to thank them, if you please."

She was determined to go, he could see that, and he was swamped with sadness for the loss of the strange little friendship they had enjoyed. "I am sorry, Evie."

"So am I," she said, with a wry lift of her eyebrows. "But it is too late to be sorry."

"Yet you could have stopped me," he cried, stung by the unfairness of it. "One word from you — one look—"

"Oh, am I your conscience now?" she said sharply. "You are a gentleman, are you not? You know how to behave towards a guest in your house. It is not for me to correct you."

There was no answer to that. "Where will you go to?"

"To my aunt in Winchester."

"The carriage will take you the whole way, and Margie will travel with you, and one of the footmen. I will not have you journeying on the common stage or the mail coach."

She frowned and opened her mouth to protest, but in the end she merely inclined her head. "Thank you. Your consideration is appreciated. If you would be so good as to write me a reference, or perhaps Mrs Armitage would do so, that I might find another employment in the future, that would be a kindness."

There was some delay while the change of plans was set in motion and the servants packed for the journey, but within an hour Eliot was handing her into the carriage. She was composed, as always. He was less so, unsure how to explain her departure to his family. And beneath the surface was sorrow and a low-burning sense of injustice that she had kissed him willingly, joyfully, lovingly and yet would leave, and in all likelihood he would never see her again.

~~~~~

JUNE
~~~~~

"Betty got a piece of skate as well as some smelts today, so that will make a good dinner with the rest of the veal pie," Aunt Dodi said. "I met Canon Waterman on the High Street and he sends his regards to you, Evie. And here is another letter for you from Essex."

Evie was in her aunt's tiny parlour, stitching one of the endless sets of clothes for the workhouse children. She set aside her needlework with a sigh. "How much did you have to pay for this one? Oh, it is only one sheet. That is something."

Aunt Dodi laughed, a deep throaty chuckle quite at odds with her delicate appearance. "Never mind the cost. We can afford a letter now and again, after all the money you sent me, and it is a good sign that Miss Barantine has not quite forgotten you."

"She is concerned about mourning protocols again," Evie said, scanning the letter. "She does not wish to do anything improper, but she would very much like to accept one or two of these evening engagements."

"Is there a young man drawing her back into the world? She is very young still."

"No, I believe Mr Nettles, the clergyman, is still her ideal. All the young men from the neighbourhood are in town just now, so I acquit her of any ulterior motive. Colonel and Mrs Spilsbury, and Sir William and Lady Wyvill are the great inducements, and none of them a day under fifty. If she accepts either invitation, she will enjoy a very dull dinner, followed by several rubbers of whist and the only conversation will concern the weather."

"Hardly a dissipated outing, and not improper for a girl in mourning," Aunt Dodi said. "But surely she has Mrs Armitage to advise her on these points now, and Lady Corbett too."

"True, but poor Violet still sees me as the fount of all wisdom regarding how a lady should behave," Evie said, with a laugh. "She starts every letter with *'Mrs Armitage says...'* or *'Lady Corbett says...'*, and then asks me for my opinion. It is very flattering, I suppose."

"Is there any other news? Of the family?" Aunt Dodi said with studied nonchalance.

Evie did not pretend to misunderstand. "Mr Edward Folkard and Mr Eliot Armitage are both at Marsham Grove at present. Violet says that Mr Armitage takes his father out in his curricle from time to time, since the weather is so fine at present. "

"So not *all* the young men are in town," Aunt Dodi said casually, smoothing the cotton mittens she wore to warm her hands, and picking up her own needlework.

"No, and I do not know why they are not," Evie said frankly. "Well... Edward is perhaps dangling after Violet, but Mr Armitage always goes to town for the season, and you need not look like that, dear Aunt, for it is nothing to do with me, you may be sure. Perhaps he is concerned about his father, and does not wish to be from home... although if there were any cause for concern, he would not take the old gentleman jauntering about the countryside, as he has taken to doing, it seems."

Aunt Dodi set her sewing down in her lap, and removed her spectacles. "Evie, are you quite sure you do not wish to talk about him? I have not the least wish to pry, but you might feel better if you unburden yourself, and do not say that there is nothing to tell, because it is perfectly obvious that *something* occurred to bring you rushing home to me. Not that I am not delighted to have you back, but you were enjoying yourself, it seemed to me, and I thought you would at least stay with Miss Barantine until she married."

How could she answer? She had told her aunt the bare bones of the story but how humiliating to admit the truth!

"I fell in love with him," she blurted. "And the worst of it was that he was not even trying. He was making no effort at all — he had no interest in making me love him, but I did anyway. And then he kissed me... He is an incorrigible rake, of course," she went on, half to herself. "Such a man must be filled with charm, whether he is aware of it or not. If he had flirted openly with me, no doubt I would have been on my guard, but how could I possibly resist him? And then when he kissed me — of course I had to leave."

"It is a pity, but you have led such a sheltered life. You did the right thing, dear, and you are safe here, you know," her aunt said. "No man can disturb us here, and you will recover your equanimity here in our little house."

Their little house. Two rooms downstairs, two upstairs and a tiny garret for the maid. The garden only a few paces long. For several years, Evie had lived there quite contentedly, asking no more of life, but now... now she had seen the world. She had moved in the Barantines' rich, if somewhat vulgar, society, and latterly she had delighted in the freedom of the Armitages' country estate, surrounded by endless open countryside and her own horse with which to explore. Now all that was gone...

Only a kiss, Eliot had said. Only a kiss, but the result was that the walls had closed in on her alarmingly, and her future was long, lonely and bleak.

11: Restlessness

It had been one of his better ideas, Eliot thought. There were Nancy and his father, missing each other and unable to enjoy a brief morning call or even write to each other, and what could be kinder than to contrive a meeting? He understood his father's reluctance to take the carriage, with Winfield a silent witness to the journey, but Eliot had his curricle, and all that was needed was a way to get his father into and out of it. At first, he could not solve the problem, for it would take two men, surely, to lift even his father's delicate frame up to the curricle seat, but one day he saw Violet's footman, Henry, carrying several buckets of coal into the house without the least effort, and the idea sprang fully-formed into his mind.

"Hoy, Henry! A moment, if you please." Henry obediently set down the buckets and loped over to Eliot. "You are a strong fellow, Henry. Could you carry my father, do you think? If it should be necessary?"

Henry nodded vigorously.

"And you can keep a secret?" Eliot whispered.

The Negro smiled, and put one hand across his mouth, with a rumble that might have been laughter.

Two days later, having obtained permission from Violet to borrow Henry, and told everyone that he planned to take his father for a little jaunt through the forest, the weather being so warm, Eliot had his curricle brought round to the front door. His father was bundled up in a heavy greatcoat, while his mother selected from an array of rugs to keep his legs warm.

"You will not keep him out long, Eliot? He is not strong, and this wind—"

"I shall take good care of him, you may be sure, Mother."

Without effort, Henry lifted Eliot's father and carried him down the steps to the waiting curricle, settling him in the seat.

"Comfortable, sir?" Eliot said.

His father grinned in delight. "Oh yes! Most comfortable. Such a treat for me. Thank you, Henry. Ah, yes, a rug. Thank you, my dear." Eliot sprang into the driver's seat, while Henry climbed up behind.

Eliot's groom held the horses' heads in disapproving silence, considering it improper to take a mere footman along on such an outing rather than a gentleman's own groom.

"Stand away, Tim," Eliot called out.

"Not too far!" his mother cried. "Do not overtire him, Eliot."

With a flick of the whip, the curricle bounced into motion. Beside him, his father laughed in delight. "Such a treat," he murmured, waving. "Such a delightful treat. Good bye, my dear!"

For a while, they drove in near silence, except for his father pointing out excitedly, "The mill! Oh, and over there, the Turners' farm. Look, that must be St Matthew's steeple." Eliot wondered how long it had been since his father had even left the house. He hated closed carriages which gave him dreadful headaches, but he could have gone out in the barouche occasionally. But then Mrs Armitage would insist on accompanying him and would fuss him enough to destroy all his pleasure in the outing. The result was that his own rooms were his whole world now, and his childlike delight in the countryside induced a great weight of guilt in Eliot's breast. How he had neglected his father! He had been so caught up in his own concerns, his own desires, that he had given no thought at all to his father, trapped at home and too gentlemanly to complain at his confinement.

"We must make this a regular excursion," Eliot said.

"Perhaps," his father replied. "I should not like Mrs Armitage to worry about me."

As they approached Epping, his father fell silent, but a quick glance at his visage showed no sign of fatigue. Instead, he leaned forward slightly and his expression was full of anticipation. He knew now where they were bound, and when they turned in through the gates of Nancy's neat little garden, he gave one brief convulsive gasp. Then they were halting, and the door burst open and Nancy's rounded form flew out to greet them, tears coursing down her weathered cheeks. Eliot's father reached down to her and she fell into his arms, sobbing. Henry jumped down and waited patiently until the two could prise themselves apart, before carrying Mr Armitage into the house.

The visit was only an hour long. Eliot stayed with the horses in the stables, while Henry waited in the house in case he was needed. Then there was the short drive home again, his father rather pink-cheeked, with a smile that could not be suppressed. Eliot's mother rushed out to inspect him as soon as they returned, declared that he had over-exerted himself and ordered a nap. He accepted without demur.

After that, the outings became a regular event, but were only permitted when there was not the least threat of rain. Eliot had never seen his father take such an avid interest in the weather before. He could not discover that Nancy did anything more than feed her visitor claret and cake, and talk to him about friends long dead and events long past, but he grew plumper and stronger under her ministrations.

~~~~~

JULY

The season was all but over, and Eliot could not remember the last time he had missed so much of it. The year Alethia's children all had the measles, one after the other, from Easter through to August, perhaps. Or the year he had set up his very first proper mistress in a cottage at Clacton-on-Sea. But otherwise, there he had been, settled in Grosvenor Square with a stack of invitations on the mantel.

This year, he could not summon much enthusiasm. Sometimes an invitation had arrived that he felt obliged to accept, and then he would dash eagerly up to town but for some reason the excitements of such occasions soon palled. After a day or two, he would be restless and longing to go home again. He told everyone that he was taking care of his ward who was still in mourning, and that was true enough, but there was more to his ennui than consideration for Violet.

At first, he could not work out what ailed him. Was he sickening for something? Was it simply his age? He was thirty now, and had been on the town for enough years to have lost sight of any
~~~~~

attraction in novelty or excess. He no longer cared to attend five different events in one night. He was no longer interested in passing the hours with people he could not even say, if he were honest, that he particularly liked. It was all show and glitter and emptiness, and he went home to his cold bed each evening in increasing dissatisfaction.

Perhaps a new mistress would relieve his boredom. It was more than a year since Hetty had moved on, after all, a longer interval than any previous, and he wondered if his restlessness would be assuaged by a fresh attraction.

One evening, at a rout in Duke Street, he encountered the familiar face of Lady Tammleton.

"Eliot! Just the person I'd hoped to see. Where have you been hiding all these weeks, my old friend? How are you?"

He smiled at the petite figure accosting him. "Well, as you see, my lady. And you are in unusually good health, if rumour is to be believed."

She gurgled with laughter. "It is true! At last Tammleton has hopes of an heir, after five years of trying. Poor fellow, the effort has quite worn him out and he has retired to the shires, exhausted. Whereas I am full of energy, and free to enjoy myself untrammelled by my dear spouse. Goodness, it is hot in here. Shall we find an open door and see if we may obtain some fresh air?"

Tucking her dainty hand into the crook of his arm, Eliot allowed himself to be led out onto a tiny balcony, occupied only by one other couple, sufficiently engrossed in each other not to notice anyone else.

"Lord, Eliot, I cannot tell you how glad I am to see you," she said in lower tones, pulling him nearer. "Marriage is a tedious business, let me tell you, and though I've never regretted my choice, and I'll always be deeply grateful to you for setting me up with Tammleton, I do miss our gay times, don't you?"

"You know you were always my favourite mistress, Lucy," he said easily. He said the same thing to all of them when he met them, but perhaps with Lucy the words were close to being true.

"There, now! And I almost believe you." She laughed, not discomfited. "As for you... Heavens, Eliot, but it's been dull with Tammleton. Respectable and pleasant, but so, so dull. There were times when I would have traded a whole year of *stupid* respectability for just one more night with you. But now... for a little while I am free of Tammleton, and my spies tell me that you're free of entanglements too. We can have some fun, just until the summer is past and I have to go back to stultifying Gloucestershire and do this whole breeding an heir business. What do you say?"

How many times had he agreed to some such arrangement? A woman already with child, her husband's eyes off her for a while... a little fun, with no expectation on either side... such a temptation, as a rule. Yet he answered her with no hesitation.

"Lucy, much as I would like to oblige you, you had better look elsewhere for your amusement."

Her eyebrows shot up. "Have I grown so frumpy, my golden-haired Adonis?"

That made him laugh, his eyes running over her delicate curves, the expensively silk-clad body, and the diamonds adorning her hair, ears and throat. "You look even more delightful than ever,

Lucy, as you are perfectly well aware, but I am not minded for the sort of scheme you have in view."

"Ah. You are hanging out for a wife, then."

"Not that, no, but..." He trailed off, not even able to put into words his own reluctance. But unbidden the image arose in his mind of his Aphrodite, with her porcelain skin and thick hair piled onto her head and her luscious lips... ah, her lips!

Lucy tilted her head, looking at him thoughtfully, and said, "I will not tease you, Eliot, but I hope she deserves you. Shall we go back in? Perhaps Markhill is here tonight, and he might serve my purpose if you will not."

It was not yet midnight, but once he had made a circuit of the room with Lucy and she had spotted one of the Berringhams and optimistically attached herself to him, Eliot had had enough. He bade his hostess farewell and made his way downstairs to await his hat and cane.

As he stood in the hall, his thoughts a thousand miles away, or a hundred, perhaps, a crowd entered from the street, lively and ripe for amusement, surrounding him with glittering jewels and shimmering silk, the feathers on the ladies' heads waving this way and that. He ignored them. Once, he would have been of their number, hopping from one engagement to the next, eating, drinking and dancing away the summer nights, falling into bed only when the sun was well risen. Sometimes it was even his own bed. Now, he was too despondent to notice them until he was hailed.

"Armitage! Well met, old friend."

"Folkard?"

"How are you? And..." He lowered his voice a shade. "...how is Evie? She is well?"

Evie... Eliot's heart lurched in sudden pain. Oh, Evie!

"She... she was well, the last I heard of her."

Folkard's face changed. "The last you heard? Do you not receive news from Essex any more, my friend?"

"She is in Hampshire," Eliot said bluntly. "Winchester. With her aunt. Not... not needed as chaperon now that Violet has my mother. And Daphne is at Marsham Grove at the moment, too."

"In *Winchester?* But—"

"Ah, my things." Eliot grabbed his hat, gloves and cane from the footman, and with a few words and a hasty bow left the house. The brisk walk round the corner to Grosvenor Square did nothing to settle his mind. His valet, recognising his mood, undressed him in silence and withdrew promptly.

Eliot tossed aside his nightcap, poured himself a brandy and settled in a chair before the open window, his slippered feet resting on the windowsill. The night was quiet, without the hooting owls or hedgerow scufflings of the country. His room faced the mews, so only the occasional late-returning carriage disturbed his thoughts.

Evie... was she the reason why he was so unsettled? He closed his eyes and his mind summoned her face without effort... the perfectly smooth, white skin, those clear brown eyes, the hair which was neither red nor brown... russet, he thought. Like an autumn leaf. If she had been with him tonight, would he have been so restless... so *bored?*

Ah, Evie! Whenever he thought of her, he was conscious of a pain just below his heart, an aching that never quite went away. It was guilt, of course. She was so gentle, so pure… and he had brought her the sorrow of unrequited love. It was unintentional, for although he had begun with great hopes of seducing her, all that had long since evaporated. He had simply enjoyed her company, and now that she was gone, he missed her unbearably. Was it love, this need for her? Or was it no more than conscience assailing him? He could not tell. All he knew was that London was empty without her.

He slept fitfully that night, and as soon as he woke, he summoned his valet to pack, and ordered his curricle brought round to take him home.

~~~~~

Essex was no better, of course. Worse, in fact, for there he had memories of Evie in every room. He could not sit at dinner without remembering her quiet presence. He could not walk in the garden without passing a dozen places that reminded him of her. And the schoolroom — impossible to go there without thinking of that kiss. If he had never kissed her, he would perhaps be better able to cope with her loss, yet it haunted him. He had never had a kiss like it. It was not merely her innocence, or the sweetness of her gentle surrender. It was that he had never taken her in his arms. Always before there had been an embrace and a close pressing of bodies. He could deduce a great deal from a lady's response to being held. Whether she placed her hands on his chest trustingly, or wrapped her arms passionately around his back, or merely held them chastely at her side — he could read a great deal into that. But when he had not held her at all… when the only contact between them was the kiss itself… it felt incomplete. He dreamt of that kiss at night, and when he woke, hot and distracted, her face loomed before him, palely beautiful.
~~~~~

There was no time to brood over kisses, however. A note awaited him from Mr Nettles, requesting the favour of an early interview. That was ominous. He came at once in response to Eliot's reply, striding about the empty breakfast parlour, arms waving.

"Not my intention, sir, you must believe me. Would never presume, never! The lady is as far above me as the sun… I do not aspire… you must understand how it is. I have always kept myself aloof, and yet… I am very much afraid…"

"We are speaking of Violet, I presume?" Eliot said, trying to make sense of this gush of words.

"Of Miss Barantine, yes, of course. Such an *angel!* But not for me, as I am sure she must be aware. She has been so kind as to… as to ask my advice about certain matters, and in terms of spiritual guidance, naturally, I have been able to oblige her but in certain other confidences— Mr Armitage, sir, I am very much afraid that Miss Barantine has… is beginning to… has developed…"

"A *tendre* for you?" he hazarded.

"Yes! And nothing could be less suitable! I, a man of the cloth with a living worth a mere few hundred pounds a year, and she, heiress to a fortune of one hundred thousand pounds. It is quite unacceptable, you do not have to tell me so."

Eliot was not about to tell him anything of the sort. Violet might be an heiress, but she was the daughter of a jewel merchant. On the other hand, Nettles might not have much of an income from the living, but he had a substantial allowance from his father, a gentleman of some means with an estate near Colchester, and his uncle was a baronet. He was not the sort of nobody whose encroachment on Violet would be widely seen as fortune-hunting.

"Come, sit down, Nettles, and have a glass of something... what do we have in here? Madeira? Sherry? Or shall I send for brandy?"

"Nothing at all, sir, I thank you. You are too kind to one upon whom you must look down with the utmost disdain."

"I do no such thing." Eliot poured two glasses of Madeira and set them on the table, pulling out a chair for Nettles. "Sit, sir, if you please, and let me tell you a little about Violet Barantine. Firstly, she is but eighteen years of age, and her affections, however ardent they may appear to be, are unlikely to be fixed. Do you know how I became her guardian? Because she had met me once, and formed an instant attachment to me. She thought that choosing me as her guardian would make me fall in love with her."

Nettles' mouth dropped open in astonishment. "But... but you could not... your own ward!"

"Quite so. But now she has turned her attentions on you, and naturally it is distressing, since she is not a girl to be deterred. But be of good heart, for her interests will shift again before too long and you will be able to rest easy."

"Oh no, I do not think it will be so, for she informs me that I have quite reformed her character and no one else will do for her. She does not *wish* to attach herself elsewhere for no one else, she tells me, could ever have the same effect on her. With another, she is quite sure that she would relapse back into her former bad habits of wastefulness and display."

Eliot sipped his Madeira, rather amused by so much impassioned principle. "As previously mentioned, she is but eighteen and has seen but little of the world—"

"Indeed, but so tractable, so docile! So biddable! So willing to be guided by a more enlightened mind."

He lifted his eyebrows at that. Violet tractable? "You have indeed wrought a wondrous change in her but—"

"It makes her *vulnerable,* do you see, sir? Vulnerable to men with weaker minds and more worldly temperaments. I wonder if she should not enter a nunnery? To keep her safe?"

His voice trembling as he tried very hard not to laugh out loud, Eliot said gravely, "No, I do not think a nunnery would suit her. She might, perhaps, like to spend a few weeks in London this autumn."

Nettles sat down abruptly in the chair provided for him. "You would truly send her away? You feel my influence is detrimental? I would never do the least thing to harm her, you must know, sir!"

"I do know it, and your influence has been most beneficial, but clearly she is bothersome to you. I will also tell you, Nettles, that I do not believe Violet is destined to end her days in Lower Marsham parsonage, and if this continues, you might feel hounded into offering for her. I would not have you teased by the chit. You stay away from her as best you can, and I shall see that she goes to town for the little season. The change of scene will do her a world of good."

"Hounded... teased... Oh. Well... that is... very considerate, sir. Very considerate indeed. I... yes, indeed, that would be for the best, I daresay."

Rather less grateful than might have been expected, he bowed himself out, and Eliot sent for Violet, where his careful plans were met with tears and protestations.

"You are sending me away?" she sobbed. "What have I done wrong? Oh, pray let me make amends! Do not, I beg you, send me away from dear Marsham Grove!"

"Just for a few weeks, and not until the autumn. The little season, Violet. A few card parties and routs, perhaps a little dancing, if you feel up to it."

"Oh... dancing... may I take Evie with me?"

"Miss Parfitt? But why?"

"Evie is my friend," she said simply. "She always knows how I should go on. Her aunt is quite well now, she says, so she will be glad to come back to me, I expect. Winchester sounds dreadfully dull."

"I do not know that she will wish to return," he said, unable to keep the bleakness out of his voice.

"No, she does not, for I have asked her several times in my letters, and she always says that I do not need her any more, but I *do*, I do. She would agree to it if you were to ask her, I am sure. If you were to go to Winchester and explain that I need her — she would come back then, would she not? And then I should be happy to go anywhere in the world, with Evie."

And his foolish heart jumped at the prospect. He had no expectation of convincing her, but at least he could see her again, and there would be no harm in that... would there?

12: The Proposal

Tuesday was Evie's day to walk into town. Ten minutes to walk through the close and past the Cathedral. Ten minutes down the High Street to the butcher to negotiate a better piece of meat than last week. Ten minutes back to the haberdasher's to buy thread, and to look longingly at the lace. Then her treat, ten minutes in Mr Peake's shop, with its wonderful smell of fresh paper, leather bindings and dust. She had no books to sell today, for her own earnings still jingled in her reticule and Aunt Dodi told her airily that she had *'a little bit put away for a rainy day, thanks to all the money you sent me'*, so they were not yet reduced to hardship. She could not at all afford the subscription to Mr Peake's little library, so generally she limited herself to ten minutes only. Long enough to read a chapter, perhaps two, and hope that the book would still be there next week. But today... today was her thirtieth birthday, and so she spent fifteen shillings on a small novel, a book of poetry and a little booklet of prayers. A small consolation for her confirmed spinster status.

On the way home, she went into the Cathedral, as she always did, sitting in the first pew, her little parcel a comforting weight on her knee. The soaring pillars and arches, and the carved ceiling so far above not only gave her the space to breathe, but also afforded her perspective on her own troubles. In such a place she was small and insignificant, her own modest sorrows no more important than those of an ant. And what, after all, had she to complain about? It was her own fault entirely. How foolish to fall for a known rake like Eliot Armitage! And even more foolish to let him know it.

Yet that in itself was not the whole of her humiliation. She had kissed him. Even when she had had ample opportunity to escape him, she had not. Instead, like a green girl she had closed her eyes and yielded to his expert lips and oh God, if only she had not! If only she had not that wondrous memory to taunt her. Sometimes she lay awake at night and wondered what it would be like to yield totally to such a man, to be his mistress, to be *his*. But that was even more foolish, she told herself sternly, and the sure road to ruin and disgrace and the loss of everything. At least she still had her reputation. It might not keep her warm at night or feed her, but at least she could sit in the Cathedral and look God in the eye with a clear conscience.

So after ten minutes of berating herself, followed by a prayer for serenity, she stood, smoothed her skirts and walked briskly home to her aunt's tiny house. There was the usual discussion of all that she had done and seen, the busyness of the shops, the approval of the thread she had brought and were there any oranges at the grocer's shop today? Then they settled down with their sewing for the day, the shifts and gowns of cheap cotton for the girls, the shirts of various sizes for the boys. They spoke little as they sewed, the clock ticking mournfully on the mantel and the occasional cart or voice outside in the close. Evie allowed her thoughts to wander, and, as they often did, they settled on an image of golden hair, deep blue eyes and a roguish smile. So hard to put him out of her mind!

Thus it was that she had no warning. When the maid came in, bobbed a curtsy and said, "Mr Armitage to see Miss Parfitt, ma'am," Evie gasped. There he was, just as her imagination had envisaged him, except for the green coat. That was new. She was so startled that she jumped to her feet, scattering pins, thread and sewing everywhere.

"Mr Armitage!"

"Miss Parfitt. I beg your pardon, it was not my intention to startle you but the maid bade me enter. May I help you?"

"Oh... no, no, it is quite all right." She knelt, blushing furiously, and gathered up her fallen sewing. "There!" She rose and stuffed everything higgledy-piggledy into her work basket. "I—" And she could not speak. Seeing him there, thinking him a hundred miles away at least and now standing just feet from her, was too much. She bowed her head, and curtsied, not quite knowing what else to do.

~~~~~

Eliot was enchanted. He had not formed any idea of what reception his unexpected arrival might elicit, but her face, lifted in a sudden burst of happiness, was more than he could possibly have hoped for. She, who was always so composed, so restrained, was full of joy at his coming. Even though she schooled her features into her usual calm expression almost at once, he had seen beneath the surface, seen her love shining through. Sweet Evie! So delightful a woman.

He would marry her!

As soon as he had the thought, he recognised the rightness of it. He would marry her, and at one and the same time correct the wrong he had done her, and assuage the aching void in his own life.
~~~~~

She would bring him contentment, of that he was sure, with her gentle, ladylike ways. She would keep his feet on the path of rectitude, and he would bring her the happiness she deserved. He would do it today, and then she would be his, she would smile at him in that heart-stopping way again and he would kiss her... Oh yes, he would kiss her.

All this passed through his mind as she scrambled to recover her composure and her sewing things. By the time all was tidy, her expression was placid once more, and she introduced him to her aunt with unruffled politeness. His manners were the equal of hers, so he seated himself beside the aunt, and engaged her in conversation. The house, the Cathedral, her late husband, the city of Winchester — all came in for comment. But eventually the aunt said, "You will take some tea with us, Mr Armitage? I shall just go and see to it." She disappeared and he was left alone with Evie.

Even then he knew better than to rush his fences. They spoke of Violet and Nettles and the plan to send her to London in September.

"I hope I can persuade you to agree to accompany Violet. If you will not, I do not know how I shall come about, for she declares that she will not go without you, and I cannot like her association with Nettles."

"He is a good influence on her," Evie said thoughtfully. "However, she will have some other fancy before long, and I should not wish him to be hurt by her thoughtlessness."

Mrs Scudamore and the maid returned soon after that with the tea and a plate of biscuits, but no cake. He guessed that they did not have visitors often enough to justify making fresh cakes every day. The plan for Violet's visit to town was gone over again.

Eliot smiled at Mrs Scudamore. "Am I too presumptuous in hoping that you can spare Miss Parfitt to my ward for a few weeks?"

"Why, certainly she may go if she wishes. It is delightful to me to have Evie's company, naturally, but I live such a quiet, retired life, well-suited to me but not ideal for one so friendly and sociable as Evie. I like to think of her in company with other gentlefolk, as she should be. She is wasted here in the Cathedral Close, and should be on a wider stage, it seems to me."

"Indeed she should," he said, smiling at Evie, but although she inclined her head in acknowledgement of the compliment, there was no answering smile.

Instead she said, "Have you had any success in locating Violet's missing diamonds?"

"I have been pursuing my enquiries," he said smugly. "It was Mr Barantine's habit to stitch valuable jewels into his clothing. However, my solicitors have talked to everyone in his employ in London and although his clothing was recovered, and all his possessions from the ship that foundered, there was no sign of the jewels. Nor were they in the possession of Mr Newbold, or either of the two gentlemen's valets. Yet Barantine had a sealed container with him, which held the legal record of the purchase of the diamonds, with the signature and seal of an attorney in Dublin. I have sent a letter to this attorney, and am hopeful of finding out something to the purpose from him." He paused, seeking some sign of approval from Evie, but her expression was impassive. "I owe it to Violet to do everything I can, especially as her inheritance is not worth as much as she once thought. After settling some debts and paying off this Newbold fellow, the brother of Mr Barantine's partner, my lawyers tell me there may not be more than fifty thousand left for Violet when all is done."

"It is still a good sum," Mrs Scudamore said.

"True, but to a girl who has been used to valuing herself higher than that, it will seem a paltry amount," Evie said. "What will the diamonds be worth, if they can be found?"

"A few thousand, no more than that, but Newbold will doubtless consider them a part of the business too," Eliot said gloomily.

"Well, I wish you good fortune, Mr Armitage," Evie said. "Even if you cannot establish what became of the diamonds, at least you will have left no stone unturned in your efforts, and that is commendable."

Her words cheered him. He rose to place his tea cup on the table before Mrs Scudamore and walked to the window of the tiny room. Such a small house, and the garden just as tiny. How could Evie bear to live here, so confined and cramped? But he could take her away from this, and place her somewhere better suited to her delicate ways.

"What a pleasant little garden," he said, gazing through the window. "Would you care to walk there with me, Miss Parfitt?"

"Oh, yes, do show Mr Armitage our peaches!" Mrs Scudamore cried, eyeing him knowingly.

Evie rose and smoothed her skirts. "Of course."

He dutifully admired the peaches, all five of them, and painfully small.

"The squirrels will get them," Evie said, smiling ruefully. "They always do. Some years we manage to harvest one or two, but usually we decide that they are not quite ripe enough, and the next day, they are all gone. We must have the plumpest squirrels in Hampshire."

The garden was no more than thirty paces from end to end, but against the far wall was a stone bench with white roses trained above it, like an arbour, as a few delicate petals lay scattered on the ground like rice at a wedding. He could not have imagined a more perfect setting for his proposal.

"Shall we sit?" he said. "I should like to talk to you privately, if you permit."

She nodded, seating herself on the bench and arranging her skirts around her. So beautiful as she looked! Her gown was a soft blue, pale and delicate, for she had left off the mourning colours she had worn when she was with Violet, and she looked utterly enchanting, her eyes demurely lowered as she waited for him to make his speech. She must guess, of course, what he was about to say, and surely her heart must be fluttering with excitement at the prospect? She loved him, she had told him, so she would be willing and eager for his addresses.

"Miss Parfitt... Evie..." he began. "How ironic it is that I should be here today, speaking to you this way. I set out all those months ago with the worst... the most *insulting* of intentions towards you. Naturally, you would have none of it. You would have none of *me.* So then I decided to have my revenge by making you fall in love with me. What a despicable creature I was! How much pain I have caused you, and how properly you reproached me for it. But in the end, revenge is yours, dear Evie, for when I set out to entrap you, I had no idea that I should myself become ensnared. Yet now I am truly caught in your web, entranced by your charms and your manifold perfections. How *good* you are, and how right to turn away from me as I was then. But you need do so no longer. I am entirely yours, Evie. Will you now be mine? Will you be my wife?"

He was, on the whole, rather pleased with his work. He had never before proposed marriage to a lady, but it was well done, he thought. She could not be displeased, although her face was calm, with no hint of her feelings. He sat back, arms folded, to await her response.

"Mr Armitage," she began.

"Eliot," he said eagerly.

"Mr Armitage, I am very flattered by your words, and honoured that you would consider making me your wife, but I regret that I must decline your most obliging offer."

The pain was as great as if he had been hit in the chest. It was inexplicable! How could she reject him, after all that had passed between them? It was utterly unaccountable.

"Why?" he croaked. "You have told me that you love me, so why refuse me?"

Her eyes flashed with sudden fire. "Need you ask? Your character is defined by your propensity to seduce women. It has been a part of your life for many years now and is too settled a state to be easily abandoned. I cannot marry a man who will inevitably bring me great unhappiness in the future."

He could scarcely believe her words, so calmly spoken yet so implacable. "But I *love* you!" he cried helplessly. "I could never be unfaithful to you! All of that, my wildness, my seductions — that is over and done with. It was over as soon as I understood my feelings for you. You must believe me—"

She rose and smoothed her skirts. "I cannot believe you."

"I swear I can make you happy!" he cried, jumping to his feet. He seized her hands, but she firmly withdrew them.

"Oh yes! For a year, perhaps two. Maybe more. But eventually you will stray and all my happiness will be at an end, and I could not bear it. It is impossible, you must see that."

"You would reject me because of what I once was?"

"Because of what you *are*. Once a rake, always a rake. A man's character is formed at an early age, and beyond that point is as fixed as stone."

"Evie, I can change, I swear it! I *have* changed. Will you not give me the chance to prove it to you?"

"I cannot. Truly I wish it were otherwise, but you must see that I should never be able to *trust* you. I am very sorry, but I cannot marry a man who will surely bring me grief."

He could find no words to convince her. Abruptly, for his legs were shaking, he sat down again. "But will you come to London? To Violet?"

Another thought flickered into his mind. She would not marry him, but she ought to have the chance to marry *someone*, a man worthy of her, as he was not. A man who was a model of rectitude and as good as she was. But she could never meet such a man here.

Her eyes clouded. "That... I do not know. To stay in your house in Grosvenor Square?"

"No, no! I shall ask my aunt and uncle to invite you. My aunt will chaperon Violet, so you will be able to dance. I should like to see you dance, and not sitting on the chaperon's bench with the matrons and dowagers, as you did that time I first saw you," he cried. "You are too young and beautiful to be relegated to the ranks of the spinsters. If you will not marry *me*, then I want you to have the opportunity to marry someone else, and to do that you must dance. Please, say you will come."

Her voice softened as she said, "I will come, for Violet's sake, so long as we will be living in your aunt's house, and not yours."

"Oh yes," he said bitterly. "You will not be facing me over the breakfast table."

"That is better for both of us," she said gently.

13: A Lady Of Delicate Sensibilities

After Mr Armitage had left, it was an hour and twenty minutes before Aunt Dodi asked the question. She talked about Mr Armitage's manners, his care for Violet, his sisters, his aunt and uncle, his house in London, his person — a great deal about his person, which had impressed her very favourably — but at length she came to the point.

"You turned him down?"

"I did."

There was a long, pregnant pause, as her aunt wavered between polite restraint and avid curiosity. In the end, curiosity won. "But why, dear?"

"Because he is not an eligible husband, Aunt. He would keep me in great comfort, but sooner or later he would break my heart."

Aunt Dodi laid down her sewing and removed her spectacles. "Oh, Evie, you have not developed romantical notions, I hope?" she said carefully. "No man is perfect, but Mr Armitage is a gentleman of means and you would have a position in society, respectability, *consequence*. He is not vicious, anyone might see that. He would treat you gently."

Evie put her half-sewn garment onto her work basket, and went to kneel at her aunt's feet. "Dearest Aunt, Eliot Armitage is a rake... a libertine. Do you understand what that means? Perhaps he may imagine himself in love with me now, or perhaps it is only guilt that drives him to offer for me, because he kissed me and harboured improper thoughts towards me, but sooner or later, another woman will catch his eye and then his marriage vows will be as naught. I do not want to be his wife when that time is reached."

"Oh!" Aunt Dodi's eyes were wide. "Oh, yes, I can quite see... oh, goodness, yes... that would be... a *libertine?"*

"A libertine," Evie said relentlessly. "I am sorry to raise such a distressing subject with you, but indeed it is so. I could not ally myself with such a man, you must see that."

"Oh, certainly! It would be unthinkable! A *libertine!* Goodness. And he looks so respectable, too. So gentlemanlike, and so eager for your good opinion. So... so... "

"Charming?" Evie said, with a little laugh. "It is an inevitable accompaniment of the rake, is it not? In order to seduce, a man must have a degree of allure, must be able to beguile even poor innocents such as I. Yet even if I succumb to his fascinations, I am not so foolish as to surrender all good sense. Better to die a spinster than to fall into the trap of a man like Eliot Armitage."

"Oh yes! Better by far. I will not conceal from you, Evie, that this is the greatest relief to me. I had thought you might be tempted by him, or you might feel that you *ought* to marry, as so many women do, but marriage is *such* a trap! One marries for financial security, but it is not a pleasant thing, to be a wife, and I was in the greatest dread that you would agree to it. Now we shall go on comfortably together, shall we not? Gracious, Evie... a *libertine!* And he seemed such an agreeable man, too."

"Very agreeable," Evie said, with a lurch of her heart that could only be grief. "Far too agreeable. But he is not for me."

Yet even as she spoke, she remembered his words, *'I should like to see you dance, and not sitting on the chaperons' bench with the matrons and dowagers, as you did that time I first saw you'.* He remembered their first meeting? He remembered her sitting on the chaperons' bench? She had remembered him, from that occasion of course, for he was by far the handsomest, most desirable man in the room, not the sort of man who would normally come within the orbit of a jewel merchant's daughter and her chaperon. Their hostess, however, amused herself by mingling the ranks at her parties and so there he had been, the rich man from Grosvenor Square, attracting the attention of Violet and Evie equally. But that he had noticed her — that was unexpected.

And the words of his proposal... *'I am entirely yours, Evie... I love you...I swear I can make you happy'.* Every word was like a dagger to her heart. She did not regret her answer, but if only he had not declared himself with such passion!

~~~~~

Eliot's smouldering anger carried him all the way back to his hotel. How dared she refuse him? How dared she take that superior attitude that he was bound to fail! He *loved* her, how could he ever wish for anyone else? But gradually the justice of her words made themselves felt. It was true that he had always done as he pleased, and taken women as he wished. Ever since he reached manhood, he
~~~~~

had indulged himself in that way. Could he now give all that up for Evie? He was sure he could, for he loved her... he would be a devoted husband, he was certain of it. And yet... at the back of his mind was a tiny seed of doubt. In five years, or ten... might his eye start to wander again? He would try very hard to be faithful, but it would not be easy for him, he acknowledged the truth of it.

Still, she would come to London. That had been a happy idea of his! It would take Violet out of the orbit of Nettles for several weeks, and Evie would have a chance to enjoy herself, and to dance. How he longed to see her dance! Should he dance with her himself? Perhaps not... perhaps it would be better not to press upon her too closely, but he would be there, watching over Violet, and he could watch Evie, too. And if he was restrained and gentle with her, she might begin to see him in a more favourable light.

Another good idea occurred to him — he would get to the bottom of Violet's missing diamonds. He had been rather dilatory on the matter, he freely confessed. It had all seemed too much trouble for gems that had clearly been stolen at some point, and although his solicitors had been asking here and there, they had not discovered anything helpful. But now he was determined to do whatever it took. He would himself talk to the manager of the shop in London. He would even go to Ireland and talk to this attorney in Dublin who had overseen the transfer of the diamonds to Barantine's hands, to the last point where the diamonds were seen and then he might follow the trail to... wherever it led. The bottom of the sea, as it may be. Or the pockets of some thief. And even if he should not succeed in finding them, if he were seen to be trying, if he were to exert himself on Violet's behalf, Evie must approve his behaviour, surely? And then her opinion of him might rise a little.

If only it might. He so badly wanted her to think well of him.

~~~~~

Eliot returned to Marsham Grove with his head full of Evie and his plans, and so he was wholly unprepared for trouble. The first sign was the physician's gig being walked outside the house when he arrived.

His father! What else could it be, and Eliot away from home just when he should not be. He leapt down from the curricle and took the steps to the front door two at a time.

But William shook his head. "'Tis the mistress, sir. Took bad yesterday with her nerves."

"Mother? Nerves?" he said, bewildered.

She was in her sitting room, stretched out on a chaise longue, moaning, one hand draped across her forehead as if she had the headache. Violet sat beside her, smelling salts in hand. Miss Robart twittered in a corner, wringing her hands. His mother's lady's maid held some burnt feathers. The housekeeper was busy opening curtains and then closing them again, as the moans from the chaise longue rose and fell in pitch. The physician was rolling down his sleeves as a maid removed a bleeding bowl. Nettles sat on a footstool, Prayer Book in hand.

"Mother? Whatever is the matter?"

"Oh, Eliot, Eliot!" She wailed. "No, I cannot— Do go away!" Then, inexplicably, she hissed, *"Traitor!"* at him.

He beat a hasty retreat. Hysterical women were not something he felt qualified to deal with. The physician followed him into the hall, where a footman helped him on with his coat.

"Whatever ails her?" Eliot said. "I have never seen her like this before."
~~~~~

"She is a lady of delicate sensibilities," the physician said, frowning at him. "She must be permitted absolute quiet, no disturbance at all. With care, and regular bleeding, she may recover her composure in a month or so."

"A *month!*"

The physician took his leave, and Eliot was left standing in the hall, feeling as if the world had been tipped upside down and thoroughly shaken, like a pepper pot.

Nettles crept out of a corner where he appeared to have been skulking. "Perhaps I may shed some light on the matter, sir? In private?"

Eliot ushered him into the breakfast parlour. "Tell me all."

"Mrs Armitage received... a shock yesterday," Nettles said, his expression grave. "Some unexpected news, brought to her in all innocence by Miss Barantine." He paused, but Eliot was too dumbfounded to utter a word. The clergyman went on, "It appears that there is a woman in Epping... a woman of disrepute, if you understand me, sir... and Mrs Armitage was brought word that... that... members of her family had been *consorting* with this person. Her husband, sir. And you yourself."

Eliot burst out laughing. "Nancy Weeks? That is what this is about?"

"It is a serious matter to a lady of refinement, such as Mrs Armitage," the man said in severe tones. "Naturally she is overset."

"Visiting an elderly lady? Is that such a serious matter? I took my father to call upon an old friend, that is all anyone needs to know."

"An elderly lady?" Nettles said. "Sir, perhaps you are not aware, but that person was once..." He lowered his voice although they were alone. "...a courtesan."

"A courtesan? Good Heavens, everyone of my father's generation had a mistress," Eliot said. Nettles winced, but said nothing. "Most of them had several. The present generation is no different, as the most cursory glance at our monarchy should reveal." He was about to walk out, but then he frowned. "Tell me, Nettles, how does Miss Barantine know anything of Nancy Weeks?"

The parson had the grace to flush to the roots of his hair. "It was an unfortunate circumstance, sir. We — Miss Barantine and I — were engaged on a mission of mercy to the dairymaid's family in Epping Street, and we happened to see your curricle as we were passing... a certain house. Naturally, Miss Barantine was curious, and asked about it until she understood the situation. Then she felt it proper to inform her hostess of the matter."

"Did she indeed! And who put that idea into her head, eh?"

"Those who conceal wrongdoing are guilty of it themselves," Nettles said haughtily.

"And those who sit in judgement on others without knowing the circumstances are guilty of sanctimonious meddling," Eliot said furiously, one finger poking the clergyman in the chest. "Get out of my sight, Nettles, and keep your piety for the pulpit."

Eliot found his father hiding in his dressing room, huddled beside the fire with a shawl around his shoulders.

"Eliot! Thank goodness! You have heard what has happened, I daresay. Poor Mrs Armitage! It is just as I feared. We should never have gone to see Nancy, I knew it. It is all my fault!"

"Nonsense," Eliot said gruffly. "Why should you not call upon a friend of long-standing? It is ridiculous to make such a fuss about nothing."

"Fuss about nothing? Your poor mother is distraught! I should have known, I *did* know, and I allowed my own selfish wishes to prevail and now look what I have done. She is very ill, poor lady. We are all to be very, very quiet, like little mice, so that her nerves may recover."

"Like little mice? Must we creep about the house, or keep to our rooms now, except for meals?"

"Oh, no proper meals! Trays in our rooms, that is all we are permitted, and I would not mind that except that the Madeira is locked away, too. I should like a glass of Madeira with my dinner," he added wistfully.

"Father, this is *your* house, you may order matters as you please. You may eat in the dining room if you like, and drink as much Madeira as you choose."

"Oh, I could not go against your mother's express wishes, Eliot. No, indeed. It is my penance for wanting to visit Nancy. Your mother has the ordering of this house, and we must not go against her."

"Then we must get you out of this house, and somewhere you will be comfortable again," Eliot said firmly.

Eliot's father could not withstand his wife's badgering, but nor could he withstand Eliot's, either. Within an hour, the valet had packed all his things, the carriage was at the door with Henry standing behind and Violet, rather bemused, had waved them off.

"Where are you taking him, sir?" she said to Eliot.

"Since there is no comfort for him in his own house, I am taking him to stay with his mistress, Nancy Weeks," Eliot said coldly. "I do not scruple to tell you this, because although you should know nothing of such matters, apparently you do. And do not imagine I shall leave you here to distress my mother any further with your interfering ways. You may begin packing, too."

Violet cried. His mother cried, too, when he told her what he had done. And two days later, they cried all over again when both Violet's carriage and the Armitage carriage were pressed into service to convey Violet, her governess, her two lady's maids and her vast quantity of luggage to St Alban's, the home of one of the Armitage sisters.

Violet had tried argument, tears, shouting and wheedling, but Eliot was implacable. To St Alban's she was to go, whether she liked it or not.

"Why can Henry not come with me?" Violet said, mulishly. "He is my *personal* footman, he should be with me."

"He is needed more by my father at the moment," Eliot said. "You can have Henry back when you go to London, but you will not need him in St Alban's. My sister and her husband live very quietly, so you will go nowhere."

"Then what am I to do there?"

"You will make yourself useful to Mrs Milton," he said relentlessly. "There are two children in the nursery, so you may help out there, if no other opportunity presents itself."

"What of Evie?" Violet said, with a final cast of the die. "May she come to St Alban's too? I shall be glad of her company, and...

and she can help me in the nursery. She was so good with Lady Corbett's children when they were here. Please, sir."

Eliot wavered. Part of him wanted to refuse Violet even that small comfort, but the image of Evie in that tiny house in Winchester rose in his mind, selling her father's books to put food on the table. Anywhere, even Cristobel's modest life, must be superior to that, and she would send money back to her aunt, he knew. "I will write to her and ask her if she might be willing," he said.

Before he took Violet to St Alban's, there was one more duty to be faced. His mother received him in her sitting room, her face pale and drawn as she lay on a chaise longue in the darkened room, the curtains half-closed against the sun. How ill she looked! She clutched a handkerchief and there were traces of tears on her cheeks. His heart lurched with pain at the sight of her... and guilt, too. This was his fault, after all. His father had understood his wife better than Eliot had, and had known how distressed she would be to learn of his mistress. Was this how all wives were, when they discovered the truth of their husband's wandering ways? He had only ever seen the brave face such women showed to the world, when inside they must want to rage and scream, or cry, or curl into a miserable ball. Why had he never realised it before?

"Mother? How are you?" he said gently, kneeling beside her and taking her thin, cold hand in his.

"Oh... tired," she said, her voice feeble. "Dr Welch has bled me again, so I shall go on better soon."

"Should I ask Daph to come back to bear you company?"

"Oh, no, no, no, not so close to her confinement."

"Then should you like to go to her? Or Alethia? Beth?"

"I could not contemplate a journey, not when I feel so low. Oh, Eliot, how *could* you? How could you encourage him to do such a thing?" A tear trickled down her wrinkled cheek.

"Forgive me, Mother. I had no idea it would upset you so. You must not blame Father, for it was all my doing. You know how easy-going he is. I had the idea and bullied him into it. I meant no harm, only to do him a bit of good by taking him to see an old friend."

"A friend! A woman like that? Oh, *Eliot!*" She sat almost upright in her indignation, before lying back again with a groan and a fresh burst of tears. Then, puzzled, she said, "An *old* friend? He has... has *consorted* with this woman before?"

"He knew her before he knew you," Eliot said quietly.

Her eyes widened as she absorbed this information.

He went on, "You would never have known anything about her, except for my stupidity, and for that I am deeply sorry. Can you ever forgive me?"

But she was crying again, her handkerchief pressed to her eyes. He crept from the room, and sent her maid in to sit with her.

14: A Visit To Pine Place

AUGUST

'Pine Place, Nr St Albans, Herts. August 17th. My very dear aunt, The heading on this paper reads 'Nr St Alban's' and it may very well be so, but I cannot at all vouch for it. If one walks for about two miles to the top of a slight rise, the spires and chimneys and smoky haze of the city are just visible on the horizon, but that is as near as I have got to it. Mr and Mrs Milton live very quiet, going nowhere, and certainly not to St Alban's, so however fine the Cathedral may be, I can give you no account of it. Mrs Milton is around forty, and her husband, as she never tires of telling us all, will be sixty at his next birthday if God spares him, which his good lady seems to doubt. I do not think sixty is such a great age, for Archdeacon Wilcox is close to ninety and as fit as a fiddle, and the elder Mr Armitage is past seventy and only slightly wobbly on steps. However, Mr Milton, at a mere nine and fifty, is invalidish, poor man, and keeps largely to his room, subsisting on weak beef broth and bread and not much else. The physician calls on Mondays, Wednesdays and Fridays, the apothecary on Tuesdays, Thursdays and Saturdays, and the parson on Sundays, which seems to cater for all eventualities. If he were my husband, I should be inclined to feed him up on red meat and red

wine and a five mile walk daily, but his lady takes after her mother and likes to fuss about him all day, which attention he seems to enjoy. There are two children, a boy of twelve and a girl of ten, who creep about the house with unnatural quietness on the rare occasions when they are permitted to leave their schoolroom. Mr Milton's sister devotes herself to their education. I am sorry to tell you that I have not been able to discover what happened at Marsham Grove to cause such uproar as to send Violet into exile. If I venture to ask Mrs Milton, she purses her lips and says only that it is a Matter Too Dreadful To Be Mentioned, and Violet will say nothing about it at all, so I am none the wiser. I hope I do not sound waspish, dear Aunt, for I am trying hard to be patient, but we have not been anywhere but church since I arrived, and Violet and I are very glum as a consequence. Or perhaps it is this horrid hot weather that frays our tempers. The only bright spot is that Mrs Bradbrook has written to invite us formally to stay with her in town next month. I have written to ask for some journals so that we may know how to dress ourselves, which I hope will lift Violet's spirits. It will certainly lift mine. Yours from gloomiest Hertfordshire, your loving niece, Evie.'

~~~~~

Pine Place was aptly named, for almost the entire grounds, which were not large, were filled with great trees which loomed far overhead. There was a small expanse of lawn at the back of the house, but otherwise the entire estate was filled with conifers. It took perhaps twenty minutes, or half an hour if one walked very slowly indeed, to follow the perimeter path, and although there were seats dotted about, and even a small statue of Eros, it was not a very inspiring outing. When Evie and Violet ventured outdoors, their boots were silent on the accumulated pine needles, and no
~~~~~

birds sang above their heads. Occasionally, they were permitted to walk further afield, accompanied by a groom to ensure they never lost their way, but usually Mrs Milton considered it too hot or too likely to rain for such an expedition.

About two weeks after Evie had arrived, a familiar curricle bowled up to the front of the house, and Mr Eliot Armitage jumped down therefrom. Evie was glad they were sitting in a room overlooking the drive so that she had the earliest intimation of his arrival, and was not taken by surprise as she had been at Winchester. When he was shown in to the morning room, she was able to rise and make her curtsy with equanimity.

She was alone there with Violet, for Miss Robart was helping in the schoolroom, but Mrs Milton soon bustled in, her face anxious.

"Eliot! How lovely to see you, naturally, but we have not a room to spare for you, and as for your man and groom—"

"Now, do not put yourself about, Bel, for I shall put up at the Hart, you know. I would not for the world inflict myself upon you, not when you already have guests. How are you, sister? And how is James? A little better in this dry weather, I trust."

"I wish I could say so, but he feels the heat abominably. Not that he ever complains, naturally, for he is a perfect saint, but he suffers greatly. Have you come from Marsham Grove? How is Mama? Is she any better?"

It was the first that Evie had heard of any indisposition in Mrs Armitage, so she listened with avid interest.

"There is nothing greatly amiss with her, as I have told you already," he said. "It is a pity she will not go to Daphne, who would love to have her."

"What, with all those children running riot? Her nerves would be shredded within a day," Mrs Milton said. "She should go to Alethia at Brighton. The sea air would do her the greatest good."

"Alethia is mingling with some very raffish society there," Mr Armitage said. "Brighton will not do, Lizzie is away from home and there is no room here. I thought she might go to Cousin Lucy, but she would not hear of it. No, Mother is better where she is. Father is well, too. I am sure you wish to know that."

There were the pursed lips again, as though Mrs Milton had sucked on a lemon accidentally. "Do come and see James, Eliot, although you must not sit with him for long. He is so easily fatigued. Are you hoping to stay for dinner? I am not sure..."

Not sure there will be enough, Evie mentally finished the sentence, as Mrs Milton drifted out of the room, shawl trailing. There never was quite enough to eat, she had discovered. Only one course, with a couple of removes, and an air of pained surprise when every dish was cleared of its contents, as if the mistress of the house could not quite adjust to the number of extra mouths to feed. Violet and Evie were not intemperate in their appetites, and Miss Robart had been banished to the nether regions — *'Oh, a governess! Oh no, not with the family, you know. It is not at all fitting.'* Evie could only hope that the provender was more plentiful in the servants' hall.

Mr Armitage followed his sister out of the room, looking as if he had stepped out of the pages of a fashion journal. So elegant, always, with his close-fitting coat, his immaculate buckskins and boots polished to a high shine. Evie had not seen him since Winchester, when he had sat on the little bench beside her under the *rosa alba* and told her without a hint of insincerity that he was entranced by her charms. Entranced! What a delightful word, and a delightful proposal of marriage, which was no less pleasing for being the only one she had ever received. She had been gratified, of course, even if she suspected that guilt had something to do with it, and gentlemanly honour, prompting him to offer for the hapless female who had fallen in love with him. If she had known nothing of him except his position as the only son and heir to a respectable family, she would have accepted him in a heartbeat, for he was in appearance and manners everything a woman could hope for in a husband.

But she did indeed know more of him. She had known of his reputation from the very day they had met at Lady Frampton's ball. On their next meeting, he had been hosting some kind of disreputable party at his house and, even more outrageously, he had tried to persuade Evie herself to become his mistress. His character was fixed in her mind as dissolute, and no amount of society polish or elegant clothing could conceal that truth.

And yet... whenever she looked at him, so handsome, with his teasing smile, she wished that it were not so.

It turned out that there would, after all, be enough food on the table to feed an extra mouth, for Mr Armitage, presumably knowing his sister well, had taken the precaution of bringing hampers of supplies from Marsham Grove. It was too soon for the autumn game birds, but there were salmon and trout, pigeons, hares and venison, a goose, any amount of green vegetables, and sweet fruit from the forcing houses.

That evening there were two courses, including four carving joints, and Mr Milton felt well enough to join them for the soup and a ragoût of hare, and to invite Mr Armitage to join him in his lair later for a glass of port. Mrs Milton was fully engaged in ensuring that Mr Milton was not too hot or too cold, was not eating too much or too little, and was not drinking anything but barley water. Miss Milton spoke only to reprimand the children, although they scarcely put a foot wrong. It fell to Evie and Violet, therefore, to entertain the guest, and since she sat next to him, it was mostly Evie. She found him pleasant company. Just as at Marsham Grove, he never said anything to disconcert her, talking easily on a variety of unexceptional topics, amusing her with some of the fashion excesses he had seen in town, and giving her news of common acquaintances. He asked kindly about Aunt Dodi, and spoke without a hint of consciousness of his brief stay in Winchester.

Violet said little to him, still cross about being dragged away from pleasant Marsham Grove and her daily rides, but when Mr Armitage mentioned someone he had seen at church, she said loudly from the other side of the table, "How is Mr Nettles? Is he well?"

With his ready smile, Mr Armitage said easily, "He is very well, Violet. He has received a letter from a colonel — I forget his name now — who was most grateful for the many pairs of stockings for his men, and would be very happy to receive more if you can spare the time, and preferably of a thicker sort, the better for preventing blisters from their boots. May I cut you another slice of the goose? Miss Parfitt? How about you? Or should you prefer the artichokes? Bel's cook has them in such a light sauce, they are quite delicious. Do try a little."

He left soon after dinner to sleep at the nearest inn, but returned the next morning when only Evie and the children were at breakfast. He gamely talked of school matters to Anthony, and of watercolours to Maria, and then drew Miss Milton into the conversation when she arrived. Evie was left to eat her plum cake and bread with as much composure as she could manage, while trying not to admire his profile.

After breakfast, he suggested they all walk in the garden, and one might have thought he had proposed an expedition to Scotland, at least, to judge by the dismay this simple idea engendered. At first, it was thought too hot, until it was pointed out that it was not yet noon and therefore still relatively cool under the trees. Then there was the risk of rain to be considered, but this was dealt with by drawing back the curtains to reveal a cloudless sky. Having disposed of these threats to health, there remained only the tricky question of what to wear for the occasion.

Evie went upstairs to the little attic room which she shared with Miss Robart to fetch her bonnet. It was too warm to need a shawl and her only parasol was still buried in one of her boxes, so in moments she skipped down the stairs again, light-headed with anticipation, to await the others in the hall. Mr Armitage was already there, and Violet arrived soon after, Miss Robart appeared from the schoolroom where she had been preparing lessons, and gradually the others drifted down the stairs. Mr Milton, naturally, was not well enough to accompany them, but Mrs and Miss Milton and both the children were well wrapped up against the slightest stray breeze. They already looked hot.

They managed one circuit of the grounds before the Miltons had had enough, and disappeared indoors to divest themselves of their surplus clothes. Evie was not willing to surrender the pleasant coolness of the garden for the stuffy morning room, so she carried on. Violet and Miss Robart gradually drew ahead of them, but Mr Armitage stayed at her side, not saying much but gently putting her at her ease. Even so, she was acutely conscious of him — his very masculinity cast an aura about her, making it impossible to think straight.

As they came to one of the benches scattered about, he said, "Shall we sit? Then you can tell me about Violet. She is looking a little out of sorts, I feel."

"She is rather downhearted, it is true," Evie said, arranging her skirts about her. "She misses Mr Nettles' friendship, but whether there is anything more to her discomfiture, I could not say." That was as close as she dared venture to mentioning Violet's sudden banishment, the reason for which was still a mystery to her.

"It is best if she forgets about him," Mr Armitage said. "Is she looking forward to going to town next month?"

"I believe so. She has agreed to set aside her deep mourning clothes, so that is a good sign. I am trying to interest her in the new fashions and the prospect of dancing again, but I cannot say that she is enthusiastic. I am by no means certain that Mr Nettles was a good influence on her, for she spends all her time knitting these wretched stockings for soldiers, and it is not natural in a girl of eighteen."

"Yet she no longer keeps everyone waiting while she decides between twenty different bonnets," he said at once, "and I cannot see that as a bad thing. She has suffered a great change in her life, which is bound to unsettle her. London will do her good, with your company to keep her in line. But what of you, Evie? You are not in your usual spirits either, it seems to me. Is anything amiss?"

Only you, she wanted to say. Instead, she gave a little laugh. "It is just this dreadful heat wearing me down, I believe. If we could but have a little rain..."

"And here you are trapped in the depths of Hertfordshire with no congenial society," he said, reaching for one of her ungloved hands where it lay in her lap. "This is not much improvement on Winchester, is it? But London will be better. Not as lively as the spring season, but I can guarantee you will not spend many evenings at home."

His hand was firm and smooth, his fingers playing idly with hers. His voice was level, but his nearness and the soft touch of his hand rendered her bereft of words.

After the briefest of pauses, he went on in the same casual tone, "My offer is still open, you know. I would love to have you to wife — my wishes have not changed at all."

His words roused her from her stupor. "Nor has my response, sir. Nothing has changed, nothing at all."

That silenced him, although he still held her hand, lifting one of her fingers after another, almost absently, not looking at her. She could not think of a single word to say to him after this. Although she scratched around in her mind, she was too disordered to string together a coherent sentence.

Eventually, he said, "Are you angry with me?"

"Angry? No, sir. Whatever should I be angry about?"

"Because I kissed you." He turned his head and now she was the one who had to look away from his clear gaze.

"But that was lovely!" she said before she could stop herself. "You said it would be and so it was. I was only upset because it made things difficult... I could not stay under the same roof with you... not after that."

"I am sorry," he said, and she could not mistake the heartfelt sincerity in his voice.

"Do not be," she said. "I chose to kiss you, after all. My own fault."

A long pause, then he went on, "It *was* lovely, though, was it not?"

She could hear the amusement in his tone, even though she was still looking down at her hand resting in his. There was a rightness to it, she decided, sitting there side by side under the trees, her hand in his, as he gently rubbed her fingers. Was he teasing her? He must have kissed dozens — no, scores — of women, and however momentous it had been for her, it could have been nothing to him. Surprise prompted her to say, "For you, too?"

He said nothing, but she was aware of him nodding.

"It puzzles me, though," she said, perfectly aware that she should stop talking to him in this intimate way and yet quite unable to do so. "I cannot tell you just *why* it was so enjoyable. Was it because it was you, or because you caught me unawares, or was it simply because it was my very first kiss?"

Another long pause, as though, unlike her, he was considering the wisdom of such a discussion. But perhaps he could not help himself either, for he said conversationally, "Would you like to find out?"

Of course she would! But it was madness, she knew that. She should remove her hand from his — should have done so long since, in fact — and she should walk away from this dangerous man as fast as she could. She should run! If she had been devastated by one kiss, how much worse would the second one be? How could her heart ever recover?

For a long, long time, it seemed to her, desire warred with her own good sense, and even though she was powerfully aware of him beside her, even though his hand still held hers, even though she could not seem to move or to speak or even to breathe, good sense seemed to have the upper hand.

But then she made the mistake of looking up, and there were those deep blue eyes gazing into hers with such a teasing expression, his lips lifted into an affectionate smile. Good sense was utterly vanquished and she was lost.

"Yes. Yes, please."

With his free hand, he stroked her cheek so softly she almost felt she dreamt it. The teasing look disappeared and his lips parted, his eyes roving over her face... the curls of hair falling over her forehead, her eyes, her nose, her mouth... lingering on her mouth, as his fingers caressed her cheek. Then he lifted her chin a little and bent his lips to hers.

She was drowning. Whatever she had felt before in that surprising kiss in the schoolroom, this was a thousand times better. Or worse, perhaps. His lips were gentle and warm, moving softly against hers, and his hand cupped her cheek. She was aware of his leg pressing against her own, of his neckcloth tickling her throat, of his other hand still holding hers, resting on her lap. She could feel her heart thundering in her ears, her breath shallow and rapid. As was his, she realised. He made a tiny noise in his throat, like a groan, and his hand gripped hers tightly, almost painfully, for a second, then slowly unclenched. She was aware of all of it, every tiny sensation heightened to overwhelming proportions.

Dimly, she became aware of her own name being called in the distance.

Violet! She must go!

She moved away from him with a gasp, her eyes shooting open. His face... oh God, his face! Such anguish there, no less than her own. But she had to go. Rising shakily to her feet, she pulled her hand from his. He made no move to keep hold of her, but he never took his eyes from hers, and his expression never altered.

Without a word, she turned and fled.

15: Dinner In Town

Eliot could not say how he got through the next hour or so. He sat immobile for quite some time, trying to work out in his own mind just what had happened to him and coming to no very clear answer. He had sat down beside Evie knowing himself to be fond of her, and perfectly ready to be leg-shackled for life. And now... *fond* would not cover the half of it... not a hundredth part of it. He was so deep in love with her that he could not quite work out which way was up and which down, although somehow it hardly seemed to matter.

Eventually Violet and the governess, whose name he could not even recall in his confusion, came upon him, and years of good manners got him through the short time remaining until his curricle was brought up from the inn and he might escape. Evie was not there to see him off, and he could not bring himself to ask after her. He was not at all sure that he could say her name without betraying himself. As it happened, Bel told him off in no uncertain terms for *'dragging the ladies all over the garden in such dreadful heat, so that Miss Parfitt has the headache and Miss Robart has had to leave the dear children and burn feathers under poor Miss Parfitt's nose'*.

Poor Miss Parfitt indeed, not even permitted to recover from her kiss in peace and quiet. But perhaps it had not been the same for her. Perhaps her world had not just melted into some unrecognisable geography where everything was oddly upside-down. Perhaps for her it was just another kiss. *'But it was lovely!'* she had said, and so it had been, that first kiss. But *this* — this was something else entirely. If only he could breathe properly, or stop shaking.

He drove home to Marsham Grove in such profound silence that even his valet was moved to ask if he was quite himself. No, he was not himself. He would never be himself again.

After just one night of his mother's maunderings, and a quick look in on his father at Nancy's to assure himself that, yes, he was contented, and even a little less frail, Eliot drove up to town. Since the Grosvenor Square house still slumbered, half the servants away for their summer visits to family, he scribbled a hasty note to his Uncle Bradbrook.

'Sir, I shall be in town for a week or so, and my cook is away. Please do not make me eat at the club every night. I promise to tell you the full story of the Scandal of Marsham Grove, with Embellishments and Full Chorus. Eliot.'

Within the hour, this brought the gratifying response that his uncle and aunt would be deeply offended if he did not eat his dinner with them every night.

Nicholas Bradbrook was his mother's youngest brother, and as different from her as it was possible to be. Having no expectations of inheritance, he had gone into the law and done so well for himself that when he married, rather late in life, he had retired from his profession and bought a neat little house in a fashionable street, near enough to Hyde Park for his lady's daily perambulations there, and only just round the corner from Grosvenor Square.

Eliot had had a little time to recover his composure by the time he presented himself at Green Street, his evening attire only slightly rumpled from frequent packing. He walked the short distance through unnaturally quiet streets, for almost everyone who could arrange it was enjoying the cleaner air and fresher food of their country estates. Those who could not lay claim to an estate of their own generally finagled an invitation from friends or remembered distant relations they had long been meaning to visit. The opening of the autumn shooting season drew many out of town, too.

The Bradbrooks had no mind for travelling or shooting or hunting or visiting distant relations, and were thus settled in town all year. They received their nephew with great pleasure. He discovered that he was not the only addition to the dinner table. Edward Folkard was there, too, for he lived with his godfather while he worked his way towards a career as a barrister. The other guest was Roger Bradbrook, who was a natural son from one of Uncle Bradbrook's many mistresses, and his father's heir. The three young men were much of an age, but while Eliot got on well with Folkard, he had never much liked Roger Bradbrook, whom he regarded as a wastrel. He was a dandy, too, and although Eliot enjoyed being fashionable as much as the next man, and was quite happy to discuss his tailor, his bootmaker and even his hatmaker, the affectations of the truly foppish drew only his disdain. He would have admired Roger if he had displayed the restraint of the buck or even the Corinthian, hiding masculine muscle behind carefully contrived coats and breeches, but Roger was a coxcomb, there was no other word for it, and his ostentatious shirt-points and neckcloths and abundant array of fobs and pins and rings, a quizzing glass always to hand, could only disgust a man of sense.

He greeted Bradbrook politely, however, and the others with genuine pleasure. He was fond of both Uncle and Aunt Bradbrook, and the more so when they plied him with interested questions about Violet and Evie, who would soon be staying with them.

"I cannot tell you what a delight it will be to have a young lady in the house," Aunt Bradbrook said, as they settled down to one of her excellent dinners. "I shall have the perfect excuse for some serious shopping, and I have already alerted a few of my particular friends that I shall expect entertainments of the most enticing variety, to lift the spirits of a girl so recently out of mourning. And she is very pretty, I understand? That will make things a great deal easier. There is nothing more dispiriting than a plain heiress, for one cannot even pretend that her popularity is genuine. And what of her governess... or chaperon, or whatever she is? I do not scruple to tell you, Eliot, that I am a trifle put out of countenance by this plan to provide her with her own chaperon. Am I not sufficient?"

"Indeed you are, dear Aunt. Miss Parfitt..." *Breathe*, he told himself, *breathe.* "Miss Parfitt will not be here as chaperon, but as a friend to Violet. I hope they will both enjoy themselves under your aegis."

"Ah," she said, and that one word encompassed so much meaning that Eliot was convinced that she saw straight through his nonchalance to the roiling emotions within. She said nothing, however, the conversation moved on and the dinner likewise. Eliot gave them all the details of the trouble at Marsham Grove, not minimising his own part in it, while they listened without comment.

"What a coil!" Aunt Bradbrook said at the end of it. "I am very sorry your poor mother has taken it so hard, but then she has always had a fanciful notion of the male sex, thinking you all paragons of virtue. It would have been better, perhaps, if she had known about

Mrs Weeks from the start. Secrets in marriage are always a mistake."

"Would you want to know?" Eliot said curiously.

"Certainly. The fact of a mistress would trouble me less than the lies it would necessarily involve. I should *hate* Nicholas to lie to me. And now I shall leave you gentlemen to your port."

Roger Bradbrook also excused himself, with murmurings about another engagement.

"Another gaming hell, more like," Uncle Bradbrook said gloomily after he had gone, passing the port to Folkard.

"Is that his current pleasure?" Eliot said easily. "I always thought women were his downfall. I set him up with the most outrageously expensive little ladybird last year, although I heard a rumour she had moved on rather quickly."

"That would be my fault," his uncle said. "I make him a good allowance, but I expect him to fund his amusements from that, and not have jewellers dunning me over the expensive trifles he has bestowed on his mistress. And as for his gaming debts! It cost me five thousand pounds last year to clear him, and I shall not do it again, and so I told him. He must think I am made of money! He runs with some very expensive sons of the nobility — Ramsey, Berringham, the Marfords — who like to play deep, but Roger has nothing like those expectations, and will have none at all if he goes on this way."

"You will not disinherit him, though?" Eliot said.

His uncle sighed. "It is very difficult. His mother died not long after he was born and I promised her faithfully I would look after the boy, and make him my heir if I should have no legitimate son.

Sentimental of me, I know, but she was my first mistress and I was fond of her. Naturally, I expected to have sons from my marriage, but Kate and I have not been so blessed. The trouble is that Roger has been raised to consider my money his by right, and — I do not like to say it of my own flesh and blood, but he is not a sensible man. He should have gone into the army or a respectable trade, like my other by-blows, but there we are. Do you have little bundles of trouble here and there, Eliot, or have you been more careful than I was?"

"There is only one that I know of, a daughter," Eliot said. "Her mother is married now, and I've set aside a suitable dowry for the girl, so that will be the end of it, I imagine. You have several to consider, do you not? Yet only the eldest is treated as a gentleman."

"Six that I know of," his uncle said promptly, "and a third son of an earl who looks rather like me, but we never mention that. The younger ones are no trouble, but Roger... maybe I should just pack him off to the army and be done with it. Then I could do something for Edward." He smiled fondly at him as he spoke. "My own godson, never in the slightest trouble, and yet I have not been able to help him."

"You are helping me with a career in the law," Folkard said, with his ready smile. "What more should any godfather do? I never expected anything more, I assure you."

"And that is precisely the difference between you two. You expect nothing, and Roger expects everything. Ah, well, let us talk of other matters. This is a bad business at Marsham Grove, Eliot, and despite what Kate says, I do not think she would want to know if I were keeping a mistress. I always thought your father managed the business very discreetly, with Nancy well looked after and Anne none the wiser, but now that it is all in the open, this hysterical nonsense about illness is unbecoming. I am fond of my sister, but she has never been burdened with excess sensibility before, and it would be more dignified to rise above it and pretend not to know. It is not uncommon for a man to have a mistress, and he cannot abandon her just because his wife has the vapours."

"I believe she is truly ill from the distress," Eliot said. "It was the greatest shock to her, for she had not the least idea."

"It may be so," his uncle said, "but now that she knows, she must learn to live with it. A great many married men keep a mistress, so her case is not so extraordinary."

Folkard looked shocked. "Mistresses and wives should never mix, in my opinion," he said sombrely. "Indeed, I am inclined to think it is better to avoid such entanglements altogether. No man *needs* a mistress, after all, married or single."

"Do you hold to that opinion from moral or practical considerations?" Eliot said.

Folkard answered him solemnly. "Naturally there are those who see nothing wrong in it. Indeed, I intend no censure, for it is the way of the world, is it not? It is for each one of us to reconcile such behaviour with the teachings of the church. For myself, I prefer to wait until I am able to marry with affection and respect."

"So should we all, but there is also the question of reconciliation with duty," Uncle Bradbrook said thoughtfully. "Take Eliot's father, for instance. The eldest son and heir to a tidy fortune, it was his responsibility to marry and secure the succession. He looked about him for years, but no one eligible captured his heart. Eventually, he made a prudent match to my sister — most suitable as to rank and fortune, but she was not his equal in character, and not able to make him truly happy. Is it not better, in such a case, for a man to discreetly maintain the mistress who holds his heart?"

"Better still, surely, not to marry without affection," Folkard said uncompromisingly. "Prudence, I grant you, is necessary too, but marriage is about more than the getting of heirs, is it not? It must also be a foundation for a lifetime of respectful companionship."

"So it has been in my case, certainly," Uncle Bradbrook said. "I was so fortunate as to meet my dear Kate, and I have not looked at another woman since that day. I sincerely wish both of you such an agreeable helpmeet, when your time comes."

Eliot found himself torn on the question. He could not feel, given his own history, that it was wrong to keep a mistress so long as she was treated fairly. After marriage it was a different matter, but for a bachelor it was a commonplace amongst men of his level of society, those with no inclination for early matrimony. It had kept him steady, he was certain, and out of worse trouble. Yet now it was preventing him from marrying the woman he wanted. Evie had told him that she loved him, yet she could not forgive him for his past... she could not *trust* him. It was the most dreadful blow, for he could not change the past.

When they went through to the drawing room, his uncle and Folkard settled down to play piquet. Eliot went through the open doors to the adjoining music room, where his aunt was at the instrument. For a while, she played on while he sat, musing over his difficulties, but after a while, she closed the instrument and came to sit beside him.

"I am interested to hear of your Miss Parfitt," she said without preamble, "for I must tell you that I have heard much of her from

Edward, since he knew her as a child, and it seems to me that he would have taken a great interest in her if she had had a dowry."

"She has no interest in him, however," Eliot said. "She views him quite as a brother, which is a natural consequence of growing up together."

"Yet it appears not to have had the same effect on him," she said thoughtfully. "His description of her did not sound especially brotherly, and I do not want the two of you squabbling over her. Indeed, Eliot, I shall take it very much amiss if either of you attempt to seduce her while she is a guest under my roof."

"Seduce her? Why should you think so?"

"Now do not pretend she is marriageable in the slightest," his aunt said, with a laugh. "She is... what, almost thirty? Never married and as poor as a church mouse, with no connections beyond a distant cousinship to the Folkards. If you have any interest in her at all, it is not as a wife. Oh! But you look conscious... Eliot, can it be that you are truly considering matrimony? And if so, it must be love, for she has neither rank nor fortune to tempt you."

He could not deny it, so he smiled and said, "I care nothing for that, as I am sure you are aware."

"Your parents will hope for a greater match than a penniless parson's daughter, Eliot."

"My mother, perhaps, but my father, I suspect, would rather see me happy, and neither of them puts me under any pressure to marry wisely, or at all."

"So you will offer for her? Or are you still contemplating?"

"Neither. I have offered twice and she has refused me as many times." His aunt's face was a picture of astonishment, making him laugh. "I know, incomprehensible, is it not? How could she possibly refuse me? Yet she has. I am too rakish for her, and she despises me thoroughly."

"Well, you have not lived a monkish life, it is true," she said, with a wry shake of her head. "Still, you are not a tenth as wild as Nicholas was in his youth. Why, he once— But never mind about that. I should not tell tales. All young men are wild when they have money to spend and no sensible occupation to fill their days. They grow more rational with the years, and a sensible woman will understand that. I have to tell you, Eliot, that if your Miss Parfitt turns up her pretty nose at a mistress or two in your past, then she is not the right woman for you. However, I shall not tease you about her, you may be sure. Tell me what you wish me to do for her. A little town polish? Some advice on fashions? To introduce her to one or two influential society hostesses?"

"Nothing that will put you out," he said, with a slight smile. "My only objective for her stay in town is for her to enjoy herself. She has lived most of her life in society of the most confined variety — a country parsonage, or the home of her widowed aunt in the Cathedral Close at Winchester. When she was in London before, she mingled only with those acquainted with the Barantines — cits, in other words. I only met her by the merest chance at Lady Frampton's, who delights in throwing a multitude of social strata into her saloon and observing what transpires. I should like Evie to experience *good* society for once. And to dance. Will you make sure she dances, my dear aunt?"

"That should present no difficulty at all, nephew." She laughed. "You may dance with her yourself, if you wish it."

Ah, if only he dared! But to stand beside her, to take her hand... Eliot could feel his composure slipping. "I shall be content to watch her dance," he said.

But of course he would not. He knew already that he would not be content at all.

16: A Departure And An Arrival

Eliot had come to town with the express intention of visiting the jeweller's shop owned by the late Mr Barantine, to see if he might find out more about the missing diamonds, or the relationship prevailing between Mr Barantine and his partner Mr Newbold, but now that the moment had come, he found himself as reluctant as ever. When he had agreed to become Violet's guardian, he had imagined an agreeable interlude showing her off in society, a succession of eager young suitors to be sternly deflected — he had particularly looked forward to this part — followed fairly promptly by a suitable match. He would, he thought, rather enjoy giving her hand in marriage, and already had a waistcoat very well suited for the purpose. The lawyers could be left to deal with the boring matter of settlements.

He had not bargained for difficulties related to her father's business. It was *trade*, after all, and therefore anathema to any gentleman. His lawyers had diligently looked into matters on his behalf, but had, in the irritating way of lawyers, presented him with an array of options. Should he care to divest himself of the business entirely, and settle Violet's share in the funds? Should he keep the business operating under the Barantine name, now well established as a source of jewellery of the most tasteful and elegant styles? And what, they asked gently, were his instructions regarding the claims of young Mr Newbold? They were more than willing, they happily informed him, to defend the matter in the courts, if that should be his desire.

So even though he wished, he very much wished, to resolve the matter, so that Evie might perhaps think a little better of him, he could not quite bring himself to do it. He dithered, therefore, spending his days improving his wardrobe, visiting his club, a few friends and Tattersall's, and dining each evening with his uncle and aunt. It was almost a week before his uncle asked him, in the most negligent manner imaginable, quite what he was hiding from.

"Or whom, one might rather say," he said, eyes twinkling, as they sat after dinner over their port. "For I have never known you to skulk about in town so much at this season of the year. There is nothing here to amuse you just now, I should have thought. I cannot imagine that our weekly card party is a great inducement. Even if you do not wish to be at home, you must have invitations enough for gatherings elsewhere."

"I am no sportsman," Eliot said, with what he hoped was a nonchalant laugh. "My year has been sadly disrupted by my new responsibilities, and this is my first opportunity to replenish my supply of neckcloths."

"You are not here for neckcloths," his uncle said.

Eliot sighed. "True enough. I am screwing up my courage to visit this *shop* of Violet's, but it all seems too tedious for words. I know I must do it, but every day there seems to be something more interesting to do. Like buy neckcloths."

Folkard shook his head with a smile. "Well, if *that* is all, should you care for company? I confess I would find it fascinating to look around such a place. The books would be fascinating."

"The books? You mean the *accounts?* You would find that of interest? Good grief."

"As should I," his uncle said. "Shall we all go? I might even buy something for Kate, if you will offer me a good price, Eliot."

"Offer you a good price? Good God, am I become a shopkeeper now?" Eliot said in disgust, but the others only laughed at him.

All three of them went to the very select establishment on Bond Street that was Barantine's, jewellers to the discerning. Mr Drysdale, the manager, was so gentlemanlike, both well-dressed and well-spoken, that Eliot would not have been ashamed to dine with him, and there were three assistants of very genteel appearance. The shop itself was appointed in the first style of elegance, and Eliot had patronised it himself in the past, purchasing items for one or other of his mistresses.

"This is not what I had expected," Folkard said, as Drysdale led them down brightly-lit stairs to the basement. "I imagined something much smaller, and less… hmm…"

"Less stylish?" Drysdale said, with a smile that showed him not at all offended. "It was always Mr Barantine's intention to cater for the most discriminating of patrons."

"The Prince of Wales?" Folkard said eagerly. "Has he indeed paid you a visit?"

"Not as yet, sir," Drysdale said sadly. "We live in hope, naturally, but His Royal Highness is firmly established in his preference for Jeffrey's. However, we have been so fortunate as to secure the custom of one or two ladies with the highest connections, the highest connections in the land, if you understand me. Naturally, one cannot mention names, but you will see when you examine the books. Do step this way, gentlemen. This is our *special* customers' room."

It was fitted out with such expensive luxury that Eliot could almost suppose himself in Carlton House. There were delicately silk-covered chairs, consoles of polished wood, gilt-framed paintings and mirrors on the walls, and exquisite Turkish carpets. Decanters of wine sat on a side table. Glass-fronted cabinets displayed the finest wares of the shop, and on the far wall was the heavily metalled door of the vault itself.

Drysdale produced a fearsome array of massive keys, and laboriously unlocked the door and an inner barred door. Inside were shelf upon shelf laden with boxes of uncut gems, bars of gold or silver, stacked boxes containing finished pieces and bags of money. Many, many bags of money.

"Would it be indelicate to enquire as to the value of all this?" Uncle Bradbrook said.

"Eighty seven thousand, four hundred and sixty pounds," Drysdale said promptly. "So it was at the last reckoning, which I take every Saturday. It was a little more than that before Mr Barantine's last, fatal journey, but he took away parures, demi-parures and single pieces to the value of seven thousand four hundred pounds, and a number of outstanding bills have been presented for settlement, for which your lawyers assured me they had your permission, Mr Armitage, sir."

"Yes, yes, they told me that everything had to be settled," Eliot said uneasily, for this was venturing too far towards business matters. "Then it is less than a hundred thousand pounds in total? I had thought that Miss Barantine's inheritance was one hundred thousand."

"The business has never been worth quite so much, sir," Drysdale said. "This past year has seen excellent returns, so this is a high-water mark."

That was disappointing, and if Newbold were to take half of everything, there would not be much left for Violet.

"Lovely work," Uncle Bradbrook murmured, gazing into one of the display cabinets. "I shall examine these rubies more closely later, but shall we have a look at the books now? Eliot?"

"I suppose we had better see them," he muttered.

Drysdale led them back upstairs, past the craft rooms where the gem cutters and goldsmiths worked, and up another level to his office, where neat shelves of ledgers and drawers of bills, paid and unpaid, testified to his methodical record-keeping. He laid out the most recent ledgers, and then, when Folkard enquired, some of the older ones as well, and Folkard and Uncle Bradbrook pored over them while Eliot paced restlessly about the room.

"How is Miss Barantine, might I be so bold as to ask, sir?" Drysdale said.

"She is well," Eliot said. "Grieved by her loss, of course, but she bears it well."

"Naturally she would," Drysdale said. "Such a charming young lady! We were always so pleased to see her when she visited, although that was seldom. Only for her birthday, when she came to thank the goldsmiths for her gifts."

"They made her presents, did they, the goldsmiths?"

"Oh, no, sir! Not personally, you understand. Her father always commissioned two pieces for her birthday — a simple one that she could wear at once, and something more elaborate, for when she should be a married lady. It was a tradition with him. Perhaps you would care to continue in the same manner, sir? To commission a piece or two for Miss Barantine's birthday in October?"

"Yes, why not?" Eliot said. That was some part of the business he understood, the commissioning and buying of jewellery. If he could not make sense of the books, he could at least give Violet the comfort of continuing her father's tradition. "Have your craftsmen draw up some sketches and I will select something."

"Very good, sir." After a moment's hesitation, Drysdale went on, "You are not quite comfortable with business, I think, sir, being a gentleman, but there are many such who oversee such investments. I hope you will not rush to sell Barantine's. It is a profitable enterprise, and perhaps Miss Barantine will wish to continue as her father did. It is hers now, after all."

"Only if we can keep it out of Newbold's hands," Eliot said sourly. Then, seeing the bewilderment on Drysdale's face, he went on, "You did not know? The late Mr Newbold's younger brother is laying claim to the whole business, on the grounds that his brother put up the money for it, and since the terms of the arrangement are lost—"

"Oh, no, sir! No, no, no! That was a loan, and it was repaid years ago," Drysdale said. "I can show you in the books. Mr Barantine had a partnership with Mr Newbold, it is true, but he merely paid him one tenth of the profits every year, in gratitude for his assistance in founding the London shop. No, the loan was repaid within three years."

"And your books can prove all this?" Eliot said in astonishment.

"Indeed, sir. Without question."

"So why did my lawyers not say so?" he said indignantly. "They are supposed to have looked into everything."

"They never asked, sir," Drysdale said. "They never mentioned Mr Newbold to me at all, or I should have told them how it was. They looked at the most recent books, and asked for a full accounting of the value of the business and went away again."

"What a splendid fellow you are, Drysdale," Eliot said. "You may increase your salary by a tenth immediately. Did you hear that, Uncle? Thanks to Drysdale, we may see off Newbold without further ado. How glad I am that we came here today."

~~~~~

Eliot engaged a new set of lawyers, who proved to be more diligent than the last. It was not to be supposed that Newbold would relinquish all his expectations immediately, but some sternly worded letters, together with a final offer of one tenth of the profits for the current year, settled the matter. The lawyers also tracked down a draft copy of the papers that Barantine had kept in his possession, which recognised his title to the business. Eliot was hazy on how it worked, but the lawyers assured him that it was sufficient to prove the case. Violet was left in full possession of her father's shop, under Eliot's tentative guidance.
~~~~~

He returned there a few days later with his uncle, the latter to collect the ruby set he had purchased for Aunt Bradbrook, and Eliot to examine the suggestions for Violet's birthday gifts.

"These are very pretty," he said, impressed despite himself. "I like these emeralds for the major set, but why pearls for this necklace? She has a number of pearl sets already. What about diamonds? She can wear those at once."

"Ah, we are a trifle short of diamonds just now, sir, especially the best quality. Mr Barantine was to bring us a great quantity from Ireland, but they appear to have been lost. You know about that, perhaps, sir?"

"I do, and it is a great mystery. Has such a thing ever happened before?"

"Never, sir, and I have puzzled greatly over it, for I cannot see how it could have happened."

"Perhaps they went down with the ship when it sank?" Eliot suggested gently.

"No, sir, for Mr Barantine kept gems stitched into his clothing for safe keeping, and yet when his garments were returned here, there were no gems at all, nor any sign that they had been torn out. The coat hems were all neatly sewn up, just as they would be when he carried no stones at all. So it is my opinion that they disappeared before he boarded the ship, sir. The papers recording the purchase are safe, and indeed he wrote to say that he had them, but... they have vanished."

"In Dublin," Eliot said, with foreboding. "I am going to have to go there, am I not? How does one even travel to Dublin?"

"The usual way is by road to Holyhead, sir, and then hop across the Irish Sea," Drysdale said cheerfully.

Eliot shuddered. "A ship!" he groaned. "What an appalling prospect."

His uncle chuckled. "There is no other way to reach an island that I know of. We shall look it up in Paterson when we get home, and plan your journey."

"It will take days to get there, I imagine," Eliot said gloomily.

"Not if you take the mail coach, sir," Drysdale said, then, seeing the look of horror on Eliot's face, added, "Perhaps five days by post chaise, sir, but there are ways of avoiding the roads. Mr Barantine liked to travel by way of Southampton. Only a day or two on the road and three days aboard ship."

Eliot grimaced. "Three days aboard ship! Heavens, no! How long from Holyhead?"

"Only a few hours at sea, sir."

"Then Holyhead it will have to be."

The plan was the subject of lively discussion at dinner that evening. Careful scrutiny of Paterson's Roads suggested that the entire journey there and back could not be completed in under three weeks.

"You will be away when Miss Barantine and Miss Parfitt arrive," Aunt Bradbrook said.

"So I will, but it cannot be helped. The weather will only get worse, and I cannot put it off until the spring, I fear. If it is to be done at all, it must be done soon, but I cannot say that I relish the prospect."

"Would it help to have some company?" Folkard said. "I should dearly like to travel a little, for I get so little opportunity, and my life is all idleness until the Michaelmas session starts."

Eliot brightened at once. "That would help, I confess. If I am to be made miserable, it would be some comfort to know that my misery is shared."

"Miserable? No! It will be an adventure," Folkard said cheerfully. "At least you will have someone other than your man to talk to. There! That is settled. It will take but a few days to make the arrangements and then we may be off."

"Now you will both be away when the ladies arrive," Aunt Bradbrook said. "Anyone might suppose that you are avoiding them, gentlemen. Or one of them in particular, perhaps."

And she chuckled, but said no more about it.

~~~~~

SEPTEMBER

Evie was heartily relieved to leave St Alban's, and the stifling household of the Miltons. The Green Street home of Mr and Mrs Bradbrook was far more to her taste, with all the delights of London to be enjoyed, and the mantelpiece already bearing a number of enticing invitation cards.

"Linen draper's tomorrow, before breakfast, and the seamstresses will be here at twelve to begin work," Mrs Bradbrook said briskly, watching as Violet's two lady's maids unpacked. She picked up some gowns to examine. "Oh, but these are very good. A little work around the hem, for skirts are a shade shorter now, and perhaps some extra trimming on the bodice, and this one will do
~~~~~

very well. And this. You have had some good advice, Miss Barantine."

"That is Evie's doing," Violet said. "I do not care for such simple styles myself, but she said it is all the crack."

"So it is. These are excellent. With a few new items, you will do very well. Miss Parfitt, may I see your wardrobe now?"

One of the housemaids was unpacking Evie's rather battered box in the room next door. "Ah, now we will need to do something about this," Mrs Bradbrook said, rifling rapidly through Evie's few gowns. "Very suitable for the chaperon's bench, but I have strict instructions to make sure you dance, so you will need something a little more modish, and these demi-trains must go."

"I have no intention of dancing, ma'am," Evie said, laughing. "That is Mr Eliot Armitage's nonsense, to imagine that I would. I am thirty, after all."

"Which is by no means too old to dance," Mrs Bradbrook said, with mock severity, her eyes twinkling. "I still enjoy a reel myself now and again, if I have plenty of time to recover before the next. I am to act the chaperon for you and Violet both, so you must dance if you are asked or I shall know the reason why. Two or three ball gowns should be enough and—"

"I cannot afford it, ma'am!"

"Nonsense! You are my guest, after all, and if I choose to take you to a ball, then you must be properly dressed for the occasion. Well, if it bothers you so much, I have some gowns that might easily be adapted to your figure with no more than a stitch or two. We are much of a height, after all, although you are too thin altogether. I like to see a little flesh on a girl, especially up top. Which reminds me… we must get you some better stays."

Evie laughed and gave up arguing. The proposal accorded too closely with her own wishes for her to resist for long. Oh, the joy of being in town again, and part of society, and to *dance!* How could she possibly refuse? She shivered with delight and allowed Mrs Bradbrook to make whatever plans she cared to devise on her behalf.

That evening, Evie waited patiently in the hall. She had never minded waiting for Violet, but tonight she had several very good reasons for not minding. Her new gown, for instance, of India muslin with gilt spangles, one of Mrs Bradbrook's hastily taken in by the seamstresses. Her silk evening cloak. A topaz necklace loaned for the occasion. Her new and deliciously soft gloves. Her satin evening slippers. *Dancing* slippers, she thought with satisfaction, feet tapping in optimistic anticipation, for tonight's evening party might well include some informal dancing.

Mr Bradbrook waited with her, together with Henry, now returned from Essex to resume his position as Violet's personal footman. Mrs Bradbrook had herself been ready long since, but was now upstairs, no doubt encouraging Violet to settle on one particular necklace or set of hair combs or whatever the difficulty was. The carriage had already been sent up and down the street twice, to keep the horses warm. Evie was amused by Violet's return to her old, dithery ways, but whether it was due to the absence of the dour Mr Nettles or the prospect of society again, it was a welcome sign, and far more normal in a girl of eighteen.

When the sounds of a carriage could be heard drawing up outside, at first Evie assumed it was the Bradbrooks' own carriage returning, but shortly thereafter the doorbell rang and the door was opened to reveal a gentleman more gorgeously attired than any Evie had seen before. His greatcoat sported so many capes that it was a wonder he could squeeze through the door, and he had to remove his hat before entry.

"Roger!" cried Mr Bradbrook, rushing forwards. "Here you are at last! We expected you back from the country days since. My son, Miss Parfitt. Roger, this is Miss Parfitt... oh, and the vision of loveliness descending the stairs is Miss Barantine."

Violet had almost reached the bottom step as Mr Roger Bradbrook removed his greatcoat in an impressive swirl, tossing it languidly to a surprised Henry, to reveal attire of such dazzling sumptuousness that Evie wondered how he could move in such clothes. His coat was moulded to his shoulders, his pantaloons clung to his thighs above Hessians so polished he might tie his elaborate neckcloth in their reflection. His shirt points rose up his cheeks, all but hiding his face.

But if Evie was more amused than impressed, Violet's face was a picture of astonished admiration.

"How do you do, sir!" she breathed.

"Dear lady!" he murmured. And when he swept her gloved hand to his lips in a flamboyant gesture, she simpered and blushed as only Violet knew how.

Evie sighed. Mr Nettles, it seemed, had a rival.

17: A Dowry

The first London engagement brought a surprise to Evie, for who should be there but Edward Folkard's uncle, the Earl of Lampeter, with his wife, two of the very last people Evie wanted to see. That, she supposed ruefully, was the disadvantage to the more superior society in which she was now moving.

"Evie?" the earl said in astonished tones when they met in Lady Cullingworth's drawing room. "Is it truly you?"

"You know Miss Parfitt?" their hostess said.

"Her mother was a Folkard," Lord Lampeter said. "We are cousins."

"Very distant, my lord," Evie said, coolly.

Lady Lampeter nodded unsmilingly to Evie and moved swiftly away, but Lord Lampeter drew her to a quiet corner.

"Tell me everything that has happened to you," he said. "It must be ten years or more since we last saw you, and we quite lost track of you after Mr Parfitt died. You went to an aunt, I believe? In Winchester?"

"I am astonished that you should remember that," Evie said.

He looked oddly embarrassed. "Naturally we always took an interest in you, for your mother's sake. Hermione lived at Folkard Hall for many years, and was quite one of the family, you know. But I thought you must have been married long since. Were there no eligible young men in Winchester? There are some very good families there, I am sure."

That made Evie smile ruefully. "However good the society, my aunt and I were not part of it, my lord. She is the relict of a canon, and still lives in the Cathedral Close. We are very quiet there, our only excitement an occasional dinner at the Bishop's Palace."

"But you have friends in town, or I should not have the pleasure of meeting you here."

Again she smiled. "I am here as the companion and adviser to Miss Violet Barantine, the young lady in the sprig muslin over there. I should not be here otherwise."

"A companion?" he said, frowning. "And she is not a relation? I do not like to think of you obliged to accept such a position."

"I am very glad of it, you may be sure, for how else could I enjoy the delights of London?" she said lightly. "Tell me of yourself, my lord, and the children. Walter must be at Eton by now, I expect."

He took the hint and talked of his own five children and all the doings of Folkard Hall until called away to be introduced to someone else. She had no further opportunity to speak to him, thankfully, but on the carriage ride home, Mrs Bradbrook said, "Goodness, but Lord Lampeter was curious about you, Miss Parfitt. He asked me so many questions! I had no idea the connection between you was at all close."

"Nor is it. We are very distant cousins, that is all. My mother lived at Folkard Hall as the poor relation until she married my father. After she died, the old countess took an interest in me as I grew up, and I was very friendly with the Folkard cousins for a while, but when the present earl succeeded, things changed and we all drifted apart." And that was as much as she wished to say about that strange time.

"Lord Lampeter wanted to know why you had never married, but I hardly knew what to say to him."

Evie laughed. "If he should ask again, you may tell him the truth — that I have no beauty, no accomplishments, no dowry, no connections and no opportunity to meet anyone suitable. There is no great mystery about it."

"Nonsense," Mrs Bradbrook said briskly. "You must not be so self-deprecating. It is true that Violet certainly outshines you, yet you have your own quieter style of beauty, and your demeanour more than makes up for any lack of accomplishments. The dowry and connections we can do nothing about, but as for opportunity... let us see what a few weeks in my company can do, shall we?"

Evie and Violet were thrust into a whirlwind of entertainments such as only London could provide. The Bradbrooks, who appeared at first sight to live a quiet, unpretentious life, knew everyone and were invited everywhere, and although their engagements were not so lively as they would be during the season in the spring, Mrs Bradbrook complaining that there was no more than one invitation per evening, it was still dazzling to two young women who had never ventured into the *beau monde* before.

It was not long before an evening party ended with impromptu dancing, and Evie found herself chased away from the chaperons' corner to participate. Oh, the joy of dancing, of releasing herself from the constraints of ladylike immobility for twenty minutes at a time! She was no great musician herself, for although she had been competently taught, she had had no instrument of her own to practise upon for many years now, but a tune never failed to communicate itself directly to her toes. Even in her most restrained evenings of chaperonage, her feet had danced to the rhythm of the musicians' playing. Now she could fling her whole body into the movements with abandon.

She supposed that her skill had not quite deserted her, or perhaps her age gave her the ability to conduct a conversation or a light flirtation with aplomb, for she soon found herself much in demand. At her first ball, she had the pleasure of never once sitting out a set, and after a week or two she even began to lose the habit of watching Violet, knowing that Mrs Bradbrook was keeping a wary eye on her, and steering her away from fortune hunters and towards the more eligible of the young men dazzled by her beauty.

It was no surprise, of course, that Violet was a great success, even in the superior society in which they now moved. As the daughter of a jewel merchant, she could not, perhaps, aspire to one of the great titles, but there were younger sons aplenty who would be very happy to marry such a lovely young lady and her hundred thousand pounds.

There were men with independent fortunes, or the expectations of them, keen to know her, too, and one of those was Mr Roger Bradbrook. Evie was not impressed by him, for although she grudgingly allowed him to be handsome enough, and his manners were above reproach, there was something about him that she could not quite like. His flamboyant style of dress repelled her, for just as she herself preferred simple elegance in her own dress, so she preferred the understated style of Mr Eliot Armitage. There was a conceit about Mr Bradbrook, too, that she disliked, although she soon realised that it was common in such society. Men of wealth and consequence held themselves with a certain attitude of disdain for lesser mortals, as if it was a privilege merely to breathe the same air as them. It was just one of many ways in which Mr Eliot Armitage now appeared to great advantage. She had always enjoyed his company, easy and unpretentious as it was, but the more she mixed with the arrogance of the *ton*, the more she missed him.

She had been surprised to discover that he had gone out of town, and only a few days before she and Violet had arrived. He had gone away to Dublin to find Violet's missing diamonds, and Evie greatly approved such an enterprise, which she had not supposed him willing to undertake. Still, she had expected him to accompany them to town, or at least to be there to help them settle in, and she wondered a little at his absence. Was he avoiding her? And if so, why? Did he do so for his own peace of mind, or did he imagine he was ensuring hers?

There was too much excitement to miss him for long, however. Their mornings were filled with shopping and fittings and leaving cards at the houses of all the Bradbrooks' acquaintances, who were numerous. Then there were callers to be received, and an array of evening engagements. Violet threw herself into this social whirlwind with abandon, unfurling her petals like a rose to smile charmingly on every personable young man within her orbit, and on one in particular. Mr Nettles, it seemed, was quite forgotten, for the new object of her affection was the foppish Roger Bradbrook. For his part, he seemed perfectly willing to indulge her fancies, and was surprisingly often at hand to squire the ladies about.

Evie was sufficiently concerned to raise the matter with Roger's father.

"No need to worry about that," Mr Bradbrook said. "Roger knows he cannot marry to disoblige me, not if he wants my fortune. Besides, Violet is not yet of age, and cannot marry without Eliot's consent, so we are safe enough. Someone new will come along to distract her before too long, and with any luck it will be someone with a more restrained style of attire."

That made Evie laugh. "Indeed, I do not believe that Mr Roger's adherence to the whims of fashion has had a beneficial effect on Violet. She bought three bonnets last week, and every one had to be reworked. Entirely inappropriate."

"And ugly," he said. "That one with all the fruit on it — monstrous ugly, especially on a girl who needs so little adornment. She should follow your lead as far as dress is concerned. You always look just the thing. It is no wonder you have so many admirers."

Evie blushed and thanked him for the compliment.

He hesitated, then said, "Miss Parfitt, there is an odd rumour in the wind that you have a substantial dowry — fifteen thousand pounds, to be precise."

She gave a gasp of astonishment. "Fifteen *thousand!* Heavens, I consider myself fortunate to have fifteen *pounds* to my name. I hope you may stifle any such talk, for it is entirely untrue."

"Is it? For it has been whispered to emanate from a very reliable source."

"Completely untrue," she said firmly. "Who is this reliable source?"

"Lord Lampeter."

She opened her mouth to protest, then clamped it shut again. Lord Lampeter! Well... that was interesting.

"Should you like me to ask him about it?" he said.

"No!" she said sharply. Then, seeing the astonishment in his face, went on in more moderate tones, "If he raises the issue with you, then by all means, but otherwise I should prefer to maintain a dignified silence on the subject. I am aware of no dowry, and if Lord Lampeter has information to the contrary, then it is for him to tell me of it himself."

Mr Bradbrook looked searchingly at her, but, to Evie's relief, allowed the subject to drop. Still, it did not stop her from thinking about it, trying in vain to suppress the simmering anger. A dowry! As if that made everything right!

~~~~~

Eliot had never been more miserable in his life. A full week had been spent on the road, a week of indifferent inns, worse food and the humiliation of hired hacks pulling his carriage. They had passed with unconscionable slowness through endless obscure counties — Warwickshire, Staffordshire, Brinshire, Shropshire and then into the desolation that was Wales. It was reputed to be a country of great beauty, with splendid lakes and forests and high mountains, but they had seen nothing of it but rain. Day after day of rain. And now they were come to the end of the world, for they had reached Holyhead, where the road ended in a grey roiling sea.

The Royal Hotel was reassuringly comfortable, providing a snug private parlour, drinkable wine, comfortable rooms and stables willing to accommodate the carriage until such time as the packet ship might return them from the alien shores of Ireland. On discovering that the packet departed shortly after six in the
~~~~~

morning, Eliot decreed that they would stay for two nights in Holyhead to recover from the travails of the journey and recruit their strength for the crossing.

"I declare, Armitage, you are as frightened of a drop of water as any man I ever saw," Folkard said, as they sampled a surprisingly good port in their parlour after dinner. "These little ships ply back and forth every day in perfect safety."

"The Irish Sea is no mere drop of water," Eliot said, but without heat. A good dinner and some decent claret had submerged the worst of his fears.

"The Holyhead to Howth crossing is not quite the Cape of Good Hope," Folkard said. "Come, man, cheer up! Why on earth did you come, when it makes you so dismal?"

"To impress Evie," Eliot said without thinking.

"*Evie?* You are doing this for Evie's benefit?" Folkard said in astonished tones. "Why? What do you hope for there? Oh, devil take you, Armitage! She is too good for that little love nest of yours, if *that* is what you have in mind. Damnation, you must not ruin her, not Evie!"

"No, no! Nothing of the sort, I assure you. I have the highest opinion of her, and I would never consider—" He broke off in some confusion, remembering a time when he had considered her in exactly that light.

"I trust you would not! She has *some* friends, I hope, who would protect her."

Eliot laughed. "Really, Folkard! What right have you or anyone else to protect her?"

He coloured, but said, "None, of course. I wish I had, but I dare not even dream of the possibility. I cannot afford to marry without money."

"I had no idea she was more to you than a childhood friend. You were supposed to take Violet off my hands, you know."

"Oh, well... Violet is very pretty and amusing company, and I liked her very well at first, until she fell into the clutches of that Nettles fellow, and became a dreary and spiritless creature, forever about her good works. Very worthy, no doubt, but I like a woman I can talk to. Like Evie." He paused, then drained the last drops from his glass. "Besides, I can hardly pursue a woman worth a hundred thousand. That makes me the worst kind of fortune hunter."

"There is no pleasing you," Eliot said lightly. "Violet is too rich for you, and Evie too poor." He reached for the port bottle and refilled both their glasses thoughtfully. "If Evie had a dowry, would you want to marry her?"

"I should certainly like to try to attach her," Folkard said eagerly. "She is everything that is good and amiable, is she not? So gentle in her ways, so ladylike, so refined... a man could be content for ever with such a wife."

These were sentiments with which Eliot could find no fault. He sipped his port, pondering. "She once said to me that she considers you in the light of a brother. Because you grew up together, presumably. That might be an obstacle."

"Pooh, there is nothing in that. If I were able to make my intentions clear, there would be no difficulty in that way. We are not so much brother and sister as friends... good friends, and is that not the perfect foundation for marriage?"

"You consider friendship to be a sufficient basis for matrimony, do you?" Eliot said. "Not affection? Love?"

"So long as there is affection on one side, and respect on the other, the marriage will be strong," Folkard said. "It is perhaps better if a wife is not head over heels in love with her husband initially so that she may weigh his strengths and weaknesses impartially, and make a rational decision. Then she will see that a sensible, respectable man, of sober habits and prudent management of his affairs, is far superior to the shallower type of fellow. Women are too easily drawn to a handsome face or fashionable clothes, when a man's character is of greater importance."

"Does it not work the other way?" Eliot said curiously. "Should not a man weigh a woman's character above her beauty or manner of dress?"

"A woman's character will be readily visible in her appearance," Folkard said smugly. "If she is beautiful on the outside, that shows that her mind is beautiful also."

"Yet this principle does not apply to men?"

Folkard frowned slightly, as if pondering whether there might be some flaws in his argument, but then his face cleared again. "Men are complex creatures, capable of displaying pleasing manners and appearance while concealing wickedness within. Women are somewhat easier to comprehend, I fancy."

Eliot's experience had not been such as to give him any confidence in this view of the world, but he was honest enough to recognise that Folkard was in almost all ways an eligible husband for a woman of no family, like Evie. In a few years, Folkard would be a wealthy barrister, and might even hope for a knighthood in later years, and in character he was unexciting but worthy. Yes, he was very eligible. He did not suppose that Evie would be responsive to his overtures, for she had made her opinion of Folkard very clear, but Eliot could not deny the man his chance with her.

"There was a letter awaiting me here from Uncle Bradbrook," he said slowly. "It seems that Evie might have a dowry after all. Lord Lampeter is spreading the word that she has fifteen thousand pounds."

Folkard froze, the port glass half way to his lips. "*Fifteen thousand?* Evie? Good God! But... Lord Lampeter? My *uncle* is spreading such a rumour? How would he know of it?"

"Her mother was a Folkard, and lived at the Hall for several years. Perhaps Lampeter knows something of Evie's circumstances that Evie herself does not."

"That seems unlikely. And yet... fifteen thousand. Five or six hundred a year, perhaps. Enough to live on. Enough to *marry* on. I shall have to talk to my uncle when we get back to town, and see if I cannot get to the bottom of it. Fifteen thousand... and Uncle Henry knows of it."

"You are on good terms with Lampeter?" Eliot said cautiously. "I thought there was a breach when they threw you out, and sent you to live with my Uncle Bradbrook."

"Not a breach, exactly. After my cousin Walter was born and I was no longer the heir presumptive, it was felt better for me to take up a career, that was all. I do not see my uncle and aunt often, but they do not cut me or anything of that nature. A breach? Heavens, no!"

Eliot said no more, but from all he had heard, Folkard had been forced to leave Folkard Hall at a moment's notice and had never been invited back. That sounded suspiciously like a breach to him. Still, it was not his business and he lapsed into silence as Folkard considered the possibility of marrying Evie, a prospect which did nothing at all to improve Eliot's dismal spirits. Dearest Evie! How could he bear it if she were to marry Folkard? But she was adamant that she would not have Eliot, so why should she not marry elsewhere?

The dark ball of despair inside him grew a little larger.

18: The City Of Dublin

The packet ship ploughed gamely across the Irish Sea, depositing Eliot and Folkard safely ashore at Howth by three in the afternoon. From there, the chaise he had arranged to meet the ship had conveyed them to Dublin. Eliot remembered little of the journey. He felt so ill and yet so thankful to have survived the crossing that he had closed his eyes and half-dozed for the short journey to the city. Their hotel was prepared for them, there was a warm bedchamber, a decanter of good wine and smooth, soft sheets. Having barely slept for several nights, he fell into bed and was asleep in moments.

He woke to trickles of sunshine creeping round the curtains, and the sound of whispered voices in the room.

"Well, it is time he was!" said Folkard's voice stridently, and the curtains were ruthlessly pulled apart.

The brilliant light dazzled Eliot. "Good God, Folkard, what are you about? Can you not let a fellow sleep?"

"You have been sleeping for almost twenty hours, you slug-a-bed. I, however, have been up betimes and have already called upon this solicitor you want to see. He is expecting you in two hours, so you had better bestir yourself if you wish to have something to eat before that. Your washing water is here, and Strood has your clothes laid out ready. I shall await you in the parlour. Hurry, now."

Eliot groaned, but obediently rolled out of bed. It took him a full hour to wash, shave and dress to the equal satisfaction of himself and his valet, but after that he descended to the private parlour he had engaged, where a vast spread of bread, pastries and meat was laid out for his enjoyment. He discovered he was ravenous, and so for some time there was no conversation with Folkard, who sipped coffee and watched him eat with amusement.

Eventually, he declared his appetite assuaged, and the two men sallied forth into the streets of Dublin, which Eliot was astonished to see were wide and lined with elegantly appointed buildings, some of an imposing size and dignity. The pavements were thronged with people, some of them dressed in a style which would pass muster in Bond Street. Their own London fashions brought them the notice of the locals, many of whom acknowledged them with a pleasing degree of deference.

"I had no idea any part of Ireland was so... so..." Eliot struggled for an appropriate word.

"Civilised?" hazarded Folkard. "One never supposed it was the endless bog of legend, but this is unexpectedly pleasant. Look at that building over there — most imposing! One might almost fancy oneself in London."

The solicitor received them with the utmost deference, willing to do all within his power to aid them, as he repeatedly assured them, but he had nothing to tell them that he had not already communicated by letter. He had overseen the transfer of Barantine's jewellery to the American gentleman and his agents, and the purchase of the diamonds, and showed them all his records of these events. He had copies of all the bills of sale. He had himself counted the coins which changed hands and could vouch for the amount, although the value of the jewellery and the unpolished stones was a matter of agreement between the two gentlemen concerned.

"What of Newbold?" Eliot said. "What was his rôle in all this?"

"Mr Newbold took no part in the discussions."

"None at all? Then why was he here?"

"The jewellery was very valuable, Mr Armitage. Mr Barantine could not walk the streets with large items of very expensive jewellery, so Mr Newbold accompanied him, and also Mr Crick and Mr Palfreyman."

"The valets? Oh, I see. So the diamonds left here in Barantine's possession? There is no question of it?"

"None whatsoever, as I mentioned to you in my letter."

"So you did, sir. So you did. Is it possible that Barantine sold the diamonds again before boarding the *Brig Minerva?* He stayed here for a few days, did he not?"

"He did, and it is possible, perhaps," the solicitor said, although he sounded dubious. "He was quite clear that he wanted them for his London shop, but something may have changed his mind. I can furnish you with a list of jewellers in the town where he might have sold them, if it would help? And solicitors, too?"

Eliot accepted the lists with expressions of gratitude, but he had no hope of finding a solution there, for if Barantine had sold the diamonds, where was the money from that sale? It was increasingly likely that the diamonds had been stolen. Nevertheless, he and Folkard dutifully made the rounds of every person named on the list, entirely unsurprised to hear that none of them had met Barantine. The jewellers had all heard of him, and a few told Eliot excitedly that they had once had the pleasure of a Barantine tiara or necklace or bracelet in the shop, but none knew anything of the diamonds.

This disheartening drudgery gave way in the evenings to much more acceptable entertainment. A note had awaited them on their return to the hotel on the first day.

'My very dear sirs, May I be the first to welcome such distinguished visitors from the metropolis to the fair shores of Ireland and to our beautiful town. Pray do me the honour of dining with me tonight at Kilrannan House. We sit down at six. Kilrannan.'

Enquiries revealed that the Earl of Kilrannan was one of the notables of Dublin, who made a point of entertaining everyone from English society who came to Dublin, for he loved above all things to hear the latest news and see the fashions and surround himself with persons of consequence.

"The Dook himself was stayin' with him, sir," the hotel chambermaid told them. "The one that drowned. 'Twas a terrible thing!"

"Falconbury? Yes, it was very sad," Eliot said. "Very sad for all those who were aboard the *Brig Minerva.*"

And yet such tragedies brought benefits, too. The Seventh Duke had died untimely, but his younger brother had unexpectedly found himself inheriting the title and the vast ducal estates. Violet had lost her father and her diamonds, but Eliot had met Evie… the sharp spear of pain in his heart made him wonder just how beneficial that had been. Yet falling in love had, perhaps, made him a better man, one who had begun to question his former licentious way of life and was prepared to exert himself for Violet. Or rather, for Evie. He was doing all of this, suffering even the dreadful sea crossing, for Evie, that she might one day think better of him.

Oh, Evie… it shocked him how empty he felt without her. He who had never grown attached to any woman before, who had bade his mistresses a fond farewell without regret, who had let two or three possible wives drift away without the slightest dismay, was reduced to shivering grief by Evie's refusals. He had an optimistic spirit, always believing that there would be a better tomorrow, but now he began to wonder. The endless years without her stretched before him, empty, desolate years, and how he was to get through them he could not imagine. But perhaps, if he mended his ways, there might be some sliver of hope for him…? He *must* hope, for how else was he to go on?

Distraction… he needed distraction, and happily the sociable Earl of Kilrannan was eager to oblige. Eliot and Folkard presented themselves at Kilrannan House at the proper time and were ushered into a saloon of grandiose if faded splendour. The earl himself was testament to the generosity of his own table, for he required the strong arms of two footmen simply to lift him from his chair, and he wheezed as he walked. He was all geniality, however, introducing them to his wife, who was almost as stout as he was, three daughters who were bidding fair to achieve a similar rotundity in the fullness of time, and a number of sons, cousins and assorted aunts and uncles.

Despite this familial over-abundance, there were several other guests, both local and passing strangers, scooped up by the earl's convivial nature. Eliot and Folkard were the centre of attention, having both novelty and the latest news from London. When they explained their purpose in visiting Dublin, they discovered that Barantine had stayed at Kilrannan House on his last visit.

"'Tis all thanks to him that we had the honour of entertaining His Grace the Duke of Falconbury under this roof," wheezed the earl. "His Grace was all set to catch the first packet from Howth, but Barantine convinced him to wait for the *Minerva*." He sighed gustily. "Ah, such tragedy, such great tragedy. Who could have imagined that a solid little ship like that, as sturdy a vessel as ever ploughed the waves, could meet with such a misfortune? And now the poor young duke is dead, and Barantine too."

Eliot made suitable murmurings, but there was not much to be said about the sinking of the *Minerva* that had not been said a thousand times, so he changed the subject as soon as was decent. He found he was not to be allowed to escape it, however, for when the ladies withdrew after dinner, he found two of the earl's sons slipping into the seats either side of him.

"So you are Miss Barantine's guardian?" one said.

"For my sins, I am," Eliot said with a smile.

"How is the poor orphaned young lady?"

"She bears her grief with fortitude," he said cautiously.

"Ah, yes, so she would, so she would. A lovely young lady, so her father said, and quite the apple of his eye."

"She is certainly very beautiful," Eliot said, and that was a statement he could make with sincerity. When she was not pouting, Violet was quite strikingly lovely. "When she is fully out of mourning, I intend to bring her out properly into society, introduce her to a few people, and she will make an excellent match, without doubt. I have high hopes for her."

"Her father left her well provided for, I am sure. A hundred thousand, he used to say. That was to be her dowry. Was it so? It would be a tragedy indeed if she should be left penniless."

"It will not be quite so much, but her father left everything to her, with only a few small bequests, so the whole of his business is hers now."

"The business? There was no other sum set aside for her? Is that not the usual way, when a father provides for his daughter, to set aside a sum in the funds?"

"Some do, indeed, but very often the provision is made and the exact sum decided only when there is a betrothal."

At once he was assailed by doubts. If the dowry was tied up in the business, then Violet's betrothal would have taken the full value of it, and then how would Barantine have been situated? He would be bankrupted by such an arrangement. That could not be right. But there was no time to puzzle it out, for the earl called down the table to him to settle, if he could, a question concerning the Queen, for he supposed that anyone living in London must be familiar with the goings-on at court. Eliot answered as best he could, and the moment was lost, but he puzzled about it all the way back to the hotel.

Dinner at Kilrannan House became a regular event, and these pleasant evenings brought the only brightness to their stay in Dublin. Their third day of investigation saw them reaching the end of their list of jewellers and solicitors, with not the slightest sign of the diamonds.

"It is as if they never existed," Folkard said dispiritedly, as they trudged back to the hotel in the rain to change before dinner.

"Yet we know that they did exist," Eliot said. "They were handed over into Barantine's care, after which they vanished off the face of the earth."

"Perhaps they were stolen," Folkard suggested. "Barantine might not have liked to advertise the fact that he had been a victim of theft. It might be bad for business in a jeweller to lose valuables in that way."

"More likely that he would have screamed it to the rooftops, and set the constables onto it," Eliot said. "Do they have constables in Ireland? There must be something of the sort to enforce the law."

"True. But then there is no explanation, or none to be found here."

"Yes, perhaps it is time to think about putting ourselves aboard that wretched ship again."

This gloomy conclusion was reached just as they arrived at the hotel, where the doorman looked at their dripping greatcoats and said sympathetically, "Ye'll be wanting some brandy sent up, no doubt, sirs."

Folkard brightened. "An excellent idea, my good fellow. Tell me, at what hour does the packet depart from Howth?"

"Eight of the clock, sir."

"Well... not quite so bad as the departure from Holyhead," Folkard said.

"It is still pretty bad," Eliot said. "Still, the sooner it leaves, the sooner it arrives. Six or seven hours — I can survive that, I daresay."

"Aye, ye'll have the wind at your backs, sirs, but the water's a trifle choppy just now. Be a rough crossing, I'll warrant."

"Perhaps we should not leave so precipitously," Eliot said nervously. "A few more days, perhaps, and the seas might be less turbulent."

"Not likely, sir, not likely," the doorman said cheerfully. "Not at this time of year. Only going to get rougher, I reckon. Oh, by the way, there's a man to wants to see you. In the coffee room."

"A man?" Eliot said. "Not a gentleman? What sort of a man?"

"Well, sir, if I had to guess, I'd say he's a gentleman's gentleman, if you understand me."

"A valet... well, he may have some information to assist our enquiries. Have him go up to the parlour while we change out of these wet clothes."

The valet, when they met him in the parlour, was a nondescript little man, dressed entirely in black, but he had none of the deferential air of a manservant. Instead, he calmly offered his card. *'James Neate, Markham, Willerton-Forbes and Browning, Inner Temple, London'*

Eliot laughed. "You are a *lawyer*, Mr Neate? I would not have guessed it."

"That is my intention," he said, eyes twinkling. "I work with Mr Pettigrew Willerton-Forbes and Captain Edgerton on behalf of the Benefactor, and it is useful to them to have someone who can mingle unobtrusively with the servant class. Sometimes information may be obtained more readily from the servants' hall than from the drawing room. I am presently engaged as a general purpose manservant to a Mr and Mrs Connell of Kilcarlow, a few miles from here, but it came to my ears that two gentlemen from London were asking about Mr Barantine and I wondered if I might be of assistance."

Eliot had no hesitation in telling Neate the whole of it, for there was no secrecy about their mission, after all.

Neate rubbed his nose thoughtfully. "I have heard nothing about any diamonds. Barantine stayed at Kilrannan House, you say? Then it is just possible that... Hmm. You will have dined there, I doubt not, but you have not been invited to stay, I take it? No, then you will not be aware that the earl and his sons run a very discreet and exclusive gambling establishment in a back room. His lordship is not at all flush in the pocket, yet he loves to entertain lavishly, and so he supplements his income by relieving some of his well-breeched guests of their money. The Duke of Falconbury was a very welcome guest, by all accounts, for he lost large sums every night in the highest good-humour."

"Sharps, are they?" Eliot said. "I thank you for warning us."

"As to that, I cannot say for sure, you understand, but there is always plenty of the best wine flowing in that house, and if a man is incautious enough to drink deeply and not check the dice or cards carefully, then more fool him. I daresay you two were too sober to be worth their while."

Folkard laughed. "Or too poor. I have not a penny to my name, and Eliot does not play high when he is with me, so I daresay the earl thought us not worth the plucking."

"That is possible," Neate said. "Only a select few passing visitors are invited to stay. Otherwise it is regulars like Mr Barantine, or my current employer, Mr Connell. What goes on is well known in the town, of course, but it is kept a secret from strangers. The earl's two youngest sons, Mr Bartholomew Tranter and Mr Christopher

Tranter, manage the gaming, so it might be worth your while to ask of them whether Mr Barantine gambled away his diamonds."

They thanked him profusely for his information, and assured him his name would not be mentioned.

The eyes twinkled again. "I have no fear of that, for I operate here under a *nom de guerre*, as you might say. But I should not like to lose my position with the Connells until my business there is concluded, so your discretion would be appreciated."

The first difficulty, Eliot discovered, was working out which of the many near-identical sons of the earl were the two concerned. Fortunately, the butler proved helpful in pointing them out, and after dinner, under cover of a rather bad musical performance from one of the daughters of the house, Eliot was able to make his way unobtrusively to Mr Bartholomew and quietly request a private interview with himself and Mr Christopher. There was a brief flash of a disconcerted expression across Tranter's face before he restored a smile to his features.

"Of course, of course. Not the least trouble in the world, my good sirs. Chris, do you come with us."

He led them across the landing to a smaller room, clearly a morning room, cold and empty at this hour of the day. The Tranter brothers lit a couple of candelabra and turned to Eliot expectantly.

"It has come to my attention that you keep a room here for special guests to play games of chance a little more liberally than would be appropriate for the drawing room," he began, and almost immediately the brothers' eyes were wary.

The older Tranter beamed at him. "You would like some play a little more exciting than Mother allows. Of course you would! Naturally we would be happy to oblige you—"

"No, no! I am not interested for myself, only in regard to the late Mr Barantine. I wondered if these wretched diamonds of his had been gambled away in this house, that is all."

The brothers exchanged glances. "We saw no diamonds..." the younger began.

Eliot cut him off with a wave of one hand. "Let me make myself absolutely plain, gentlemen. I am not in the least concerned with your little enterprise, nor do I care if you or anyone else won those diamonds honourably at the card table or by dice. I do not even care if you were fleecing Barantine, for he must look out for himself."

"No, no! We would never have fleeced *him*!" Bartholomew Tranter protested. "He was one of our *regulars*."

That made Eliot laugh. "I accept your word on the point. All I wish to do is to discover, if I can, what became of them, for I know they were handed into Barantine's possession and they were not found with him when he died. Somewhere in between those two points they vanished, and they were not sold, or he would have had the equivalent in coins. Gambling them away seems like a very plausible explanation."

There was a long silence, as the brothers mulled it over, looked at each other, thought some more. Then Bartholomew sighed.

"I believe, brother, that we ought to confess the whole, do not you?"

19: Green Street

The Tranter brothers led Eliot and Folkard downstairs, through a door and then a second door, concealed by a curtain, and finally up another flight of stairs. The large room at the top was furnished in the same opulent but faded style as the other parts of the house that they had seen, but the room's purpose was revealed by a number of card tables. A footman setting out decanters and glasses on a sideboard was hurried out of the room with a gesture.

"This is our gaming room," Bartholomew Tranter said. "It was Mr Barantine's favourite place in the world, he was wont to say. He never played in London, for he could easily have lost his entire fortune there in a night, and his business partner was very stuffy about it, he said. He would harass him for weeks if he thought he had been at the tables. So Mr Barantine came here three or four times a year to meet his American agent and do a little business, and beguile away the evening hours in here."

"Did he win or lose?" Eliot said, intrigued by this new view of Violet's upright father.

"He won," said the younger sourly. "No profit from him."

The elder laughed. "He won games of skill, it is true. Whist or piquet — no one could touch him there. Well, one person, perhaps. But he played faro and hazard and vingt-et-un as well, and brought in less sensible players, so we made our share that way and it worked to our advantage. He brought us the Duke of Falconbury, and induced him to stay on until the *Minerva* called here, and we made a small fortune from that poor duke. I never saw such an appallingly bad player so happy to throw his money away. We were very happy Barantine brought him our way."

"He also brought us Ellsworthy," the younger brother said.

"Ah, yes. The duke brought *him*," Bartholomew said. "He was only a clerk, seemingly, but one hesitates to disoblige a duke. Mind you, anyone would have taken Ellsworthy for a gentleman, so we had no qualms about it. Pleasing manners, very well-spoken, good quality clothes. One could take him into any company. But he was devilish good at all the games of skill. Piquet was his preferred game, and he won almost every time, until he met Barantine. He spotted Ellsworthy at once, and when his opponent rose from the table, Barantine challenged him to a game. Well, they played all night! I think it was past dawn when they finally gave it up, and that only because Barantine had lost all he had. Close to a thousand he lost, and if Ellsworthy would have taken rolls of soft or vowels they would be playing still, I suspect. But he said no, he never took anything other than coins on the table, because he knew of someone who had gambled away everything he possessed in such a fit, and took his own life after. He never wanted to be responsible for such an eventuality, he said."

"Barantine was desperate to play him again, though," Christopher said. "Had never enjoyed himself so much in his life, he said, to play against someone of such skill, and even win the odd *partie,* was a delight beyond measure. For several nights they were both there, and Barantine pleaded with him, but Ellsworthy was adamant. He would lose a little at vingt-et-un, then win a hundred or two at piquet or whist, and that would be the end of it. But then—" He glanced at his brother. "You tell it, Bartie. I can hardly bear to think of it, even now. It makes me feel sick."

"That is because you are too young to remember the last time, brother. Besides, we did nothing wrong. Barantine wanted to play high, but he had not the coins for it. One night, the last night he was here, he won a hundred pounds from the poor duke, so when everyone else was gone, he proposed a more serious game — piquet at a hundred pounds a *partie.* I am a tolerable player, not as good as he is, but I could give him a run for his money, so we settled to it. No one was here but Chris and myself, so you will have to take my word for it."

"Your word is good enough," Eliot said equably.

"Well, then we settled to it and he won several hundred quite easily. But then he began to lose, and in case you have any doubts, no, there was absolutely nothing underhand going on."

"I believe you," Eliot said, seeing the sincerity in his eyes.

"In no time, it seemed, he was out of money, so he offered his vowels and we have always accepted them when offered — we are not so restrained as Ellsworthy! — and we played on, and he went on losing. I expected him to stop, but he never did. I was not keeping track, but there must have been fifty thousand on the table, and I will be honest with you, Armitage, it looked like a good night's work to me. Barantine was a rich man, and even if he lost it all, he had enjoyed himself and he would be back in three months and might win it all back. So when he scooped up the notes and said, *'Let us lay this to rest — one last game for the title to my business',* I accepted the bet. And he lost again. He signed the title over to me, shook my hand, told me he would expect me to give him the chance to win it back next time he was in Dublin and that was the last we ever saw of him."

"You have the title to the business?" Eliot said in astonishment. "But I thought you were going to tell me about the diamonds!"

"No, we never saw any diamonds. It was the business he lost. Chris, fetch the papers from the safe, will you."

The papers meant nothing to Eliot, but Folkard read them carefully. "Yes, these are the missing documents."

"And do they say anything of Newbold?" Eliot said.

"No, but that hardly matters. See here, where it says that Lethbridge Barantine has sole ownership? It is crossed out, you see. Then the name *'Conway Tranter'* — one of your older brothers?"

"Aye. That was five years ago, the last time Barantine got reckless. It was a year before he won it back."

"Then *'Lethbridge Barantine'* again, and now *'Bartholomew Tranter'* and the date, and Mr Barantine's signature. Mr Tranter owns the business in its entirety."

"But what about Violet?" Eliot said, appalled.

"She will still get the Bruton Street house."

"Leased."

"Oh. Well, the contents, then."

"A few sticks of furniture, and the clothes she stands up in! She will be penniless."

Bartholomew coughed. "This is why we have said nothing, why we find it so distressing. We would not for the world be the means of depriving Miss Barantine of her inheritance. We wondered if we should just burn the papers and be done with it. What do you think?"

"You cannot do that!" Eliot said sharply. "These are legal documents, after all. Folkard, bring your lawyer's mind to bear on the case. How can Violet's inheritance be restored to her? What is to be done?"

"Why, nothing," he said calmly. "Mr Tranter owns everything and Violet owns nothing and that is the end of the matter."

"And we still have no idea where those *wretched* diamonds are," Eliot said disgustedly.

~~~~~

'Green Street, London. My dearest Aunt, We are living such hectic lives, you would be astonished, I daresay. I was used to think that our time at Bruton Street was busy, but that is nothing to how we now spend our days, and Mrs Bradbrook assures me that the spring season, when everyone who is anyone is in town, will be such a whirlwind of excess that we shall barely have time to breathe. So far this week we have been to the theatre not once but twice, enjoyed two routs, two card parties, one musical soirée and a ball in the Venetian manner. Apart from the strange liveries of the footmen and a rather bad painting of Venice on one wall, I distinguished nothing especially Venetian about it. In answer to your question, no, the loss of the younger Mr Armitage and Mr Folkard is not felt at all, not in the least, since we have so many young men to compensate for their absence. We are very gay without them, I assure you. As to your other question, Mrs Armitage is said to be a little better and
~~~~~

has gone to Brandeth Hall to support Lady Corbett in her imminent confinement, although since the lady has produced some eight or nine offspring already, it is to be supposed that she will know what to do tolerably well. I am still none the wiser as to the cause of the difficulty in August, and although I try to suppress my curiosity in Christian restraint, I do not manage it very well when everyone knows but me. I am glad that your cold is better and has not affected your lungs. Do try to stay indoors while the weather is so horrid. How astonishing that the roses are still in bloom, despite all the wind and hail. Pray give my regards to the Bishop when you see him on Tuesday, and be assured that I am in perfect health and spirits, and treated most kindly by the Bradbrooks, who ensure that I want for no comfort. Yours from lively London, your dissipated niece, Evie.'

~~~~~

Evie could tell Aunt Dodi that she did not miss Eliot, but she could not be so dishonest with herself. Every hour of the day brought some reminder of him. When she danced, she wished he were her partner. When she sewed, her thimble reminded her of how he had caught her unawares and she had scattered her sewing things. The thimble had rolled under a chair and only been discovered two days later. When she played whist, she saw his hands shuffling, dealing, placing a winning card with a smile of triumph. When she wore her favourite bonnet, it reminded her of his kiss. Oh, his kiss...! And when she woke each morning, restless and unrefreshed, she imagined opening her eyes to see his face on the pillow beside her, peaceful in sleep, his golden hair tousled. And no matter how much she berated herself for such madness, she could not get him out of her mind.
~~~~~

Mrs Bradbrook perhaps noticed that she was not in spirits, for she said one day at breakfast, "I believe you are a little tired, my dear. Have we worn you out with our junketing?"

"Oh no! Not at all, but... I did not sleep well last night. There were noises in the street until the small hours... a group singing with great gusto..."

"Should you prefer a quieter room? I can give you one at the back of the house, but it is not so commodious as the one you now have."

"No, indeed, I am perfectly satisfied... pray do not be concerned, ma'am. What are your plans for the day?"

"Violet has asked me to go shopping again, so I thought we might go to Bond Street. Then we might call in at Hookham's to obtain something new for you to read, for I know you have read everything you had at the last visit."

"How kind you are, ma'am, although Mr Bradbrook has enough books to occupy me in between visits to the library."

Mr Bradbrook looked up from his letters to smile at Evie. "Mostly legal tomes, and not of much interest to you, I daresay. You must ask Eliot to show you the library he has in Grosvenor Square when he gets back. More than enough reading there even for you, Miss Parfitt. Well, you will want the carriage for your expedition, Mrs Bradbrook, so I shall walk round to the club later."

"No, indeed we shall not need it. It is no distance to walk, and Henry may carry our parcels for us. Henry is such an asset to the household. I shall be very sorry to see him go."

Pushing back his chair, Mr Bradbrook rose to leave. "Do not tire Miss Parfitt with all these schemes, Kate. Not everyone has inexhaustible energy, as you do. At least Violet has the good sense to lie abed in the mornings to recruit her strength. How many do we have for our card party tonight?"

"I should be able to make up four or five tables, even without Violet and Roger."

Mr Bradbrook was halfway to the door, but now he stopped, a little frown on his forehead. "Violet and Roger?"

"They are to go to the theatre with the Boremans, if you remember. Jack Boreman is a very personable young man with perfect manners and a restrained style of dress, who will make an excellent contrast with Roger. A distraction for Violet, perhaps."

"Ah!" he said, smiling. "You are so clever, my little kitten, and I adore you, did I ever tell you that?"

"Only every day, Nicholas," she said, going rather pink.

He planted a kiss on one cheek and then, almost as an afterthought, on her lips, before he left the room, chuckling to himself.

"Well! My goodness!" Mrs Bradbrook said, adjusting her cap, although it needed no attention. "Nicholas is such a romantic at heart, and as much now as the day we were wed."

Evie got up to pour herself some more chocolate from the pot on the sideboard, to give her hostess time to compose herself. Or perhaps it was to compose her own jangled nerves, for she could not help thinking of Eliot at such a moment. Would he be so romantic after several years of marriage? Would she wish him to? But she knew the answer to that — of course she would. She yearned for such closeness, such intimacy. She had enjoyed something of that nature with her father, but how much greater would it be with a husband? But such thoughts were foolish. She was not going to marry, ever.

When Evie returned to the breakfast table, Mrs Bradbrook said brightly, "Did I tell you that I had a letter from Eliot yesterday? No, for you were not by... you had gone to the park with Violet and Roger. Poor Eliot! He is having such a miserable time of it — the rain, the incessant travelling, roughness of the ocean. But he and Edward have arrived safely in Dublin, you will be happy to hear."

"Oh yes! So glad... he was not looking forward to the journey, I think." She tried to appear unconscious but a little warmth spread into her cheeks, and she turned industriously to her toast.

"He is a very bad traveller altogether. I wonder he undertook such a mission when he dislikes it so much, but there, I expect he has his reasons."

"He wishes to find Violet's diamonds," Evie said, rather puzzled. "What other reason could there be?"

Mrs Bradbrook chuckled. "My dear Evie, he is trying to win your favour."

Evie was struck dumb, shaking her head and blushing furiously.

"Now, now, you must know how it is. When a man is refused, it puts him very much on his mettle. Eliot is trying to convince you that he is worthy of you, in the hope that you will change your mind."

"But I shall not! I *cannot!* No matter how many good deeds he accomplishes, his character is still fundamentally flawed."

"Because he kept mistresses in his past? That does not make him irredeemably wicked."

"No, but it makes him a bad risk as a husband. I could not bear it if he were to return to his bad habits. I do not want to put all my trust in a man who could make me so unhappy."

"And are you happy now?" Mrs Bradbrook said gently.

Evie lifted her chin defiantly. "Mr Armitage has... has disturbed my equanimity somewhat, it is true, but that is merely a temporary affliction. I shall make a recover, ma'am."

Mrs Bradbrook looked at her thoughtfully. "It does seem a shame, for you are very well suited in so many ways, and it would be such a splendid match for you. The Armitages are very wealthy, and you would want for nothing."

"Money does not sway me," Evie said quietly. She sat motionless, hands clasped tightly in her lap. If only the subject could be forgotten! She experienced enough difficulty living with her decision believing that it was only Eliot who knew of it, but to be the means of disappointing his family, too, was beyond anything. "I dare not take the risk."

"All marriage is risky, Evie. One never knows one's husband until one is well and truly married to him, and even then there may be surprises. A substantial income is a great comfort if the surprises are unpleasant ones. I confess that I hesitated over Nicholas, for he had a dreadful reputation in those days."

"Did he?" Evie said, startled. "He seems a paragon of respectability to me."

"And so he is now, but he was wild when he was young. Not gambling or anything of that nature, for he was always careful with his money, having so little of it then, and he worked hard in his career and did very well. But women! He was a notorious rake, and cuckolded half the peerage, if even a portion of the tales be true. My father warned me against him, that he would never be faithful to one woman. I dithered for months, head over heels in love but not wanting to take the risk, just as you are doing. But one day, he brought me here, to this house, and told me it would be mine if I married him, and he would give up his work and be a gentleman so that I could be a lady, because I was the only thing he wanted in his life. I know it is shallow of me, and he teases me about it to this day, that I only accepted him to get this house, but it seemed to me that if he were going to make me unhappy, then at least I should be unhappy in comfort. But he never has... made me unhappy, that is."

Before Evie could gather her wits to respond to this, a knock on the door heralded the footman. "A note delivered by hand from Lady Shearsmith, ma'am."

"Ah, Lydia is a good creature. I asked her— Thank you, William." She waited until the footman had left and the door was firmly closed before opening the sealed letter. "Ah, it is as I suspected. There, read it, my dear, for none have a better right."

Evie took the sheet from her, and began to read Lady Shearsmith's sprawling hand.

'My dear Kate, Charles finally got Lampeter alone and it is as we thought. There is the sum of fifteen thousand set aside for Miss P and it was Lampeter himself who put up the money, having affectionate memories of her mother and a sincere wish of seeing her satisfactorily married, since she is a penniless orphan with no

prospect of a match otherwise. What a magnificent gesture, but then he has a reputation for charitable works, although very humble about it. I hope Miss P makes a splendid match. Lydia. Post Script - do you suppose Lord L is this mysterious Benefactor who has been handing out great sums of money to those affected by that awful shipwreck?"

20: Rakes And Gamblers

Evie was furious with Lord Lampeter. To the world, it must seem like a benevolent gesture towards a poor relation. So generous! So selfless! But she knew better, and what was almost more galling was that now she would look at every single dance partner, every gentleman who had paid her the least attention, and wonder if he was seeing, not Evie, but fifteen thousand pounds. Such a useful amount! A welcome addition to a man of moderate fortune and a godsend to a man of lesser means.

At the very first opportunity, she went to see Mr Bradbrook in his book room. He rose with his warm smile and led her to a chair beside the fire.

"Now, Miss Parfitt, tell me what troubles you."

"It has come to my notice that this sum of fifteen thousand pounds, supposedly my dowry, was set up by Lord Lampeter himself. He has admitted it."

"Yes, I have heard something of that."

"You did not mention it, sir."

He rubbed his nose thoughtfully. "It was a trifle awkward. You had not authorised me to make direct enquiries of his lordship, unless he should raise the subject himself, yet I could not help feeling that there was something more to the matter than mere charity to a distant cousin. Lampeter's philanthropy is well-known, of course, but his benevolence usually takes the form of orphanages and schools, establishments of that nature, and I have never subscribed to the notion being bandied about that he is the Benefactor of the *Brig Minerva*. This was the first time I had heard of him bestowing a sum of money on an individual not of his immediate family. Your relationship is of the most distant kind, and not such as would even oblige him to acknowledge you, if he chose."

"It is a large sum of money to give away, too," Evie said. "His good works tended to be of the self-sustaining sort. The orphans lived on what they could grow or make, and the scholars paid something for their tuition. Fifteen thousand handed over to a smug husband is a different matter. Janey will not like it one bit."

"Janey? Oh, Lady Lampeter. No, she does not, seemingly. Indeed, this makes it even odder. I was sufficiently concerned that when I encountered him at my club recently, and alone, I asked him directly about it, and he admitted that it is his own money. He was shocked to discover that you are as yet unmarried and living in much reduced circumstances, and wished to do something to help you. There is no more to it than that. The money is held by his own lawyers, and will be handed over as soon as you marry. He also said that you may have the income from it at once, if you wish."

"I want nothing from him!" she said angrily.

"Hmm." He gazed at her over his spectacles. "Is there… something between you and his lordship, Miss Parfitt? Not a romantic entanglement, obviously, but—"

"Nothing at all! There is *nothing* between his family and mine, not friendship, not openness, not even an invitation to the tenants' Christmas ball. My mother was the over-worked and little-valued poor relation at Folkard Hall. After she died, the old countess used me as the sensible older child to watch her granddaughters. Oh, I benefited from the arrangement, for I joined the lessons with their governess, and learnt to ride and dance, but I was convenient, too. Then, once I was no longer needed, I was ignored. They treated me as if I did not exist, Mr Bradbrook, no longer fit company for the Folkards of Folkard Hall. So for Lord Lampeter to decide to be charitable towards me after all this time is the outside of enough!"

He nodded gravely. "I understand. You are bitter, and who could blame you? This money must seem like the greatest insult. Yet it would not be sensible to allow your hurt to overcome prudence. It is a generous offer, on his part, with no conditions attached. Perhaps Lampeter now sees how his family has wronged you, and wishes to make amends. A man may change over the years, as the carelessness of youth gives way to the sobriety of maturity. He may wish to correct the injustice of the past."

"Some injustice can never be corrected," she said, although with less heat, her anger subsiding in the face of Mr Bradbrook's reason. He was right, of course — it was madness to refuse a sum that would make her independent. It would give her the choice to live her life as she wished, to marry or not, and to keep both herself and Aunt Dodi in perfect comfort.

He said nothing, for perhaps he could see that she was beginning to consider the possibilities.

"I will think on all you have said," she said quietly, rising to leave. "Thank you for listening to me. You are a good, kind man, Mr

Bradbrook, and I understand why Mr Eliot Armitage and Mr Edward Folkard speak so highly of you."

"No need to thank me, my dear. There is nothing I enjoy more than the company of a charming young lady, and you bring a little brightness into my dull day."

She laughed. "You are a flatterer, sir. Mrs Bradbrook tells me that you were a notorious rake at one time, but I find that hard to believe. A flirt, perhaps, but—"

"Indeed, it is true enough, although those days are behind me now. I have grown fearsomely respectable of late."

"And you simply... stopped? You lost interest in women?"

"No, no! A man never loses interest in women until he is shrouded and coffined, but that is a general admiration of all the wonderful qualities of womankind. The wandering from one woman to another, as the bee flies from flower to flower — that is a different matter, and I did a great deal of that in my youth. Then I met my dear Kate, and I never needed any other woman after. She is everything to me. One may still admire, but as for me, I shall never stray."

This was such a new idea to Evie that she was mesmerised — a rake who could abandon his wild ways, and settle down in faithful and loving married harmony? She had not even known such a thing was possible.

"Can a man truly change his character?" she said wonderingly. "Can a rake reform, or were you especially fortunate in your wife?"

"Kate is one in a million, it is true," he said, smiling warmly, "but there is more to it than simply meeting the right woman. There are two kinds of rake, Miss Parfitt. One kind enjoys the thrill of the chase, the challenge of seducing a victim, and the greater the challenge, the more he will delight in it. The virtuous innocent is his target, and he cares nothing for the ruin of her reputation. Once he has won her, he loses interest and moves on to fresher prey. That kind will never reform his ways, for marriage does not give him the excitement he is seeking. But the other kind glories in women — their beauty, their gentle natures, their soft skin and lustrous eyes, all their feminine charms. He loves women in all their magnificent variety, but he delights in finding one in particular with whom he can be at ease, a friend he can talk to. That kind, if he is lucky, will meet a woman who encompasses all the wonders of womanhood in combination, and if he can win her, he will be contented for life. I am of this second kind." A slight hesitation. "And so it is with Eliot, I believe."

Evie left the room in thoughtful mood.

~~~~~

In Dublin, Eliot made contact with Mr Neate again, to explain all that he had learnt and to ask his advice.

"We are no nearer to finding these elusive diamonds," he said, "and now we have a new twist, in that two of the Tranter brothers appear to be the owners of Barantine's business. Far from improving my ward's financial position, I seem to have reduced her to poverty."

Neate laughed. "No, her father did that. This will have to be tested in court, of course, but the intention is clear and it is a debt of honour. The title to the business was staked in a game of chance and the Tranters won it honourably, or so they say. Even if they did not, if Barantine did not complain at the time, then there is nothing to be done now. They have the papers in their possession, with
~~~~~

Barantine's signature and date, and assuming there is no forgery involved, I should regard it as quite settled. Take them back to London with you and let the lawyers see to it. No, it is the diamonds that make me anxious. How much were they worth?"

"Several thousand pounds," Eliot said.

"Five thousand seven hundred pounds," Folkard said. "Barantine also had close to two thousand in cash, but he lost that in his gaming frenzy."

"And none of the diamonds were offered for sale to any jeweller in the town?" Neate said.

"So they say, but if they were stolen and sold surreptitiously, they would not admit to it," Eliot said.

"If that had happened, word would have leaked out, and would have come to someone's ears," Neate said. "I have asked a few likely fellows about stolen diamonds, but no one has heard anything, and these are the sort of people one might expect to have caught such rumours."

"You mix with some interesting types," Eliot said.

Neate grinned. "It goes with the job, sir."

"But what am I to do now?" Eliot said plaintively. "If the diamonds are not to be found, must I tamely go back to London and tell Violet she is not a great heiress at all?"

"The diamonds appear not to be in Dublin," Neate said thoughtfully. "Nor were they recovered from the *Minerva*, either from the possessions of those who drowned or from the ship itself, yet it seems to me that the answer must lie on the ship. If Mr Barantine had disposed of them before boarding or even aboard ship, that might well have been discussed openly after the ship departed from Dublin."

"There were survivors, were there not?" Eliot said. "One of them might have overheard something, perhaps."

"Perhaps. Two were part of the crew, the Second Mate and the deck boy. Both were interviewed exhaustively for the inquiry into the sinking, and every last moment of their time was accounted for, and every word spoken or heard was related. Mr Willerton-Forbes and Captain Edgerton also talked to them several times, as part of their work for the Benefactor. I do not believe there is anything still to be discovered from them. Mr Ellsworthy received an injury to the head and remembers nothing of the voyage at all."

"Might one of them have stolen the diamonds?" Folkard said. "They could then have swum to shore after the wreckage with the jewels in a pocket, and no one any the wiser."

"Unlikely, because if the ship had not hit that rock, there would have been a hue and cry as soon as Mr Barantine woke and found the diamonds missing, and the ship and crew would all have been searched," Neate said. "Also, none of the survivors lives in a style that would suggest they had ever had such a fortune. The Second Mate spent his bounty from the Benefactor within a few months, and is now back at work. The deck boy bought a small farm for his family, where they live in a quiet way. Mr Ellsworthy bought himself a horse and some new clothes, but otherwise lives a modest life as secretary for a local ship-owner. But Mr Ellsworthy knew Mr Barantine in Dublin, and so he might have some memories that would confirm that the Tranters had won the business."

"It is not unknown for memory to return, at least in part, even after a severe blow to the head," Folkard said. "He might recall something of the voyage by now."

"Well, we had better talk to this Ellsworthy, I suppose," Eliot said with a sigh. "Is he a Dublin man?"

"He originates from Carlisle, but he is presently to be found in Cornwall, precisely where the *Brig Minerva* deposited him."

"*Cornwall?* How the deuce are we to get to Cornwall from here?"

Neate smiled. "Why, by ship, of course, Mr Armitage, and there is one due in Dublin Port in three days which happens to be calling at Penzance. That is very close to Pendower, where Mr Ellsworthy lives."

"But my carriage awaits me at Holyhead!" Eliot cried. "This is impossible! I am happy to search for Violet's diamonds, but I did not bargain for traipsing from one end of the country to the other."

"Cheer up!" Folkard said, giving him a hearty slap on the back. "It is an adventure, my friend. You may write to your coachman at Holyhead and have him take the carriage back to London, or wait for us somewhere along the way — Salisbury, say. We shall just have to suffer the indignity of a hired post-chaise." He laughed. "Do not look so miserable — this is fun, and you have the pleasure of a longer sea voyage to look forward to."

Eliot groaned.

"Dublin to Penzance? I should say it is no more than eighteen hours—" Neate said.

"Oh God!"

"—if the winds are favourable. But you will find the ship very comfortable, I am sure. It is quite a famous vessel."

"But is it safe?" Eliot said.

Neate laughed. "Oh, very safe. It *did* have a small accident once upon a time, but it has been fully restored to seaworthiness. It is called the *Brig Minerva.*"

"Oh God! Oh God! Oh God!" Eliot wailed, head in hands.

But the others just laughed at him.

~~~~~

Eliot never wanted to see another ship as long as he lived. The promised eighteen-hour journey had turned into four and twenty of the most hideous hours he had ever experienced. He lay in his bunk being banged against first one wall and then the other and then the strap that prevented him from being tossed onto the floor, until he hardly knew what was coming next. His stomach refused to believe it was empty and kept trying to unburden itself. He wished he could die at once, and be done with such torture. Folkard agreed that the sea was wild, and he felt slightly queasy himself, but the Tranter brothers strolled about the ship in the greatest good humour, admonished Eliot for succumbing like a girl to a slight swell, and ate and drank their way through his share of the provender. Even Strood, normally an indifferent traveller, pronounced the journey tolerable.

It would have been ironic, if Eliot had been of a mind to appreciate it, to consider that he lay hoping for death in a vessel which had already brought so much death. It seemed ghoulish to send the *Minerva* to sea again after all its travails, but it had been successfully refloated and taken back to Southampton, where the
~~~~~

damage was found to be easily repaired. Within a few months it was back in service, for a ship was still a ship, after all, and too valuable for sentimentality.

When they arrived in Penzance, Eliot's friends half-carried him the short distance to the hotel, where he lay in bed quietly until the world had stopped lurching up and down, and he began to feel some confidence that he might, after all, survive. By the evening of the second day, after a stroll about the town and a good dinner, he felt himself fully restored and ready to contemplate the prospect of moving on the following day. A pair of post-chaises was procured, the hotel settled with and by ten o'clock they were on their way, and if the road was winding and muddy and hideously rutted, at least there was no water beneath them.

Pendower was a small, picturesque coastal village, boasting a single inn and no more than a handful of habitations larger than a fisherman's cottage. The largest of these was Pendower House, where Ellsworthy resided. It was the very place where his unconscious form had been carried after the sinking and where he had slowly healed from his injuries, and there he still was. The house belonged to the local land-owners, the Chandrys, but was currently also the residence of a baron, and so they were greeted by liveried footmen and a troop of grooms as their post-chaise drew to a halt.

Eliot had written ahead to inform Ellsworthy of their purpose, and he was awaiting them at the door. He was a nondescript sort of man, with nothing about him to excite attention or command admiration. His features would blend into a crowd, and his attire, while clearly well-made, was worn in the careless manner of one with no aspirations towards style or fashion. He received them graciously, however, without undue deference, and with the well-turned phrasing that in different company would cause him to be mistaken for a gentleman. Only a slight burr betrayed his humble origins. Perhaps the noble company in which he now found himself had infused the humble clerk from Carlisle with a little society polish.

He showed them into a sizable book room, where a young woman was setting out glasses and platters of pastries. She was too well-dressed to be a servant, and Ellsworthy introduced her as a daughter of the house, Miss Virginia Chandry.

"You will not object to Miss Chandry's presence, I am sure," Ellsworthy said. "I have no secrets from her."

No wonder he had stayed where he was, with such a temptation. She was pretty rather than beautiful, but with a pleasing figure and the clear, unselfconscious gaze of a woman who knew her own worth. After offering them a very good Madeira and placing the pastries within their reach, she withdrew to a chair in a corner and calmly picked up her sewing.

Ellsworthy remembered the Tranter brothers, and made polite enquiries about their family before turning to Eliot. He seemed relaxed, but Eliot thought there was some wariness about him as he explained again the reason for their visit.

"I understand that you remember nothing of the voyage, but you might, perhaps, have some information from Dublin which would assist us. Perhaps Barantine mentioned that he had gambled away his business? Or was he unusually cast down before boarding?"

"Not in the least," Ellsworthy said. "Indeed, he seemed to me to be in very good spirits, and he mentioned nothing of his business to me, that I can recall. But then, he was an habitual gambler, and such people take their losses lightly. They always think they will come about, although they rarely do. It was Mr Newbold who mentioned the matter. He was very distressed that his friend had been so reckless with his livelihood."

"He told you that Barantine had lost the title to the business?"

"He did."

"Hmm... that confirms all that the Mr Tranters have told us. That is helpful, thank you. And I suppose neither of them told you what had happened to the diamonds Barantine bought in Dublin? I do not expect you to know, for we have asked that question of every likely person in Dublin, to no avail. He certainly had them in his possession when he left the lawyer's office, but they have vanished into thin air."

"He did not tell me, but then he did not need to. I knew precisely what he had done with the diamonds, for he gambled them all away to me."

"What!" Eliot cried, sitting more upright. "He *gambled* them... then you have them?"

"Unfortunately not." Ellsworthy pulled a small velvet pouch from a pocket and shook the contents onto a table, perhaps eight or nine uncut stones. "This is all that remains of them."

"Ah," Eliot said. "You had better tell us all about it, Mr Ellsworthy."

21: Obligation

The story Ellsworthy told was all too plausible. Having enjoyed playing piquet against him, Barantine wished to continue but Ellsworthy refused to take his vowels.

"I know it is bad form, but I have this terrible fear of causing a man to be swept up in a frenzy and lose his entire fortune, so I will only play against someone who can place physical coins on the table at the start of play, when they are calm and sober. Then I will play until one or other of us has won the entire amount, or until the gentleman wishes to stop. For several days Mr Barantine asked me to relent, but I would not. But then, the day the *Minerva* arrived in port, he came to me privately in my room at Kilrannan House, and placed a bag of diamonds on the table before me. *'I have no more coins,'* he said, *'but I have these, which are of the same physical nature.'* He told me they had a value close to six thousand pounds, and he was quite ready to lose the entire amount, so desirous was he of playing against me. I knew nothing then of his wagering his business, so I accepted his offer, and we played in his room, and I came away six thousand pounds the richer, gentleman, won honestly, for I would not stoop to cheat. But you will have to take my word for that, since no one else was in the room except for Mr Barantine's man, whose name was Crick, and he is drowned, too."

"I believe you," said the elder Tranter. "I watched you play over several nights, and I never saw the least sign of anything untoward in your play."

"Aye, I will vouch for it, too," his brother said. "We watch newcomers like hawks, as you may imagine, especially — and you will forgive me for saying this, Ellsworthy, I am sure — especially those who are quiet and unobtrusive, as you are. But your play was always above reproach."

"Barantine would never have taken him on if there had been anything havey-cavey about him," the elder Tranter said.

"It matters not, since the diamonds are all but gone," Eliot said edgily. "You have sold them, I suppose?"

"I did not know what to do with them at first," Ellsworthy said. "Mr Barantine said he hoped I would keep them, so that the next time we met he might perhaps win some of them back. I planned to look for work in Southampton, and he had a shop in Winchester, so it would have been easy to meet. It would have been a great pleasure to us both, for he was a fine player."

"If he was so good, how was it that you won everything?" Eliot said sharply.

"We had played for twelve hours, and we were both exhausted," Ellsworthy said, his voice soft by contrast. "The spoils were fairly evenly divided at that point, but he suggested one last *partie*, winner to take all, and so that was what we did. It could just as easily have gone the other way."

"And again, we have to take your word for it," Eliot said.

Ellsworthy gave a rueful smile. "You are suspicious, and I do not blame you. This is precisely why I was unsure what to do. I am only a clerk, gentlemen, raised in an orphanage and living on my wits and what work I can find. Who would believe that Mr Barantine willingly gambled such a prize, or that I had won it honestly? And there was his daughter to consider. It seemed to me that I should return the diamonds to her, if I could. I wrote to an old friend who is an attorney, and he came to see me here."

"Mr Titmuss!" Miss Chandry cried from her corner. "I remember him coming, for it pleased me that you were not friendless in the world."

He smiled at her, and the affection between them was easy to read. "I am not friendless, no. He came here and I told him of my dilemma, and asked how I could return the diamonds to Miss Barantine, but he advised against it."

"The devil he did!" Eliot said.

"He said it would raise questions and draw attention to my unorthodox acquisition of the gems, which was exactly what I wished to avoid. He pointed out that Miss Barantine was a great heiress and would hardly miss such a sum, great as it seemed to me. But still, I did not feel comfortable keeping the stones myself, so I gave them to my friend to sell and distribute the proceeds to charitable endeavours. I kept a very few stones, enough to make Miss Chandry a necklace one day."

"You can furnish me with the direction of this Titmuss person, I suppose?" Eliot said.

"Of course. He will verify all that I have told you of his part in these affairs." He hesitated, gazing thoughtfully at Eliot. "Was my friend correct in his assumption, Mr Armitage? Is it true that Miss

Barantine has a great fortune of her own, and would not miss the paltry sum of six thousand pounds?"

"There was no fortune," Eliot said curtly. "Everything was tied up in the business, which Mr Bartholomew Tranter now owns. All my ward now possesses is one thousand pounds from the Benefactor, a few necklaces and bracelets and her clothes."

Ellsworthy's eyes widened in shock. "She has nothing?"

Miss Chandry laid down her sewing and moved forward to lay a hand on Ellsworthy's shoulder. "She has her own attractions, I am sure. Is she pretty, Mr Armitage? Is she graceful and well-spoken and accomplished? Is she charming or clever? Can she sew and cook and keep house?"

"She is a great beauty and much admired," Eliot admitted.

"Then she will do well enough, fortune or no," she said firmly. "Money is not everything. A woman may be penniless and yet find her place in the world, respected and loved by those who know her well."

At once Evie's face rose unbidden in Eliot's mind, and he could not deny the wisdom of Miss Chandry's words. Evie was penniless, and yet she was respected and loved. Even before this mysterious dowry rumour, she had found her place in the world, living contentedly with her aunt in Winchester. Dear, uncomplaining Evie! The thought of her softened his disposition towards Ellsworthy.

"Will you take what is left of the jewels to Miss Barantine?" Ellsworthy said earnestly. "It is not much but—"

"No," Eliot said quietly, with a smile. "You came by them honestly, and they are yours to do with as you please. Have them made into a necklace for Miss Chandry, and be assured that I shall take care of Miss Barantine. She is my ward, after all, and my responsibility."

"But you must take this to her," Ellsworthy said, pulling another velvet pouch from his pocket. "Mr Barantine promised his daughter the finest of the diamonds for her own. Before we played, he gave it into my care for safe keeping, in case he should gamble that away too. I was to return it to him when we reached Southampton, when he was sure it would be safe for him to have it again." He opened the pouch and slid out a single, huge stone. "Pray tell Miss Barantine that her father did not forget his promise to her."

~~~~~

They stayed one night in the inn at Pendower, dining at Pendower House with the baron and his numerous relations, before setting off on the long journey back to London with their two post-chaises, one for Eliot, Folkard and the Tranter brothers, and another for the two valets and the luggage. The bad roads to Holyhead had been miserable, with the prospect of the sea voyage ahead of him to depress his spirits even further, but the bad roads out of Cornwall troubled him less.

Partly this resulted from the presence of the Tranters, who always had some little anecdote or jest to beguile away the tedium of travelling, and were happy to relieve him of coins at their evening whist table.

The other part of it was the little puzzles that Ellsworthy had inadvertently set him, not so much about the diamonds but the man himself. He was raised in an orphanage in Carlisle and lived by his wits, so he said, and yet he was well-spoken and clearly well-educated. When the gentlemen had gathered round the baron after dinner and the conversation had, by some chance, turned to Henry
~~~~~

VIII and the dissolution of the monasteries, Ellsworthy had talked with both eloquence and erudition, and without a trace of the working man's burr he had affected earlier. He was a first-rate card player, yet the Tranters were convinced he was no sharp. And what to make of a man who earned his living as a secretary on a salary of a few hundred a year if he was lucky, who *gave away* diamonds worth six thousand pounds?

From time to time, Eliot drew forth his pocket book, wherein Ellsworthy had inscribed the name and direction of the attorney who had assisted him - *'Wm. Titmuss Esq, Harebell Cottage, St Peter's Cross, Hants'.* And how did an orphan from Carlisle come to know an attorney in Hampshire? Casual questions had elicited the information that he had left Carlisle at an early age, lived in various northern towns before settling in Liverpool, whence he had made his way to Dublin. No mention there of Hampshire. He had been on friendly terms with the Duke of Falconbury, too, and how had that come about? A more unlikely comradeship was hard to envisage.

With such thoughts the miles flew past, and with each milepost, each toll gate, each overnight stay his spirits rose, for soon he would see Evie again. He could scarcely wait.

~~~~~

The clock on the mantel in Mr Bradbrook's book room ticked mournfully, in keeping with Evie's mood. She did not want Lord Lampeter's fifteen thousand pounds, but since it was being forced upon her, she would ensure some good came of it.

"You will have an income of six hundred pounds a year, Miss Parfitt," the solicitor said. "When you marry, naturally your husband will assume the management of your little nest egg, but until that happy day, someone from the bank will deliver the interest to you
~~~~~

personally, if you wish, or you may authorise a gentleman — Mr Bradbrook, say — to collect it for you. Sign here, if you please... and again here. Thank you. Should you prefer to receive your interest quarterly or only on Lady Day?"

"Quarterly, if you please, but I should like it to be paid to my aunt in Winchester," Evie said.

"I daresay that can be arranged," the solicitor said uncertainly, with a quick glance at Lord Lampeter, who gave a brief nod. "Yes, that can be arranged, although... but never mind. My lord, may I trouble you for your signature also? And again here. So obliging of your lordship. And Mr Bradbrook, sir? Just here... and here. And I shall add my own signature. Excellent. Such a pleasure to do business with you, my lord, Miss Parfitt, Mr Bradbrook. This copy is yours, Miss Parfitt, and I shall keep the other safe. So very much obliged... greatest pleasure... good day to you all. A very good day."

Lord Lampeter rose to leave also, his face solemn. "I am pleased that you are willing to accept my gift in the spirit in which it is offered, Evie, in memory of your mother. Alas, poor Hermione! We should have done more for her at the time."

"Indeed you should," Evie said, icy spears of anger making her voice harsh. "Do not make the mistake of supposing that I accept it willingly, my lord, but since I cannot prevent you from bestowing it upon me, I may as well make use of it to free my aunt from want."

"That is commendable," Lord Lampeter said gruffly, "but when you marry, your husband may have other ideas on the subject."

"I shall take no husband." Even as she said the words, grief tore through her... no husband, no Eliot, no kisses that melted her insides like summer butter. Never again.

He grunted. "Well, that is as you choose, of course. I hoped this money would make it easier for you to find a husband, but if it pleases you to help your aunt, I shall not cavil at that." He looked at Evie thoughtfully. "I hope we can be friends, at least." When she said nothing, he went on, "Come for dinner tonight. No, not tonight, for we dine out... tomorrow, then. You too, Bradbrook, and your wife. We sit down at seven."

"That might not suit Lady Lampeter," Evie said.

"My wishes prevail in my own house, I hope," he said, frowning. "Until tomorrow, then." And without another word, he was gone.

Mr Bradbrook chuckled. "A man used to having his own way, I fancy, or else his wife is excessively compliant."

"Not Janey!" Evie said, laughing. "She arrived at Folkard Hall as the poor relation — they always had some distant cousin or other living there, for the convenience of having someone to order about. Within a day, she had taken me in the strongest dislike. Within a month she had her claws into Henry, and within a year, or not much more, she had married him, become a countess and produced an heir. She will not be pleased at the invitation."

"Oh dear! Well, it is short notice and we shall have to cry off from the Iversons tomorrow, but Kate will certainly want to dine at Folkard House. We have never crossed the threshold before, you know, so she will be very much obliged to you. Miss Parfitt..." He stopped, eyeing her uncertainly.

"Please say what is on your mind, sir."

"Very well, then. I will not enquire what lies at the root of this business, and the world will no doubt see it as just another instance of Lampeter's benevolence, but fifteen thousand pounds is an excessive amount of goodwill towards a very distant relation, no matter how many slights may have accrued over the years. There is more than just neglect involved, to my mind, and your strong dislike of the man speaks to some deeper issue. However, that is your secret to keep, my dear. But there is one matter I would ask you to consider carefully. Are you sure you fully appreciate the implications of this money that Lord Lampeter has put forward? Bear in mind that he has not made the capital sum over to you, only the interest, and if you should decide to marry—"

"I shall not!"

"But if you should, he will have the ability to influence your choice. Any suitor will have to apply to him for your dowry, and he will be able to decide how much to settle on you, or even to refuse altogether. It gives him great power over you."

"I am more concerned by the obligation to meet him socially," she said ruefully. "Having successfully ignored me for thirteen years, it would have been a kindness to have ignored me for another thirteen, and thirteen more after that, but now the acquaintance is unavoidable, I fear. I thank you for your warning, however, but it is unnecessary, for I shall never marry, I believe."

He gave her a rueful smile. "So I thought, once, until I met my beloved Kate, so do not set your mind entirely against the possibility. One never knows what turn of events may occur. However, if you choose to embrace spinsterhood, at least you may do so in some comfort. It is a relief to me that you now have some independence, and you are sensible enough not to be duped by fortune-hunters — or Roger, come to that. He is in debt again, the foolish boy, and this time I am determined not to rescue him from his own improvidence. Since his difficulties are of too urgent a nature to wait for Violet to come of age, I was afraid he might cast his greedy eyes on your fifteen thousand."

"Oh dear!" Evie said. "I am so sorry. He seems to have a knack of getting into scrapes, but I assure you I am in no danger from him. What will become of him?"

"I have given him a week's grace to come about, if he can. If not, the army may be the making of him, but I do *not* want him idling away his time in town any longer, that much is certain. His character is too weak to resist the expensive temptations here. If only I had not promised his mama to raise him as my heir! It was a foolishly sentimental vow, and now I am bound by it."

"Must one be bound for ever in such a case? Is it a matter of honour? Or could you perhaps reach some amicable agreement with Mr Roger, a fixed sum made over to him to discharge all obligation? He might be happier to have the power of purchasing a small property of his own, where he may live his own life without feeling that he has to meet your expectations, and you would surely be happier to lose the constant drain on your purse."

"What an excellent idea, Miss Parfitt. I shall suggest it to him."

~~~~~

'Green Street, London, a Sunday or possibly Monday in September, but do not ask me the date, for I cannot tell you. I know I wrote to you only a few days ago, but here I am at midnight or thereabouts writing again, for I was just dropping off to sleep when a carriage rattled past the house making such a racket that I was wide awake at once. It is now sitting motionless two doors down from here, awaiting its customer, and since it will disturb me again as soon as it starts into motion, I shall take advantage of my wakefulness to bore you with my nocturnal ramblings. Now that I am a woman of
~~~~~

means, I find myself looking askance at the gentlemen who dance attendance on me. Is it some aspect of me that draws them, or is it my money? After all, I am thirty years old, without great beauty or wit or accomplishments, so what else could it be? Worse, to my mind, is that they are none of them such as to set my heart racing. Mr Hawes greets me with poetic effusions and then talks incessantly about his estate in Staffordshire and his summer in Brighton with a viscount. Mr Durham says nothing at all, but gazes at me with huge puppy eyes. Mr Whyte's shirt points are frayed and his waistcoat stained. Young Mr Iverson, who is eight years my junior, blushes and stammers whenever I speak to him, although I forgive him for he is the most graceful dancer imaginable. As for Mr Carver, who is old enough to be my father, he speaks of my manifold attractions, but his eyes stray downwards in the most disconcerting manner.'

Here she stopped, chewing the feather of the quill pensively. The real problem was that whenever she thought of them, her mind was immediately filled with the more agreeable image of Mr Eliot Armitage. He was handsome, he was articulate, he was sensible and he was always immaculately attired. And he was in love with her, her heart whispered. Eliot cared nothing for her dowry. But she could not trust him, and so that was that, she told herself briskly, and not the slightest need to mention him to her aunt.

'We attended Morning Service today or perhaps it was yesterday at St George's, which is a fine building indeed. London has some splendid churches, it has to be said. The sermon was not so interesting as at Grosvenor Chapel, but there was a splendid turnout of the nobility in all its variety. We saw Lord and Lady Lampeter there, for it is their nearest church, and Lady L even inclined her head an inch or two in my direction, which is progress. If I stay for another year, I might extract a bow from her, and if I am very fortunate, in

five years or so she might even smile on me. I do not depend on it, however. Her pelisse was far too overwrought for church, in my opinion, but she wore the most ravishing—'

The night-time peace was shattered by a high-pitched scream of such ferocity that Evie dropped her pen, splattering ink all over the paper.

Then, as she waited, heart racing, to hear more, there were raised male voices from far below, another scream, less intense, and then, terrifyingly, a great crash.

Evie jumped up and ran for the door, grabbing a candlestick and the poker as she went.

22: A Change Of Fortune

As Evie flew down the stairs, the sounds of disturbance grew louder. Another crash, more yelling, a female voice shrieking "Stop it, stop it at once!" and then an ominous silence. She rounded the final turn of the stair to find a scene of chaos in the hall. A console was overturned, its vases of flowers and porcelain bowl of calling cards dashed to pieces on the floor, their contents scattered. In the midst of the debris, a man, incongruously garbed in Mr Roger Bradbrook's garish greatcoat, lay motionless. Henry sat astride him, one fisted hand raised as if to strike. Violet, cloaked and bonneted, cowered in a corner, a candelabrum wobbling in her hand.

"Violet, whatever is going on?" Evie said, keeping to the bottom stair to avoid walking barefoot across shards of broken porcelain. "Why are you not in bed?"

Violet gave a convulsive sob, but simply shook her head.

A deep male voice said, "Running away. *Scoundrel!*"

Henry could speak? In all the unfathomable oddity of the situation, that was the oddest of all, and for a moment Evie could think of nothing else. But then she took in the band box and portmanteaux beside the door, Violet dressed for travel, Mr Roger's distinctive hat rolled into a corner... and she remembered the carriage waiting outside.

"You are *eloping?"* she cried incredulously. "Good God, Violet, you are the most foolish child I have ever met!"

The sobs intensified. Henry slowly lowered the raised fist, and cautiously stood up. The figure on the floor groaned, but did not move. Even though she could not see his face properly, for it was covered in blood, she knew it was Mr Roger, who had presumably thought to meet his debts by rushing Violet to Scotland for a hasty marriage.

The door from the service stairs opened and the valet and footman peered out uncertainly, one bearing a lamp, the other a poker. Behind them, the flickering light of a single candle illumined the housekeeper's head, incongruously swathed in a very feminine lace cap. From the main stairs, Mr Bradbrook descended with rapid steps.

"What has happened here?" he said.

"Henry has just prevented Mr Roger from eloping with Violet," Evie said.

"I see," he said, in such calm tones that she wondered if he had even understood, but his sharp eyes raked the scene and he must have seen the truth of it.

Behind him, from the half-landing, came Mrs Bradbrook's worried voice.

Mr Bradbrook turned to her. "Ah, Kate, will you take Violet back to her room, if you please? Violet, go upstairs now, you will go nowhere tonight. William, help Henry carry this fool of a son of mine into the book room. Drake, some more lights. Mrs Wickmore, can you organise a couple of housemaids to clean up this mess? Miss Parfitt, I—"

"A bowl of water and cloths first, Mrs Wickmore," Evie said briskly. "We must tend to Mr Roger's injuries."

Mr Bradbrook opened his mouth to speak, then thought better of it. Henry bent down and lifted Mr Roger single-handedly into his arms, then carried him into the book room, the footman scuttling behind with the lamp. Mr Roger groaned again. Henry looked at Evie for instructions on where to lay his burden.

"On the floor, Henry. Better not get blood on the furnishings. Yes, just there. Mr Bradbrook, there is a carriage waiting on the street. Perhaps you could—?"

"Of course. William, go and get dressed. Oh, and get that luggage out of the hall. Miss Parfitt, is Roger badly injured?"

"I cannot say until this blood is cleaned up. Ah, well done, Mrs Wickmore, that was quick."

"It's not very hot, madam, but—"

"No matter. It will do. Thank you, I can manage now."

"But if he starts to come round, madam, he might—"

"I have Henry here," Evie said. The housekeeper withdrew, and Evie began to clean Mr Roger's face. "There now, it is just his nose, Mr Bradbrook. No great harm."

"Thank God! I was afraid... well, Henry, you are such a great big fellow, I thought for a moment you might have killed him. Not that he would not have deserved it, mind. Fool of a boy! Miss Parfitt, shall you mind if I go and make sure that carriage is sent away? It would not do to have awkward questions asked by the neighbours, and the longer it stays on the street—"

"By all means," Evie said. "Henry is protection enough."

For a while the only sound in the room was Evie dipping a cloth into the bowl, squeezing, mopping blood... dip, squeeze, mop. Henry had taken up a position where he could watch Mr Roger's face as it emerged from its mask of blood, and there he stood, motionless.

"I think you must have known this was coming, Henry," Evie said after a while. "You did not undress and go to bed like everyone else, so you must have had some inkling."

She glanced up at him, and he nodded.

"You have been watching her more carefully than I have. Of course, no one notices a footman. There you stand in the background, wherever Violet goes, seeing all the little signs that I should have seen." Guilt assailed her. It was her job, after all, the one responsibility for which she was employed, to protect Violet from unscrupulous fortune hunters, and she had failed. She had been so wrapped up in her own affairs that she had taken her eyes off Violet. "You have done well, Henry. Thank you."

He nodded an acknowledgement.

She paused in her ministrations to look fully at him. "Oh, you are silent again? I should dearly like to know why you choose not to speak when you are fully capable of it, but only if you wish to tell me of it."

Still he said nothing, and she turned back to her patient. She had supposed that he had been born mute, or perhaps a childhood illness had rendered him so. She had even toyed with the idea that he had been punished as a slave with some hideous mutilation. But that he should voluntarily remain silent was not an idea which had crossed her mind.

He cleared his throat. "I was insolent." She spun round to face him. "As a boy. Master told me... be silent or he cut my tongue out. I was silent. Like it better. Habit now. Except... angry. Talk then."

She smiled at him. "I am honoured by your confidence, Henry, but no one will learn your secret from me."

He nodded again, with a little smile.

~~~~~

OCTOBER

The streets of London were the most welcome sight Eliot had seen for an age. Lights shone warmly through the dusk, casting a golden shimmer across rain-slick cobbles, and even the pie-seller's calls sounded melodious, for soon, very soon now, he would see Evie again and this strange hollow place inside him would not ache so badly.

The chaise stopped first at Green Street to deposit Folkard and his luggage, where the footman told them everyone was out.

"Dining at Mr and Mrs Iverson's, sir, with a ball to follow."

Folkard's face registered disappointment. "What a pity! Are *all* of them out, William? Miss Parfitt too? Oh, well... I suppose there is no dinner for me, either."

"You are expected, sir. Mrs Garman has a roast capon for you, and some damson tarts."

"Capon," Folkard said disconsolately. "I am not fond of capon."
~~~~~

Eliot could not help laughing at his dejection. "Come round to Grosvenor Square, if you like. Mrs Carpenter will have something more substantial than capon, and we will have a four for whist after."

"I had sooner be dancing at the Iversons'," Folkard said, but he willingly got back into the carriage.

Eliot had written ahead to prepare the household for his arrival with the Tranter brothers, so there were hot baths awaiting them and an excellent dinner. There was also a veritable mountain of letters, most of which he set aside to deal with later, but there was one hand-delivered from Aunt Bradbrook, which he opened at once.

'Eliot, Lake tells me you are expected today, and if it be so, you will find us at the Iversons this evening. I mentioned your possible return to Mrs I and she, good soul that she is, said you would be most welcome to join them, if you are not too fatigued from your journey. The dancing commences at nine. Kate Bradbrook.'

"There you are, Folkard. You shall have your dance at the Iversons' house after all."

He looked dubious. "Your coachman will not thank you for dragging him out again."

Eliot laughed, and pulled aside the curtain to reveal the square. "You see that house opposite, with all the torches? That is the Iversons' house. If I were to open the window, we could hear the music, I expect. Can you walk so far without fatigue, do you think?"

Folkard laughed and thought he could probably manage it without exhausting himself. Within a very few minutes, therefore, they were disposing of hats, gloves, coats and canes in the Iversons' hall, mounting the stairs to the upper floor and being announced.

No one noticed them. A wall of noise assaulted their ears, of music and loud voices and shrieks of laughter, and the overheated air washed over them. The Iversons had long since abandoned their post at the head of the stairs to receive guests, and the room was too crowded for Eliot to catch sight of them, but one of the sons loomed up before them, greeted them affably, murmured, "You know everyone, I am sure, Armitage," and disappeared back into the throng.

"There she is!" Folkard cried, his face alight with excitement.

And there she was indeed. Eliot's heart lurched at the sight of Evie spinning and leaping down the lines of dancers with another of the Iverson sons, smiling — no, *laughing* — at him, as he gazed at her with an expression of adoration. They reached the bottom of the set and stopped, glowing, delighted with themselves. Dear God, she was so extraordinarily beautiful that Eliot could barely breathe. And her gown — in full evening dress she was a sight to behold, her silk skirts swirling around those long legs of hers, and spangles in her hair. Folkard waved vigorously to her, and her gaze settled on him momentarily, then flickered to Eliot and onwards, to take in the Tranter brothers. Then she turned her lovely eyes back to her partner, and Eliot was left with the bitter ashes of grief and longing and jealousy.

He distracted himself by taking the Tranters around the room, introducing them here and there, finding them partners for the next dance. He supposed he should dance himself, but he was too agitated. All he could do was to lean against one of the marble pilasters which ornamented the room and watch Evie and wallow in his own misery. He had wanted to see her dance, and now that his wish had been granted he found that it brought him no pleasure at all. After the Iverson boy, and he could not have been much above twenty, she danced with a fop, then a shabby sort of fellow and then with Folkard. Then there was an older man who leered at her in a way that made Eliot want to hit him very hard. He knew he should leave, or at least take himself off to the card room, but he could not tear his eyes from her. Sometimes her gaze fell on him, her expression puzzled, but then she would turn back to her partner, all smiles. It tore at his insides, and he had no idea what to do about it.

"Armitage? How are you, old friend?"

"Hmm? Oh, Berringham... I am well. And you?"

"Perfectly fit, but very much in need of one of your little parties, old friend. Lucy has gone off to Gloucestershire to produce the heir and I— Are you listening to me, Armitage? Who are you glowering at? Ah, Lampeter's little secret, eh? She's not my style, but—"

Eliot turned his attention full onto his friend. "What do you *want,* Berringham?"

"I told you, an invitation to one of your discreet little parties."

Puzzled, Eliot blinked at him. It was so long since he had thought about his old habits that he was momentarily taken aback. "Oh... no more parties. Not of that type, at least."

"So Lucy was right — you *are* looking to be a tenant for life! Who would have thought it?" He chuckled. "I wish you joy, Armitage. Lord, you succumbing to matrimony! Whatever is the world coming to?"

Still laughing, he drifted away, and Eliot went back to watching Evie.

"Eliot? How was your journey?" It was Aunt Bradbrook, her head tipped to one side quizzically.

"Oh... we survived it, despite the best endeavours of the Irish Sea."

"Did you meet with success?"

"Success?"

"Violet's diamonds — did you find them?"

"Oh... well, yes and no. Long story." That brought him back to himself with a crash. There was another cause for misery, for his news would distress them all. "How is Violet? I have not seen her yet."

"She is well enough, but she is staying with a friend in Richmond for a few days. Also a long story, if you must know. She and Roger— Eliot, are you listening to me?"

"Hmm?"

"Oh, Eliot, do go and *talk* to Evie, instead of standing here watching her and looking miserable."

But he could not, and after a while he sought out his hosts to thank them for the hospitality he had barely noticed, and then quietly crept home.

~~~~~

"Do you mean that Violet is entirely penniless?" Evie's voice was sharp with distress.

They were gathered in Uncle Bradbrook's book room on the morning after the Iversons' ball, just the Bradbrooks, Evie and Eliot himself. His valet had brought him the news of Violet's failed elopement with his shaving water, his eyes gleaming with excitement. For the servants it was just another titbit of gossip to exclaim over in the basement, but to Eliot it was one more
~~~~~

manifestation of his utter failure as a guardian. Who would have expected that the care of one young lady would be so difficult?

"Not quite penniless," Eliot said, spreading his hands helplessly. "She has the thousand pounds bestowed on her by the Benefactor, and the contents of the Bruton Street house. Her gowns, her carriage, her jewels. Everything her father gave her."

"That does not provide an income, however," Uncle Bradbrook said. "One cannot eat bracelets and rings, nor pay the milliner with them. Even if everything were to be sold, how much would that raise? No more than a few thousand pounds, perhaps, if one is inclined to be optimistic."

"It is quite certain that the business is lost?" Aunt Bradbrook said. "Can it be challenged in law?"

"We will take a legal opinion, of course," Uncle Bradbrook said, "but Edward said it looks quite solid to him, with Barantine's signature and the date and so forth. Also, his will did not explicitly name the business as a bequest to Violet, which might have permitted a challenge. He simply left her everything he owned, and if he no longer owned the business—"

"Yes, yes, I see. It is all very distressing, and such a disappointing end to your efforts, Eliot."

"I hoped to recover some small part of her fortune, and ended up losing all of it," he said miserably. "Such a pity that everything was tied up in the business."

"Yes, that was certainly imprudent," Uncle Bradbrook said. "However, she is still a remarkably beautiful girl, and we need not despair of settling her comfortably enough. She will not, perhaps, be able to look so high as before for a husband, but she surely has suitors enough, does she not, Miss Parfitt?"

"She has *admirers,"* Evie said, frowning. "It is hard to say which of them is serious, or would be undeterred by a change in her fortunes. Poor Violet!"

"Do not say *'Poor Violet'*, as if she were a sweet, innocent little thing who ill-deserves such misfortune," Aunt Bradbrook said, eyes narrowed. "I am very cross with her. However foolish Roger may have been, he at least had some reason for his madness, but I had thought Violet to have more sense."

"She has never been greatly endowed with common sense," Evie said ruefully. "I knew that, and should have been watching her more closely. I have been a very bad chaperon. I fully expect to lose my position, Mr Armitage, so you need only tell me when you wish me to leave."

"Never!" he said without thinking, then, seeing her startled expression, he went on rapidly, "I hope you will stay for as long as Violet needs you. You must not blame yourself for her misbehaviour. No doubt the two of them cooked it up in secrecy. How could you have known?"

"Henry knew," she said simply. "And I *must* blame myself, for my primary function was to teach her to be a lady. If she thinks that eloping is acceptable in a lady, then I have failed utterly."

"She knew perfectly well that it was wrong," Aunt Bradbrook said acidly. "She told me so, but she declared herself too much in love to resist. Roger can be very persuasive, you know. The blame lies entirely at his door, I feel."

"What have you done with Roger?" Eliot said.

Uncle Bradbrook sighed. "Gone to a friend of mine in the north. I have told him that I will settle all his debts here, and make him over the sum of ten thousand pounds besides, but after that all obligation on either side will be at an end. It will deplete my resources considerably, but I shall return to my legal work for a while, just until we are on an even keel again."

"And Violet? She is at Richmond, I understand?"

"Some old friends from the City have just settled there," Evie said. "It will do her good to have a few days away from the hurly-burly of town, and it will remind her of how far she has come." When Eliot frowned, trying to puzzle that out, she added, "They are quite dreadfully vulgar. Now that she has seen the superior society in which you move, she will feel the contrast and perhaps she will be encouraged to strive for betterment. Although... it will be difficult if she no longer has a fortune."

"I shall make sure she has a sum to offer," Eliot said. "I cannot afford a hundred thousand, but something... ten thousand, perhaps. That could be drawn from my own money without any need to ask Father's help. I do not want her dwindling into spinsterhood for lack of a dowry."

Evie laughed. "She can always come and live with me and Aunt Dodi in Winchester, sewing clothes for the poor children in the workhouse. I never thought to find myself better off than Violet, but now I have an income of six hundred pounds a year, Mr Armitage, thanks to Lord Lampeter. Riches indeed to me."

"How will you spend this largesse, besides supporting Violet?" he said lightly.

"Books... lots of books."

But her eyes glittered dangerously as she spoke and he thought it best to ask no more. She was right, though — it was ironic indeed that penniless Evie was now richer than the great heiress she had been hired to chaperon. Life was very strange, sometimes.

23: Friends And Relations

Sometimes, Evie woke and everything felt calm... normal. If she slept deeply, her mind seemed cleansed of all its worries and she awakened refreshed and ready for the day. She might even enjoy a few minutes of this peaceful state. Then she remembered... so many horrid things to remember. Violet had tried to elope. Her fortune was gone. Evie herself was financially independent, but forever beholden to Lord Lampeter for his benevolence. And then there was Eliot...

He looked so tired and dispirited that her heart ached for him. He had gone to so much trouble to find Violet's lost diamonds, only to lose the rest of her fortune as well, and he had taken it hard. No one seemed able to convince him that it was not his fault, and now he was subdued and utterly cast down, quite unlike himself.

If only she could talk to him! Yet he hardly came near her. That night at the Iversons, the first time she had seen him in two months, her insides had turned somersaults of joy at the sight of him. But he had said not a word to her, had not even approached her, merely glowering at her from the side of the room as she danced. Since then, she had scarcely seen him.

Edward, on the other hand, was unavoidable. He was there at the breakfast table, then if the ladies went out during the morning he offered to accompany them, and in the evenings there he was still, ready to attend them to whatever engagements lay before them.

"He is in love with you," Violet whispered to Evie one evening, when the ladies were alone after dinner.

"Nonsense," she said robustly. "If anything, it is your company he seeks out, not mine."

Violet shook her head, the curls on either side of her face dancing. "He always liked you very well, Evie, and now that you have a dowry, he can afford to marry you. He could not afford to marry me, not any more," she added sorrowfully.

Poor Violet! She had returned from her sojourn in Richmond chastened by her failed elopement, and in penitent mood, only to discover that her punishment was even worse than she had feared — her entire fortune was lost. She had wept a little, until Evie showed her the reddened nose this engendered, but had accepted that she must put a brave face on things and continue to go out and about in society just as before. She was young enough that she could not be downcast for long, and she had the small consolation of the diamond her father had chosen for her.

"He kept his word," she said, her eyes glowing. "Papa always kept his promises, and Mr Armitage is to have it made into a pendant for me, to remember him by. It is a pity my fortune is lost, but I shall just have to be sure to marry a very rich man. Mr Armitage knows any number of rich men."

"There are also your papa's old friends," Evie said cautiously. "Young Mr Fairchild, for instance, or Mr Glover. Perhaps we should call on Mr Glover's aunt one day."

"Papa wanted me to marry a *gentleman*. A lord, if possible, but definitely a gentleman, and he refused Mr Glover three times, if you remember."

Evie did remember. Violet had sulked for a week after the third attempt, until a fortuitously-timed invitation had cheered her up again. She was never out of countenance for long, for her belief in her own ability to attract admirers never waned. Even after her change of circumstances, she was entirely convinced of her own powers.

At first it seemed that she was correct in this assumption. Wherever she went, her adoring flock crowded around her, and Evie persuaded herself that it was only her cynical eye that imagined them less assiduous in their attentions. But before long, it became clear that penniless Violet was not nearly so appealing as heiress Violet. Gentlemen who had once fought for the honour of a second dance with her now contented themselves with one. The crowd jockeying for the right to lead her into supper dwindled to just one or two. Invitations were thinner on the ground than previously. No one was so crass as to cut her, but there was markedly less enthusiasm.

Finally, the day came when Violet was obliged to sit out a dance altogether, for lack of a partner. Evie was claimed by Edward, but she saw the tears hovering on Violet's lashes.

"Edward, I am quite worn out after that last reel. Why do you not ask Violet, instead? She has more energy than I have."

Before he could speak, Violet cried, "No, no! You look so well together, and Mr Folkard has been waiting for his turn with you all evening."

"Miss Barantine, I should be very happy—" Edward began gallantly.

"No, you must not pity me," she said firmly. "A lady does not show disappointment, is it not so, Evie? I shall sit quietly here until Mr Folkard brings you back."

"Very well, if you are quite sure, but do not wander away or talk to any gentlemen you do not know, for Mrs Bradbrook is in the card room just now."

Edward led her to the nearest set. As they waited for the musicians to strike up again, he said, "Poor Violet! Has she ever lacked for a partner before?"

"Never, to my knowledge. She is learning some harsh lessons, I fear."

"Yet she puts a brave face on it," he said, with some admiration. "I thought she would throw a tantrum or insist that you should sit out the dance too. She is growing into a well-behaved young lady."

"Indeed she is," Evie said, pleased by such a clear sign of approbation. Perhaps, with ten thousand pounds from Eliot, there was a possibility of a match after all.

"That is all your doing," he said. "You have taught her well."

"Oh, but she is very sweet-natured beneath the frivolous exterior," Evie said absently, twisting her head to watch Violet. "I could not teach her if she would not attend to me. Who is that lady beside her? I do not know her."

"I have hardly seen a soul I recognise," Edward said. "It is Armitage who is acquainted with all these people with their fancy titles, and he is not even here. This is supposed to be a simple card party, you know, but the rugs were rolled up and musicians in place before we arrived, champagne everywhere and have you seen the spread laid out in the supper room? Berkeley Square is a cut above Green Street, that much is certain."

"Where has she gone?" Evie said, scanning the room. "Oh, there she is, just disappearing behind that curtain. We must go after her."

"Of course," he said, without enthusiasm.

Evie darted between the dancers, and made her way towards an alcove formed by thick marble pillars, half hidden by draped curtains. Violet was sitting on a chair, sobbing piteously, while the unknown lady sat beside her, murmuring into her ear.

"Oh, Violet!" Evie cried, kneeling at her feet. "Do not cry so."

"I know, I know, my nose will go red, but I cannot help it, Evie, truly I cannot. I have never been so humiliated! Mr Watson, whom I thought was so gentlemanly, saw me sitting alone and... and he walked past me as if we had never been introduced! That was very bad of him, was it not?"

"Indeed it was. Oh, thank you, Edward. Why is it that ladies' handkerchiefs are so inadequate? Would you be so good as to fetch Violet some water, if you please?"

He disappeared, and the unknown lady said gently, "I have smelling salts, if required. My mother taught me to be prepared for any eventuality. However, pray tell me at once if my presence is intrusive." She was so beautiful that Evie was sure she would have remembered her, had they ever met before, and her gown, her jewels, the clever way her hair was styled placed her in the first rank of elegance.

"Not in the least," Evie said at once, rising again and sitting on the other side of Violet. "I am very grateful to you, although I do not think we shall require the smelling salts. Violet is not at all vapourish, and she will be better directly."

"I shall, I shall!" Violet said, with the slightest of sobs. "Thank you so much! You have been very kind, and I have kept you from the dancing. I am so sorry."

"Not the least need to apologise, for I do not dance tonight," the lady said smiling. "I live next door, and am only here for a little while so that Mama can tell her friends about my sister's betrothal. You have a little more colour now that your friend is here. I shall leave you to her care, Miss Barantine." She rose gracefully to her feet, her expensive silk gown swirling elegantly around her.

"You know who I am," Violet said artlessly. "But I do not know *you.*"

"I am Lady Ruth Grenaby."

Violet gasped. "Oh! You are a *real* lady! So your father must be... someone very important. An earl or—"

She smiled at Violet's artlessness. "The Duke of Orrisdale. My father is a duke."

"Ohhh!" Violet's eyes were round with wonder. "I have never met a duke's daughter before, not that sort of a lady. Evie — my friend, Miss Parfitt here — is teaching me to be a lady, although... I am not an apt pupil, I fear. Evie is the most ladylike person I know, but you are a *proper* lady."

Lady Ruth laughed, and exchanged a speaking glance with Evie before sitting down again. "I assure you, Miss Barantine, that a title does not make me special."

"Oh, but it must do," Violet said earnestly, her tears quite forgotten. "Your father is a *duke*, which is almost like royalty, whereas my father is... or was— May I say, Evie? I need not be ashamed of him, need I?"

It was Lady Ruth who answered. "You should never be ashamed of your family, Miss Barantine. Your father was a jewel merchant, I have been told, and he died on the *Brig Minerva*, and now you have lost the fortune you expected to inherit. So I have heard, but none of that is your fault."

"You know all about me," Violet said wonderingly.

"We have something in common," Lady Ruth said quietly. "I, too, lost someone on the *Brig Minerva...* the Duke of Falconbury. We... had an understanding."

"Oh, how dreadful for you," Violet said, instinctively reaching out a hand for Lady Ruth's. "And now you have no one to marry, so we have that in common also, for I begin to think that no one will ever wish to marry me, now that I have no money."

"You are too young to consign yourself to spinsterhood," Lady Ruth said, smiling. "Not every man wants or needs to marry for money, and you now have one incomparable advantage over me, Miss Barantine — when a man does offer for you, at least you will know that he loves you and is not simply a fortune-hunter. I, on the other hand—"

"Yes?" Violet said. "Oh, you mean gentlemen might offer for you just because you have a lot of money?"

"I must marry suitably," Lady Ruth said briskly. "The daughter of a duke must marry the son of a duke, if she possibly can. My marriage was agreed between my father and his almost ten years ago. Now that he is drowned... well, he has a younger brother who is the new duke, and to my father, one brother is much the same as another."

"But that is quite horrid!" Violet cried. "An *arranged* marriage... to have no choice in the matter!"

"It is expected of me," Lady Ruth said simply. "I have grown up knowing of it, so I do not repine. But you may choose your husband according to your inclinations, and I do not think you will be without offers."

"Oh, but Evie is *thirty* and has never had an offer at all because she was poor," Violet said.

Lady Ruth glanced at Evie, amusement in her eyes. "Just because a lady remains unwed does not imply that she has received no proposals of marriage. I am sure Miss Parfitt could have married at any time, had she chosen to."

Evie did not disabuse her of the notion. How could the daughter of a duke possibly understand the life of a parson's daughter? She who had always moved in the upper echelons of society could not imagine the stifling confinement of Evie's small village, ignored by the local gentry who took their cue from the Hall, and surrounded by farmers and millers and farriers, who thought themselves several rungs of the ladder below the vicar's daughter. Marriage was a choice she had never had, until very recently.

Edward returned just then with a glass of water and anxious enquiries, and then there was all the business of introductions to be made, which Evie watched with curious detachment. She had spent over two years with Violet, gently setting her on the path to proper decorum in society, and here she was, mingling with the grandson of an earl and the daughter of a duke, performing introductions as if she had been born to it. Now she knew how mothers felt when their fledgling daughters first took wing, and no society mama could be prouder than Evie was at that moment.

Even she was surprised, however, when Lady Ruth said, "If you are quite well now, Miss Barantine, perhaps you would care to take a turn about the room with me?"

Violet turned to Evie with big eyes. "Oh, may I, Evie? Please say I may."

"Of course."

When they had gone, Edward sat down beside Evie. "That is a very good connection for her. They live next door, you know, the Grenabys. They are only in town briefly to buy wedding clothes for the younger daughter, who has snagged a baron already, and not even out of the schoolroom. Yes, a very good connection for Miss Barantine. Who knows what may come of it?"

"Very little, I suspect," Evie said, laughing. "Lady Ruth has a kind heart, she knows Violet's history and she saw her distress, but Violet is hardly a fit companion for a duke's daughter. They will not be strolling down Bond Street together, I imagine."

"Still, it will do her good to be seen with Lady Ruth, and it has cheered her up. Violet is never downhearted for long, I believe, and I shall dance with her later. She will like that," he added, in the tone of one convinced of the efficacy of such a treat. "We have missed the end of *our* dance, Evie. I suppose you have not a vacancy later?"

"I am afraid not, and now I must listen to Mr Hawes expounding the great virtues of Kellingborough again for twenty minutes. I wish this evening had been the card party it was advertised to be. Ah well."

"Shall I see you tomorrow?" Edward said, suddenly looking anxious.

"Of course!" she said, startled. "We live in the same house, remember?"

He half-smiled, twisting his lips in unexpected agitation. "But I should like to see you *alone*. I have... something to say to you."

Evie was aware of a flutter of fear. He was not going to be foolish, was he? But perhaps it was about Violet? She answered him calmly, however. "I shall be in the book room at... oh, eleven o'clock, shall we say? Mr Bradbrook has a meeting with his lawyers, and Mrs Bradbrook is taking Violet and several of her hats back to the milliner, so I shall be alone."

"Excellent," he said, with such a wide smile that her heart plummeted. Surely it must be about Violet.

~~~~~

It was not about Violet. Evie knew as soon as Edward came into the room that it was going to be difficult. He had not been at breakfast, and now she could see why — he wore a new coat and had styled his cravat into some complicated arrangement that did not suit him at all. She could not forestall him, however. He would say what he planned to say and then... she would have to deter him. She waved him to a chair, and waited for him to do what he must.

He talked for some time, a speech that he had obviously laboured over painstakingly. She embodied all the virtues of
~~~~~

womanhood, apparently, and — a surprise — he had been in love with her for years. Never before had he felt there was any hope for his suit, for he had no money of his own and his prospects of advancement, optimistic though he was, were in the future. But now she had a dowry, and that, combined with his own hopes of a career, was enough to encourage him… and so on and so forth.

She waited, head lowered, for his eloquence to expend itself. Then, calmly, she said, "I thank you for the honour you do me, Edward, but I must refuse your very obliging offer."

"Evie, you have not considered…"

"I do not need to consider. It is impossible."

"But why? We get along so well! We have always been friends, have we not? And now we could be something more than friends. You must see—"

"No, Edward," she said gently. "I do not love you… could never love you."

"Only because you have not yet had time to think about—"

She rose to her feet, obliging him to rise also. "Edward, I must repeat, and I wish you will accept my word and say nothing more on this point — it is impossible. I do not… have *never* regarded you in that light, and that will not change."

"You do not know that! If you but consider—"

"No! We grew up together, and I view you as a brother, nothing more. I cannot *ever* see you as a husband. Please respect my wishes in this matter, and speak of it no further."

"But why, Evie? Love is hardly a reliable guide to happiness in matrimony. Respect, liking, a certain affinity... you must see that we are so well suited. I shall not accept a refusal so ill-founded."

She heaved a sigh of pure frustration. "Edward, I wish you nothing but good, but I cannot possibly marry you."

"Why ever not? You have given me not a single rational reason why not."

Anger rose up in her to choke off all her carefully restrained answers. He wanted a rational reason, and he should have one, though the skies fall.

"Very well, then. I cannot marry you because you may be my brother. My father was not Thomas Parfitt, and could very well have been your father."

"No..." he whispered.

"It is the truth," she said coldly, "so never speak to me on this subject again."

24: Failure And Guilt

Eliot's clever plan to find Violet's diamonds so that Evie would think better of him had ended in such disaster that he had abandoned any hope of soon winning her regard. In time, he felt, if he behaved with restraint, she might begin to see him in a different light and perhaps he might try courting her seriously, but for now it seemed as if all hope was lost.

"You did your best," she had said to him in kindly tones, but the sentiment reminded him forcefully of a master at Eton who had spoken to him in exactly that manner after he had performed abysmally in an attempt to translate from the Greek. Failure was failure, however gently received, and it was only when he accepted the depths of that failure that he understood how much he had depended upon succeeding. He had told himself that his concern was for Violet, but he could not deny the truth — that he would do anything within his power to raise himself in Evie's esteem. Without her approval, his life was nothing at all.

Eliot gradually settled into a level of misery that enabled him to function on a daily basis. He could not avoid Evie entirely, for he had to see Violet from time to time, but he contrived only to meet her in large gatherings where his constraint might pass unnoticed.

Whole days passed by where he exchanged no words with her at all. On some evenings there was dancing, and then he had the exquisite pain of watching a succession of partners enjoy her company, as she bestowed happy smiles upon them. He told himself that if ever he should see her sitting down, partnerless, he would dance with her, no matter how difficult it should be. But she never sat out a dance, so his resolve was never tested.

His guilt over Violet gnawed away at him, too, and for the first time he began to take more interest in her, squiring her on morning calls and shopping expeditions, and taking her riding, or driving in his curricle. She very much enjoyed the latter, sitting up beside him and maintaining a continuous commentary of trivia. One day he took advantage of an hour of sunshine to drive her to Hyde Park.

"Evie says that the Bruton Street house must be got rid of," she said to him as they rattled out of Green Street onto Park Lane. "She says that you have kept up the lease, and all the servants are still there. That is a great expense which I cannot afford, and there are my lady's maids, too, and Miss Robart and Henry and—"

"There is no great rush to make sweeping changes," Eliot said.

"But I must learn to live within my means, as Evie does," she said earnestly. "A lady must never exceed her income. If I sell my jewellery—"

"No, no! Let us not be too hasty," he said, wheeling the curricle neatly into the park. "You are still under my guardianship, and even when that ends I will not abandon you, so there is no need at all for you to be selling off this and that, as if you were friendless."

"Not immediately, perhaps, but I must be sensible, as Evie is. She has fifteen thousand pounds now which provides an income of six hundred pounds a year, and she says that she will live very comfortably on that. If I were to sell everything that Papa left me — the jewels and the carriage and all the furniture from Bruton Street — do you think it would be so much? Would it be a great deal less? I should like to know, so that I might prepare myself."

She turned her great eyes on him, and he could not be unmoved by her sincerity. Gently, he said, "Would it be helpful if I were to have an inventory taken of the contents of Bruton Street, and everything valued? That would give us an idea."

"That would be lovely! Thank you! You are very kind to me, but I do not wish to be a charge upon you, dear Mr Armitage, not when you have been so generous and have tried so hard to find my diamonds. Perhaps I could be employed, like Evie. Do you think I should talk to Mr Tranter about working in Papa's shop? I know a great deal about jewels and—"

"Under no circumstances will my ward work in a shop!" Eliot said in such a stern tone that Violet visibly quailed. "Do consider my position, Violet, and give up any such idea." Seeing her dismay, he went on more softly, "It is still my intention for you to have a full season next spring, and I cannot do so if you are engaged in any form of trade. There will be a ball for you at my house in Grosvenor Square, and it will not be my fault if you do not have a wonderful time. I would not have the world say that I had behaved shabbily towards my ward and obliged you to live like a pauper."

She pondered this new aspect, and then nodded slowly. "That would be very bad. Evie was always used to say that I should behave well to reflect credit on Papa, and now I must reflect credit on *you*, must I not? As best I can," she added mournfully.

"You are a great credit to me, Violet, and also to Miss Parfitt's teaching."

"Oh yes, Evie always knows how to go on, even though she is not a *real* lady, not like Lady Ruth. Just imagine how proud Papa would have been to know that his daughter was acquainted with a duke's daughter. She is so affable and kind, even to me, but Evie says that great ladies often are, although Lady Ruth's mama was not at all affable, and gave me such a look! I did not like her at all. Will you truly give me a proper season? For I should like that very much. If I am to be poor, I shall do my best to be content, but I confess I do like to dance and enjoy myself."

"And so you shall, Violet, so you shall," he said. "Perhaps you will dance your way to a husband, who knows?"

"That would be very agreeable, especially if he is rich, for I do not much like being poor. However, I do not expect it to happen, for look at poor Evie. She is very ladylike and not so very plain, is she?"

"She is not at all plain!" he said, startled.

"Naturally all her friends must think so, and she is very kind and virtuous, so any man would be glad to marry her, one would suppose, and yet here she is, thirty years old — *thirty!* — and never had a single offer until Lord Lampeter gave her a dowry. So I expect I shall be a spinster, now that I am poor."

Eliot's head spun. "Evie has received an offer?"

"Oh, several. Mr Durham, Mr Carver — he asked her three times, imagine how much in love he must be! Oh, and Mr Folkard."

Folkard... how could Eliot have forgotten his interest in Evie? He had been so swept up in himself he had never seen the danger.

"She turned him down?" he said, as his heart seemed to stop beating.

"All of them!" It was safe to breathe again. "She told them she was very much obliged but she has no thought of matrimony at present. She told me so that I might know how a lady should reject a proposal. She turned down all of them, and I must say I do not blame her, for Mr Durham is not at all agreeable and scarcely speaks a word and even put his proposal in a letter, can you imagine it! And Mr Carver is very old, so she would not like to be married to him, I daresay. Mr Folkard is agreeable enough, though, so perhaps she has not refused him." His heart lurched again, as Violet rattled on, quite impervious. "Oh, look at the trees! Such delightful colours! I should like a pelisse in that colour, and a bonnet with feathers dyed to match. I think I should look charmingly in it, but I daresay Evie would not agree, for she never likes my ideas about clothes. Oh, is that a squirrel? How sweet he is."

Eliot did not agree either, but Evie... now that was a different matter. She would look splendid in autumn colours, and he liked the idea of the feathers. How beautiful she would look! Dear Evie, with that glorious hair... how he yearned to see it tumbled about her shoulders, to run his fingers through it... So much longing, so much pain! If only he could escape from London, and these tormenting thoughts that drove him half mad. And yet it was such sweet torture, to see her, to speak to her sometimes, to watch her dance. He loved to watch her dance...

But not with Folkard. And please God, let her not marry Folkard.

~~~~~

Eliot invited Folkard to dinner at Grosvenor Square. He deliberately chose a night when he knew the Tranters would be out later, so although he had to sit through an hour of them discussing their promising talks with the lawyers, and how competent a manager Mr
~~~~~

Drysdale was, and how much they were learning about jewels, as soon as the covers were cleared and the port set on the table, they excused themselves and departed, and Eliot had Folkard to himself.

"They are going to stay on in town, it appears," Eliot said. "I imagined they would go back to Dublin fairly soon, but they seem rather settled."

Folkard made some non-committal noises. His head was down, staring at the table, and he pushed his port glass from one hand to the other, back and forth, back and forth. He had contributed very little to the conversation all evening, but with the Tranters in the room, the lack had not been felt. Now the silence was profound.

"Are you quite well, Folkard?" Eliot said. "You seem a touch under the weather."

"I am well, but... I have received a blow, Armitage. A dreadful blow, and of a most unexpected nature."

"Then I am sorry for it. If you wish to speak of it, I am accounted a good listener, but if you prefer to—"

"It is Evie!" Folkard said, looking up suddenly with fire in his eyes. "She said such things—! It cannot be true, and yet... if she invented such lies, she is not what I believed her to be."

"Evie would never lie," Eliot said, beginning to be alarmed by these revelations.

"So I thought too, but... damnation, Armitage, she told me she could not marry me because we are *brother and sister*."

Whatever Eliot had expected, it was not that. For a moment he was too shocked to speak, but beneath the astonishment was a little ripple of pure joy — she had refused him! She would not marry

Folkard after all, and Eliot would not be called upon to face that test of his fortitude.

Tentatively, he said, "Her father and your mother?"

"No, no! I doubt my mother ever met Parfitt. There has always been a chaplain at the Hall, so no one went to Parfitt's church. No, she meant her mother and my father... or one of my uncles, perhaps."

"Or one of your uncles... you mean to say that she does not know who her mother's lover was?"

"Lover! That is not how Evie sees it, not at all. *'A violent assault',* she called it, and her mother tried to take her own life after it."

"Good God!" Eliot cried. "And she claims your father was the perpetrator? Or one of your uncles?"

He gave a rueful shrug. "She makes no precise claim, for her mother made none, but... shall I tell you the whole of it? As Evie told me? And then you may judge for yourself whether she is lying or not."

"Evie does not lie," Eliot said again.

"Wait until you hear all before you make up your mind," Folkard said sombrely. "This is what she told me. Her father was parson at St Andrew's in Greenhill — a tiny village, nothing but farm workers living there. One morning he was taking his usual early morning walk when he happened to be passing Black's Pond — quite a sizable lake, in fact, with a wooden fishing pier. He saw a woman there, which was unusual enough, being not long after dawn, but she was standing at the end of the pier. Not doing anything, just standing there. Then, as he watched, she threw herself into the water."

"Poor woman. And this was Evie's mother, I collect?" Eliot said. He felt he should stop Folkard, for Evie had surely spoken in confidence, but he was too bound up with the story to extricate himself.

Folkard nodded. "Hermione Folkard, from a distant branch of the family, taken in as an act of charity to make herself useful. Parfitt was a good swimmer, so he dived in and rescued the woman, and took her home to the parsonage. She was very unwell after her dip in the pond, so the apothecary and later a physician were called to attend her. They knew who she was, and they discovered signs of this supposed violent assault. The physician told Parfitt that Hermione should not go back to the Hall, for some reason, so Parfitt called the banns and married her. Can you see how incredible all this is? For surely they were lovers before! Why else would he marry her instead of—?"

"Just tell the story as Evie told it," Eliot said curtly. "You may add your own interpretation later."

"Very well, very well. No need to snarl at me. Nine months later, Evie was born, and Parfitt told her he never so much as laid a finger on Hermione, but we only have his word for that. A year or two after that, Hermione died. She had never been in health again after her swim — that part was well known. After her marriage, I doubt she even left the parsonage. Parfitt related all this to Evie when she was fifteen, and here is the part I truly cannot credit. The part I have already told you — perhaps it may have happened just as she says, but the rest? No, this goes too far. Parfitt told Evie that her father must be *one of the Folkard sons*. Can you believe it? Here is his reasoning. He said that the rest of the family had all gone up to town, even the chaplain, but the three boys were still there, waiting to go up to Oxford. My father and my two uncles. They were very close in age, and they were all up at the same time, that year. That night, when the *'violent assault'* took place, would have been their last night at the Hall, they were on their own in the house with only Hermione for company, so Parfitt decided it must have been one of them who ravished Hermione. *That*, you see, is the flimsy foundation upon which Evie refuses me, but it is far more likely that it was one of the footmen or... or a groom or some such. My father and his brothers were not the only males at the Hall."

"Did Hermione never reveal the name of her attacker?"

"Apparently not, which makes the whole story ring even more false."

"On the contrary, it makes it more credible," Eliot said soberly. "If it had been a footman or a groom, she would surely have said so. No reason not to. Besides, no servant would take the risk. It is a hanging offence, after all. But a son of the house? I can see her keeping quiet about that, and also being so distraught that she would wish to take her own life. If she accuses one of them and he denies it — she is ruined to no good purpose. If she keeps quiet, she is still ruined."

"You prefer to think the worst of them, then? You do not see any other possibility?"

"There are plenty of other possibilities, but this one is the most likely, to my mind. Consider, Folkard — three young men, of an age to be a bit wild, any one of them could have drunk a touch more than was good for him, got a bit too frisky with her, and things went too far. I have never been in such a case myself, but I know plenty who have. Things happen, sometimes. What matters is afterwards.

These three were all raised as gentlemen, they should have known that there was an obligation to make things right. If, instead, her assailant simply took off and abandoned her — that would be enough to bring any woman to despair."

"But it could have been *anyone,*" Folkard said. "To presume that it was a gentleman—! It is such a despicable accusation."

"No one accused anyone," Eliot said pensively. "In fact, it seems to me that a great deal of effort went into *not* accusing anyone. Hermione herself seems never to have revealed who her attacker was. The parson married her to avoid any hint of a scandal. Neither the apothecary nor the physician seem to have reported their concerns about the *'violent assault'* to the magistrate. And Evie's father told her the story as soon as she was of an age to understand, in order to avoid any misalliance with the family — with you, specifically. All of that speaks very clearly of a strong suspicion on everyone's part that this was not the act of a footman."

Folkard chewed his lip worriedly. "That does seem... very logical. Nevertheless, it is still speculation. There is no evidence, other than the beliefs of people long dead and Evie's faith in her father's veracity."

"There is one other piece of evidence that should not be forgotten," Eliot said. "Lord Lampeter's dowry to Evie. Fifteen thousand pounds! That is great generosity towards a very distant relation with no conceivable claim on the family... unless it is some belated effort to make amends."

"Good God!" Folkard said. "Guilt money?"

Eliot nodded. "It seems to me that Lord Lampeter's conscience is greatly troubling him."

25: Making Amends

'Brandeth Hall, Surrey. My very dear Eliot, Happy news! Daphne is safely delivered of a son, several weeks earlier than anticipated, a long, difficult birth, but bravely borne by my stalwart girl. The infant is not so robust as one would like, so would you be so good as to collect Nurse from Marsham Grove and bring her to me here, together with all the items listed on the enclosed sheet. I know you will be happy to perform this small service for your sister, and you can have no engagements in town at this present. Indeed, I am surprised you are still there and have not yet gone home. For myself, I do not foresee any possibility that I may be spared before Christmastide, and since Elizabeth finds herself in a delicate condition again, I may be summoned to Heath Manor before the spring. I cannot tell you when I may be at home again. Your very fond Mother."

~~~~~

Eliot did not quite see why Lord Corbett could not bestir himself to drive about the countryside with infant supplies, or even send a servant, but then he remembered the customary chaos in that household and the vast number of children to be kept, if humanly possible, on the right side of total anarchy, and he concluded that
~~~~~

neither his lordship nor the servants could be spared. He obligingly drove into Essex, where to his surprise he found his father once again in residence. Why had he left Nancy's care?

"Where is he, Powell? In the library?"

"Yes, sir. He has a Mr Wakes with him."

Mr Wakes? One of Nancy's sons? That was interesting.

He knocked, and when his father called out, he went inside. "Are you busy, Father? I will leave you in peace, if so."

"Ah, Eliot! How delightful!" his father said, beaming at him. "What an unexpected pleasure. I am never too busy to see you. Come in and meet my son, John Wakes. John, your half-brother, Eliot."

The two men bowed to each other, albeit rather warily. Despite the close connection, they had never met, nor expected to. Mr Armitage had always kept his two families well apart.

"Your mother is well, I hope, sir?" Eliot said, wondering if that was the reason for the visit, although his father would hardly look so cheerful, if so.

"Perfectly well, thank you," Wakes said rather stiffly.

"John and his family are to move into Nancy's house," Mr Armitage said. "That way, Nancy will see more of her grandchildren, and John and his wife will have the benefit of a bigger house and the garden. It will be good for all of them. Do you not think it a good idea?"

"Very good," Eliot said, although surprised. Nancy had told him that her sons were ashamed of her and seldom visited, yet now one of them was to move in with her. "It will be company for Nancy, too," he said cautiously.

"Precisely so," his father said happily. "I do not like her to be on her own. Well, John, my attorney will draw up the papers, and it will all be settled within a few days."

"Thank you, sir. I am very much obliged to you."

"Eliot, ring for Powell to show John out, will you?"

When Wakes had gone, Eliot poured Madeira for his father and himself, and sat in the wing chair vacated by Wakes. He was burning with curiosity to know about the papers being drawn up, but he asked no questions. That was his father's affair, after all, and he could keep it to himself if he wished. Instead he said, "I thought you were comfortably settled with Nancy, Father."

"Oh, I was, very comfortably settled. She looked after me so well, Eliot, but I could not stay there for ever, you know, not when it distressed your mother so much. I could not impose such an injury upon her. Your intentions were good, but my conscience would not permit me to stay any longer with Nancy. She was in want of company, but it did not need to be mine. I wrote to both the boys and asked them to come and see me. Well, Mark is in the army and not able to do so, but John came and we arranged matters to the satisfaction of all parties. They will look after Nancy and share the house with her, and I will ensure that the house and a suitable sum is made over to them after her death. It is not a large amount, so it will not diminish your inheritance by much."

"Heavens, Father, as if I cared about that. It is much better to see Nancy taken care of."

"I was sure you would see it that way. I have not seen John for years, but he has grown up to be a fine young man. A little thoughtless when he was younger, but then which of us is perfect in youth, eh?" He chuckled. "Now that he is married with children himself, he understands how he hurt his mother by his previous neglect. He told me also that the one thing he and Mark wanted as boys was for me to acknowledge them openly. I saw that they were educated and established in careers, but it never occurred to me to do more than that. John was thrilled to come here, to walk in through the front door to see his father. Who would have guessed it? I am minded to invite him and his family to visit in the future."

"Mother may not like that," Eliot said.

"Perhaps not, but I do owe a duty to my own sons... and my grandchildren. It was different when your mother knew nothing of Nancy, but now that she knows, she must understand that *all* my children have a claim on me, not just the legitimate ones."

"Will she come home, now that you have returned?"

"Perhaps. In her own good time, no doubt," he said, eyes twinkling. "She is enjoying herself at Daphne's. You heard the news, I take it? Another boy. Just at the moment I believe Daphne needs her more than I do. Powell has found me a new footman, as sturdy as Henry, to help me get about. I went out for a little drive in the barouche yesterday. Yes, I am managing perfectly well." He raised the glass to his lips with a smile of satisfaction.

~~~~~

Eliot collected Nurse, and drove back to London and then out to Surrey, a two-day journey, for Nurse could not possibly proceed a distance of fifty miles in a single day. Since she regaled him throughout with embarrassing tales of his own infancy, and stopped
~~~~~

in every place larger than a hamlet in case there should be an apothecary with stocks of a particular ointment she regarded as indispensable, he was heartily glad to reach Brandeth Hall. He was then obliged to stay for two nights at the particular request of Lord Corbett, who fell on his neck as only a man trapped in a house full of females and children can do.

There was one advantage to all this bustle, which was that Eliot had less time to brood over Evie. In town, there was the constant risk of meeting her at an evening engagement, or even on the street. She lived only a five-minute walk from Grosvenor Square, and he was perpetually aware that he had only to turn his steps in that direction to see her again. In Essex and in Surrey there was no such temptation, and although Marsham Grove held memories, they were not unpleasant ones.

Evie was brought forcibly to his mind on the journey back to town, however. He had stopped at Kingston to rest his horses, only to find a carriage with a familiar coat of arms in the yard.

"Lord Lampeter?" he asked the ostler.

"Aye, sir. In the best parlour. Problem with the axle. Just waiting on the wheelwright now."

"Is Lady Lampeter here also?"

"No, sir. Just his lordship."

Eliot hesitated, but they would both be confined to the inn for an hour or two, at least. He scribbled a note on the back of one of his cards — *'If you are minded for company, I am in the coffee room. Armitage.'* Within two minutes, Lord Lampeter's balding head and prominent nose appeared round the door.

"Armitage! Come upstairs."

The servants were busy setting the table for a meal, but Lampeter poured wine for them both and gestured Eliot to one of the sagging wing-chairs beside the fire.

"Are you coming or going?" Lampeter said. "Up to town or down to the shires?"

"Up. My Surrey sister has just provided her husband with another son — the third or fourth, I have lost count rather — but I have escaped at last."

Lampeter gave a grunt that might have been laughter. "Your sister has done well. Janey only managed two. What about yourself? Not setting up your nursery yet?"

"Plenty of time for that," Eliot said easily.

"Oh, certainly. I was almost forty before I took a wife, but there were rumours swirling that you might— Well, people make too much of these things, I daresay. Just because a man turns down an offer of a certain kind does not necessarily imply that he has turned to matrimony."

Eliot had no trouble interpreting that. Lady Tammleton's search for a little fun had been much talked of in the clubs, and his refusal was equally well known. He smiled and said nothing.

After a moment, Lampeter went on, "There was a great deal of talk about this ward of yours, Armitage, and some people wondered if you had an interest there. She is a great beauty, after all, and you are something of a connoisseur."

"What, marry my own ward? That would be a great breach of trust."

"Oh, indeed. I never gave it much credence. I was sorry to hear that her father gambled away her inheritance. That is a great misfortune. How has she taken it?"

"Rather well, in fact. She is a good-hearted girl, even if she is a bit hen-witted sometimes."

"And Evie? How is she going on? I have not seen her since... for a few weeks. I do not go into society much when Janey is not with me."

"Miss Parfitt is well," Eliot said, wishing his heart did not beat faster just at the mention of her name. He wanted to talk about her, to ask about the strange story she had told Folkard, but he had no idea how to broach the subject.

"She has suitors, I hear?" Lampeter said, leaning forward slightly. "She may receive an offer soon, I understand? So the word is."

"She has already received offers," Eliot said, and Lampeter nodded, seeming pleased. The opening was too fortuitous, so Eliot went on quickly, "Edward Folkard offered for her."

"Edward?" Lampeter almost dropped his glass. "Did she—?"

"She refused him." Dare he mention it? He had to... "She told him some story about them being brother and sister."

Lampeter had gone white. "Was that why she refused him?"

"Apparently. Is there any truth in such a story?"

He held his breath, but Lampeter frowned. "Why would *Edward* offer for her? Fifteen thousand can hardly be an inducement to him, after all. His godfather is a wealthy man."

"Until recently, Mr Bradbrook's heir was a natural son, who lived expensively and has almost ruined his father. Folkard never had a feather to fly with of his own, and will not until he is fully trained as a barrister. He managed to keep himself very well on a minuscule allowance and the kindness of friends. I stabled his horses for him, for instance. It appears that he has always had a fondness for Evie... Miss Parfitt, but could not afford to consider marriage until you so generously provided her with a dowry."

"Good God! I had no idea," Lampeter said. "But she will not have him?"

"No, because she believes him to be her brother. Is it true?" he said, relentlessly, for now, if ever, was the moment for Lampeter to confess.

Instead he stared into the air, as if he was not attending. "I always wanted to do something for Edward, but Janey so disliked the idea, and he seemed to be well-placed. Then after Arthur was born, it seemed unlikely— Two sons should be enough." He turned sharp eyes on Eliot. "You will not repeat these foul rumours, Armitage."

"Naturally not, sir."

He grunted. The servants had long since placed food on the table and disappeared, so he said, "Eat with me, and give me your opinion of a new venture I have in mind."

It was one of his charitable enterprises, and Eliot valiantly tried to take an interest in the affair, without much enthusiasm. He had always tried to look after the family's tenants, and elderly servants were pensioned off to a cottage somewhere and sent annual presents of fruit and game, but he had never considered the possibility of setting up orphanages or homes for fallen women.

"Is it expensive?" he asked after a while, the idea rolling around in his mind. "These establishments of yours must cost a pretty penny."

"Lord, no!" Lampeter said. "I cannot afford to throw thousands into philanthropic endeavours. A few hundred to buy a small property with a bit of land they can work to feed themselves, and to train them for some useful work, and then they are sufficient unto themselves. I am not made of money!"

"Yet you could afford fifteen thousand for Evie," Eliot said smoothly. Lampeter half-choked on a slice of mutton, and Eliot went on hastily, "I have even wondered whether you might be this mysterious Benefactor who has given a thousand pounds to all those affected by the sinking of the *Brig Minerva*. A man of your wealth and known charitable nature — it is a not unreasonable supposition."

Lampeter wiped his lips with a napkin and took a long draft of his wine, then, perhaps to give him time to compose his thoughts, he refilled the glasses. "I am not the Benefactor, no. Surely it must be the new Duke of Falconbury, in memory of his poor brother? Although I have heard the Prince of Wales mentioned, and one or two of his brothers. Few men could afford such a prodigious sum, and certainly I could not."

Not the twenty-six thousand given away by the Benefactor, yet he had managed to find fifteen thousand for Evie. It did not add up aright, but Eliot could not persist with his questions in the face of Lampeter's obvious reluctance to discuss it. Even so, one thing was very clear — Evie was indeed Folkard's sister, and Lampeter knew of it and felt sufficient guilt in his own complicity to bestow a very large dowry on her.

When the servants returned to clear the table, Lampeter called for a bottle of port, and poured two glasses.

"You see Evie regularly, I suppose, on account of your ward. Is she well? And happy? Will you give her my good wishes when you see her?"

"She is well, she seems happy and I will convey your good wishes to her when next I see her," Eliot said neutrally.

"Which she wants no more than my money, I dare say," Lampeter said, his bushy eyebrows lowering. "Does she hate me, would you say?"

"Hate is an emotion entirely alien to her," Eliot said.

Lampeter sighed, and swirled the port in his glass. "And yet she has every reason. She is my conscience, Armitage. I am known as a philanthropist, a man of charitable works, but it is all because of Evie. She is a living reminder of my dark past, which haunts me still. What is done can never be undone, no matter how bitterly one regrets it."

Eliot held his tongue, unwilling to interrupt the flow of reminiscences. Was Lampeter finally about to reveal the truth of Evie's parentage?

26: Consequences

Eliot waited, as Lord Lampeter sipped his port thoughtfully.

"Do you have brothers, Armitage?"

"None, only sisters."

"You cannot know then what brothers are like, how they egg each other into mischief. I had two of them. William was the heir, older but not wiser, always ripe for any game. Arthur was the gentle younger brother, easily led. I was the sensible middle brother, or so I thought. But we were very close in age, so we did everything together and whatever we did, William was the instigator, Arthur followed and I... I followed too. Sometimes I protested, but mostly I followed. So that was why things went awry that night."

For a long time he was silent, staring into the fire, lost in his memories, and they must have been unpleasant ones, judging by the grim expression on his face. After a while, he set his glass down on the table and looked up at Eliot.

"I tell you this because perhaps Evie should know... or Edward, perhaps, for it concerns him, too. I am too much the coward to tell them directly, but you are a stranger to me and that makes it easier. You may judge how much to tell them — all of it or nothing at all, that is for you to say, but secrecy does no good, and it eats away at me. I have confessed to my chaplain, but that did not help, so I will unburden myself to you, Armitage, if you will hear me."

"You may tell me whatever you wish."

Lampeter grunted, and leaned back in his chair. "It was the last night before we went up to Oxford — William's final year there, Arthur's first. The only year we would all be there together. The family had already gone to London, for Parliament was sitting, so we were alone in the house, except for Hermione. She was a little mouse, scuttling about here and there, running errands for Mother, running the house, essentially. An unpaid housekeeper. She even looked like a mouse, with her brown hair and her dull brown dresses. Little noticed, as a rule, but we needed a four for cards, so she was summoned. We had been drinking steadily for some time by then, so we had got beyond the slightly bosky stage. Before long, the game was abandoned and William set about teasing Hermione. Had she ever been kissed, had she an admirer, that sort of thing. She was a few years older than us, and had been at the Hall for perhaps ten years by then, so we were all familiar with each other... not friends, exactly, but comfortable together. So it seemed like a harmless game. And when William started to kiss her, it did not seem wrong, exactly. A little pleasure for her."

Eliot shuffled uncomfortably, remembering his own behaviour with Evie. Had he not argued exactly the same way? And she had roundly berated him for his presumption.

"Hermione never protested," Lampeter went on. "She neither encouraged nor discouraged him, she just sat there and allowed him to do it. And so, being William, he went a bit further and then a bit further again, and we, drunk as we were, thought it all a grand game and did nothing to stop him. Even when he committed the ultimate insult against her, we simply stood and watched. *'She wanted it,'* he said afterwards. *'She wanted me to.'* It was Arthur who said that he should not have done it, that it was wrong. And William said—"

He broke off abruptly, his breathing ragged, anguish etched on his face.

"No, I *will* tell all," he said in a low voice. "William said that if we all did as he had done, then none of us could be blamed for it. And God help us, we did. Afterwards, Hermione — poor, innocent Hermione — said, *'May I go now?'*, for all the world as if we had asked her to bring us some more wine or some such. And away she went, quite calmly, and we never saw her again. We looked for her later, but she had vanished. I suppose she went to her parson."

"She went to a pond and tried to drown herself," Eliot said starkly, so that Lampeter winced. "Parfitt fished her out and took her home."

"God! Poor girl. I never knew that, but that explains why we could not find her. We left at first light, very much the worse for wear, but as we sobered up, the enormity of what we had done began to dawn on us. William was inclined to laugh it off as boyish high spirits, but Arthur and I were not having that. Arthur decided that he would go home as soon as he could get permission to see how Hermione did. If she were with child, he would marry her... or even if she were not. William thought that was foolish, that we could pay her off. He had a small inheritance of fifteen thousand pounds which he offered to put into a fund for her. William always thought that money solved everything. We decided that she should have the choice — the money or a husband.

"The fund was set up, Arthur arranged his return and then we heard that she had married Parfitt. Well, that seemed to resolve matters for her, but for us it was otherwise. One cannot simply walk away from such wickedness without paying the price. There are always consequences. William learnt no lesson from that night, but grew steadily wilder. He married, as had been arranged for some years, but he was seldom at home. He must have been to every brothel in England before the consequences of that caught up with him and destroyed his health. Arthur determined to wrong no other woman, so he married early, too, and after Edward was born he took himself off to India to make his fortune, where he died within a six-month. And I… I swore off women altogether, and became a philanthropist. That was my penance.

"Hermione died when Evie was about two, and my mother decided to educate Evie alongside William's daughters. I never saw the point of that until Evie was sixteen or so. By that time, Father was failing, William was ill and so Mother announced that I was to marry Evie. All that time, she had been training her to be a countess. Mother thought she was meek, you see, and would make a conformable wife. Is she meek?"

Eliot smiled. "Not in the least. She has great strength of character."

"Ah. She would have done very well for me, then. Better than Janey. Of course, it would not do. She could have been my own daughter! Or a niece at the very least, and I was obliged to tell Mother some part of the truth. She dropped Evie instantly — a bad influence on William's girls, supposedly, although I could not see the logic in such thinking. Edward had to go, too, in case he took it into his head to marry Evie. Janey was summoned from some far-flung outpost of the Folkard family and I was told to marry her and get on with cutting Edward out of the succession. And what with William dying, and having to clean up the horrendous messes he left behind, and then Father and trying to get the estates in order, I confess I forgot about Evie and Edward for many years. I assumed Evie had married long since, and Edward was in a good position with his godfather, so although my conscience never stopped prickling, I truly believed that they were not suffering."

"I believe that was true," Eliot said. "Neither of them has a resentful nature. Evie lacked for good society, but she never repined, and Folkard is content to be working towards a career in the law."

"Yet I must do something for him, I believe. Evie's fifteen thousand — I had forgotten all about that fund, but it reappeared when I was disentangling the family finances a few years ago. I left it intact, with the thought that it might do for my younger son. Well, he is but six years of age, so he can wait. But Edward... yes, I might do something for him. An allowance, perhaps..."

Eliot smiled. "Now you sound like your older brother. Money is not the answer to every question. You would do Folkard more good if you were to accept him back into the family again. Why not invite him to Hampshire occasionally? He is your nephew, after all."

Lampeter straightened in his chair. "That is a capital plan, Armitage. I wonder I never thought of it before."

"Lady Lampeter would dislike it, perhaps?" Eliot hazarded.

Lampeter chuckled. "Janey has some decided opinions, it is true, but she is mellower these days. Besides, she will do as I wish. Yes, I shall do it. My conscience will never be untarnished, but I may yet lighten the stains."

Eliot sighed. "We all make mistakes, God knows, but we can live with the past if we set the future in order. Besides, much good has come from that one dark episode in your life."

"My charitable works, you mean?"

"That too, but I was thinking about Evie. She may have been conceived in great wickedness, but she has lived her life in unblemished virtue, bringing happiness to all who know her. I can never regret her birth."

~~~~~

Eliot arrived back at Grosvenor Square to the news that the auctioneer he had engaged to value the contents of the Bruton Street house would be grateful if he would favour him with a little of his time.

"No time like the present, eh, Mrs Lake?" he said.

"Indeed, sir. Will you be in for dinner, sir? The Mr Tranters are both dining out this evening."

"In that case, I shall dine at the club."

The walk round to Bruton Street invigorated him after hours cooped up in the carriage, and the colour of the trees and the piles of fallen leaves that crunched under his feet reminded him of Evie's lovely hair. So many things reminded him of Evie!

The Barantine house was one of the largest on Bruton Street, an elegant affair, the door opened by a stately butler and a bewigged footman. Inside, the hall gleamed with gilt-framed paintings, silver candelabra, polished mahogany and rows of marble busts on plinths. The furniture was of an Egyptian style with a few solid Tudor pieces, the busts were Roman and the sconces on the wall looked almost convincingly medieval.
~~~~~

"Mr Nagle is in the library with Miss Robart, sir," the butler intoned, when he enquired for the auctioneer.

"Oh, Miss Robart is here, is she?"

"She knows the library better than anyone, sir. Miss Parfitt is in the drawing room with Mr Nagle's assistant."

Eliot's unruly heart somersaulted, but he had no need to see Evie, he told himself. "Better show me to the library, then."

The library was a small room, but presumably its former owner regarded the floor-to-ceiling bookshelves on three walls as sufficient justification for the name. Poring over a large globe in one corner were Miss Robart and a gentleman in the neat grey wig and black coat of the professional man.

"Oh, Mr Armitage! What an unexpected pleasure!" Miss Robart cried. "Miss Parfitt and I were quite agreed that you could not possibly call today, for how could the Metropolis compare with the beauties of Surrey? And even if you should by chance arrive today, Miss Parfitt said that it would undoubtedly be too late in the day for you to appear."

"And yet here I am," Eliot said, smiling at these effusions. "How are you, Miss Robart? Well, I trust?"

"Oh yes, yes, indeed, Mr Armitage. So very kind in you to enquire, but I am quite well, very well indeed. Apart from a very slight cough, on account of the damp weather I believe, but nothing to signify. Nothing at all to signify. How very kind of you to ask, sir. Too kind to an old governess like myself. Quite beneath your notice."

Eliot said all that was proper, and after no more than ten more minutes in this vein, he finally was able to turn to the auctioneer.

"Hardly a cut book in the place, sir," he said cheerfully. "The late Mr Barantine liked to buy books, seemingly, but he was less keen on reading them."

"Oh no," Miss Robart said. "Mr Barantine himself was not a reader, but he wished to have books about the place. He wished to create a proper environment for his daughter to flourish, you see, with great art and works of literary merit."

"As to the great art..." Mr Nagle coughed deprecatingly. "There is a painting in the drawing room that I should be obliged if you would examine, sir, and perhaps favour me with your opinion."

"I know nothing of art," Eliot said cheerfully. "One painting is much like another to me. Books... now there I might take an interest, but I can say nothing on the subject of art." But seeing the dismay on the man's face, he took pity on him. "Well, you may show me this painting, if you will."

The auctioneer led the way up the stairs, and Eliot had plenty of time to prepare himself for the sight of Evie. But when a loitering footman threw open the door, the room was empty. Eliot let out a long breath, not quite sure whether relief or disappointment was uppermost in his mind.

"There, you see, sir?" Nagle said, moving directly to the large, ostentatious painting above the fireplace. "The late Mr Barantine was sold it as a Rubens, and paid a deal of money for it, seemingly, but I do not think so."

"It is certainly full of movement," Eliot said. "And the figures are lively, and rather lifelike, I should say, although rather plumper than is fashionable just now."

A flicker of irritation crossed the auctioneer's face. "Yes, but—Ah, Miss Parfitt!"

Eliot spun round, his heart seeming to stop beating. There she was, as composed as ever, neatly dressed in dark blue. Miss Robart also dressed in plain colours and simple styles, but where she invariably looked drab, like the governess she was, Evie always looked elegantly restrained, like the lady *she* was. And breathtakingly beautiful... she took his breath away, anyway. However could Violet think her plain!

"Mr Armitage!" Evie said, executing a neat curtsy. "How did you leave Lady Corbett? Well, I hope."

"I... Yes, she..." Lord, if only he could breathe. "She is well."

"And the baby? He thrives?"

"Yes, he... he is coming on very well."

She gave a little laugh, and he thought her cheeks were slightly flushed. He was staring, of course. Those lips... so soft, so mesmerising... She was like an oasis in the desert to him, and he drank in the sight of her. If only he could stare at her for ever! He forced himself to break his gaze. "You are well, Miss Parfitt?"

"I am very well, thank you, Mr Armitage. What do you think of our supposed Rubens?"

"Rubens..." he said, but could find nothing intelligent to say on the subject of Rubens. He had only ever seen one previous example, which was of a similar style, but the subjects of Barantine's Rubens seemed somewhat more warmly clad, and he could hardly mention that.

Evie's eyes crinkled with amusement. "Here is the original bill of sale, Mr Nagle," she said. "It was in the safe, as we thought."

"Excellent. Ah yes, at that price, it seems unlikely... but I will speak to the gentleman named here as the selling agent. Thank you, Miss Parfitt. I shall finish my work in the library and then move on to the nether regions."

"The kitchens?" she said. "Is there much value in pots and pans?"

"The wine and silver cellars," he said, beaming. "Who knows what delights may be found therein?"

He bustled out of the room, the door clicking shut behind him, and Eliot was left with Evie. He could feel the blood pounding in veins, and she was a little pink, but she spoke composedly.

"Is wine a valuable commodity, Mr Armitage? It is not a subject upon which I have much expertise."

Breathe. Deep breath. "It can be. A well-managed cellar, built up over many years, can be very valuable. Although more pleasurable drunk than sold, in my opinion."

She smiled but said nothing.

Terrified that she would find some excuse to go away, he rushed on, "Um... this room is very pleasant. It has... a little more elegance than the other parts I have seen."

"It is but recently improved. Mr Barantine asked for my advice, and I am quite pleased with the result."

"So you should be," he said. "It is a delightful room. The rest of the house is... less tasteful. If that is the result of Barantine's efforts, then yours are more aesthetically pleasing. What sort of a man was he?"

"He was not a man of great learning or intellect, for his education had been rudimentary, and he had but little appreciation for the refinements of civilisation. He bought books by the yard, and art to fill the spaces on his walls — four landscapes, of such a size, for the dining room, half a dozen Roman emperors and a still life for the entrance hall, two stern gentlemen in wigs for the drawing room and one famous artist to hang over the fireplace as a subject for conversation. There was no pretence about him, however. He knew his place in the world and never wished to step outside it. His only ambition was for Violet, that she should marry a gentleman and to that end he wanted her to be taught to be a lady. He dreamt of seeing her the mistress of a fine house in the country, surrounded by lawns and woods and a trout lake. For some reason, he was very keen on the trout lake. I should go and drag Miss Robart out of the library, I daresay."

A twist of fear — she must not go, not yet! "Miss Parfitt..." he began, not quite sure what he would say, but he had to think of something, anything.

"Yes?"

But he knew what he must say. "I have a confession to make. Folkard shared with me something that I believe you had told him in confidence... about your mother. I feel you ought to know that, but you need not fear that I will betray the secret."

"Oh, I do not mind *you* knowing," she said, with a little smile that gave him a glow of warmth. "I should have wished to keep it from Edward, however. He was... quite upset. I am not even certain that he believed me, but everything I told him is exactly as I had it from my father, and he would never invent such a tale."

"It is all true," Eliot said sombrely. "I met Lampeter on the road only this morning, and he told me the whole sordid tale. Your poor mother! It was despicable, what happened to her, and the worst of it is—" He stopped, wondering at the wisdom of such words, but perhaps she deserved to know. "Even Lampeter does not know who your father is."

"It hardly matters," she said. "It makes no difference to me. My father — my *real* father — lived in the parsonage and raised me and loved me, and no wrongs perpetrated upon my mother change that. But what they did to *me*, and to Edward too — that is the wrong that angers me still. For sixteen years, the Folkards were kind to both of us, in their way. The old countess was always stiff-rumped and distant, and the old earl barely knew my name, but I was treated as one of the family, as if I were a sister to William's three daughters, a responsible older sister, entrusted with their care. Those girls were my *friends*. But when I was sixteen, everything changed. Edward was sent away and I... I was shut out, somehow. They never said or did anything explicit, they simply... withdrew. And then Janey came and married Henry, and *she* made it very clear that I was no longer welcome. It was as if I no longer existed, and that world I had grown up knowing, that *society* was lost to me for ever. To this day, I have no idea what happened."

"They discovered the secret of your parentage." Eliot said.

"But why would that change anything? I am the same person, no matter who sired me."

"Not when they planned for you to marry into the family," Eliot said gently. "You could have been a countess now, Evie."

"No..." she breathed, but he could see her understanding the problem.

"And then Lampeter told them why it was impossible. Folkard was sent away for good, you were shut out and Lampeter himself was hastily married off. But they made a mistake in not telling Folkard the truth, poor fellow. Lampeter thought he was Uncle Bradbrook's heir, and too wealthy to be tempted by a mere fifteen thousand pounds, or perhaps he thought separating you was adequate protection, but he certainly should have told him."

"But what a dreadful thing to tell a man about his own father, that he... *ravished* a defenceless young woman!" Evie cried. "No wonder the family tried to keep it quiet, and it would have been better to maintain that silence indefinitely, and not try to assuage the guilt by giving me money thirty years after the event."

"Lampeter is trying to make amends for the past," Eliot said. "It may be late in coming, but it is well-intentioned."

"There is no making amends," she said softly. "What is done cannot be undone. We cannot change the past, no matter how much we may want to."

Her voice was filled with sorrow, and he knew that she was not talking about the Folkards any longer. He wanted to plead with her, to tell her that whatever was in his past was finished with and he was a different man now. Yet somehow he could not. How many times had he seen men make the same mistakes over and over? Sensible men, like Barantine, who repeatedly risked his entire fortune on the turn of a card, and had left his daughter near to destitution as a result. Less sensible men, like Roger Bradbrook, who compounded gambling folly with elopement. Even his former mistress Lucy Tammleton, who could not resist another affair, even now she was very well-married.

And what of Eliot himself — he had once been so confident that he would never lapse into his bad habits again if he could only marry Evie. Now he was far from certain of his own strength of character.

27: A Dinner For Friends

Violet's birthday arrived in typical October weather — with steady rain and winds strong enough to tear the last few leaves from the trees. Eliot's carriage collected Evie, Violet and the Bradbrooks in Green Street and then drove the short distance to Bond Street and the discreet entrance to Barantine's, jeweller of distinction, as the sign above the door proclaimed. The Tranter brothers and Mr Drysdale were there to greet them and show them around, before the little ceremony where the jewellery Eliot had purchased for Violet's birthday was handed over by the very craftsmen whose skills had created them. The main pieces, a demi-parure in emeralds, were enclosed in a large box carved and inlaid with mother-of-pearl in a very pretty design of birds. The smaller set, an amber and pearl necklace, was in a smaller, flat box, very plain, with just the word *'Barantine'* engraved on the lid. And this year there was an extra box, containing the special diamond Barantine had kept for his daughter, now made up into an elegant pendant.

The jewels were admired, Violet thanked everyone very prettily — she was getting so accomplished at making little speeches, Evie thought with some pride — and then they withdrew to the elegantly appointed downstairs room, where champagne and sweetmeats were laid out for them.

Mr Tranter coughed discreetly, then said, "We have another birthday present to offer Miss Barantine, if she would like it, and if her guardian permits, of course." He made a little bow in Eliot's direction. "Now that my title to the late Mr Barantine's business is confirmed, I have it in mind to make a small change. My brother and I have always shared everything we have, and as he is to help me manage the business, I wish to make him a part-owner. And since it would be wonderful to have a member of the Barantine family still connected, I should like to offer Miss Barantine a share also — one third, with no direct involvement in the business, naturally, for she is quite a lady and cannot be associated with trade. A partnership, in the manner of the late Mr Newbold's partnership with the late Mr Barantine, and equal shares between the three of us. What do you think, sir?" he said to Eliot.

"I have no objection, so long as Violet is not required to work in the shop," he said, smiling.

"Oh no, indeed not, sir! Nothing could be further from our thoughts! All we would ask is that Miss Barantine's wears jewels from the shop occasionally, and if anyone should enquire, to inform such persons of the origins of the items. That is all."

"Oh, but I do *that* already," Violet said. "All my jewels came from Papa's business, and naturally I say so when anyone asks. Which they often do."

"Would Violet have a share of the profits?" Eliot asked.

"Certainly, certainly! A one third share, just as my brother and I will take. We cannot say exactly how much that will be, since the success of the business varies from year to year, but it will not be less than one thousand pounds a year. Once or twice Mr Barantine made ten thousand pounds clear profit in a year, but more usually it is four, five, six... So we can say with certainty that your share each year will not be less than one thousand pounds, Miss Barantine."

Violet blinked. "But that is more than Evie had from her fortune! Does that mean I shall be rich again?"

"Not rich, precisely," Eliot said, "but you will be a lady of independent means. Sadly, it means you may become a target for fortune hunters again."

"But I shall not be duped a second time," she said firmly. "Indeed, I am determined not to marry for years."

"Ah now, that would be very sad," said Mr Tranter, taking her gloved hand in his, and raising it to his lips. "Not all men are devious scoundrels, out to rob you of your money. There will also be honourable men who will admire and cherish you for your beauty and good nature and charming ways, and it would be the greatest pity to turn them away because you have been burned once."

"But how shall I know which ones are devious scoundrels and which ones are honourable men?" she said, her great green eyes gazing up into his turquoise-blue ones.

"You will know because an honourable man will allow you the time to make up your mind and will not press you. An honourable man will make sure you know him well enough to judge his character. An honourable man will be faithful, and will wait for as long as it takes you to understand your own heart. Marriage is for life, Miss Barantine, so it is not a state to be entered into in haste."

"Oh yes!" she breathed, mesmerised. Neither noticed that he still held her hand.

Evie sighed inwardly. It seemed that Violet's resolution to avoid matrimony might already be crumbling in the face of male charm. She caught Eliot's eye, and saw him trying not to laugh.

"He is very personable," he whispered, as they followed the others back up the stairs, "but since he has just given her a third of his own income, we may acquit him of fortune-hunting."

The next destination was Bruton Street, to deposit the emerald demi-parure in the safe with the other valuable jewellery that Violet's father had given her over the years. It was Violet's custom on her birthday to look at all the previous presents, to remind herself of the happy day when she would be old enough to wear such elaborate pieces. Henry gently lifted every box from the safe, which took some effort for they were large and heavy, and laid each one on a cloth-covered table. Fifteen, perhaps twenty boxes, each one beautifully made, but the contents were even more so — diamonds, rubies, sapphires, huge pearls, emeralds and a myriad lesser stones winked and twinkled. Beautiful, and valuable too, but even if every one were to be sold, they would only raise a small fraction of the one hundred thousand pounds that Violet should have had.

Violet sighed over them, and shed a few tears as she remembered her previous birthdays, when her father had been there.

"Which is your favourite?" Evie said.

"I like them all," Violet said, as she always did. "Which is yours?"

"The new set is exquisite," Evie said, picking it up, "but the swirling pattern of these rubies is so—" She stopped as she lifted the second box. "Why is this one so much heavier?"

"Different wood in the box?" Eliot suggested. "The set is slightly larger."

"But it is *vastly* heavier. Feel them both."

"So it is. How odd."

He set the box down on the table and carefully lifted out the items of jewellery and then the silk lining. And there below was something gleaming — a bar of solid gold. Quickly he looked in some of the other boxes. Every one contained a gold bar.

Eliot began to laugh. "So the dowry was not tied up in the business after all. Violet, I believe you have just become exceedingly rich again."

~~~~~

It had long been in Eliot's mind to hold a dinner at Grosvenor Square to thank his aunt and uncle for their hospitality and discuss Violet's future, but having the Tranters under his roof had inhibited these plans. Now, however, they had taken lodgings near to Barantine's shop on Bond Street, and Eliot was able to issue his invitation. There were to be only six of them, and even with the dining table reduced to its smallest size, it would be far too large for the party.

"Shall I put up the round table in your study, sir, as you do for your gentlemen friends?" the housekeeper asked.

"No, I should not like to entertain ladies in such a small room," Eliot said, remembering too many riotous evenings there. "We will eat in the library."

She blinked in surprise. "In the library, sir?"

"Why not? It is a handsome room, and Miss Parfitt will certainly want to see it."
~~~~~

The anticipation of her pleasure in the room fortified him whenever his spirits faltered, which was often. He very much hoped that the evening would erase the memory of her unfortunate first visit to Grosvenor Square, when she had inadvertently been shown into one of his parties for his male friends. In the event, it was Violet who mentioned it, as soon as she was shown into the drawing room.

"Oh, I remember this room!" she cried, as soon as the greetings were over. "This was where you were holding your party for pretty ladies when we first came here. Do you remember, Evie? They were wearing French fashions, of the sort you will not allow me to wear, for they were rehearsing a tableau about the troubles to perform at Carlton House. Although..." Her brow wrinkled. "I do not recall reading about it, and everything that goes on at Carlton House is reported in the newspapers, is it not?"

"Possibly not everything, Violet dear," Evie said solemnly, although how she kept her countenance Eliot could not imagine.

"Ah, good evening, Henry," he said hastily, seeing the imposing figure of the footman in the background. "And how are you? Well, I trust?"

The Negro nodded, with a little smile.

"Henry is always well," Violet said. "I do not think he has ever even suffered from the headache. Oh, he wrote a little note for you, Mr Armitage."

She pulled a screw of paper from her reticule. Unfolding it, Eliot read, *'How is Mr Armitage Senior?'*.

"Why, thank you for asking, Henry. My father is very well. I had a letter from him a few days ago, and he sounds in very good spirits."

"Is he still with—" Violet said, before blushing scarlet as she remembered she was not supposed to know about such things as mistresses.

"He is home at Marsham Grove," Eliot said gently.

Violet, still blushing, cast an apologetic look at Evie before subsiding into the nearest chair. Evie began admiring the room, Aunt Bradbrook joined in, and the awkward moment passed.

Eliot felt sick with excitement when they went down for dinner. He so badly wanted Evie to like the library, to understand that he had arranged for them to eat there for her sake and yet he was afraid that it would not be sufficient to crack the shell of her composure. So little did, and yet he knew the warm, loving woman who lay inside that shell — he had kissed her, touched her, felt her trembling response. He could not bear to hear platitudes from her.

She surprised him. "Oh, how Miss Robart would love this room!"

"Miss Robart? I thought *you* would love it, with your affinity for books."

"Oh, I do love it, of course — how could I not? It is a magnificent collection, and the room itself of such splendid proportions, a perfect setting for dinner. But I am not such a great reader as Miss Robart. She would rather read than anything else on earth, and would be contented for ever if she had access to a library like this. I love to read, but I enjoy many other activities, too, and if I am offered the choice of a ball or a card party or a dinner with good friends instead — well, the books would just have to wait. Where shall I sit, Mr Armitage? A round table is confusing my sense of the proper order of things."

"Eliot must choose his seat, and that will be the head of the table," Aunt Bradbrook said.

He laughed. "That is the point of a table that is perfectly round — there is no head and no foot, and we may all sit where we please."

"That will never do!" his aunt said with mock severity. "Sit where we please? What anarchy is that? You may sit there, Eliot, then I shall sit on your right hand, and Evie may sit on your left."

"No, indeed," Evie said, but her eyes were laughing. "I am only the paid companion, so Violet must take the more honoured place beside our host, and I shall sit next to her."

"But then you would oblige me to sit beside Edward," Uncle Bradbrook said. "Since we have equal numbers of each sex, I claim my rightful share of the ladies."

"Then you had better sit beside Violet, and Evie may sit on your other side," Aunt Bradbrook said. "That leaves Edward to sit between Evie and me. There! We have arranged it most satisfactorily, despite your efforts to confound us, Eliot."

Eliot found there was an exquisite pleasure in facing Evie across the table. Often when he looked at her, he found that she was watching him, a little smile playing on her lips, as if she enjoyed it, too. If someone made a witty remark, or some mishap occurred, her eyes sought his to share the joke. It felt so intimate, it was almost like being married, except that she would leave at the end of the evening with the others, but somehow there was no pain in that. For now, for a few fleeting hours, she was his and he was content.

While the servants were there, they talked of general matters... of books, given the setting, of the rather grand ball they would attend in a few days, of dancing and Evie's suitors. There was altogether too much talk of Evie's suitors.

"Mr Hawes has gone back to Somerset... or is it Sussex, Evie?" Violet said.

"Staffordshire," Evie said smiling, her glance catching Eliot's.

"Oh. Anyway, he has gone, and Mr Carver too. He said his mama was sick, but I do not believe it. But now there is Lord Burnsford. He is a *viscount*, Mr Armitage, and he sends Evie roses every single day."

"Which is not the way to win my favour," Evie said severely. "How could I approve of a man so wildly extravagant?"

"What should a man do, then, to win your hand?" Aunt Bradbrook said. "Would you favour a more practical gift — a bolt of flannel, perhaps, for your winter nightgowns, or a chaldron of coal?"

"Tallow candles!" Uncle Bradbrook put in. "Very economical."

"How unromantic!" Violet cried. "Surely he must write poetry in your honour."

"If he could write good poetry, that might be acceptable," Evie said. "So few people do, however, and bad poetry would instantly end any regard I might have felt for the writer, so it is not advisable. A man who hopes to win my regard need only be considerate of my wishes, and take the trouble to arrange matters in such a way as to bring me pleasure. I prefer thoughtfulness to gifts, always."

Her eyes lifted as she spoke, falling on Eliot with such warmth that he was almost overcome. He could only smile at her, and bask in what he hoped was her approval.

When the servants had withdrawn, Eliot raised the matter that was preying on his mind.

"Violet, it will soon be time for you to leave Green Street and return to Marsham Grove, for I fear we have taken advantage of my aunt and uncle's hospitality for too long. But that leaves me with a problem. My mother is still from home, and not likely to return for some time, which means that you and Miss Parfitt will be unchaperoned. I propose to remain in town for the winter, therefore, and—"

There was a chorus of protest at this.

"You cannot allow such considerations to keep you from your own home," Evie said, and she sounded pleasingly upset by the prospect. "I am surely not of an age to need chaperoning, Mr Armitage, and will be sufficient chaperon for Violet."

Eliot was about to protest, but Aunt Bradbrook leaned across to lay her hand on his. "You are very scrupulous in such matters, and one cannot fault you for that, but let us not be hasty. Let us not rush to make plans for circumstances which may not arise. We still have several engagements to attend before Violet can leave town, and much may happen between now and then. When the time comes we shall discuss it sensibly, and if a chaperon is necessary then I could come to Marsham Grove, or one of your sisters might come, or Evie's aunt in Winchester, perhaps."

Eliot brightened. "Would Mrs Scudamore be willing, do you think?"

"I think she would be delighted," Evie said.

"If it should be necessary," Aunt Bradbrook said, with a smile at Evie. "Who knows what may happen in the next week or two?"

And Evie, composed, serene Evie, blushed deeply and gazed at the walnut she was rolling about with her fingers.

Eliot understood. From the bliss of an evening in Evie's company, he was thrust into the cold, roiling sea of despair. She would marry — that was what this was about. Evie would marry one of her innumerable suitors, and how would he go on, without hope?

~~~~~

He had no wish to attend this wretched ball, but his aunt left him no choice.

"Lord Burnsford's mother has come to town especially for the occasion, so it would be a great insult if you were to refuse to go. For Evie's sake, Eliot, please."

Evie looked beautiful, of course. She wore a gown he had not seen before, of turquoise silk with a simple net overgown, and a necklace of small diamonds that was probably Violet's. It was some time since he had seen her at a large gathering of this type, and he could see at once that the men who hovered around her now were of a different type. Gone were the oddities, the men she would never look at twice. In their place, men of solid worth — the viscount, a squire's son, several gentlemen of the shires. Not exciting, but men of unblemished reputation, able to give her the settled home and respectability she deserved.

For a while, he watched, mesmerised, as she danced with first one, then another. He could not tell, or perhaps he was too closely involved to be impartial, if she favoured one above another. She smiled equally on them all, or so it seemed to him. People came, spoke to him, went away again, but he could not tear his eyes from Evie, as she danced, light-footed, her skirts swirling about her, smiling, always smiling...
~~~~~

And then it was all too much.

Heartsick, he staggered out of the ballroom onto the wide balcony, lit by many lanterns, the autumnal air warmed by braziers, and down the steep steps at one end of it. There on the bottom step he sat in near darkness, head in hands, and gave way to utter despair. He wished her well and happy, of course he did. He was not so bitter as to begrudge her the happiness she so amply deserved. If only he need not see it! If only he could crawl away to Essex and hide until she were safely wed. Or perhaps when she had a couple of babes. In five years, or perhaps ten, the pain might have receded and he could face her with tolerable composure. But not yet. Not now!

He had no idea how long he sat there, wallowing in misery. The music for the cotillion had stopped and some other tune had struck up — a reel, he thought. What did it matter? He could not go back in there and smile and make light conversation. Let them dance on without him.

It was her perfume that first drifted into his consciousness. Roses… she always had the faint scent of roses about her that reminded him of the bower in the garden at Winchester. He knew she was there behind him, coming down the steps. With a swirl of silk and shimmering net, she sat down beside him.

"Not dancing?" she said, pulling off her long gloves.

With an enormous effort, he turned to her with something resembling a smile. "I came out for some air. It was so hot—"

"Ah, no!" she cried, putting one hand on his. "You must not pretend, not with me. I see the pain in your eyes. Let there be complete honesty between *us*, at least."

Honesty… he could give her honesty, if she wanted it. "I could not bear to watch," he said, his voice ragged. "To see you so happy, dancing with all your admirers. To know that soon you will choose one and—"

"No," she said. "I will never choose one. I shall never marry any of *them*." A pause, as she gazed at him, her eyes so clear in the half-light. "Does that help a little?"

He nodded. "A little. But you will never marry *me*, either. I have realised, you see — and this is what brings me to despair because it is irresolvable — that I can never be worthy of you. No matter how much I may strive to improve, how much I may hope to convince you of my sincerity and that I have reformed all my bad habits, it is impossible. You were right after all. I can never be sure that I will not relapse. I am weak and frail, and so there is always the possibility that I will fall."

"Then you are making progress," she said, giving his hand a little squeeze.

"Am I?"

"Of course. A man who talks of *'never'* and *'always'* and makes grandiose promises has no understanding of mankind. You are weak and frail and *human*, as are we all. And at least you are never *boring*," she said with asperity. "Unlike my troop of suitors. They are all so respectable and worthy, but there is not one of them who makes my heart beat faster. Not one of them makes me lie awake at night wondering what it would be like to be married to him… not one of them makes me want to kiss him. To be honest, I never consider them at all. But every morning, I wake and think — I could have been married to him by now. I could have been lying in his arms. He could have been holding me. You kissed me, Eliot, twice you kissed me but you never held me. You have no idea how I *ache* to be held by you."

Time ceased. He stopped breathing, his heart no longer beat, he could not move or speak. There was no music, no ball, no world, nothing existed except Evie's lovely face. She was not looking at him now, but he could see in the dim light that a single tear had made its way down her cheek. It shimmered a little, and he longed — how he longed! — to wipe it away with one gentle finger, to feel the warmth of her skin, to touch her. But he could not move. He could not speak. He could only listen, and pray for the words that would make his miserable life bearable again.

"I think sometimes," she went on, still not looking at him, but her hand was warm on his, "that perhaps it would be worth it. To have a year or two or three of perfect bliss, no matter what came after. I wonder a great deal about that. All marriages have their difficulties, do they not? And yet they survive them, and grow stronger for the challenge. Then I look at your uncle, whose reputation was every bit as bad as yours in his youth, and yet here he is, utterly devoted to your aunt. And I wonder if perhaps I am throwing away a whole lifetime of happiness in fear of some imaginary trial that might never happen. Do you not think?"

He could only nod his head, quite unable to speak, mesmerised by her beauty, marred as it was by that solitary tear. She turned her head to look at him, and he saw in her eyes, as clear as if she were speaking the words, the hope there, the longing, the *love*.

"Do you..." he began but his voice was not quite under his control. A deep breath, then he made another effort. "Do you want to try?"

"I cannot say. It is too *difficult*," she said, with sudden passion. "My heart wants to, but my head... my head says it is madness. That is what love is, I think, a kind of madness, that consumes all rational thought. I know I should be prudent, but prudence makes me so miserable. You watched me dancing with those dull men and thought I was happy. How could you so mistake me? Can you not see the emptiness in my heart that only you can fill? I see your pain, so surely you can see mine? It eats away at me, Eliot. I am never free of it, and I so badly want to be, even if it is only for a while. Prudence... I am *sick* of being prudent. I know, without the least doubt, that if I turn away from you now, I will regret it for the rest of my life."

"Evie..." he whispered. She was so close to him that her perfume wound itself around him, bound him to her, and her hand still lay on his, creating a physical bond between them. There had always been that bond, he realised, a deep connection that tied them together in some visceral way. "Evie... I love you so much."

"And I love you too. I want you... I want to be yours." She smiled at him, and everything melted inside him. He loved her so profoundly, so *completely* that nothing else in the world mattered or even existed but her.

"I will do my best," he said, "my *utmost* to keep you happy for ever, but do not hate me if I fail."

Her free hand reached out and touched his cheek and he uttered a little cry. Eyes closed, he leaned into her hand, kissed it, brought his own hand to hold it there against his face. And then came the moment he had longed for, dreamed of, until it consumed every waking hour of his life. Her lips touched his, warm and soft and tasting of wine and syllabub and the salty tang of her tears.

Almost before he was aware of her and long, long before he was ready, she drew away.

"Don't stop! Please... do not stop." He opened his eyes and she was so close that her breath was warm on his face.

"Hold me, Eliot," she whispered. "Hold me tight and make me yours."

She smiled up at him, closing her eyes and parting her lips. He took her in his arms and kissed her and it was glorious.

28: An Unexpected Visitor

Evie woke to the joyous certainty that her life had changed utterly. The hollowness inside that had haunted her for months was gone. Instead, she was filled with the glow of happiness. Eliot had touched her and kissed her and *held* her — held her so tight that she had melted into him, her being fused with his as if they were one person. It had felt so perfect, so right, and now everything was different. He would be with her for ever. She could not recall exactly what had been said, but they would be together, that was all that mattered. One day, very soon, she hoped, she would wake to find his golden head on the pillow beside her, those dark blue eyes watching her, his lips curved into that lazy smile she loved so much. And then he would hold her again...

No one had ever held her before, not that she could remember. Certainly not her father. His love for her was deep and abiding, but he had never hugged her or even touched her. Her nurse had had a brisk manner that confined itself to rubbing her back when she fell over or hurt herself. The Folkards were too dignified to embrace. She had never had a lover. Not until now, when the desperate need to be held had overwhelmed her.

She was up long before Mrs Bradbrook's maid came to help her dress, and she was the first down to breakfast. He would come soon, she was sure of that. They had parted in haste last night, thrown into panic by Violet's clear voice on the balcony above them — *'Evie? Are you out here? No, she is not here, ma'am.'* And then the lower murmur of Mrs Bradbrook's voice, gradually dwindling as they returned to the ballroom to seek her elsewhere. There had been a mad scramble to find her discarded gloves in the dark and put them back on and get inside before anyone suspected that she had been so scandalously engaged. As if it mattered now! But there had been no time for more than a few hasty words — *'Come to me—' 'Yes, yes!' '—soon, very soon' 'Tomorrow...'*

Now it was tomorrow and she could not wait, could not bear the endless wait for him to come to her, to see his face again and his smile, that intimate smile that was just for her. She crumbled bread and a Bath bun and watched the hands on the clock crawl — were they even moving? How soon would he come? Not before noon, she supposed.

But he did. They were all still at breakfast, even Violet, who rarely descended so early, when he was shown in. Evie dropped her knife onto her plate with a clatter and jumped to her feet, aglow with excitement. She saw her own delight reflected in his expression. After the most perfunctory of greetings to the others, he turned to her, eyes afire.

"Miss Parfitt, may I have a few words with you — alone?"

"Oh!" That was Violet, understanding at last.

Mr Bradbrook's voice held a measure of amusement. "There is a fire in the book room."

They left without another word, hastened into the book room, shut the door. And then she was in his arms again, being held, being kissed... very thoroughly kissed. It was a long, long time before they surfaced, laughing, still locked together, his arms wrapped around her as if he would never let go of her.

"What was it you wanted to say to me?" she said.

"I have no idea. Everything goes out of my head when I am with you."

She giggled, resting her cheek on his shoulder with a sigh of contentment. "I am not quite sure what it was that we agreed upon last night," she murmured into the soft wool of his coat. "Did we agree upon anything?"

"Only that I am weak and foolish, but for some astonishing reason you love me anyway. Evie, will you help me to be worthy of you? Will you guide my footsteps to a future far better than my past? Will you be my helpmeet, my friend, my beloved wife? Will you marry me?"

"I will."

"You are quite resolved? No more doubts?" A little frown marred his high forehead.

"No doubts. I want to be with you," she said, and it was the simple truth. "I want to be yours, and the sooner the better. Today! Can it be done today? Is there not some kind of licence?"

"A special licence, yes. *Today!* Oh lord, yes, let us do that, if we can. I am not sure if I can get one, but I will try."

A loud rap on the door was followed, after a slight interval to allow them to separate and smooth rumpled clothing, by Mrs

Bradbrook. "I hate to intrude, but Nicholas has an appointment in town and he refuses to go until he knows whether it is all settled."

Evie laughed. "Tell him it is settled. We are to be married as soon as Eliot can arrange it."

"Today!" Eliot said. "Doctor's Commons… I must go at once. I will be back as soon as I can."

"Oh," Mrs Bradbrook said, eyebrows raised as she watched his disappearing back. "Today… that is very sudden. Are you sure you will not take a little time… wedding clothes and so forth?"

"I have already wasted three months," Evie said with sudden passion. "I shall not waste another day… another hour!"

Mrs Bradbrook chuckled. "Far be it from me to argue with such ardour. Whenever you come back down to earth, we shall have a pleasant time visiting all the warehouses. Come and have some breakfast, for although you have been dissembling rather well, I have not seen a bite pass your lips this morning."

"Oh, I cannot eat!" Evie said distractedly, but she allowed herself to be shepherded back to the dining room.

Mr Bradbrook smiled knowingly and disappeared at once, but Violet and Miss Robart were whispering together. Violet jumped up and rushed round the table to Evie, her face tearful.

"Oh, Evie, I did not *know!* I should have realised… I have been terribly selfish, caught up in my own affairs, I never noticed! Mrs Bradbrook says you have been attached for *months* and I never guessed a thing. And is it true? You are to be married?"

Evie could only nod, and that brought forth another flood of tears.

Miss Robart, too, was dabbing at her eyes with a crumpled handkerchief. "Oh Miss Parfitt, how romantic, how wonderfully romantic! And Mr Armitage such a charming gentleman. So happy you will be, so very happy. And Grosvenor Square! You will live at Grosvenor Square!"

"So I will," Evie said, rather surprised that this had not previously occurred to her. "And at Marsham Grove... and there will be no difficulty with chaperons."

"As I suspected," Mrs Bradbrook said smugly. "I rather hoped you would have reached an understanding by the time you remove to the country. Lord, such excitement! So much happy news at last."

The ladies settled to their usual morning employments in the parlour, or rather, Mrs Bradbrook and Violet did so, the one marking up her household accounts and the other pretending to net a purse, but in fact chattering unstoppably about Evie and Eliot. She was fascinated by the romance which had been going on right under her nose, yet of which she had remained oblivious. Now she wanted to have all the details laid out for her, of when Eliot had first begun to court her and when Evie had first detected signs of love in herself and how she had recognised them and, above all, what did it *feel* like to be in love? Evie began to suspect that Violet herself had never experienced any feelings of true affection for the several gentlemen of whom she had appeared to be so enamoured.

For her own part, Evie was waiting. Just as she had been waiting for Eliot to come, now she was waiting for him to come back and tell her how soon they were to be married. Today, possibly. Please let it be today! But if not, she could wait a few more days... or weeks, perhaps, if they had to call the banns. But until she knew, she could not do anything. There were letters to write, arrangements to make, any number of things to be done, she felt sure, but until Eliot returned she was unable to do any of them. So she held a piece of sewing in her hands, and even placed the occasional stitch, but mostly she sat, waiting.

Two ladies of Mrs Bradbrook's acquaintance called to talk over the ball, and were thrilled to be the first recipients of the exciting news.

"Ah, I guessed as much," one of them said, triumphantly. "I knew something was in the wind as soon as Lucy Tammleton told me—"

Her friend hushed her at once, and quickly changed the subject.

When they had gone, Evie said, "Who is Lucy Tammleton?"

"An old friend of Eliot's," Mrs Bradbrook said. "Violet, my dear, I have a letter to write. Would you be an angel and run down to the book room and fetch me some more wafers?" When Violet had gone, Mrs Bradbrook went on, "Lady Tammleton was Eliot's mistress some years ago. When their arrangement came to an end, he introduced her to Lord Tammleton, who liked her well enough to marry her. Earlier this year she approached Eliot to... reignite their former intimacy. He refused, and she was indiscreet enough to tell people so. There was much speculation that he was on the brink of matrimony."

"I see," Evie said, feeling that she ought to be distressed by this information, yet was not. It was all in the past, after all.

"You will find that you bump into several of his former mistresses as you move in society, and some of them will find it amusing to tease you about it. Make sure he tells you of them, so that you are not taken unawares. Do not let them concern you."

"I do not," Evie said. "What he has done in the past is over. It cannot be undone, but it cannot hurt me, either. All I have ever worried about is what he may do in the future — if he reverts to his old ways, *that* would hurt me incalculably."

"It is the risk we all take when we marry," Mrs Bradbrook said equably. "One never knows what a man is like until one has lived with him for a number of years, and it is the same on the other side. The gentlest, most sweet-natured girl may turn into the most shrewish wife imaginable. The cards are dealt face down, and we never know what they are until we turn them over. I was dealt a wonderful hand, and I suspect you have been, too, my dear."

"I hope so," Evie whispered.

Violet returned, and then more callers were announced and Evie was required to exert herself once more, trying not to watch the clock on the mantel, not to count the minutes and hours passing. Those visitors, too, left but not long after, the heavy tread of feet on the stairs promised another arrival. Was it Eliot at last? Surely it was Eliot!

"Mr Nettles, madam," the footman said.

There was complete silence as he entered the room, gazed around until his eye fell on Violet and then bowed.

"What a pleasant surprise, Mr Nettles," Evie said, trying to keep her voice level, although her astonishment was great. "Mrs Bradbrook, may I present to you Mr Nettles, who is the new vicar of Lower Marsham. Mr Nettles, Mrs Bradbrook's husband is brother to Mrs Edmund Armitage of Marsham Grove."

Bows and curtsies were exchanged, it was established that all were in good health and Mr Nettles confirmed that he had left his parish in good order, and his parishioners in prosperity and health. After that, it was hard to avoid the burning question in everyone's mind.

It was Violet who voiced it. "But what are you doing in London, Mr Nettles? Is it church business?"

He looked startled. "Church business? No, nothing of the kind. I should not have thought *you* would be in any doubt of my object, Miss Barantine."

"No, indeed, how should I know what brings you to town?"

"Ah, but that is so like you, always so unassuming. I am sure that, in your heart, Miss Barantine, you have been expecting me long since, but it took me some little while to obtain a curate to perform the offices for me on Sunday."

"You are mistaken, sir," Violet said, her voice trembling. "I have not been expecting you in the least, in my heart or... anywhere else, and I am greatly puzzled as to your meaning."

He chuckled. "No, no! Your modesty is charming, but I am sure you comprehend me perfectly."

"Mr Nettles, I believe you should speak plainly," Evie said with asperity, "for we are all at a loss to understand your meaning."

He looked at her with a frown, as if weighing whether to believe her or not. "Naturally I came as soon as I could after I heard the news. Miss Barantine, all is well, and you need not despair any longer for I am here to rescue you."

"To rescue me? From what, pray?"

"From sorrow and despair. From grief and longing. From—"

"Really, Mr Nettles, get to the point, if you please," Evie said sharply.

"Yes, do," Violet said, "for you are making me very nervous, talking about despair and grief in that way. It is very lowering, Mr Nettles."

For a moment his mouth flapped open like a fish, then his eyebrows snapped together. "Very well. Since there is now no obstacle to our marriage, Miss Barantine, I propose to—"

Violet squeaked in alarm. "Obstacle? *Marriage?"*

Mr Nettles leapt up from his seat and crossed the room in two strides of his long legs, to hurl himself at her feet. He grabbed her hand, which brought another squeak, as she leaned as far away from him as she could.

"Oh, pray, sir—" she began, but he would not be deterred.

"Miss Barantine... Violet, do not be afraid! As always, you bear your troubles nobly, but you may now safely place your future and... and your *person*," he rushed on, reddening slightly, "in my hands. Now that you have lost your fortune, I may set aside my scruples and marry you, just as you have long wished."

"Oh, no, sir! No, no, no! You quite mistake the matter."

He sat back on his heels. "You have not lost your fortune?"

"Yes... no... I mean, I did indeed lose my fortune, but then I found it again, or at least Evie found it for me, although it is of no consequence for even if I *had* lost it, I should not wish to marry you." He stared at her, dumbfounded. Perhaps feeling that something more was required, she added, "But indeed I am very much obliged to you and... and honoured and so forth." She threw Evie a desperate glance, but Evie was too busy trying not to laugh to help her. "It is so very kind of you, but I do not believe I wish to marry anyone... I mean, I have no thoughts of matrimony at this present."

The tiniest laugh escaped Evie's control, and she had to hastily turn it into a cough.

Mrs Bradbrook was made of sterner stuff. "Mr Nettles, I am certain you will be glad of some refreshment after your long journey. Will you not come downstairs and we shall see what Mrs Garman can find for you. Some cold meat, perhaps, and a glass of Madeira."

"I do not take wine at this hour," he said reprovingly, but he rose to his feet obediently.

"Some tea, then, or coffee," she said coaxingly. "Soup, perhaps."

"A little broth would be acceptable," he said grudgingly, as she led him out of the door.

As soon as he had gone, Evie burst out laughing.

"Did I do it right, Evie?" Violet said anxiously. "I mentioned honour and obligation... and I remembered to say I have no thoughts of matrimony, just as you told me. Oh, poor Mr Nettles! Do you think he has been harbouring a secret passion for me all this time? And now I have quite blighted his hopes."

"Dear Violet, did you not notice that he said nothing at all about his passion or love or anything of the sort? He said he could set aside his scruples now that you are penniless and marry you *'as you have long wished'*. He believes he is fulfilling *your* hopes."

"Oh dear. Then he is quite mistaken," Violet said. "I own there *was* a time when I looked favourably on him, but I never imagined myself as a parson's wife, living in that poky little parsonage. Mr

Nettles made me realise how selfish I was and how much good I could do with my money but I was never so unselfish as to want to live without a carriage or a footman or a lady's maid or new gowns or any of the luxuries I have always had. I know Papa spoilt me, but I should be miserable living in poverty. You are such a good person that you can do it without complaining, but I shall never forget how fierce you looked when you told Mr Nettles that there was no virtue in poverty — no *dignity* in it. Mr Nettles is not exactly poor, but he does not like to spend money on anything if he can help it and that is worse in a way — to have money but not enjoy the comforts of life. I do so like the comforts of life," she added wistfully.

"So do we all," Evie said. "That is not my reason for marrying Eliot, but it is a great relief to know that I shall never be poor again."

"Exactly so!" Violet said, leaning forward earnestly. "Is it selfish of me to wish to live as I have always done? When I thought my fortune was quite gone, I did not repine a great deal, or at least I tried not to, because I hoped that I might marry a very rich gentleman, but it is quite shocking the way gentlemen who seemed to admire me turned away from me when they thought I was poor, and how gentlemen flocked around you as soon as you had a dowry. That is not right, is it? They are nothing but fortune hunters, and I am sorry to say it of Mr Bradbrook's son, but he was one, too, and it was very wrong of him."

"Indeed it was," Evie said, smiling at so much righteous indignation.

"But Mr Armitage is so rich that he cannot possibly care about your money," Violet said triumphantly. "And you waited thirty years for exactly the right gentleman to come along and appreciate all your virtues, and he waited for you, too. Is it not charming? You are so in love! I never saw you look that way before, nor Mr Armitage...

so *happy* and excited and glowing and... oh, I have not the words! But I have decided that I shall not rush to marry before I am twenty-one. I shall wait until I am absolutely certain, when I glow like you and Mr Armitage do, because then I will know it is truly love and not just a passing fancy."

"How very wise you are growing, Violet," Evie said. "But this is exactly why it is better to see a little of the world and improve your understanding of people before you take the plunge into matrimony."

Mrs Bradbrook bustled into the room just then. "Lord, what a prosy bore Mr Nettles is! But Nicholas is back, and I have left him to deal with him. Violet, you have not changed your mind about marrying him, have you? Good, because he would go on about how you had led him on and such like nonsense, so I took the liberty of mentioning that you were induced into an elopement by Roger. Mr Nettles was so shocked that he decided you are no fit companion for a clergyman and has withdrawn any claim to your hand. I hope you have no objection. Now, of course, he is itching to get back to Essex, but I have told Nicholas on no account to let him leave this house."

"But why, ma'am?" Evie said. "Surely the sooner he is gone the better?"

"If Eliot returns with a special licence, then it will be very convenient to have a clergyman already on the premises, do you not think? Should you care to put on a different gown, just in case? The green muslin is so very pretty, and although it is not quite new, you have not worn it so very much."

"Oh, yes, and Lidderdale will do your hair for you! You must look beautiful for your wedding," Violet said.

"Let us see if there is to be a wedding today before we worry about gowns and hair," Evie said, laughing.

"Even if there is no wedding, there is a betrothal to celebrate," Mrs Bradbrook said firmly. "That is worth a change of gown and a rearrangement of your hair, is it not?"

Meekly, Evie went. At least it would pass the time waiting until Eliot returned. So much waiting... but she did not mind. The hollowness inside her had gone, replaced by the steady flame of love.

29: Epilogue

NOVEMBER

Eliot drifted through the autumn days in a haze of delirious happiness. Evie was his, and the world was a place of sunshine and roses, no matter the darkening evenings and showers of chilling rain. Nothing could dent his joy. Sometimes Evie went shopping with Aunt Bradbrook to buy wedding clothes, or there were fittings by the *modistes*, but for most hours of the day they were together. When callers came to congratulate the newly-married pair, they received them side by side. When they made calls themselves, they were together. And when they attended evening engagements, Evie was on his arm, wearing one of her new gowns and her wedding gift jewels, looking radiant.

"I like to see you in your finery," Eliot said complacently, as the carriage brought them home from the theatre one evening. "These new clothes suit you well. I only wish you had had something new for your wedding."

"It did not matter to me," she said. "I was nearly married in my ancient grey wool, except that your aunt persuaded me into the muslin instead."

"It was rather a scramble, though," he said. "Rushing off to Doctor's Commons, and then within five minutes of my return, we were married, and no cake or flowers or any ceremony. We hardly had time to catch our breath."

"It was perfect," she said softly, with what sounded like a sigh. "I only wanted one thing — you — and there you were. There was nothing I would change about it. Mr Bradbrook giving my hand to you, Miss Robart and Violet crying, Mrs Bradbrook and Henry as witnesses, Mr Nettles— I do not know how it is, for he is an ill-humoured man in other ways, but as a clergyman he brought solemnity and majesty to the traditional words, and imbued the office with gravitas, despite being called upon at such short notice. I was very moved."

"But it was not what you expected, I am sure."

"I expected nothing. Marriage had never been a likely prospect for me, so there was no image in my mind of how my wedding should be. I enjoyed every moment of it, and especially afterwards, when we walked home arm in arm through the dusk as husband and wife." Another, heavier, sigh. "It was a perfect day, my love."

"I believe you are right," he said.

Such bliss could not shut out the world for long, however.

"I am obliged to call on Lord Lampeter today," Eliot said one morning, as they sat in the little breakfast parlour at Grosvenor Square.

Evie set down her coffee cup. "Obliged to?"

"It is about this dowry of yours. He has come up to town specifically to discuss it with me, so I must go, I feel. However, I can refuse it, if you prefer not to be beholden to him. There is no need for it, after all, since you already have a good settlement."

"That is true, for you have been very generous. At present, the interest is going to Aunt Dodi," she said slowly. "She was so thankful to have it, for she has struggled for years on next to nothing. I should not like to deprive her of it before she has even had the first quarter's interest. Yet Lord Lampeter retains the capital, and I would certainly like to cut that connection, if I could."

"If he truly intends it as a dowry, then he should make the capital over to me, as your husband, and the arrangement with your aunt can continue. Is she content in Winchester? I wondered if you would like her to make her home with us. The interest would give her some independence if she wishes to travel about, visit friends, that sort of thing, but she would be living here most of the time. What do you think? Would she like to live in town?"

"Oh! Would you really wish to do that? I should like it of all things, but we will have Violet and her household with us as well, at least until she marries. Shall you like to fill your house with so many people? You have been used to live here on your own."

"And a great, empty place it is for one bachelor to rattle around in. I have six unused bedrooms, just begging to be filled. There will be plenty of room for Mrs Scudamore, if she wishes to come. You may write and invite her whenever you like. Tell her that I will fetch her myself whenever it suits her. We shall be at Marsham Grove until January, but then we shall all be fixed here in town until the summer."

"Your mama and papa may not care to have my aunt imposed upon them, Eliot, especially after all the upheavals they have suffered this year. I know that they appear to have settled their differences, but—"

"I have already suggested it to both of them, and they are very happy with the idea. It has been in my mind for some time now. Besides..." He reached across the table to take her hand. "My love, you are an Armitage now. Mrs Scudamore is my aunt as much as yours, and I have a great fondness for her since her little garden provided such an idyllic setting for my first proposal."

"It was very romantic," she said, laughing. "How could I have been so foolish as to turn you down?"

"I cannot imagine," he said complacently. "It was rather well-phrased, too, though I say so myself."

"It was. You said you were entranced by my charms." She sighed. "Such a delightful proposal, sir. All of them were delightful, but I liked the last one the best."

"Oh? Why was that?"

"Because it was the one I accepted."

~~~~~

That evening, Eliot dined alone with Evie for one final time. It was their last day in town, for tomorrow would bring the journey to Marsham Grove with Violet and her entourage, and before long Evie's Aunt Dodi would be there too, and in December Eliot's relations would arrive for Christmas. Their honeymoon was over, and they would never have the house to themselves again. There would be no more leisurely breakfasts or dinners, just the two of them. It was foolish to repine over such things, but he could not help wishing that he need never share her with anyone, even such dear friends as Violet and Aunt Dodi. They lingered over the dessert, but
~~~~~

eventually she withdrew, leaving him alone. When he went through to the drawing room with his port, only a sip or two taken, for he could not bear to be separated from her for long, she was lying on the chaise longue, a book in her hands. She laid it aside with a glad smile, and made to sit up.

"Ah, no!" he said at once. "Stay as you are, so that I may sit at your feet and adore you, as is only proper." He fitted the words to the deed, settling on the floor beside her, and taking her hand in his.

"How absurd you are!" she said, her smile widening, laying her head back upon the cushion.

"But I *do* adore you," he said softly, lifting her hand to his lips and kissing it. "You are perfection, my love."

"Perfection? What nonsense you talk."

"Perfect for me, darling one. I want you to understand that what I feel for you is like nothing I have ever experienced in my life before. You know my history... you know there have been many women in my life... but there has never been anyone like you. I have never felt for any of them as I do for you. I cannot... I do not have the words... but I love you so profoundly... so deeply... that I cannot even understand it myself. Everything is different now. It is like being in a foreign country, where even the air is different. I am not the same person I was when we first met."

She gazed at him with her clear brown eyes. "This is very serious!"

"It is the truth, however. Everything changed, and I even know when it happened. It was that kiss at Bel's house. We sat on that bench under the trees and kissed and... everything was different."

"The second kiss? Not the first?"

"No. The first kiss was lovely." He laughed, and pressed his lips against her palm. "You said it was, and you were right. But the *second* kiss... oh Lord, the second kiss! I hardly remembered how to breathe after that."

She chuckled. "Really? And yet I was disappointed—"

"Were you?" He sat up a little straighter. "I disappointed you? Or the kiss was the disappointment?"

"No, no! Not the kiss! It was..." She sighed. "Oh, it was *wonderful.* But... I wanted you to hold me. I expected you to take me in your arms and you did not."

"I was afraid..."

"Of what?"

He kissed her palm again, with a little sigh. "Of frightening you away. You had already refused to marry me twice, remember, and in such terms as precluded any possibility of a change of heart. And yet... it seemed to me that there was *something* between us, something that could not be denied. You talked so openly of kissing, and... Evie, I felt as if the most beautiful butterfly in the world had settled on my outstretched hand. You were right there, asking me to kiss you and I was utterly *terrified* of spoiling the moment and driving you away, perhaps for ever. So it seemed to me that I dared not take you in my arms. I had to allow you the possibility to fly away whenever you wanted. I could not *constrain* you... so I only touched your cheek... like so... in case you felt the need to flee."

She leaned into his hand, closing her eyes. "Perhaps you were right. Perhaps I would have panicked if you had held me then. But it haunted me afterwards, that you never had."

"It haunted me, too," he whispered. "I wanted to so badly, my darling. But although we tiptoed around each other for a while, I am so, so glad that we chose not to wait to marry. This little interlude has been so wonderful, just the two of us, but tomorrow we will be at Marsham Grove with Violet and everything will be different. At least you need not skulk in the shadows with Miss Robart, as you were wont to do. You may take your place at the head of the table."

"It does not seem right, though," she said. "That is your mama's place. Is she ever going to come home?"

He shrugged with a huff of breath. "Who can say? Perhaps at Christmas, but there is always one or other of my sisters who needs her, and she seems happy to be where she is truly useful, in a busy household. Father is happy, too. Even his health is better since he was at Nancy's. No doubt I was wrong to interfere there, but I cannot regret it, and it has worked out well in some ways. Nancy has her own family around her now, and Father will have us, even if Mother is away. We will look after him."

"Indeed we will. It pleases me that he is in contact with your half-brothers."

"That is my feeling, too," Eliot said. "Perhaps Roger Bradbrook was over-indulged, but it is only right for a father to acknowledge *all* his children, I think. In fact... Evie, you should know that I have a daughter who lives at Clacton-on-Sea. Would it distress you if I were to take more interest in her than hitherto? I have always taken care of her and her mother, and made sure they want for nothing, but as we have seen with Nancy's sons, such children also need to be openly acknowledged."

"Every child should know who his father is, if possible," Evie said quietly. "Sometimes children are born out of wedlock, but they should never be swept out of sight, as if they were nothing at all. A child has two parents, and it is wrong to pretend otherwise. It is not the child's fault to be born in one situation or another."

Eliot nodded, then said with a rueful smile, "I am not certain that Mr Nettles would agree with you. He would no doubt preach a fiery sermon on the subject."

"I hope we need not take Mr Nettles as a guide to our behaviour," she said. "He has very little Christian forgiveness in him, for a clergyman. Everyone makes mistakes from time to time. It is how they behave afterwards that matters. That is where honour and strength of character show themselves. Nor is it right to judge people by what they were in the past. I have learnt my lesson there, as you have cause to know. The past is gone. What a person is now — that is the only thing that matters."

He caught up her hand again and kissed the tips of each finger in turn. "You are a forgiving soul, my dearest one. Then let it be so, and may the past lie quietly and never trouble us, for we have the most glorious future ahead of us."

"Let us hope so," she said.

He smiled at her. "I intend to make it so."

THE END

The final book in the series is *The Duke*, wherein all will be revealed regarding the Benefactor, the mysterious Mr Ellsworthy and the sinking of the *Brig Minerva.* You can read a sneak preview of chapter 1 after the acknowledgements. For more information or to buy, go to http://marykingswood.co.uk

Thanks for reading!

If you have enjoyed reading this book, please consider writing a short review on Amazon. You can find out the latest news and sign up for the mailing list at http://marykingswood.co.uk.

Family trees: Hi-res versions are available at my website http://marykingswood.co.uk

A note on historical accuracy: I have endeavoured to stay true to the spirit of Regency times, and have avoided taking too many liberties or imposing modern sensibilities on my characters. The book is not one of historical record, but I've tried to make it reasonably accurate. However, I'm not perfect! If you spot a historical error, I'd very much appreciate knowing about it so that I can correct it and learn from it. Thank you!

Isn't that what's-his-name? Regular readers will know that characters from previous books occasionally pop up. Mr Hawes of Kellingborough was last seen dangling after Fanny in *The Seamstress*, until Ferdy lured him away to London with introductions to all his noble relations. Lawyer Mr Willerton-Forbes, his flamboyant sidekick Captain Edgerton and the discreet Mr Neate have been helping my characters solve murders and other puzzles ever since *Lord Augustus*. Mr Jonathan Ellsworthy, mysterious survivor of the *Brig Minerva*, and his good friend Miss Ginny Chandry were last seen in *The Clerk.* Lady Ruth Grenaby, who befriended Violet, will reappear in *The Duke.*

About the Silver Linings Mysteries series*:* John Milton coined the phrase *'silver lining'* in *Comus: A Mask Presented at Ludlow Castle*, 1634

Was I deceived, or did a sable cloud
Turn forth her silver lining on the night?
I did not err; there does a sable cloud
Turn forth her silver lining on the night,
And casts a gleam over this tufted grove.

Ever since then, the term *'silver lining'* has become synonymous with the unexpected benefits arising from disaster. The sinking of the *Brig Minerva* results in many deaths, but for others, the future is suddenly brighter. But it's not always easy to leave the past behind...

Book 0: The Clerk: the sinking of the *Minerva* offers a young man a new life *(a novella, free to mailing list subscribers)*.

Book 1: The Widow: the wife of the *Minerva's* captain is free from his cruelty, but can she learn to trust again?

Book 2: The Lacemaker: three sisters inherit a country cottage, but the locals are surprisingly interested in them.

Book 3: The Apothecary: a long-forgotten suitor returns, now a rich man, but is he all he seems?

Book 4: The Painter: two children are left to the care of a reclusive man.

Book 5: The Orphan: a wilful heiress is determined to choose a notorious rake as her guardian.

Book 6: The Duke: the heir to the dukedom is reluctant to step into his dead brother's shoes and accept his arranged marriage.

Any questions about the series? You can email me at mary@marykingswood.co.uk - I'd love to hear from you!

About the author

I write traditional Regency romances under the pen name Mary Kingswood, and epic fantasy as Pauline M Ross. I live in the beautiful Highlands of Scotland with my husband. I like chocolate, whisky, my Kindle, massed pipe bands, long leisurely lunches, chocolate, going places in my campervan, eating pizza in Italy, summer nights that never get dark, wood fires in winter, chocolate, the view from the study window looking out over the Moray Firth and the Black Isle to the mountains beyond. And chocolate. I dislike driving on motorways, cooking, shopping, hospitals.

Acknowledgements

Thanks go to:

All those fine people in Albany, Australia who restored the *Brig Amity* and gave me the germ of an idea.

Allison Lane, whose course on English Architecture inspired me.

Shayne Rutherford of Darkmoon Graphics for the cover design.

My beta readers: Barbara Daniels Dena, Amy DeWitt, Megan Jacobson, Rosemary Paton, Quilting Danielle, Melanie Savage, Rachel Daven Skinner of Romance Refined

Last, but definitely not least, my first reader: Amy Ross.

Sneak preview of The Duke: Chapter 1: The Duke Of Falconbury

FEBRUARY

Lord Randolph Litherholm picked up the nearest quill pen. As usual, there were precisely three laid out for his use, trimmed and prepared with meticulous care by one of his under-secretaries, but he always took the nearest to hand. He dipped the pen in the inkstand and wrote his name at the spot indicated by his attorney. The parchment was removed to be sanded by another of his under-secretaries, and a second parchment was placed before him. The pen was dipped a second time, his name inscribed, the parchment removed by yet another under-secretary.

In stately procession, the two parchments were carried around the mahogany desk, as large as many dining tables, and placed in front of the bluff, middle-aged farmer sitting on the opposite side, stiff in his Sunday best coat. He too chose a pen, dipped, signed, then dipped and signed again, laying his pen down with a sigh of obvious relief and a wide smile. Beside him, his country attorney, in a dazzlingly white neckcloth, no doubt bought new for the occasion, smiled also.

Then Max Lorrimer stepped forward with the sealing tray and the ducal seal for the final part of the ceremony. He himself, as the most senior secretary, undertook to melt the wax and apply a measure to each parchment, while Ran merely pressed the seal into the molten wax.

And then it was done. There were glasses of Madeira and dishes of sweetmeats and fifteen minutes of laboured conversation with the farmer and his attorney, every word no doubt to be remembered and carried back to their northern fastness, to be related to red-cheeked wives and daughters and wide-eyed neighbours, the glories of Valmont described in grandiose terms. Of the owner of so much splendour, less grandiose terms would be employed. Lord Randolph, the farmer would say, shaking his head sorrowfully, was nothing out of the way at all, and wore only a plain black coat, pale pantaloons and a triflingly simple neckcloth, such as a cheap attorney might wear, with not a bit of jewellery to be seen, apart from a paltry signet ring.

When the visitors had been shown out, and the steward and various attorneys and secretaries dispersed to their usual tasks, Ran retreated to his own office, a much smaller and less imposing apartment one floor below.

"So... another wretched mine," Max said, his eyes brimming with laughter. "Your revered father would *not* have approved."

"Pooh! We have had the salt mine for ever, not to mention those tin mines in Cornwall. Coal is no different," Ran said, with a shrug. "And very profitable, which Father would most definitely have approved. Good management of the estate, that was his watchword."

"How many mines is that? Four? Five?"

"Six," Ran said. "What else do you have for me today, Max? Let us get down to business."

For more than an hour, they discussed estate matters — tenant houses, farming prospects, the shooting and fishing rights on a distant holding, some property in London that the lawyers were looking into. Secretaries and attorneys and footmen came and went, bearing letters to be signed, or notes of domestic matters, or occasionally whispering in Max's ear. Eventually, however, the stream of decisions to be made and letters to be signed and sales or purchases to be approved dwindled to a trickle, and the attorneys and under-secretaries disappeared. Only Max, Ran's oldest friend outside the family, remained.

"Come now, Max," Ran said at length. "Are we finished for the day? Pour me a glass of something, will you, and tell me what is in your mind, for you are unusually subdued."

Max obediently went to the sideboard where the decanters stood, and with the experience of many years' acquaintance, poured two glasses of Ran's favourite Canary.

"You are aware of the date, of course," he said, sliding the glass across the battered deal table that served as Ran's working desk.

"Of course. A year since the *Brig Minerva* sank. A year since my brother died. How could I forget?"

"I beg your pardon. I did not mean to imply that you had forgotten. But Hammick is still in Boston, no doubt eating his head off at your expense, and awaiting further orders."

Ran sighed. "I am aware..."

"He has been to every single church on the east coast of America, and enquired of every family of consequence, and has found not the slightest indication that your brother married while he was there, nor fathered a legal heir. Not that anyone imagines that Gervase would have married without notifying you."

Another sigh. "No, you are quite right. There is no hope now of such a thing. Hammick may be relieved of his quest."

"There is another letter from Mr Willerton-Forbes, as well."

Ran groaned. "Does the fellow *never* give up? I neither want nor need the Benefactor's money."

Max laughed and shook his head. "He cannot give up! Do but consider his position, Ran. He has been charged by this mysterious Benefactor to transfer one thousand pounds to every survivor or next of kin of a victim of the *Brig Minerva.* He cannot complete his task without seeing you, and I daresay you are now the very last. How it must irk him! He must wish of all things to put the whole behind him, but he cannot, since you refuse to see him."

"Very well, very well! Make an appointment for him, if it must be so. And now, that must be all? May I go and do a little shooting? Ah... there is something else?"

"His Grace the Duke of Orrisdale arrived about two hours since."

Ran jumped to his feet. "And you only tell me now?"

"He gave strict instructions that you were not to be disturbed. Brent will have taken care of him, you know, and His Grace said that he would be happy await your pleasure in the Porcelain Room."

Ran laughed. "Of course he would! But I shall not keep him waiting any longer."

The Porcelain Room was not one of the larger chambers at Valmont, being no more than an ante-room between two far more imposing apartments, but it was a charmingly elegant place, full of lightness and wintry sunshine. Here, amongst the delicate glass cabinets and multitude of pale oak shelves, stood the Duke of Orrisdale, a man of fifty, who was a looming figure half a head taller than Ran, and broad as well. He was not precisely fat, but he looked as if his tailor had been surreptitiously increasing the seams of his coats for some years now.

"I beg your pardon for not receiving you when you arrived," Ran said as he entered.

The duke did not glance up from the vase he held in his hands. "No need, no need," he said absently. "Your people have looked after me very well. This is a lovely piece, Litherholm! Not so fine as Sèvres, but almost so. Limoges, I think?"

"I cannot tell you," Ran said, smiling. "Mama was the expert. And Gervase, of course. Have you been given your usual room?"

"Oh yes, yes, no need for you to worry about that. Everything made ready within the twinkling of an eye, just as I like it, although I gave you not the least warning. But I could not let the day pass without notice, you know. Yet here you are, still in your black coat. It is a year now, Litherholm, a full year since your brother's tragic death. You might leave off the mourning garb now."

"True," Ran said colourlessly.

"Aye, well, you must do as you think best, and I am not one of those thinking you should have stepped into Falconbury's place long since. It was very proper of you to wait and see if the lad might have fathered an heir while he was in foreign parts." He looked at Ran from beneath bushy eyebrows. "You have found none, I take it."

"No."

"Hmm. So you will claim your seat in the Lords now? I assure you there will not be the least difficulty there."

"When I go to town in the spring, I shall see about it," Ran said.

"Ah, excellent! That is what I wanted to hear." With a reluctant sigh, he set down the vase he had been holding and picked up a snuff box. "Now this is exquisite. Sèvres, of course."

"Is it?"

The duke chuckled. "You may have an excellent head for the management of your estates, Litherholm, but you are a philistine in matters of the decorative arts. Indeed it is Sèvres, and a finer example I never saw. Your mama had a wonderful eye for such things, and your brother too, but I daresay there will be no more added to the collection now that the dukedom is in *your* hands, eh? Shall you make many changes, once you assume the title?"

"Probably not. I like Valmont the way it is." He waited patiently, guessing that the duke was getting to the point in his roundabout way.

"How old are you now, Litherholm?"

"Eight and twenty, sir."

"The years fly by so. And my Ruthie is almost one and twenty."

Ran shivered. "And how is the Lady Ruth?" he said politely.

"Well enough, well enough, but… she has waited a long time, Litherholm."

"I am aware, Duke."

"Not that I will put any pressure on you, none at all, for that is not my way, and after all, the understanding was with your brother. They got on so well, right from the start, and although we never minded him jauntering about the world, for they were both very young then—" He stopped, twisting his lips thoughtfully.

Ran said nothing, for what after all was there to say?

"Well, we should like to know where we stand, that is all," the duke said bluntly. "There is Susan barely eighteen and already settled — not general knowledge yet, but I do not scruple to tell you — so you see, it would be as well if we could fire Ruthie off first. That is the proper way of it, the eldest daughter before the younger. The Duchess wants to hold a Grand Ball at Mallowfleet for Ruthie's birthday next month, and it would be the ideal time for an announcement… if there is to be an announcement. But it is for you to say, you know."

Taking a deep breath, Ran said, "You will not find me in the least unwilling, but…"

"But?"

"Ruth is such a beauty, and so accomplished… everything that any man could hope for in a wife. I understand why she would wait for Gervase, but I cannot imagine that she would be happy to accept me in his place. She must surely have a myriad of suitors… what about Claythorpe? His name was mentioned last season, was it not?"

"Pft, we were very taken in there! It is true that he was very attentive, and we did think... an earl, too, which would have been tolerable, and if she had liked the idea... but then it all went off, and he had the nerve to tell me later that he found her too cold and reserved. My Ruthie, as well-bred a daughter as ever lived! Aye, she has had suitors enough, but she has always been content to accept our choice for her. She is a good girl, and knows her duty to her mama and to me. She will certainly accept you if you make the offer."

"But I am so different from Gervase," Ran said. "Will she mind taking second best?"

"She will be taking the Duke of Falconbury, not some paltry younger son. It may not be precisely the husband she expected, but the position is the one she has been destined to occupy for years. You will not find her a troublesome wife."

"No, no! Indeed not, but I should like to talk to her before anything is irrevocably settled. To assure myself that she is happy with the arrangement. Will you bring her to stay here for a few days? So that we may get to know each other a little better? Then, if she wishes it, I shall come to Her Grace's Grand Ball and make my offer in form."

"That would be sensible," the duke said. "Next week, perhaps. Good, good, so that is all settled. You still keep your usual hours here? I shall have a lie down upstairs, then, before changing for dinner."

With obvious reluctance, he returned the Sèvres snuff box to its place. Impulsively, Ran picked it up and pressed it into his hand.

"Keep it, as... a token of my esteem, and gratitude."

"Well now... well now... how very kind! Your brother would not have given away a family heirloom so readily, you may be sure."

"I am not my brother," Ran said sadly.

After handing the duke over to the butler, Ran made his way to a small side door that gave onto the western gardens. Here he collected a weather-beaten felt hat and a greatcoat of an old-fashioned style, and set off along one of the wide gravel paths through the parterre. Valmont was loosely based on the style of the Palace of Versailles, and the gardens, too, were laid out in a formal French manner, with an array of parterres and bosquets, pools and fountains, grottoes and a large labyrinth. Although there were shrubberies and even a so-called wilderness, these were artfully arranged and carefully managed. The more modern fashion for natural landscapes and deer parks had not yet overtaken the Litherholm family. Gervase, perhaps, would have swept away the formality and replaced it with something that looked just like any other garden, but Ran loved the straight lines and closely clipped hedges.

At the far end of the reflecting pool was a large, temple-like building in the Roman style, with lofty pillars topped by a pediment bearing the Litherholm coat of arms. The family mausoleum was not a cheerful place, but Ran did not regard the gloomy atmosphere. He strode up the steps and pushed open the great wooden door. High windows admitted enough light for him to make his way about halfway down one side. Here stood a black marble sarcophagus, very plain, engraved only with the words *'Gervase Septimus Litherholm, Seventh Duke of Falconbury'*.

"Well, you old rascal," Ran said, sitting cross-legged on the dusty floor. "A whole year, and now there is no escaping it. I am to have your title, whether I wish it or no, and I am to have your bride, too. You should have married Ruth before you left, you little idiot, and then I should be helping her to raise your son to be a true Litherholm, instead of trying to squeeze myself into a mould to which I am patently unfitted. Or maybe you would have stayed at home if you had had such a good reason. Whatever were you thinking, to go gadding about to the New World like that, and then getting yourself drowned? Perfectly imbecilic thing to do. And now I have to try to step into your shoes, and that is going to be so hard, Ger. So hard... I am a perfectly good steward, but there is more to being a duke than nurturing the estate for the next generation. And then there is Ruth... how can I make her happy, brother? What an idiot you are, to make her fall in love with you and then die. I shall do my best, God knows, but I shall always be second best. Always." He paused, the lump in his throat almost choking him. Resolutely, he got to his feet. "But I shall do my duty, as ever. Sleep well, you old rascal. Sleep well."

Slowly he made his way back across the gardens to the side door. Brent, the butler, was waiting inside for him, his face impassive. He was a solemn man of about sixty, who had served three Dukes of Falconbury, had seen everything and was the most imperturbable man Ran had ever known. Nothing ever rattled his poise.

"His Grace is resting on his bed, my lord," Brent said, deftly removing the greatcoat and accepting the elderly hat. "Monsieur has taken the liberty of preparing some roasted sweetbreads, knowing as how His Grace is so fond of the dish, and Mrs Cromarty is to make a chestnut soup."

"That is very thoughtful," Ran said. "I can always depend on you all to rise to the occasion, even when His Grace arrives without notice. You have brought up some of the good claret from the cellar, I expect."

"Naturally, my lord, and the port His Grace the Sixth Duke laid down. Ah, there is a small tear in the pocket of this coat. I shall inform Mr Giggs."

Ran turned, looking the butler in the eye. "Do you know, Brent, my brother bought this coat when he first went up to Oxford, and as for the hat... I cannot tell you how ancient it is."

"I believe it was your father's, my lord."

"There you are, then. Tell Giggs he may dispose of them as he sees fit. He may leave my old olive driving coat here for my garden strolls. And pray tell him also that he may put away all my black coats. My year of mourning is over. For tonight, he may lay out my new blue coat, the Weston, and the cream waistcoat."

"Very good, my lord."

"And Brent... I shall be taking my seat in the Lords in the spring, so I suppose we had all better get used to the title, eh? Tell the other servants, will you."

The butler bowed deeply, and then his face creased into a most unaccustomed smile. "Yes, indeed I will... Your Grace."

END OF SAMPLE CHAPTER of *The Duke.* For more information, or to buy, go to http://marykingswood.co.uk.

Printed in Great Britain
by Amazon

65433728R00220